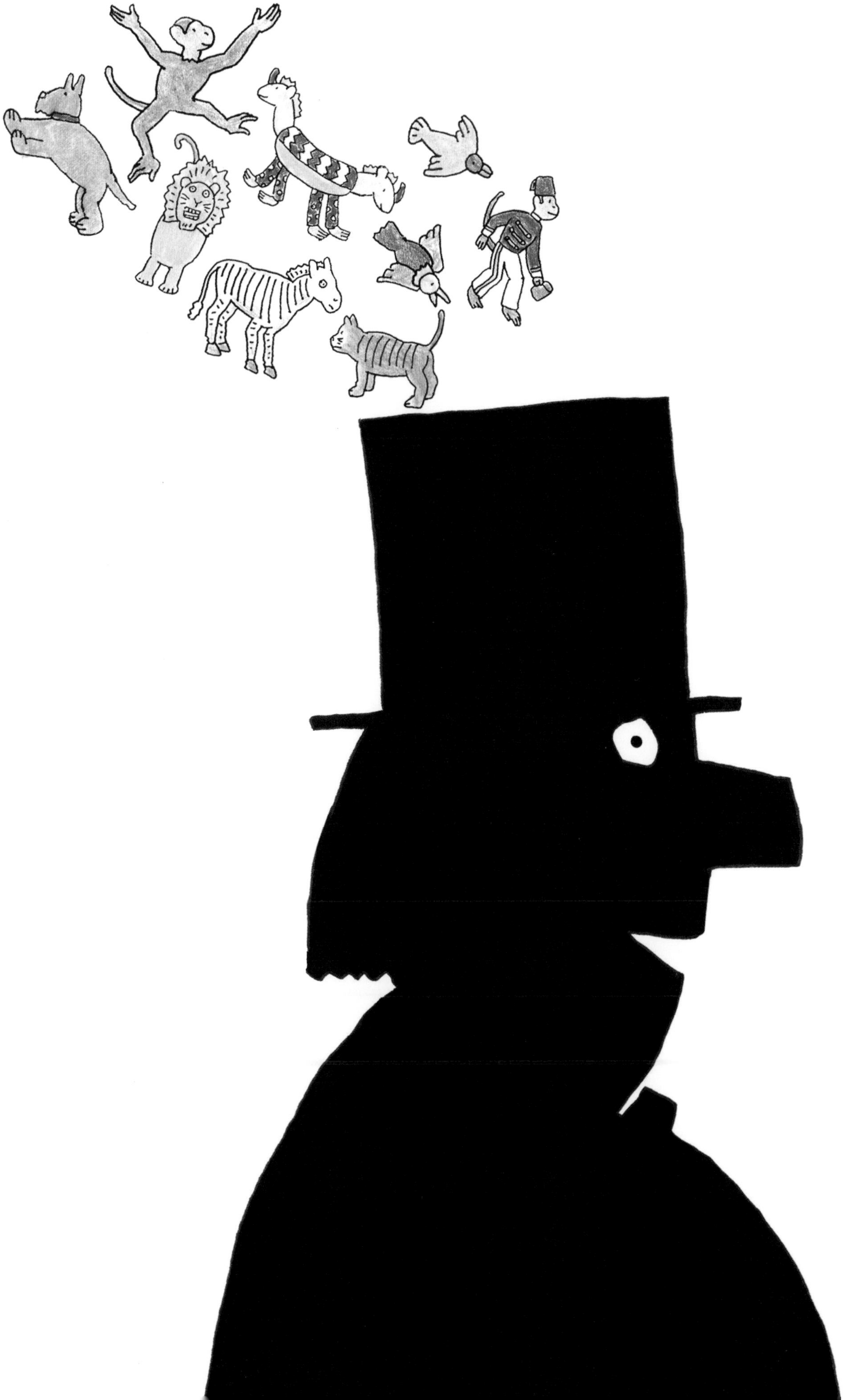

Published in 2015 by Creative Editions

P.O. Box 227, Mankato, MN 56002 USA

Creative Editions is an imprint of The Creative Company

www.thecreativecompany.us

Edited by Kate Riggs. Art directed by Rita Marshall

Printed in China

Library of Congress Cataloging-in-Publication Data

Chwast, Seymour.   Dr. Dolittle / Seymour Chwast.

Summary: American artist Seymour Chwast reinterprets Hugh Lofting's *The Story of Doctor
Dolittle* for a 21st-century, graphic-novel-influenced audience, formatting the text in a comic style.

ISBN 978-1-56846-258-5

1. Graphic novels. [1. Graphic novels. 2. Animals-Fiction. 3. Physicians-Fiction. 4. Veterinarians-Fiction.
5. Human-animal communication-Fiction.] I. Lofting, Hugh, 1886-1947. *Story of Doctor Dolittle* II.
Title. III. Title: Doctor Dolittle.

PZ7.7.C48Dr 2015   741.5'973-dc23   2014038207

First edition 9 8 7 6 5 4 3 2 1

HUGH LOFTING'S CLASSIC STORY ADAPTED BY SEYMOUR CHWAST

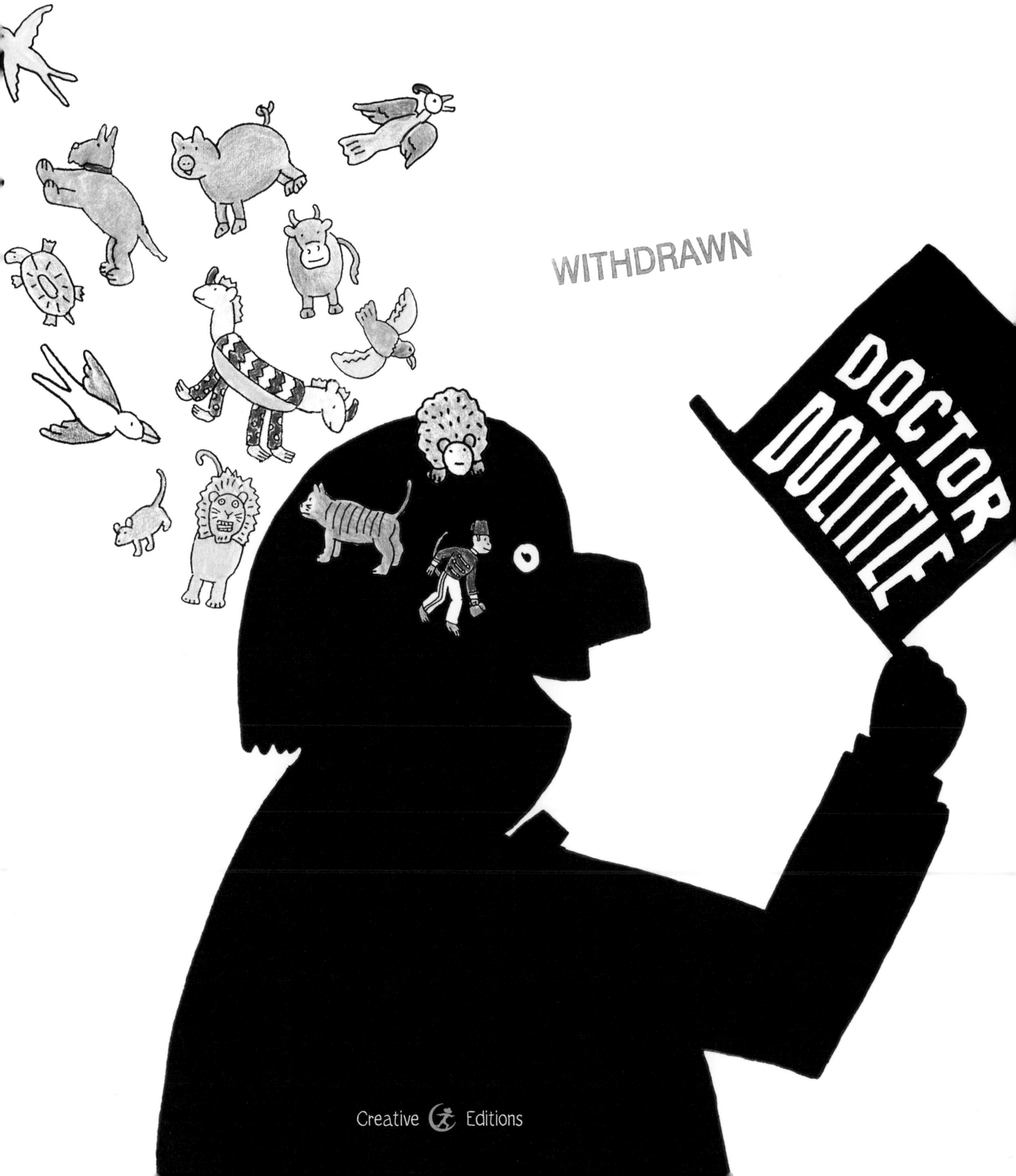
DOCTOR
DOLITTLE

Creative Editions

Introduction

Stories about a kindly veterinarian named John Dolittle first appeared in book form in the 1920s with the publication of *The Story of Doctor Dolittle*, by English-born author Hugh Lofting (1886-1947). When Lofting served in the trenches as a member of the British army during World War I, he wrote home to his wife and young children not of the grim realities of battle but of an imaginary doctor who could talk to animals. These letters became the basis for the initial book of the Dr. Dolittle series. Lofting followed *The Story of Doctor Dolittle* with 11 more Dolittle novels, including the 1923 Newbery Medal-winning sequel, *The Voyages of Doctor Dolittle*. The final volume, *Doctor Dolittle and the Secret Lake*, was published a year after Lofting's death, in 1948.

Lofting himself supplied the original artwork and used the books as a vehicle for spreading messages of peace and compassion in an uncertain and increasingly violent world. In the process, he created an icon of children's literature, Dr. Dolittle, who would stand the test of time.

Taking inspiration from the original tales, iconic American author and illustrator Seymour Chwast here reinterprets Dr. Dolittle for a 21st-century, graphic-novel-influenced audience. Although the text itself has been reimagined to fit the format, the general plot of *The Story of Doctor Dolittle*, along with the sentiments and ideals behind it, remain the same: Dr. Dolittle's world is one of childlike wonder and hope. It is a world that beckons us to seek adventure and encourages us to be caretakers of all creatures, great and small.

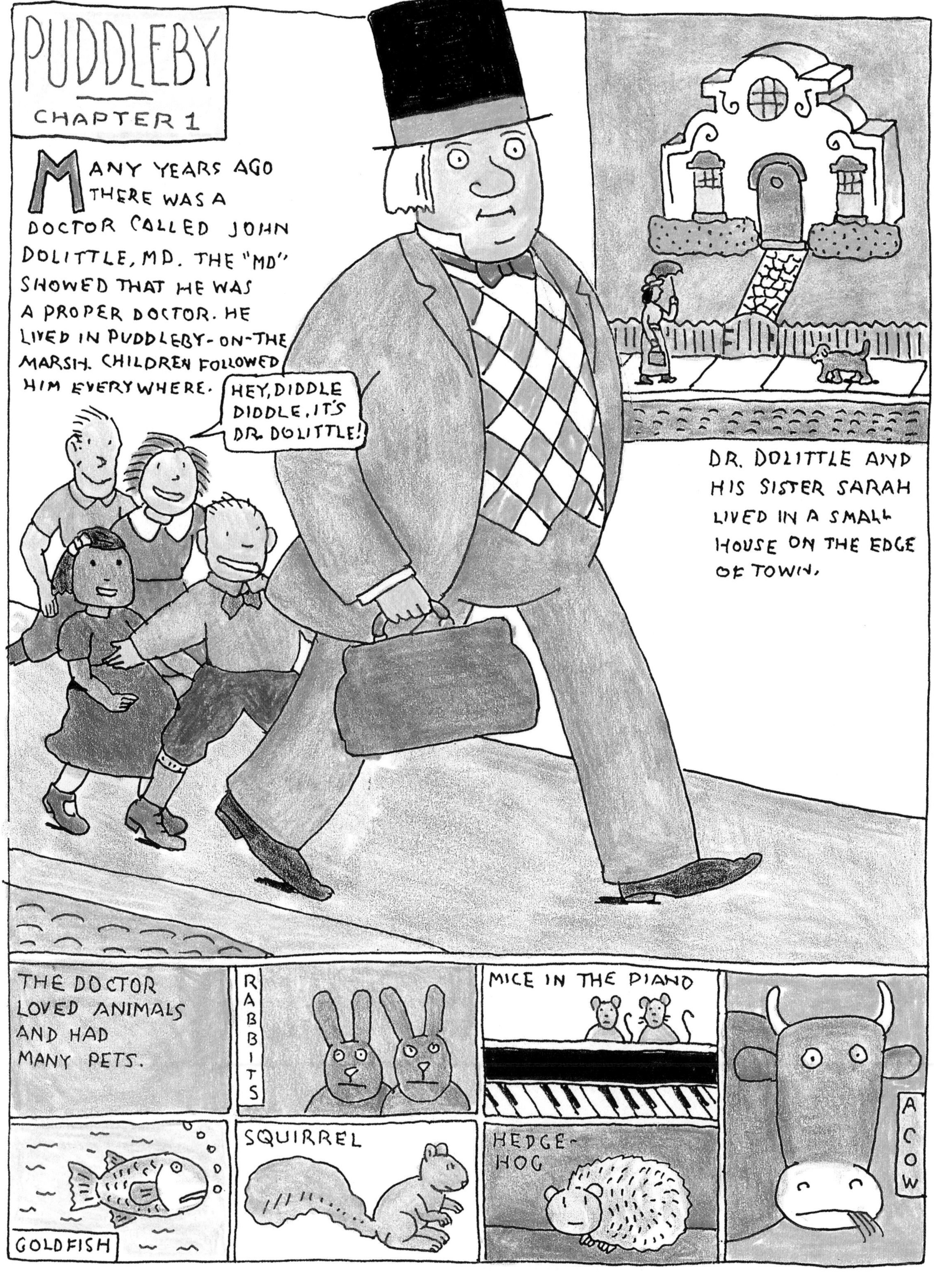
PUDDLEBY
CHAPTER 1
MANY YEARS AGO THERE WAS A DOCTOR CALLED JOHN DOLITTLE, MD. THE "MD" SHOWED THAT HE WAS A PROPER DOCTOR. HE LIVED IN PUDDLEBY-ON-THE-MARSH. CHILDREN FOLLOWED HIM EVERYWHERE.
HEY, DIDDLE DIDDLE, IT'S DR. DOLITTLE!
DR. DOLITTLE AND HIS SISTER SARAH LIVED IN A SMALL HOUSE ON THE EDGE OF TOWN.
THE DOCTOR LOVED ANIMALS AND HAD MANY PETS.
RABBITS
MICE IN THE PIANO
A COW
GOLDFISH
SQUIRREL
HEDGE-HOG

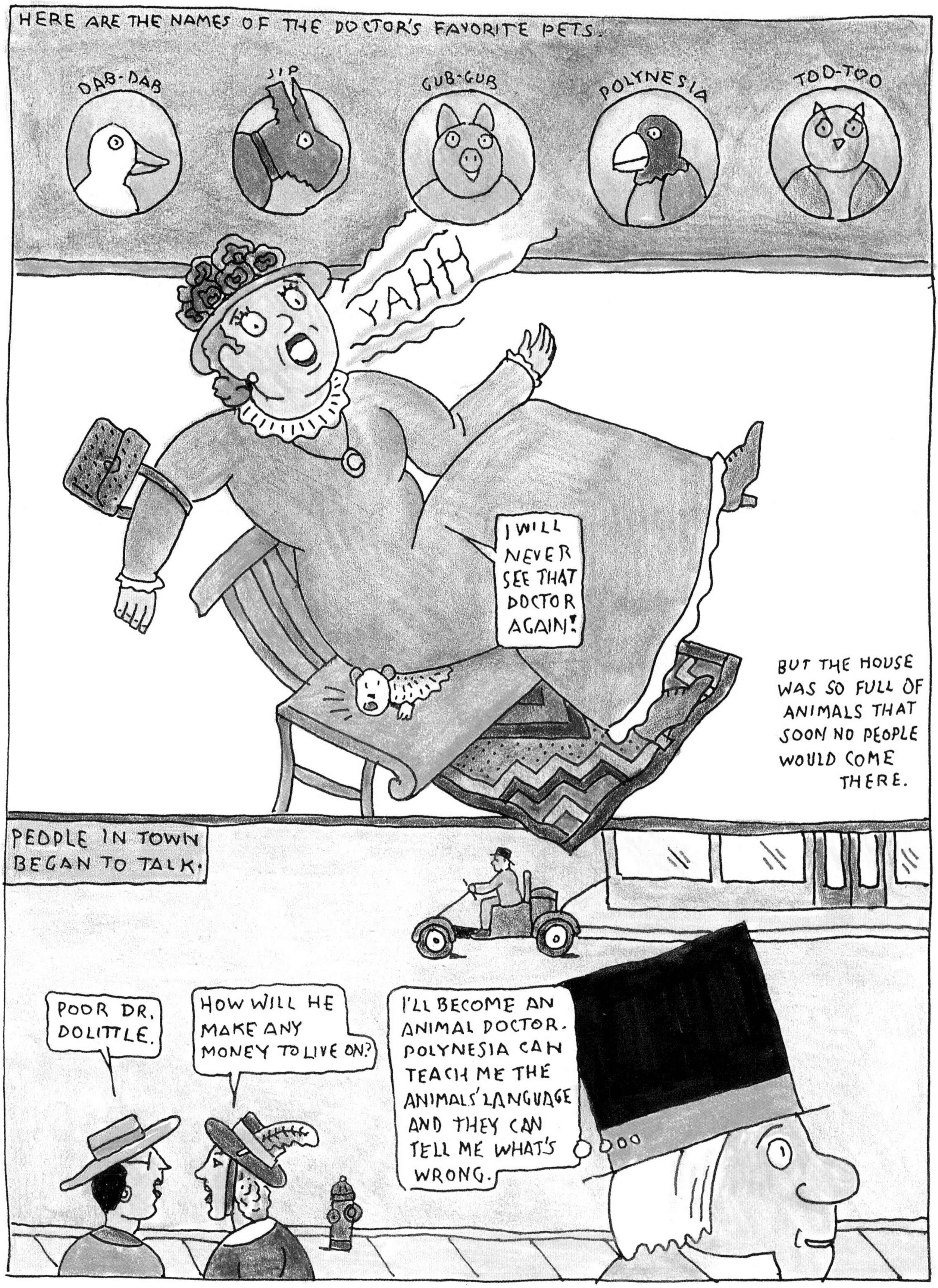
HERE ARE THE NAMES OF THE DOCTOR'S FAVORITE PETS.
DAB-DAB
JIP
GUB-GUB
POLYNESIA
TOO-TOO
YAHH
I WILL NEVER SEE THAT DOCTOR AGAIN!
BUT THE HOUSE WAS SO FULL OF ANIMALS THAT SOON NO PEOPLE WOULD COME THERE.
PEOPLE IN TOWN BEGAN TO TALK.
POOR DR. DOLITTLE.
HOW WILL HE MAKE ANY MONEY TO LIVE ON?
I'LL BECOME AN ANIMAL DOCTOR. POLYNESIA CAN TEACH ME THE ANIMALS' LANGUAGE AND THEY CAN TELL ME WHAT'S WRONG.

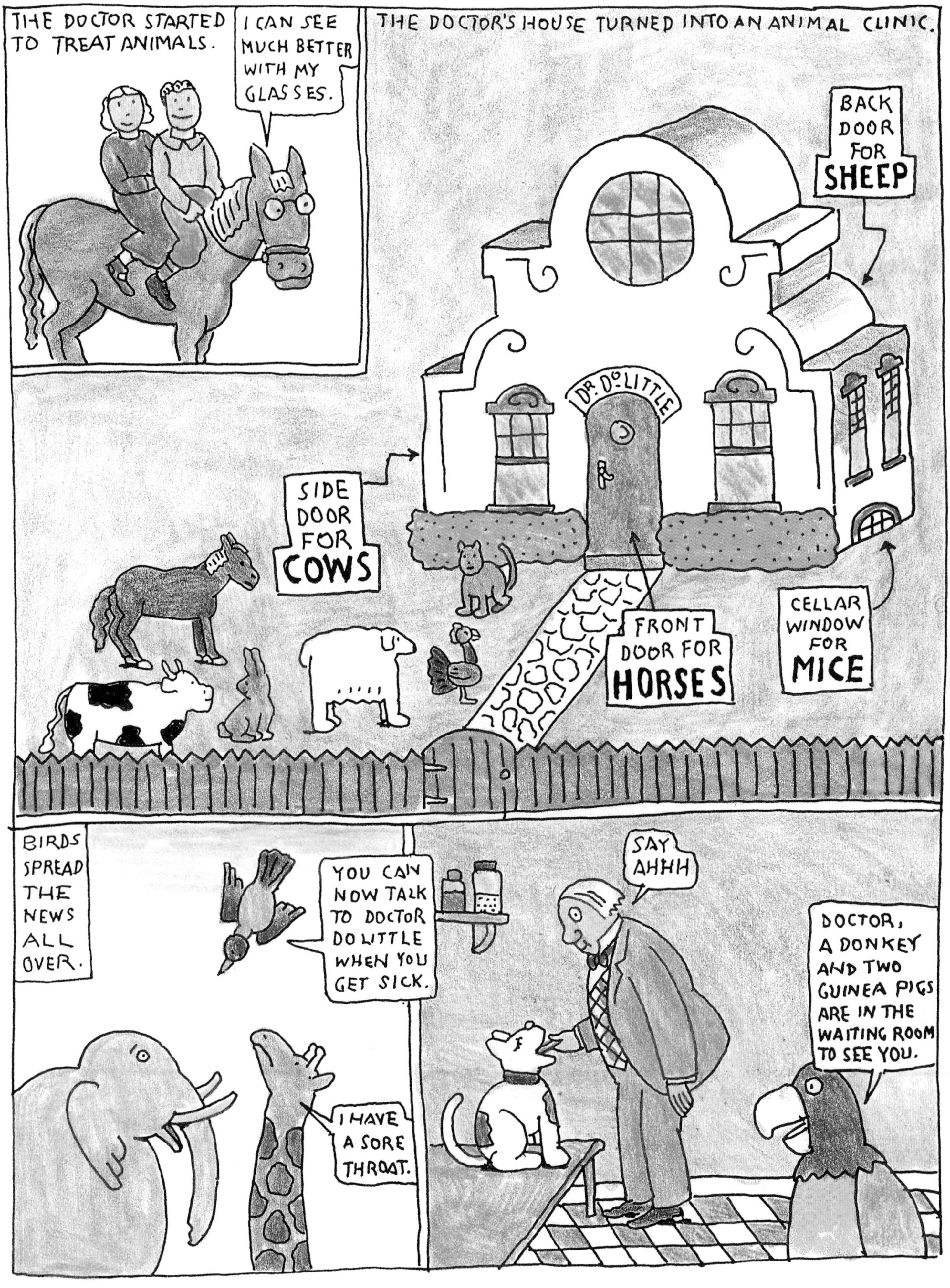
THE DOCTOR STARTED TO TREAT ANIMALS.
I CAN SEE MUCH BETTER WITH MY GLASSES.
THE DOCTOR'S HOUSE TURNED INTO AN ANIMAL CLINIC.
BACK DOOR FOR SHEEP
DR. DOLITTLE
SIDE DOOR FOR COWS
FRONT DOOR FOR HORSES
CELLAR WINDOW FOR MICE
BIRDS SPREAD THE NEWS ALL OVER.
YOU CAN NOW TALK TO DOCTOR DOLITTLE WHEN YOU GET SICK.
I HAVE A SORE THROAT.
SAY AHHH
DOCTOR, A DONKEY AND TWO GUINEA PIGS ARE IN THE WAITING ROOM TO SEE YOU.

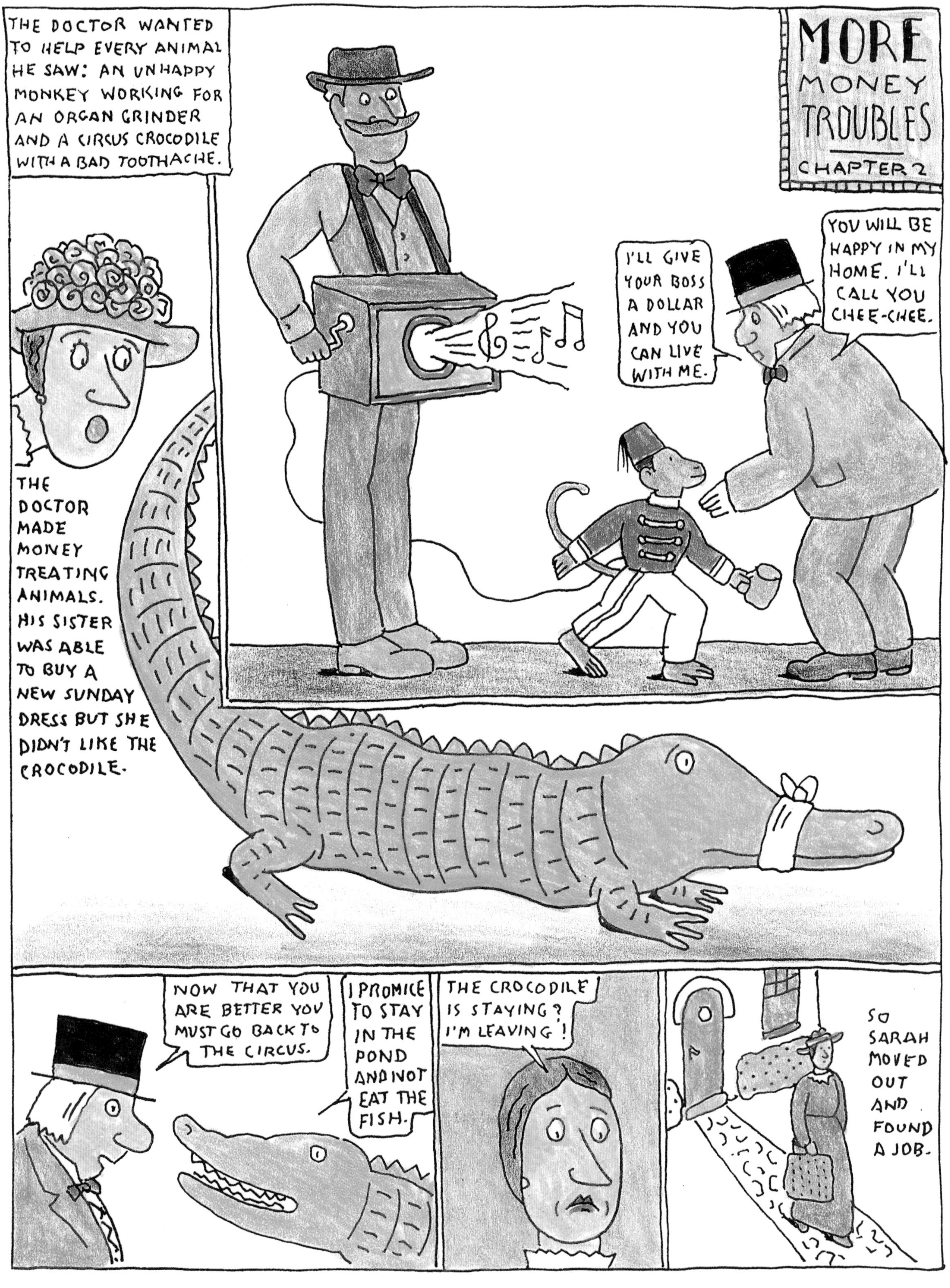
MORE MONEY TROUBLES
CHAPTER 2
THE DOCTOR WANTED TO HELP EVERY ANIMAL HE SAW: AN UNHAPPY MONKEY WORKING FOR AN ORGAN GRINDER AND A CIRCUS CROCODILE WITH A BAD TOOTHACHE.
I'LL GIVE YOUR BOSS A DOLLAR AND YOU CAN LIVE WITH ME.
YOU WILL BE HAPPY IN MY HOME. I'LL CALL YOU CHEE-CHEE.
THE DOCTOR MADE MONEY TREATING ANIMALS. HIS SISTER WAS ABLE TO BUY A NEW SUNDAY DRESS BUT SHE DIDN'T LIKE THE CROCODILE.
NOW THAT YOU ARE BETTER YOU MUST GO BACK TO THE CIRCUS.
I PROMICE TO STAY IN THE POND AND NOT EAT THE FISH.
THE CROCODILE IS STAYING? I'M LEAVING!
SO SARAH MOVED OUT AND FOUND A JOB.

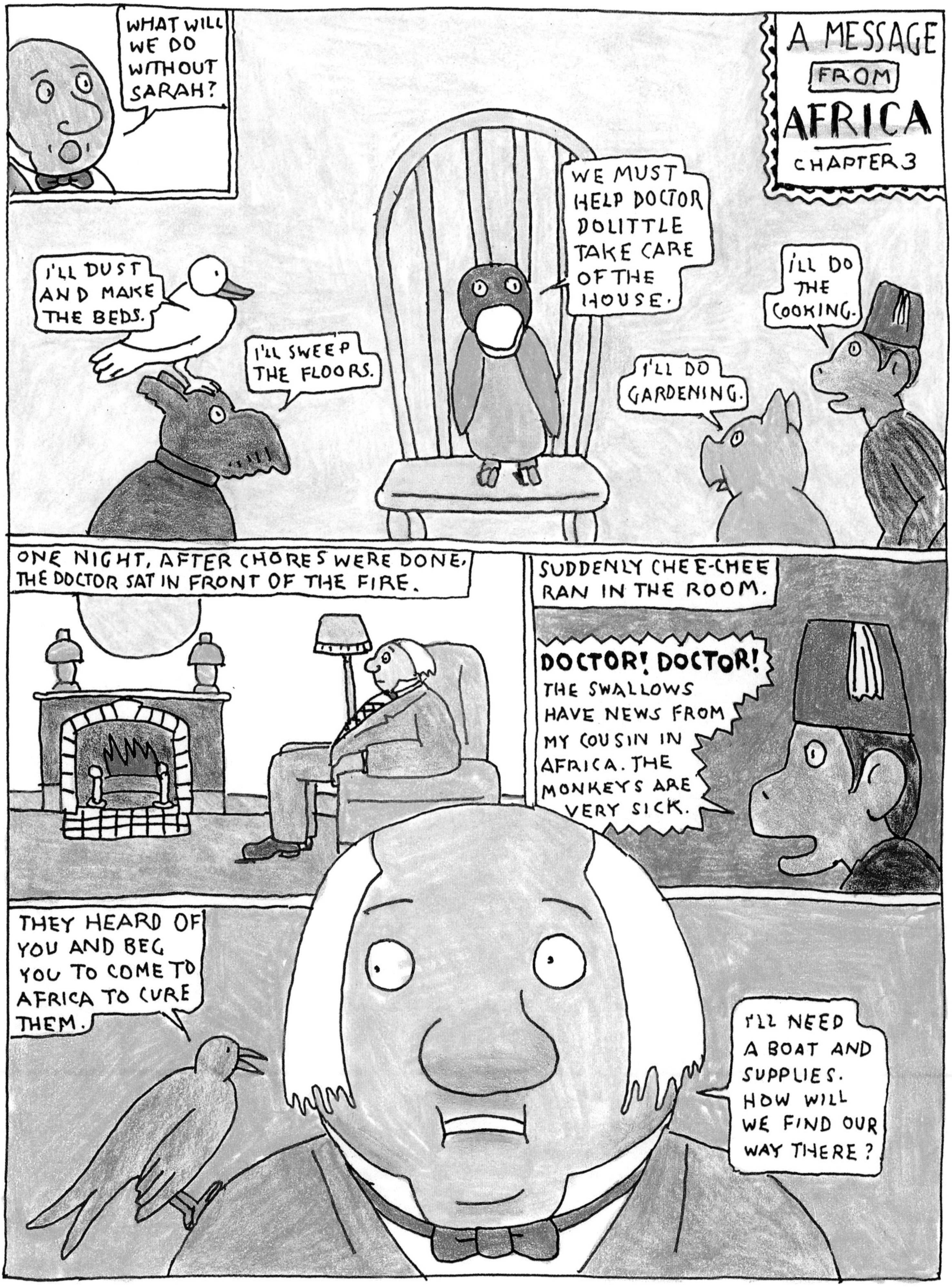
A MESSAGE FROM AFRICA
CHAPTER 3
WHAT WILL WE DO WITHOUT SARAH?
I'LL DUST AND MAKE THE BEDS.
I'LL SWEEP THE FLOORS.
WE MUST HELP DOCTOR DOLITTLE TAKE CARE OF THE HOUSE.
I'LL DO GARDENING.
I'LL DO THE COOKING.
ONE NIGHT, AFTER CHORES WERE DONE, THE DOCTOR SAT IN FRONT OF THE FIRE.
SUDDENLY CHEE-CHEE RAN IN THE ROOM.
DOCTOR! DOCTOR! THE SWALLOWS HAVE NEWS FROM MY COUSIN IN AFRICA. THE MONKEYS ARE VERY SICK.
THEY HEARD OF YOU AND BEG YOU TO COME TO AFRICA TO CURE THEM.
I'LL NEED A BOAT AND SUPPLIES. HOW WILL WE FIND OUR WAY THERE?

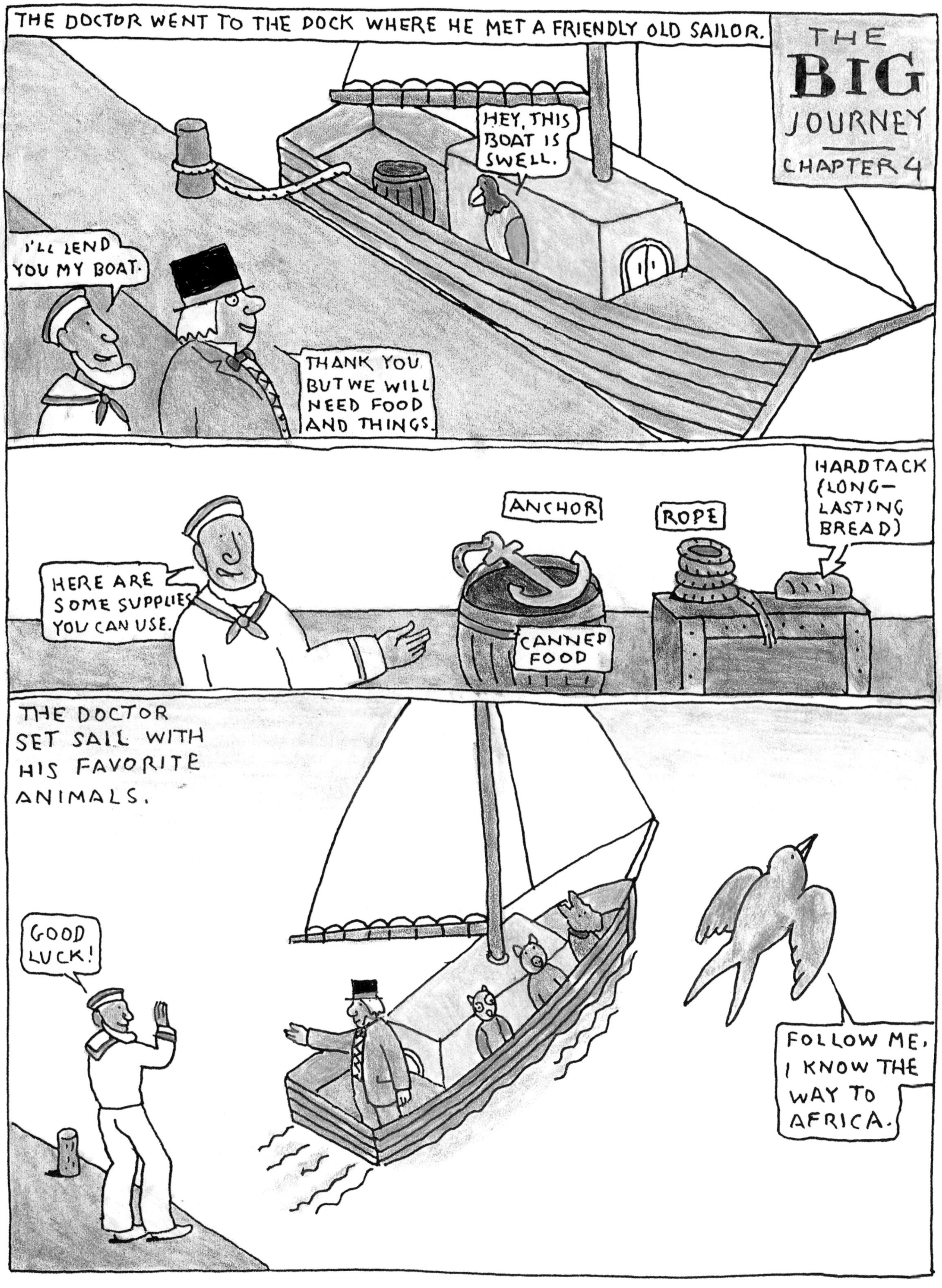
THE DOCTOR WENT TO THE DOCK WHERE HE MET A FRIENDLY OLD SAILOR.
THE BIG JOURNEY
CHAPTER 4
HEY, THIS BOAT IS SWELL.
I'LL LEND YOU MY BOAT.
THANK YOU BUT WE WILL NEED FOOD AND THINGS.
HERE ARE SOME SUPPLIES YOU CAN USE.
ANCHOR
ROPE
HARDTACK (LONG-LASTING BREAD)
CANNED FOOD
THE DOCTOR SET SAIL WITH HIS FAVORITE ANIMALS.
GOOD LUCK!
FOLLOW ME, I KNOW THE WAY TO AFRICA.

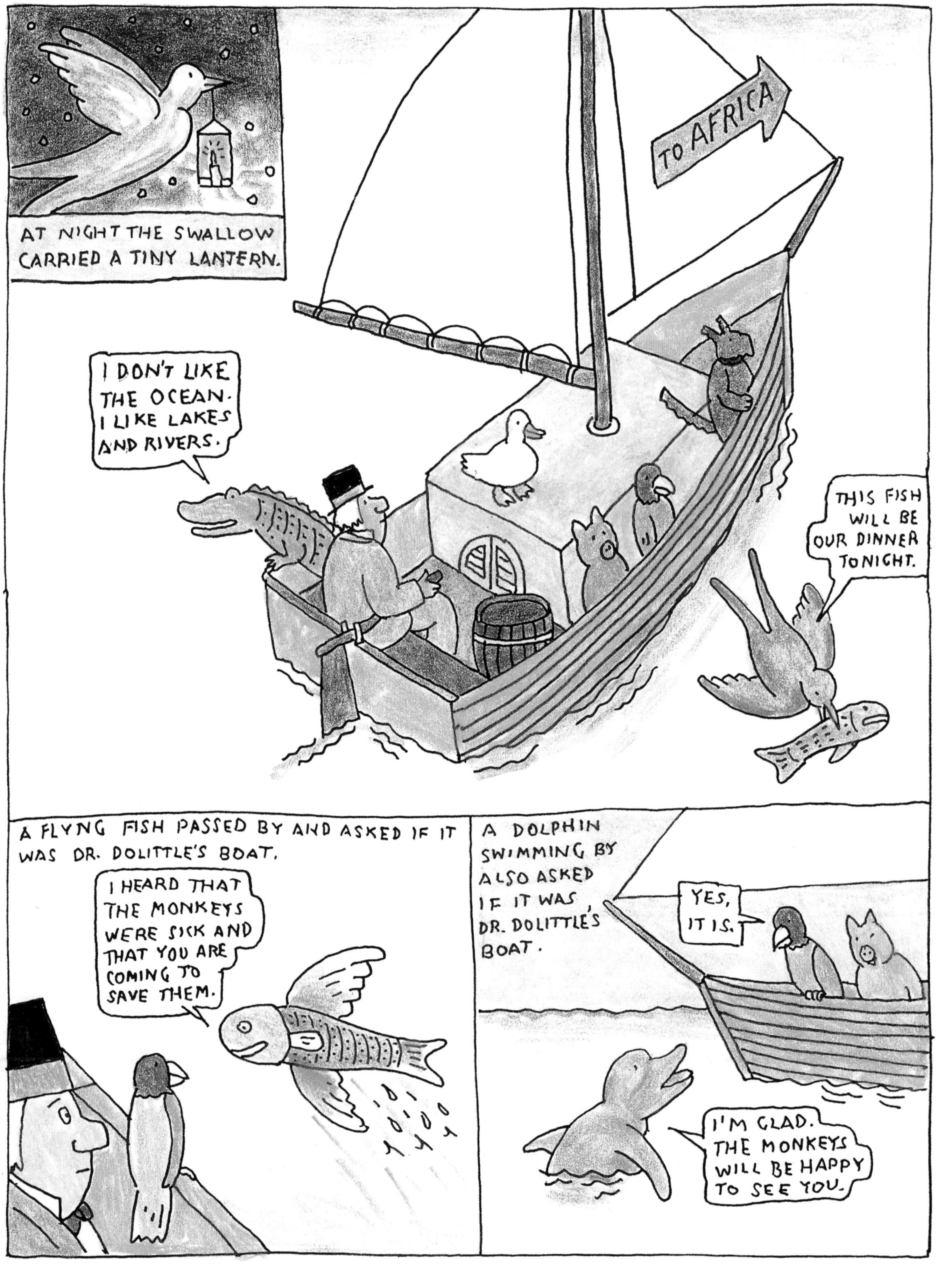
AT NIGHT THE SWALLOW CARRIED A TINY LANTERN.
TO AFRICA
I DON'T LIKE THE OCEAN. I LIKE LAKES AND RIVERS.
THIS FISH WILL BE OUR DINNER TONIGHT.
A FLYNG FISH PASSED BY AND ASKED IF IT WAS DR. DOLITTLE'S BOAT.
I HEARD THAT THE MONKEYS WERE SICK AND THAT YOU ARE COMING TO SAVE THEM.
A DOLPHIN SWIMMING BY ALSO ASKED IF IT WAS DR. DOLITTLE'S BOAT.
YES, IT IS.
I'M GLAD. THE MONKEYS WILL BE HAPPY TO SEE YOU.

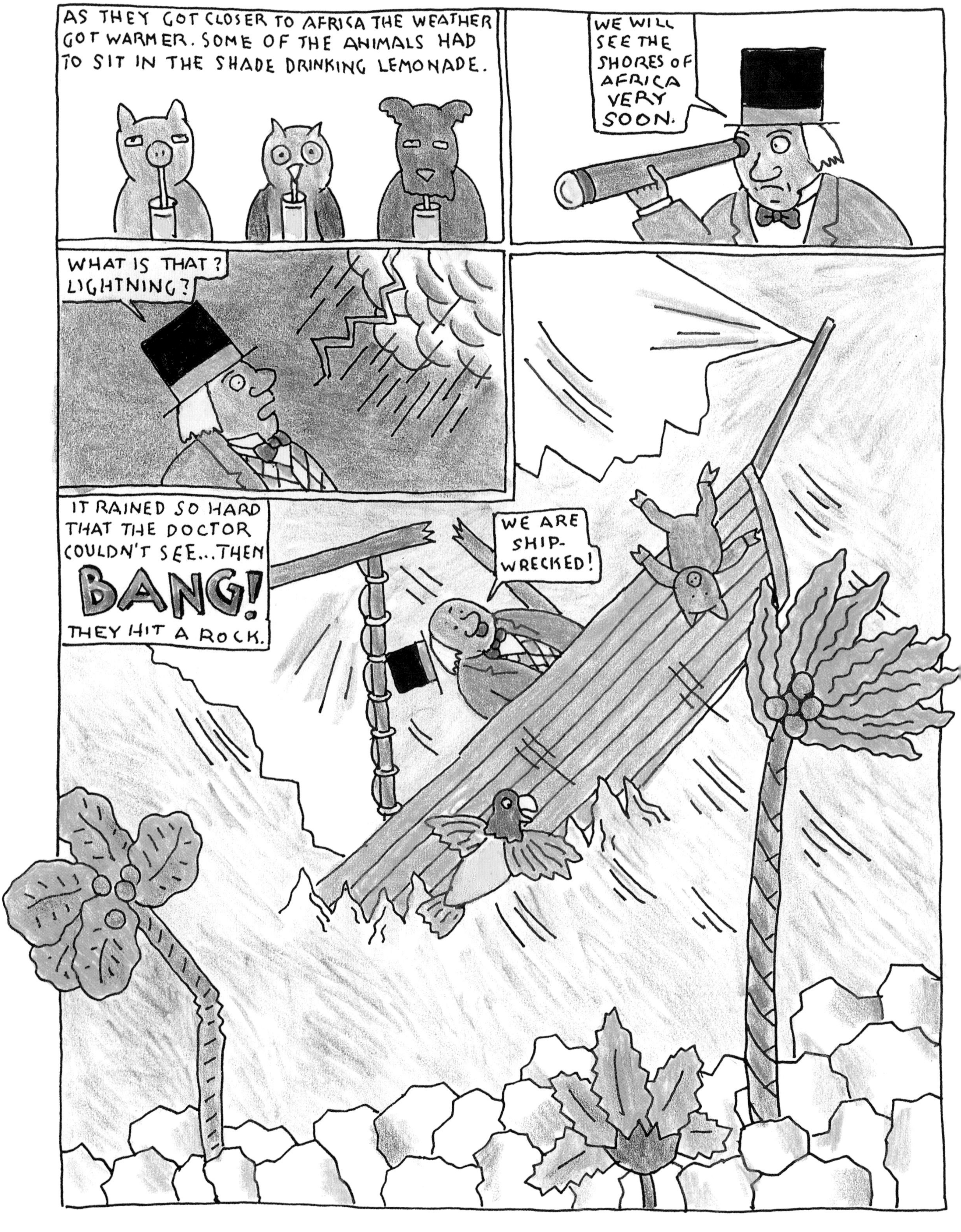
AS THEY GOT CLOSER TO AFRICA THE WEATHER GOT WARMER. SOME OF THE ANIMALS HAD TO SIT IN THE SHADE DRINKING LEMONADE.
WE WILL SEE THE SHORES OF AFRICA VERY SOON.
WHAT IS THAT? LIGHTNING?
IT RAINED SO HARD THAT THE DOCTOR COULDN'T SEE...THEN BANG! THEY HIT A ROCK.
WE ARE SHIP-WRECKED!

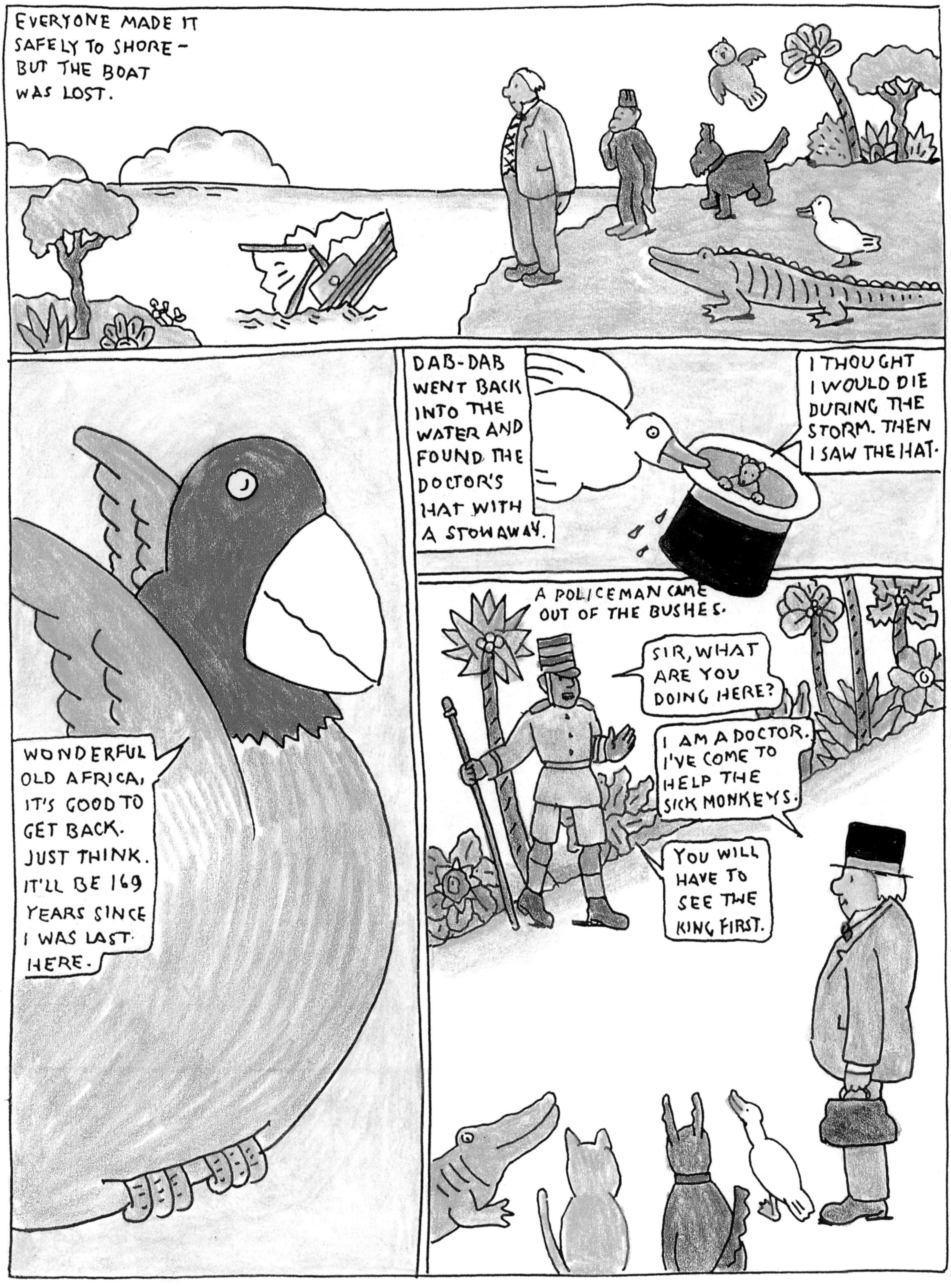
EVERYONE MADE IT SAFELY TO SHORE - BUT THE BOAT WAS LOST.
WONDERFUL OLD AFRICA, IT'S GOOD TO GET BACK. JUST THINK. IT'LL BE 169 YEARS SINCE I WAS LAST HERE.
DAB-DAB WENT BACK INTO THE WATER AND FOUND THE DOCTOR'S HAT WITH A STOWAWAY.
I THOUGHT I WOULD DIE DURING THE STORM. THEN I SAW THE HAT.
A POLICEMAN CAME OUT OF THE BUSHES.
SIR, WHAT ARE YOU DOING HERE?
I AM A DOCTOR. I'VE COME TO HELP THE SICK MONKEYS.
YOU WILL HAVE TO SEE THE KING FIRST.

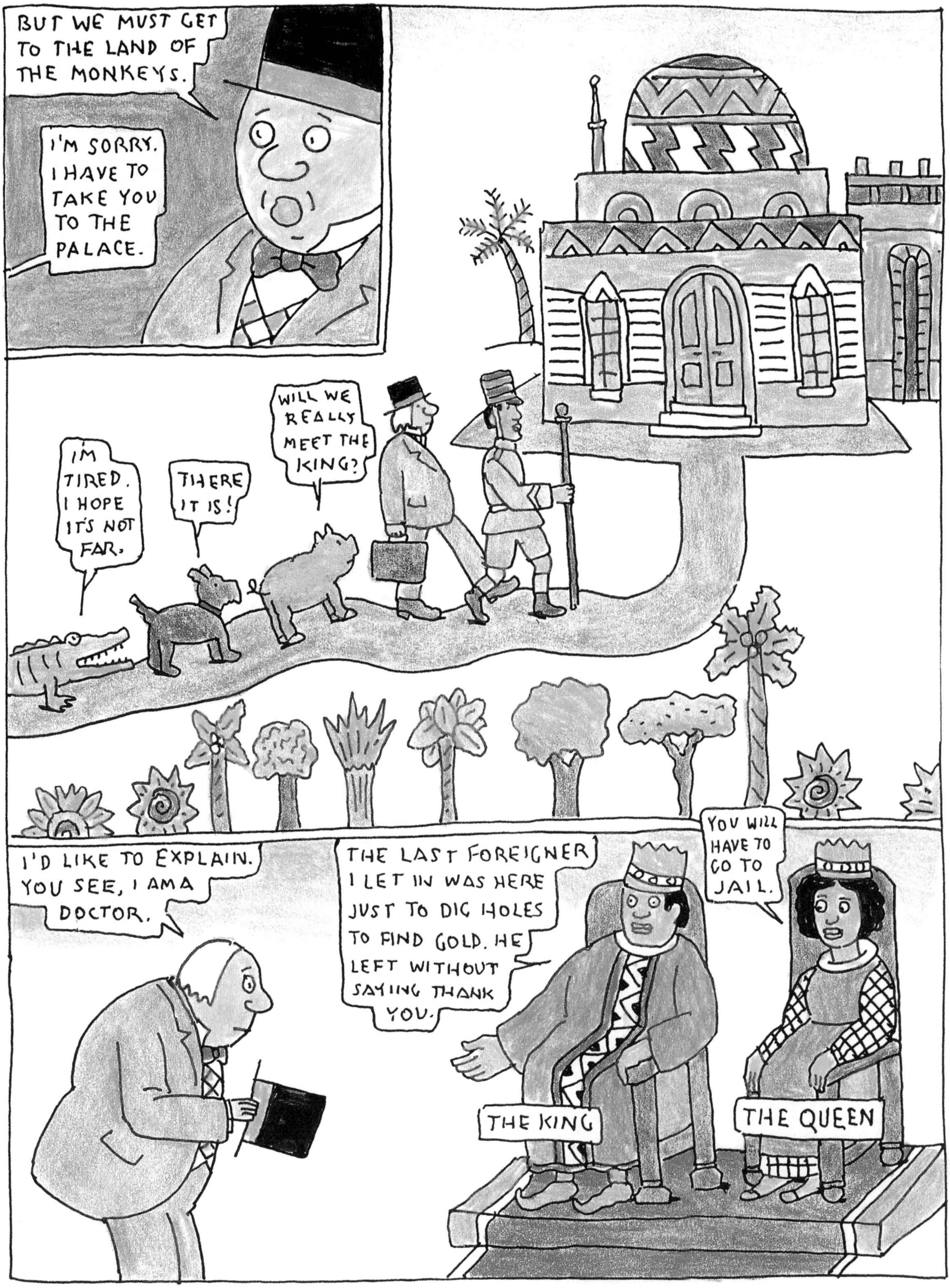
BUT WE MUST GET TO THE LAND OF THE MONKEYS.
I'M SORRY. I HAVE TO TAKE YOU TO THE PALACE.
I'M TIRED. I HOPE IT'S NOT FAR.
THERE IT IS!
WILL WE REALLY MEET THE KING?
I'D LIKE TO EXPLAIN. YOU SEE, I AM A DOCTOR.
THE LAST FOREIGNER I LET IN WAS HERE JUST TO DIG HOLES TO FIND GOLD. HE LEFT WITHOUT SAYING THANK YOU.
YOU WILL HAVE TO GO TO JAIL.
THE KING
THE QUEEN

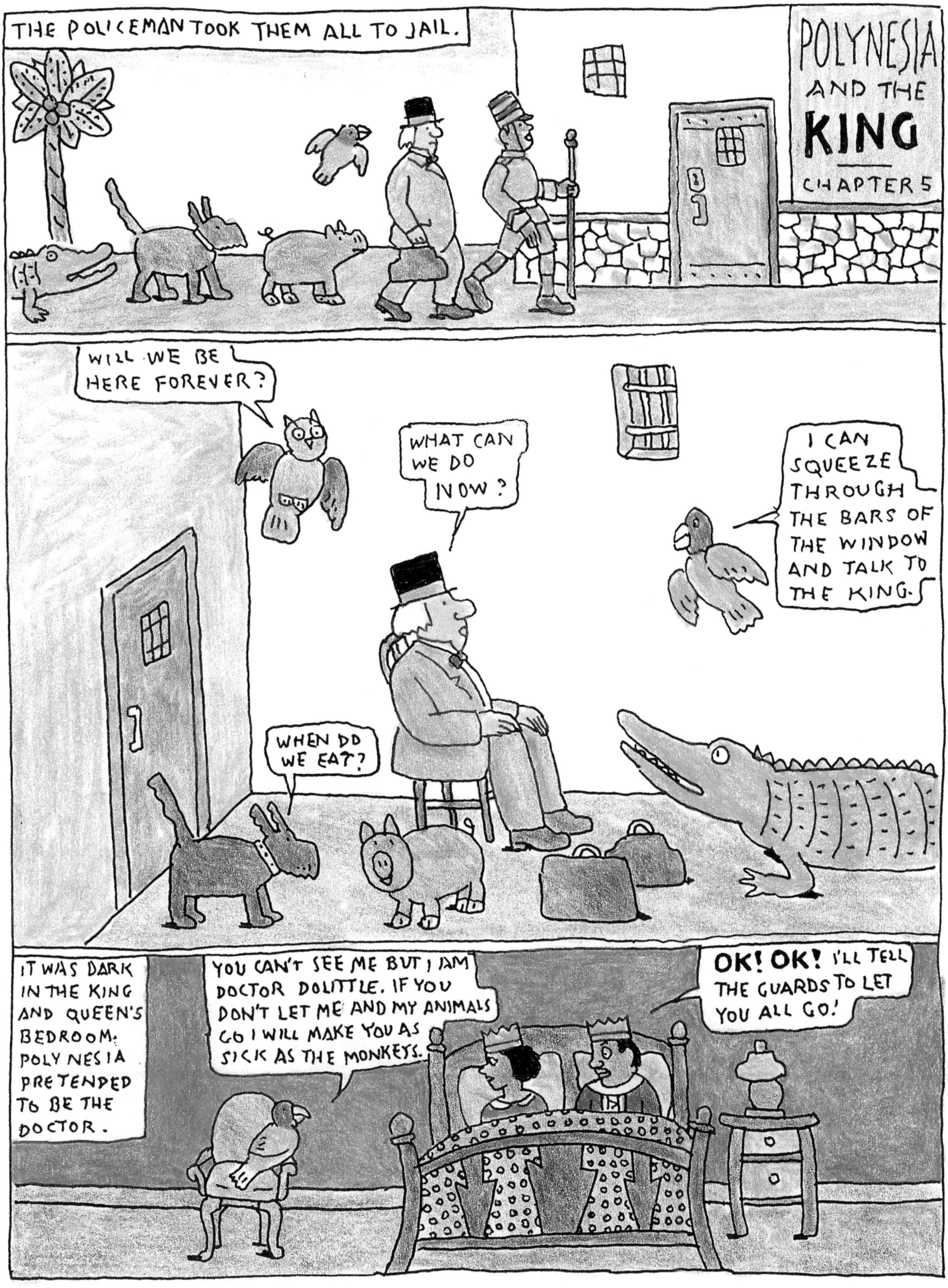
THE POLICEMAN TOOK THEM ALL TO JAIL.
POLYNESIA AND THE KING
CHAPTER 5
WILL WE BE HERE FOREVER?
WHAT CAN WE DO NOW?
I CAN SQUEEZE THROUGH THE BARS OF THE WINDOW AND TALK TO THE KING.
WHEN DO WE EAT?
IT WAS DARK IN THE KING AND QUEEN'S BEDROOM. POLYNESIA PRETENDED TO BE THE DOCTOR.
YOU CAN'T SEE ME BUT I AM DOCTOR DOLITTLE. IF YOU DON'T LET ME AND MY ANIMALS GO I WILL MAKE YOU AS SICK AS THE MONKEYS.
OK! OK! I'LL TELL THE GUARDS TO LET YOU ALL GO!

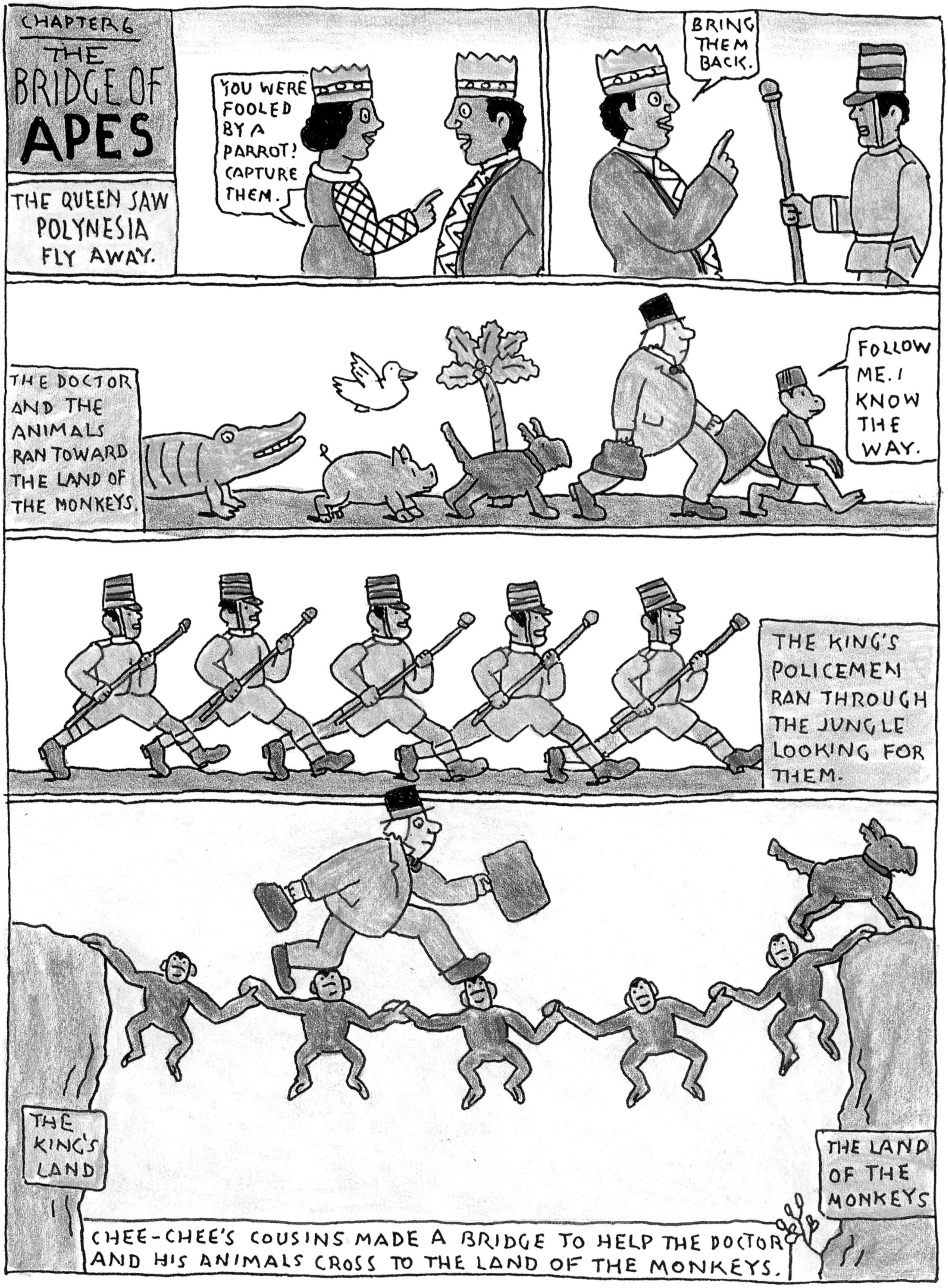
CHAPTER 6
THE BRIDGE OF APES
THE QUEEN SAW POLYNESIA FLY AWAY.
YOU WERE FOOLED BY A PARROT! CAPTURE THEM.
BRING THEM BACK.
THE DOCTOR AND THE ANIMALS RAN TOWARD THE LAND OF THE MONKEYS.
FOLLOW ME. I KNOW THE WAY.
THE KING'S POLICEMEN RAN THROUGH THE JUNGLE LOOKING FOR THEM.
THE KING'S LAND
THE LAND OF THE MONKEYS
CHEE-CHEE'S COUSINS MADE A BRIDGE TO HELP THE DOCTOR AND HIS ANIMALS CROSS TO THE LAND OF THE MONKEYS.

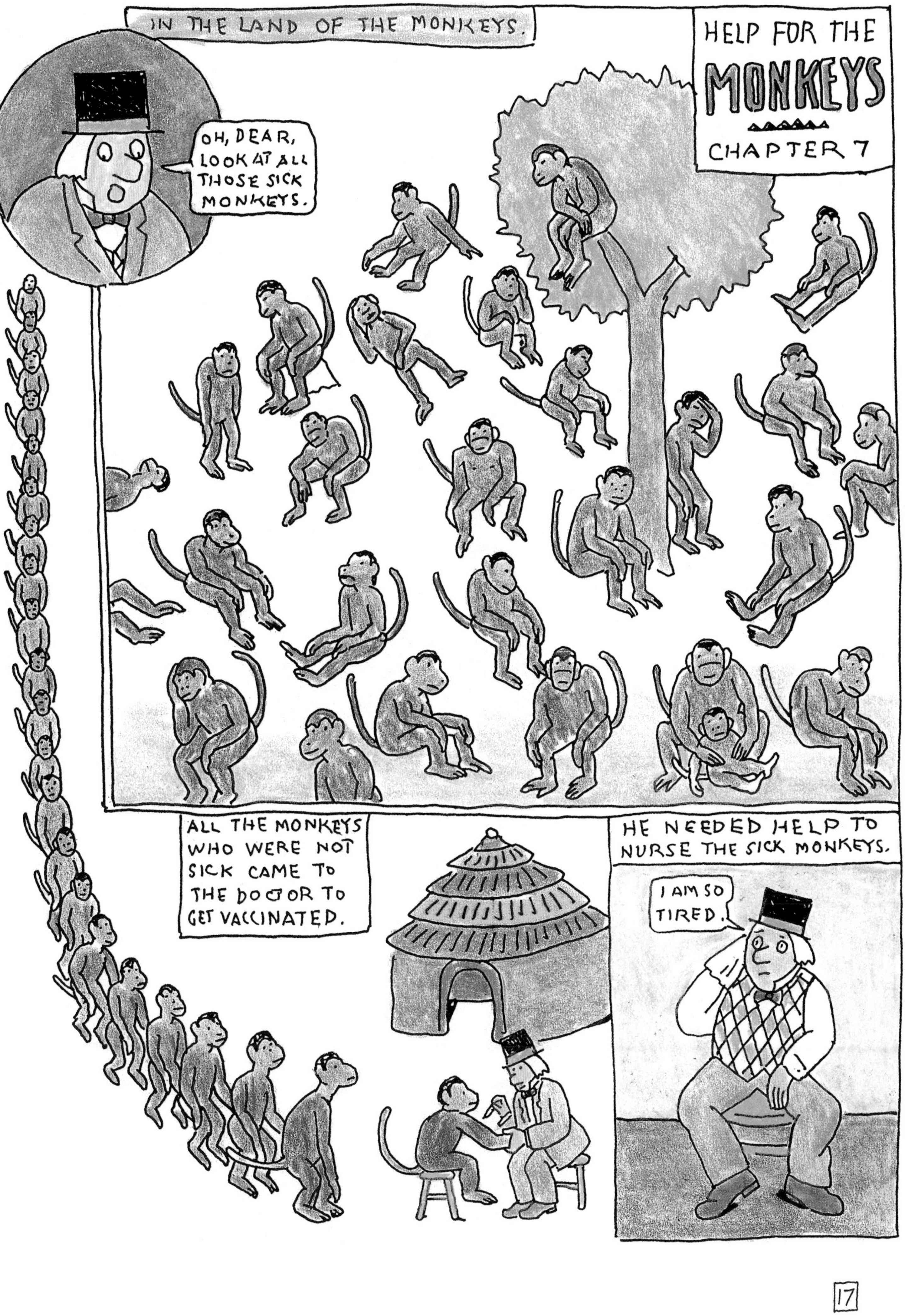

IN THE LAND OF THE MONKEYS.
HELP FOR THE
MONKEYS
CHAPTER 7
OH, DEAR, LOOK AT ALL THOSE SICK MONKEYS.
ALL THE MONKEYS WHO WERE NOT SICK CAME TO THE DOCTOR TO GET VACCINATED.
HE NEEDED HELP TO NURSE THE SICK MONKEYS.
I AM SO TIRED.

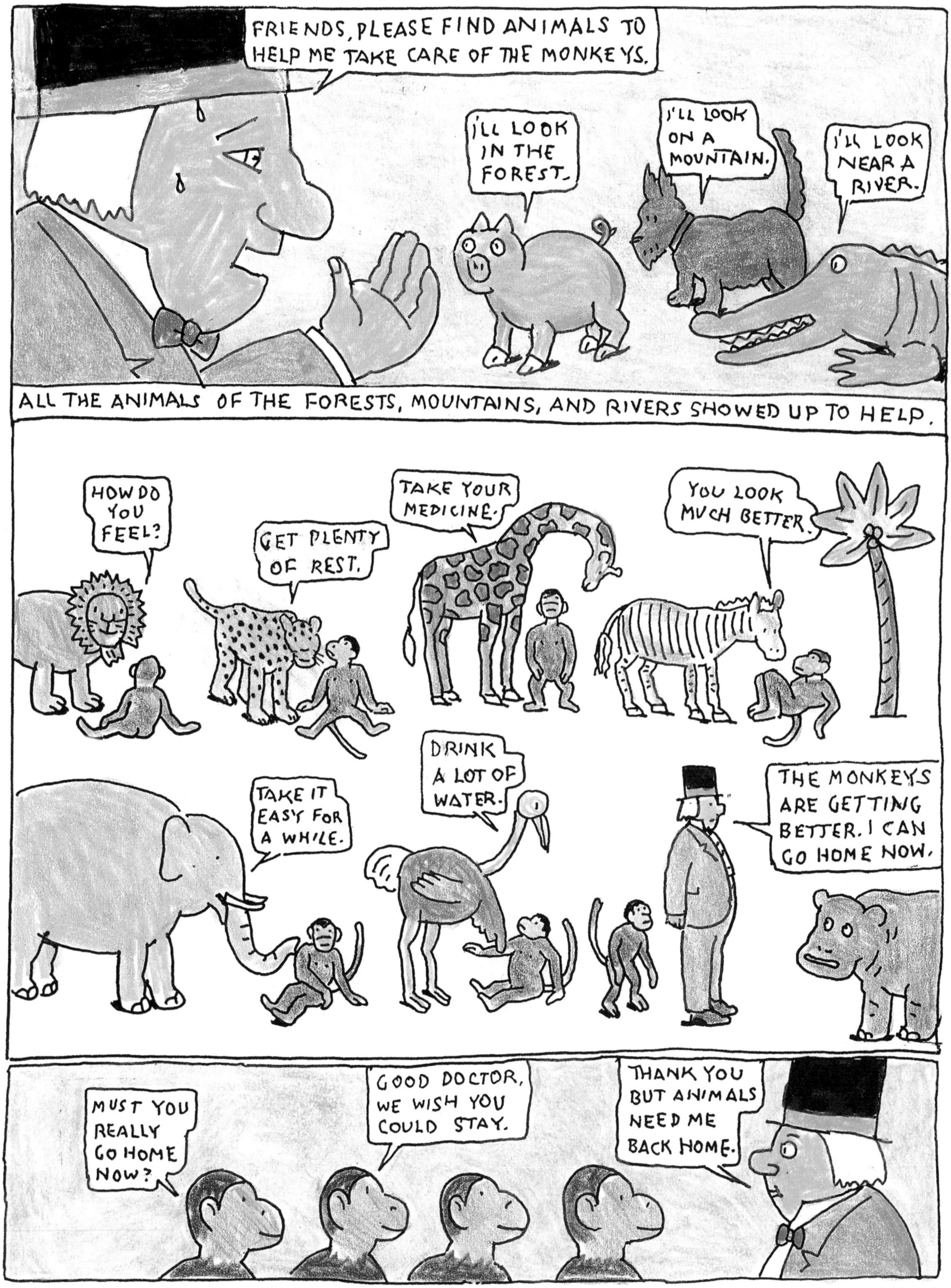
FRIENDS, PLEASE FIND ANIMALS TO HELP ME TAKE CARE OF THE MONKEYS.
I'LL LOOK IN THE FOREST.
I'LL LOOK ON A MOUNTAIN.
I'LL LOOK NEAR A RIVER.
ALL THE ANIMALS OF THE FORESTS, MOUNTAINS, AND RIVERS SHOWED UP TO HELP.
HOW DO YOU FEEL?
GET PLENTY OF REST.
TAKE YOUR MEDICINE.
YOU LOOK MUCH BETTER.
TAKE IT EASY FOR A WHILE.
DRINK A LOT OF WATER.
THE MONKEYS ARE GETTING BETTER. I CAN GO HOME NOW.
MUST YOU REALLY GO HOME NOW?
GOOD DOCTOR, WE WISH YOU COULD STAY.
THANK YOU BUT ANIMALS NEED ME BACK HOME.

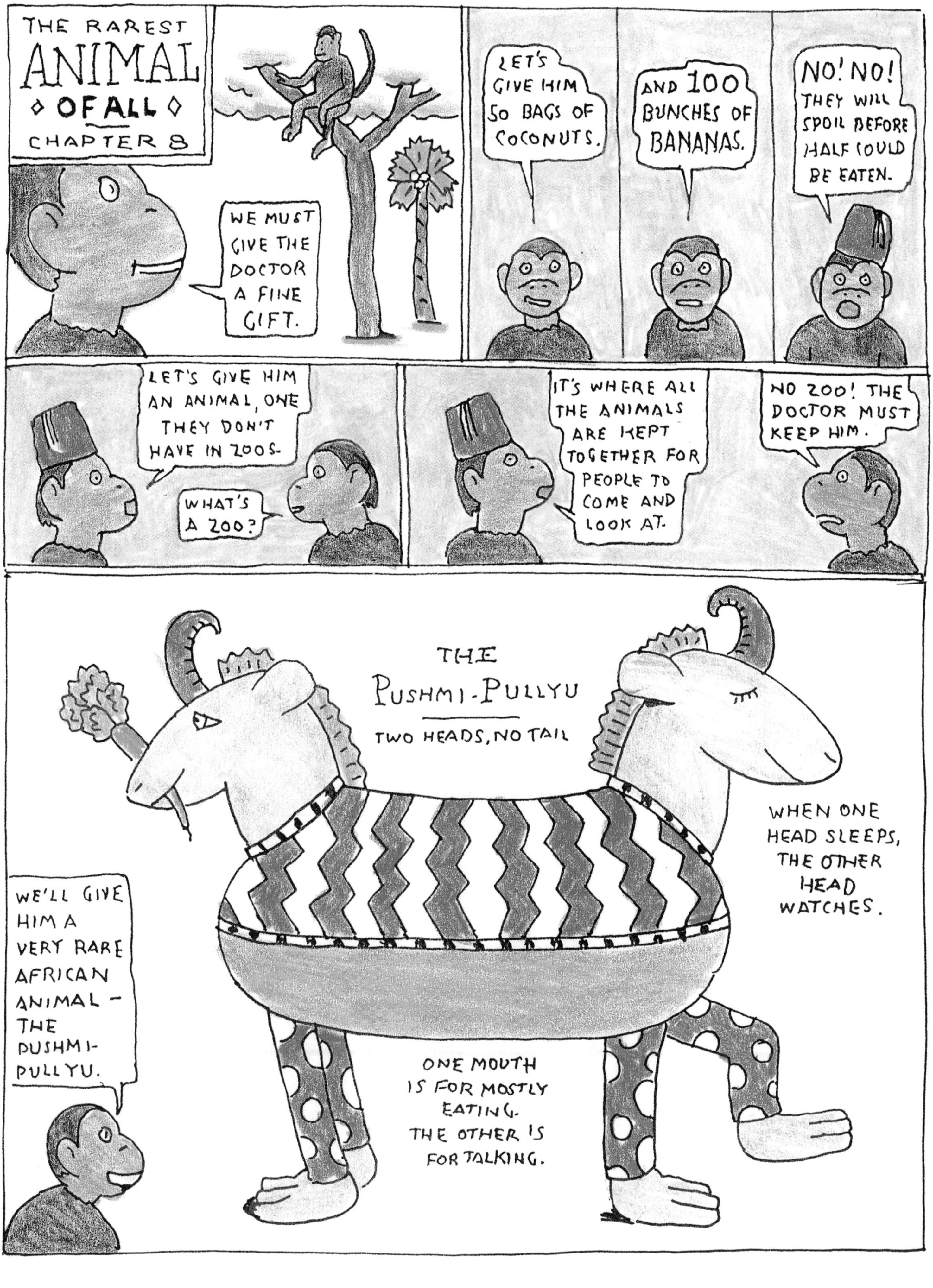

THE RAREST ANIMAL OF ALL
CHAPTER 8
WE MUST GIVE THE DOCTOR A FINE GIFT.
LET'S GIVE HIM 50 BAGS OF COCONUTS.
AND 100 BUNCHES OF BANANAS.
NO! NO! THEY WILL SPOIL BEFORE HALF COULD BE EATEN.
LET'S GIVE HIM AN ANIMAL, ONE THEY DON'T HAVE IN ZOOS.
WHAT'S A ZOO?
IT'S WHERE ALL THE ANIMALS ARE KEPT TOGETHER FOR PEOPLE TO COME AND LOOK AT.
NO ZOO! THE DOCTOR MUST KEEP HIM.
WE'LL GIVE HIM A VERY RARE AFRICAN ANIMAL – THE PUSHMI-PULLYU.
THE PUSHMI-PULLYU
TWO HEADS, NO TAIL
WHEN ONE HEAD SLEEPS, THE OTHER HEAD WATCHES.
ONE MOUTH IS FOR MOSTLY EATING. THE OTHER IS FOR TALKING.

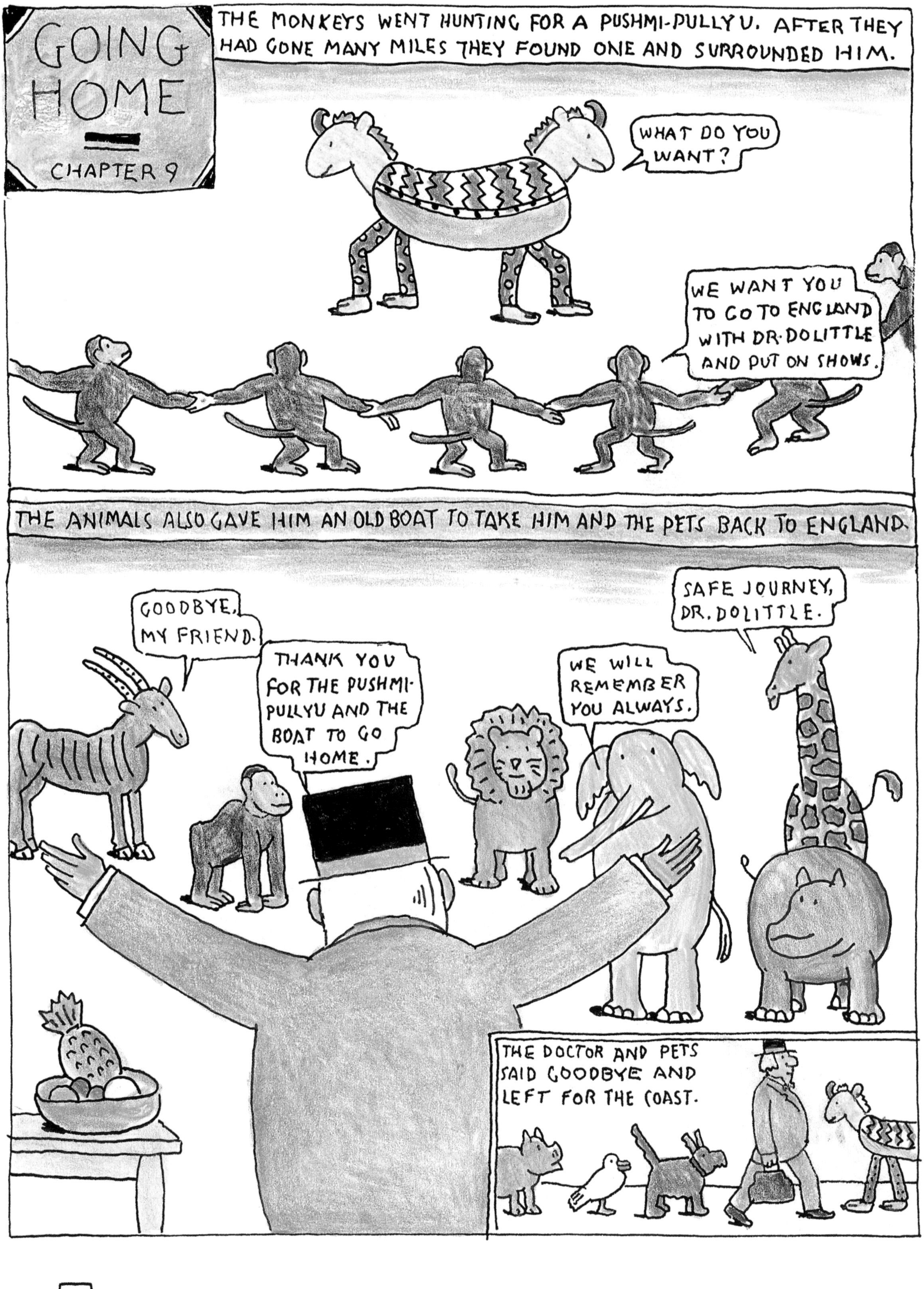
GOING HOME
CHAPTER 9
THE MONKEYS WENT HUNTING FOR A PUSHMI-PULLYU. AFTER THEY HAD GONE MANY MILES THEY FOUND ONE AND SURROUNDED HIM.
WHAT DO YOU WANT?
WE WANT YOU TO GO TO ENGLAND WITH DR. DOLITTLE AND PUT ON SHOWS.
THE ANIMALS ALSO GAVE HIM AN OLD BOAT TO TAKE HIM AND THE PETS BACK TO ENGLAND.
GOODBYE, MY FRIEND.
THANK YOU FOR THE PUSHMI-PULLYU AND THE BOAT TO GO HOME.
WE WILL REMEMBER YOU ALWAYS.
SAFE JOURNEY, DR. DOLITTLE.
THE DOCTOR AND PETS SAID GOODBYE AND LEFT FOR THE COAST.

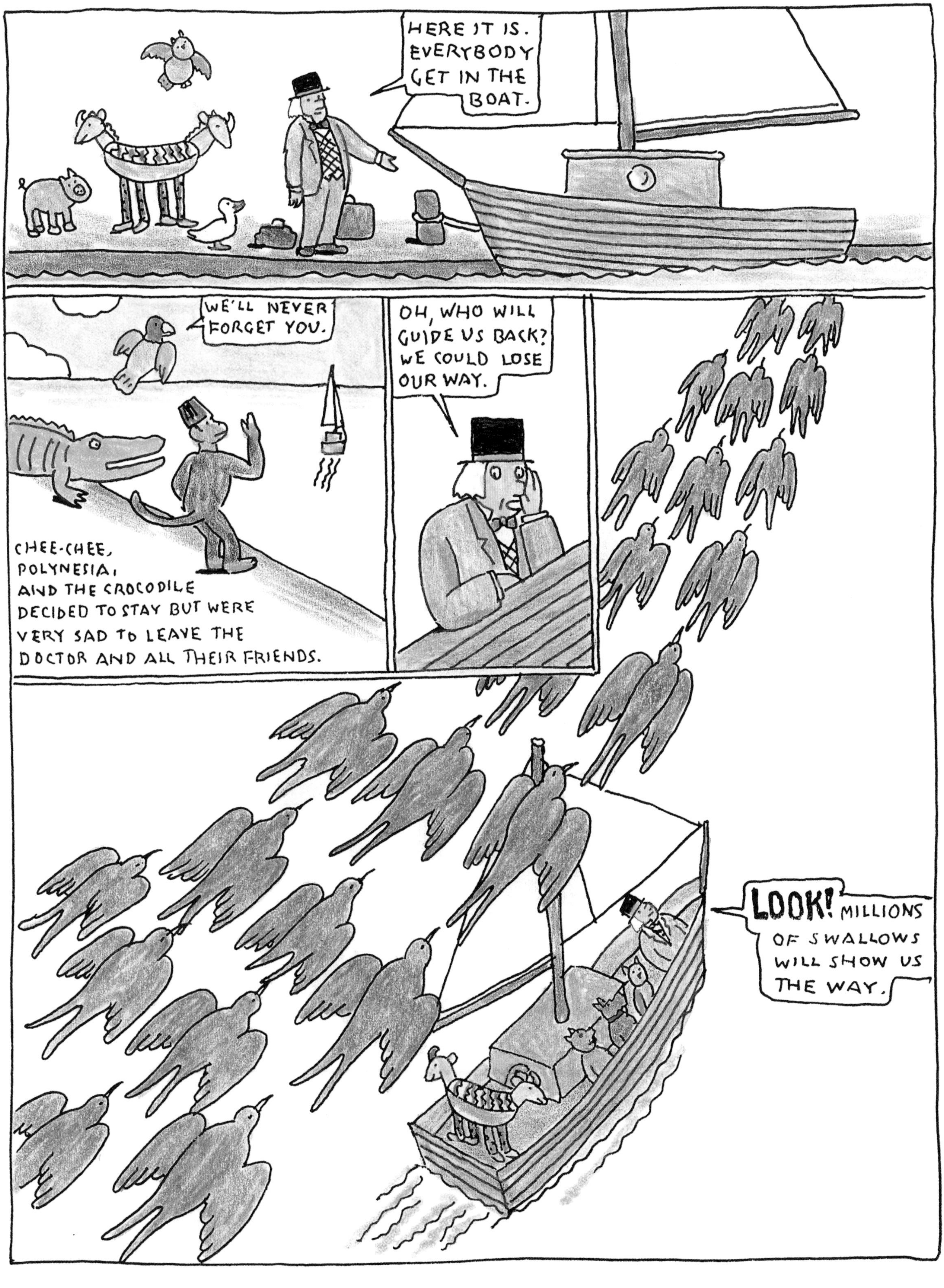
HERE IT IS. EVERYBODY GET IN THE BOAT.
WE'LL NEVER FORGET YOU.
CHEE-CHEE, POLYNESIA, AND THE CROCODILE DECIDED TO STAY BUT WERE VERY SAD TO LEAVE THE DOCTOR AND ALL THEIR FRIENDS.
OH, WHO WILL GUIDE US BACK? WE COULD LOSE OUR WAY.
LOOK! MILLIONS OF SWALLOWS WILL SHOW US THE WAY.

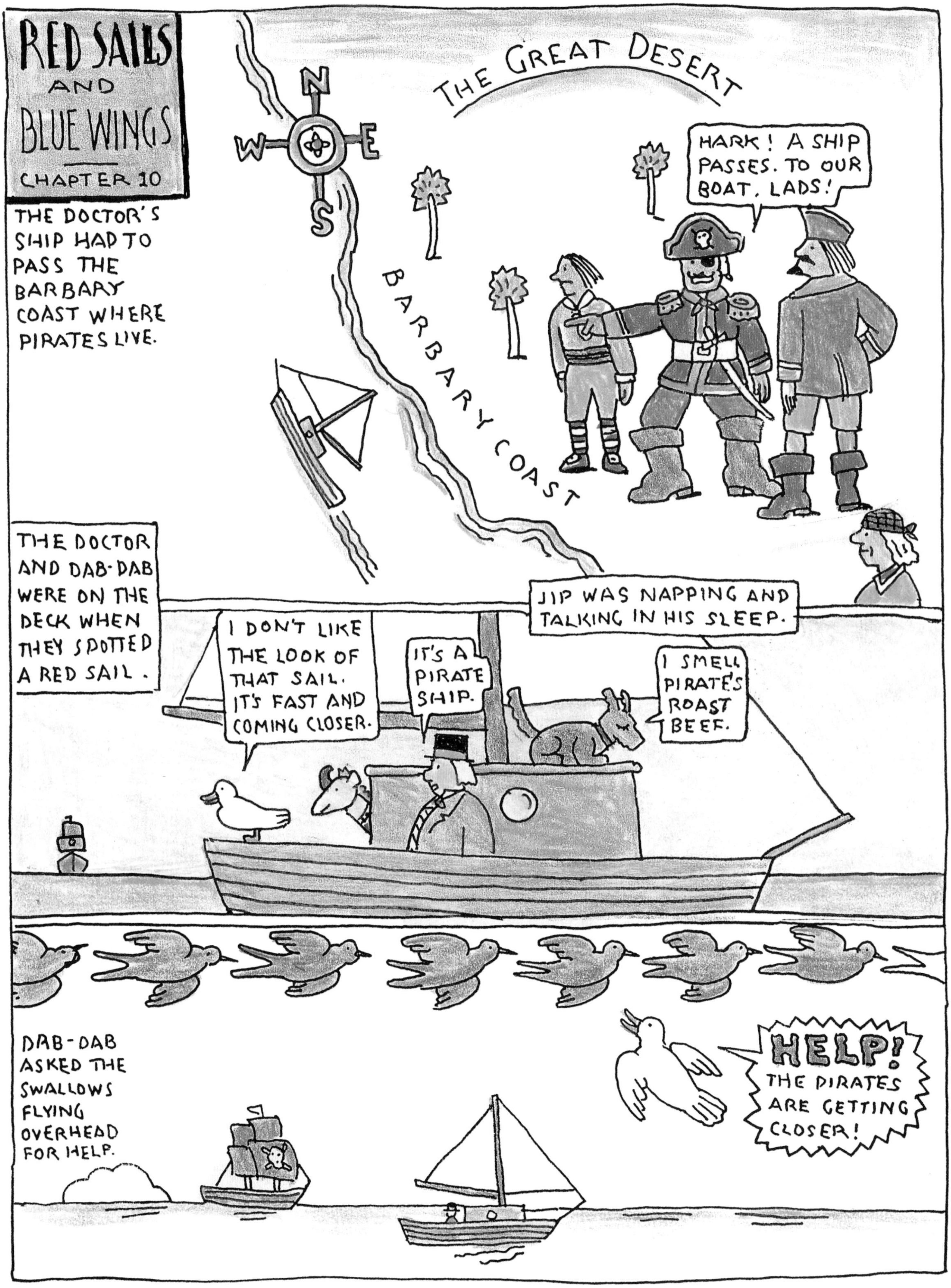
RED SAILS AND BLUE WINGS
CHAPTER 10
THE DOCTOR'S SHIP HAD TO PASS THE BARBARY COAST WHERE PIRATES LIVE.
N
W
E
S
THE GREAT DESERT
BARBARY COAST
HARK! A SHIP PASSES. TO OUR BOAT, LADS!
THE DOCTOR AND DAB-DAB WERE ON THE DECK WHEN THEY SPOTTED A RED SAIL.
JIP WAS NAPPING AND TALKING IN HIS SLEEP.
I DON'T LIKE THE LOOK OF THAT SAIL. IT'S FAST AND COMING CLOSER.
IT'S A PIRATE SHIP.
I SMELL PIRATE'S ROAST BEEF.
DAB-DAB ASKED THE SWALLOWS FLYING OVERHEAD FOR HELP.
HELP! THE PIRATES ARE GETTING CLOSER!

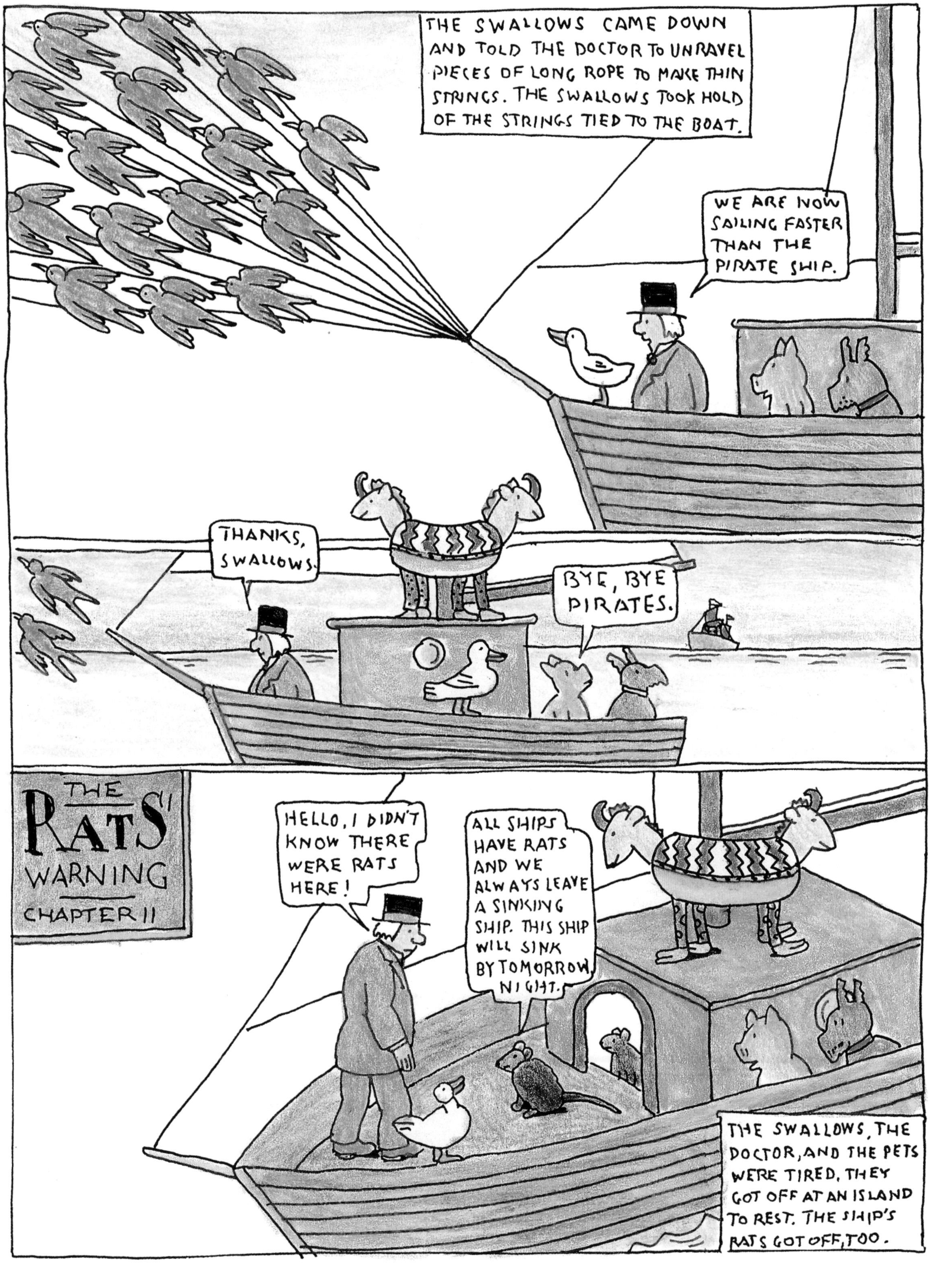
THE SWALLOWS CAME DOWN AND TOLD THE DOCTOR TO UNRAVEL PIECES OF LONG ROPE TO MAKE THIN STRINGS. THE SWALLOWS TOOK HOLD OF THE STRINGS TIED TO THE BOAT.
WE ARE NOW SAILING FASTER THAN THE PIRATE SHIP.
THANKS, SWALLOWS.
BYE, BYE PIRATES.
THE RATS' WARNING
CHAPTER 11
HELLO, I DIDN'T KNOW THERE WERE RATS HERE!
ALL SHIPS HAVE RATS AND WE ALWAYS LEAVE A SINKING SHIP. THIS SHIP WILL SINK BY TOMORROW NIGHT.
THE SWALLOWS, THE DOCTOR, AND THE PETS WERE TIRED. THEY GOT OFF AT AN ISLAND TO REST. THE SHIP'S RATS GOT OFF, TOO.

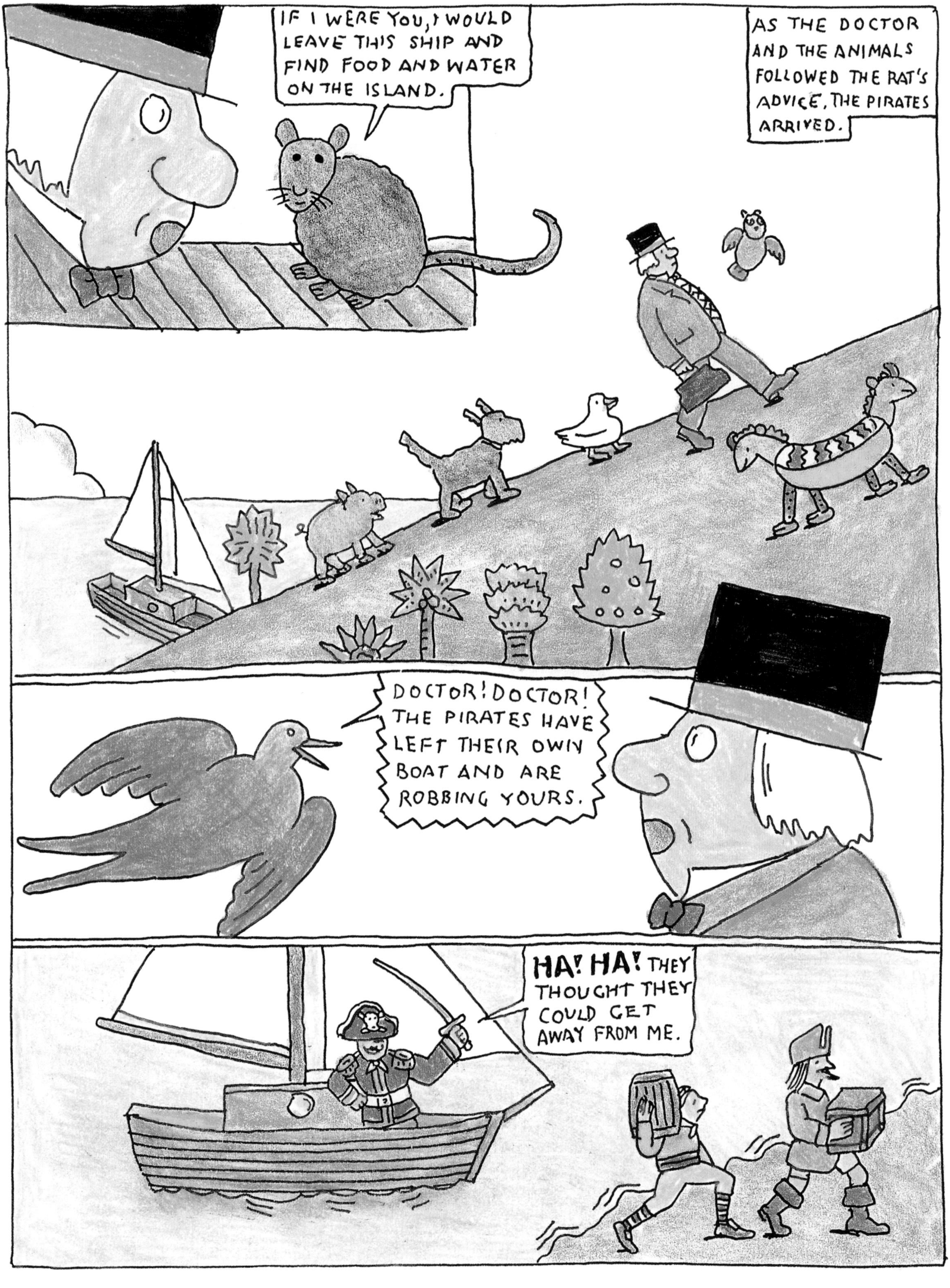
IF I WERE YOU, I WOULD LEAVE THIS SHIP AND FIND FOOD AND WATER ON THE ISLAND.
AS THE DOCTOR AND THE ANIMALS FOLLOWED THE RAT'S ADVICE, THE PIRATES ARRIVED.
DOCTOR! DOCTOR! THE PIRATES HAVE LEFT THEIR OWN BOAT AND ARE ROBBING YOURS.
HA! HA! THEY THOUGHT THEY COULD GET AWAY FROM ME.

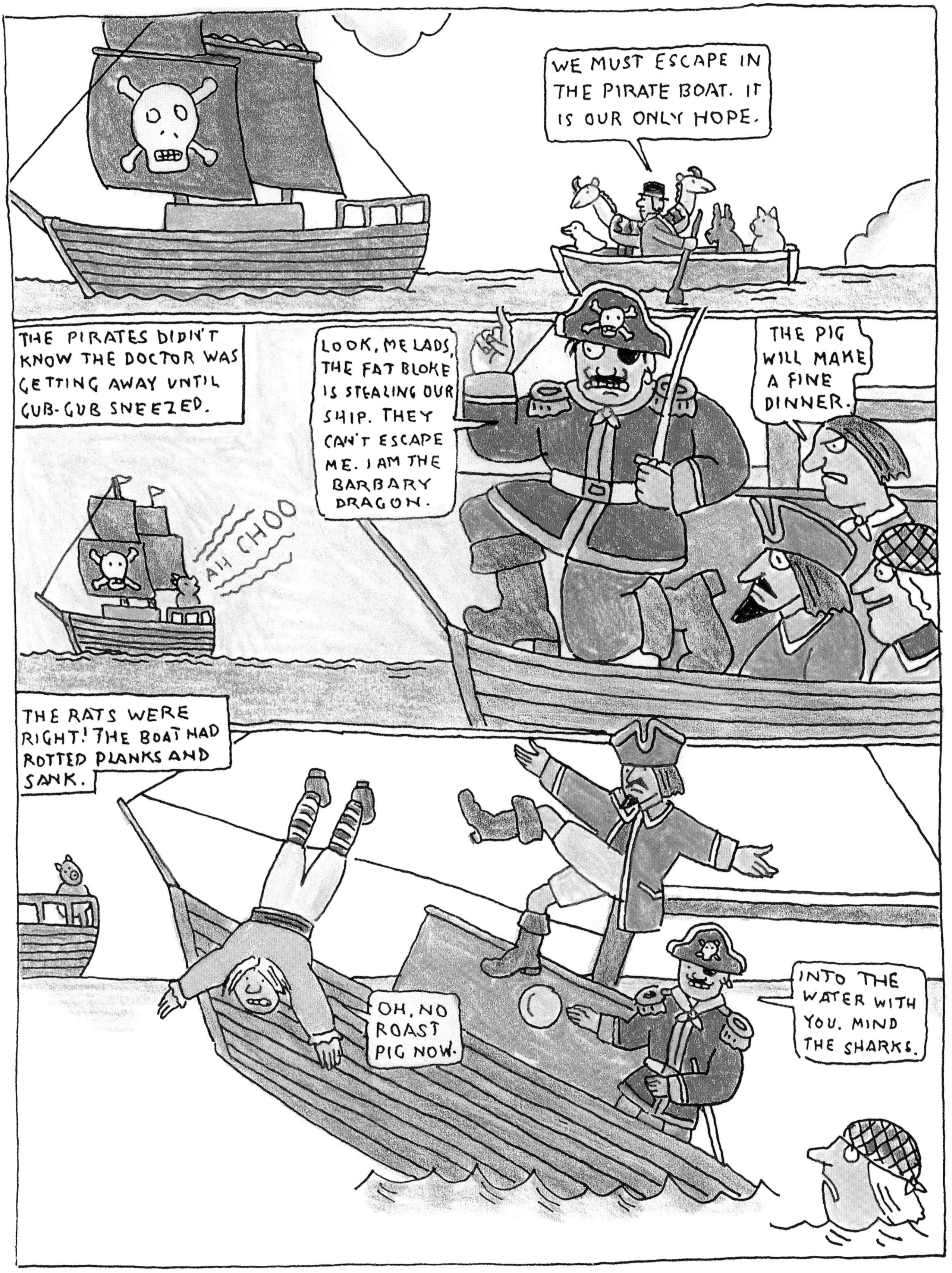
WE MUST ESCAPE IN THE PIRATE BOAT. IT IS OUR ONLY HOPE.
THE PIRATES DIDN'T KNOW THE DOCTOR WAS GETTING AWAY UNTIL GUB-GUB SNEEZED.
AH CHOO
LOOK, ME LADS, THE FAT BLOKE IS STEALING OUR SHIP. THEY CAN'T ESCAPE ME. I AM THE BARBARY DRAGON.
THE PIG WILL MAKE A FINE DINNER.
THE RATS WERE RIGHT! THE BOAT HAD ROTTED PLANKS AND SANK.
OH, NO ROAST PIG NOW.
INTO THE WATER WITH YOU. MIND THE SHARKS.

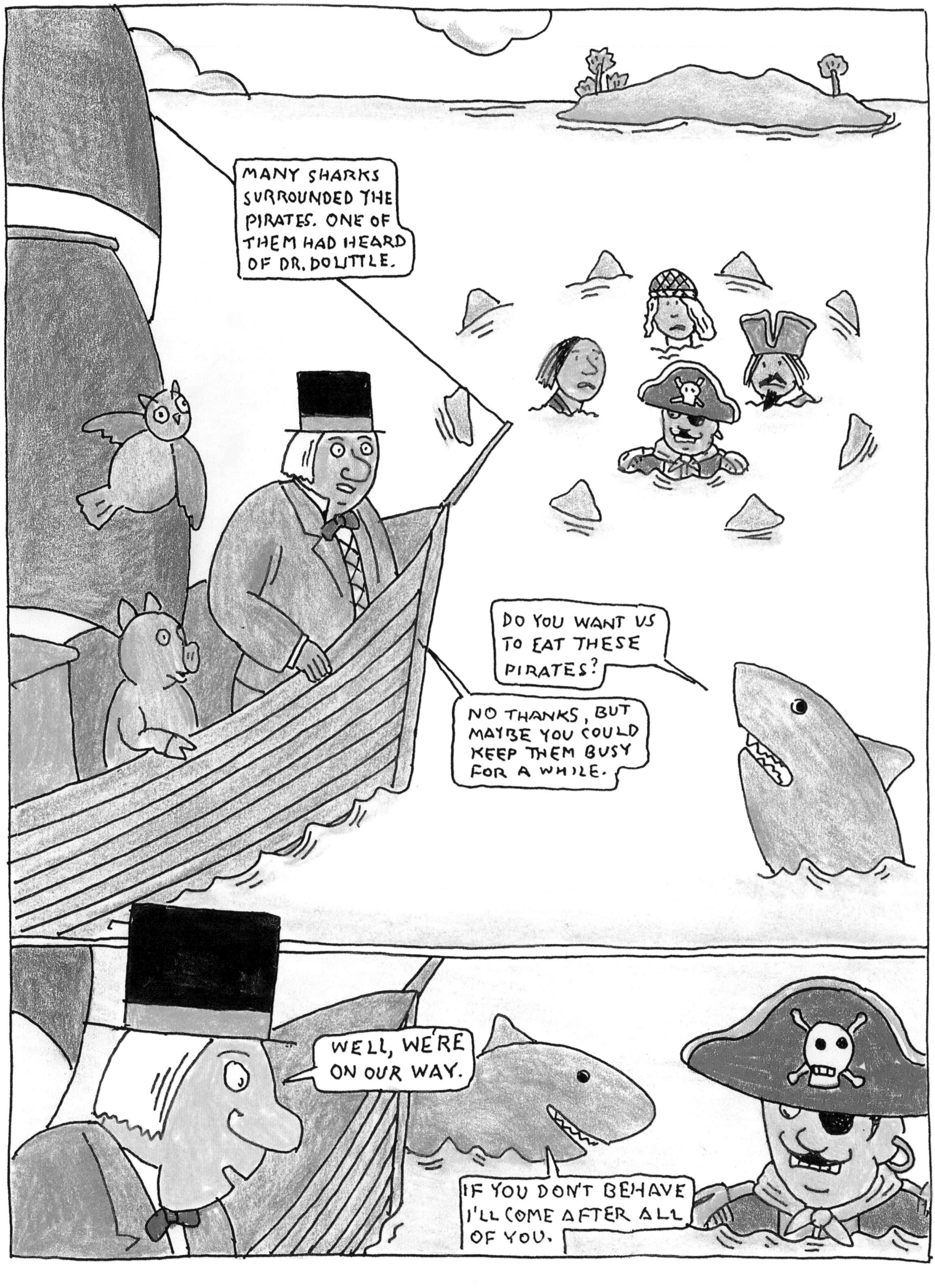
MANY SHARKS SURROUNDED THE PIRATES. ONE OF THEM HAD HEARD OF DR. DOLITTLE.
DO YOU WANT US TO EAT THESE PIRATES?
NO THANKS, BUT MAYBE YOU COULD KEEP THEM BUSY FOR A WHILE.
WELL, WE'RE ON OUR WAY.
IF YOU DON'T BEHAVE I'LL COME AFTER ALL OF YOU.

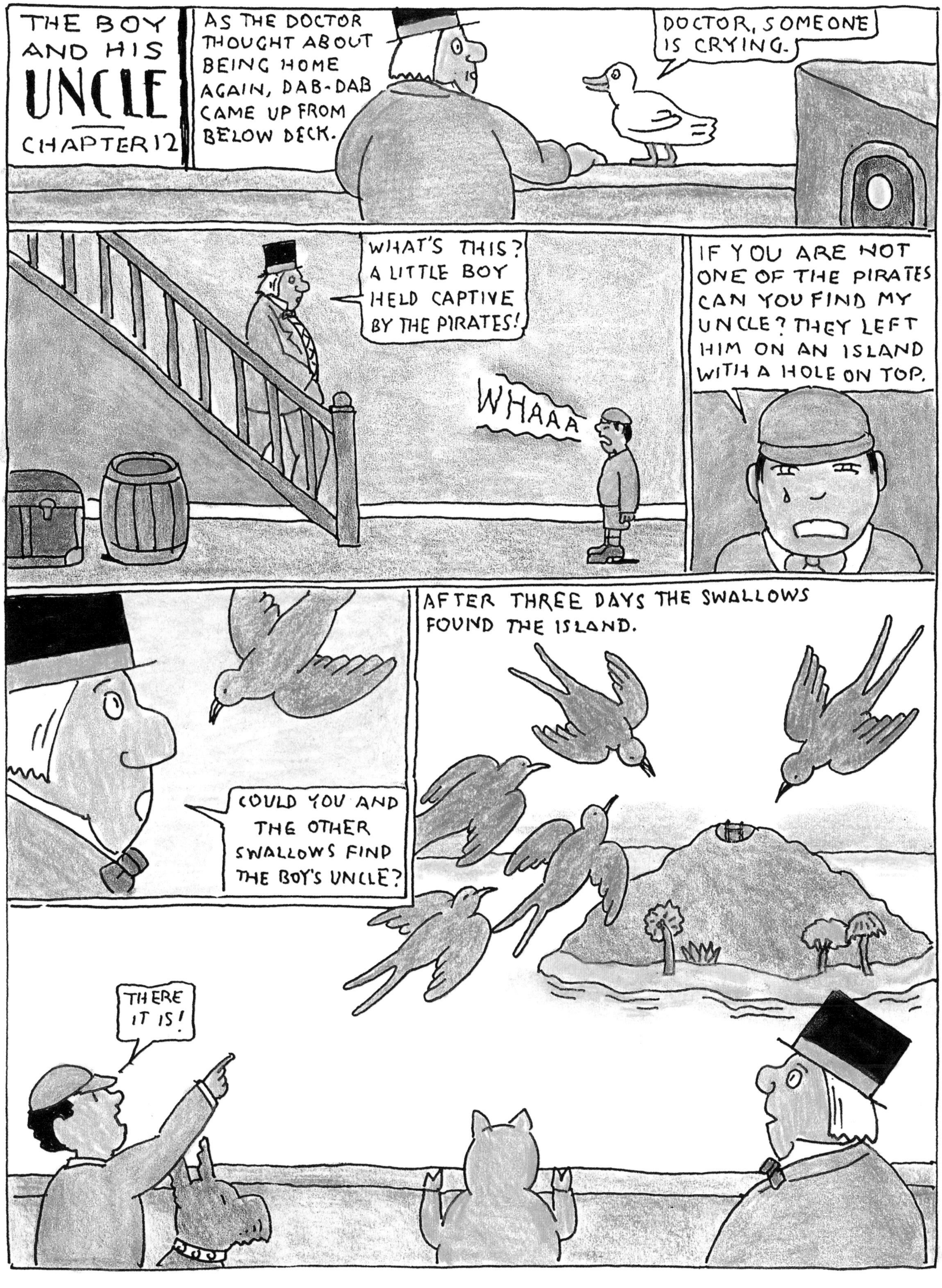
THE BOY AND HIS UNCLE
CHAPTER 12
AS THE DOCTOR THOUGHT ABOUT BEING HOME AGAIN, DAB-DAB CAME UP FROM BELOW DECK.
DOCTOR, SOMEONE IS CRYING.
WHAT'S THIS? A LITTLE BOY HELD CAPTIVE BY THE PIRATES!
WHAAAA
IF YOU ARE NOT ONE OF THE PIRATES CAN YOU FIND MY UNCLE? THEY LEFT HIM ON AN ISLAND WITH A HOLE ON TOP.
COULD YOU AND THE OTHER SWALLOWS FIND THE BOY'S UNCLE?
AFTER THREE DAYS THE SWALLOWS FOUND THE ISLAND.
THERE IT IS!

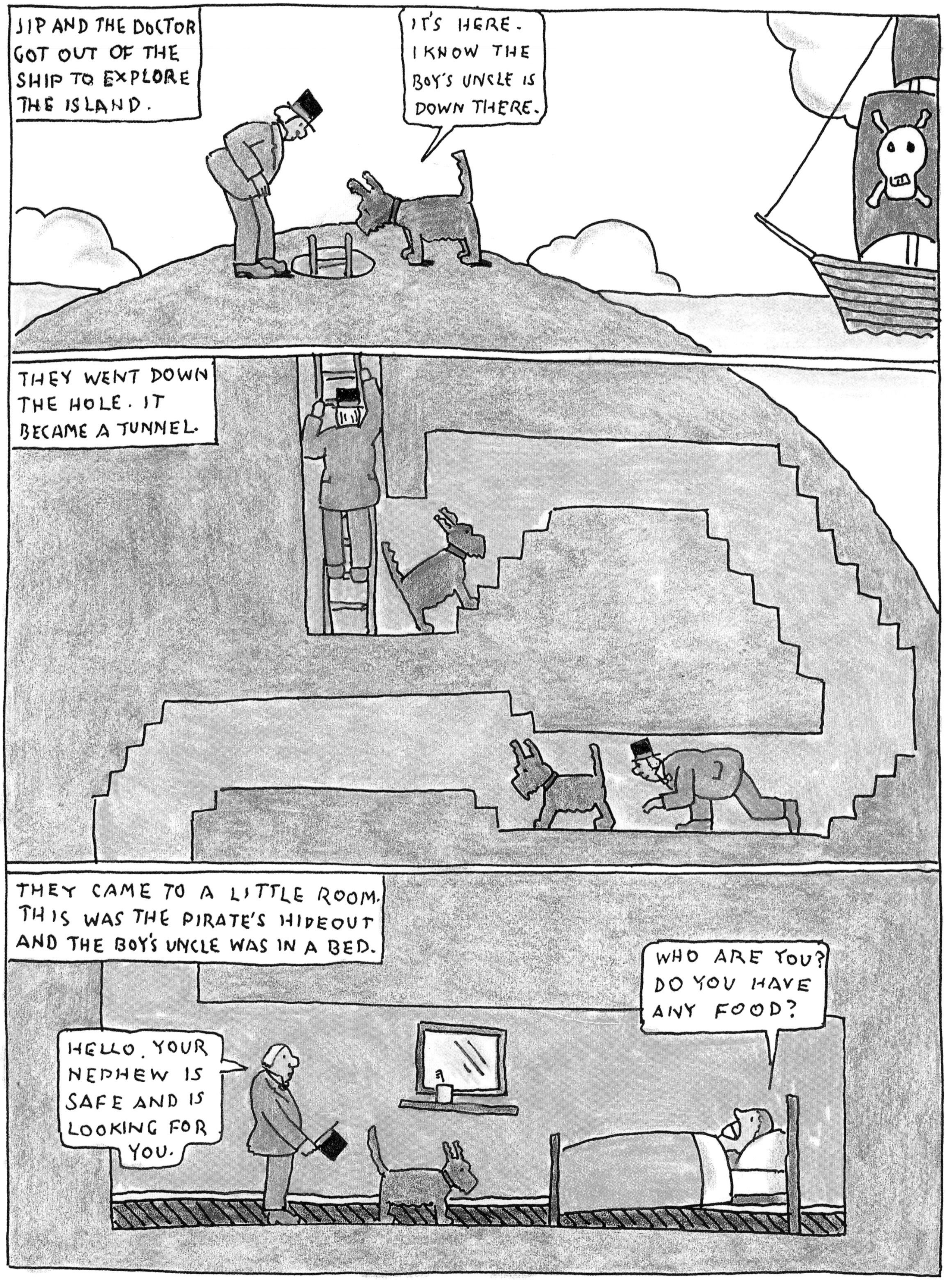
JIP AND THE DOCTOR GOT OUT OF THE SHIP TO EXPLORE THE ISLAND.
IT'S HERE. I KNOW THE BOY'S UNCLE IS DOWN THERE.
THEY WENT DOWN THE HOLE. IT BECAME A TUNNEL.
THEY CAME TO A LITTLE ROOM. THIS WAS THE PIRATE'S HIDEOUT AND THE BOY'S UNCLE WAS IN A BED.
HELLO. YOUR NEPHEW IS SAFE AND IS LOOKING FOR YOU.
WHO ARE YOU? DO YOU HAVE ANY FOOD?

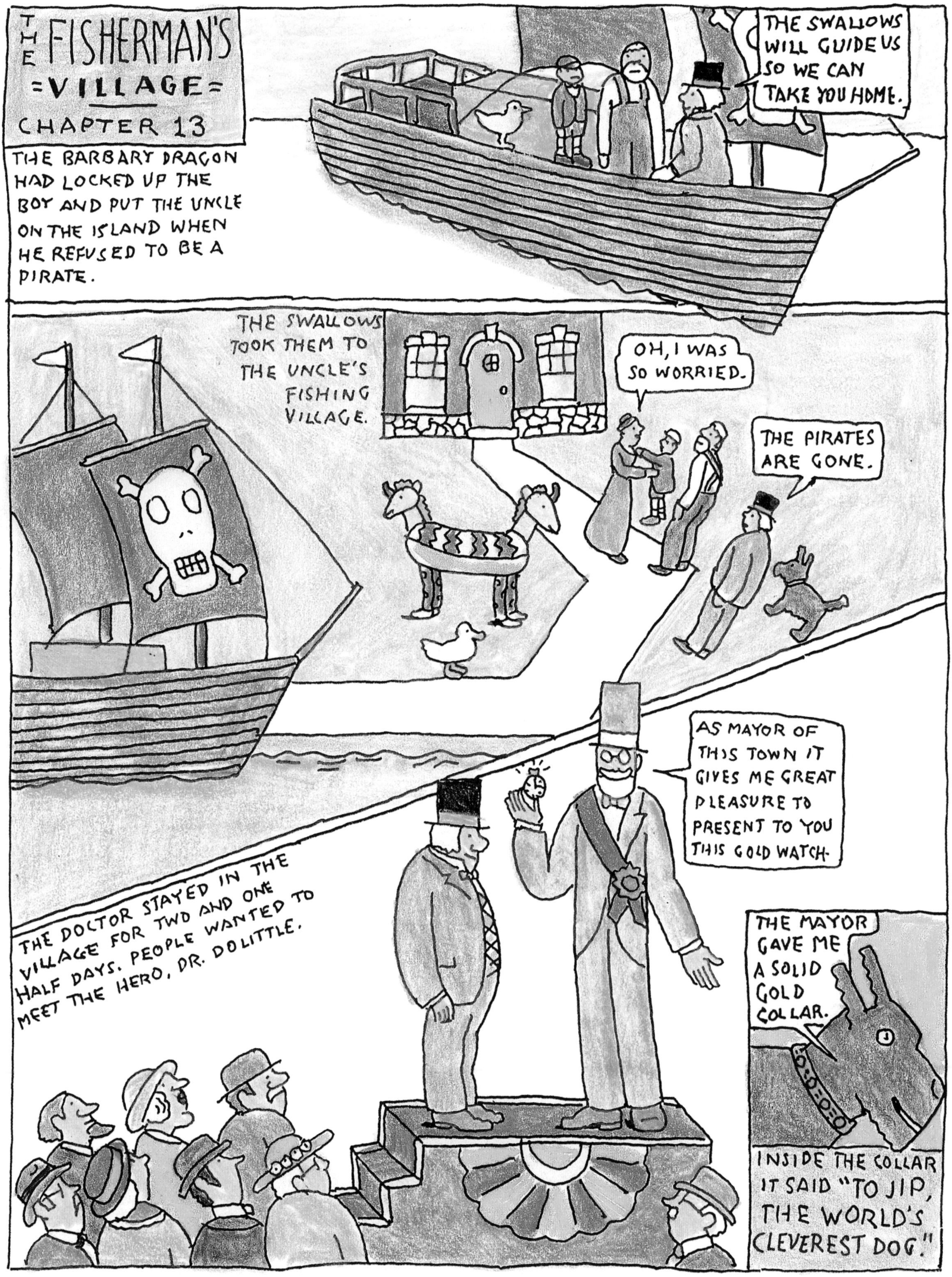
THE FISHERMAN'S VILLAGE
CHAPTER 13
THE BARBARY DRAGON HAD LOCKED UP THE BOY AND PUT THE UNCLE ON THE ISLAND WHEN HE REFUSED TO BE A PIRATE.
THE SWALLOWS WILL GUIDE US SO WE CAN TAKE YOU HOME.
THE SWALLOWS TOOK THEM TO THE UNCLE'S FISHING VILLAGE.
OH, I WAS SO WORRIED.
THE PIRATES ARE GONE.
AS MAYOR OF THIS TOWN IT GIVES ME GREAT PLEASURE TO PRESENT TO YOU THIS GOLD WATCH.
THE DOCTOR STAYED IN THE VILLAGE FOR TWO AND ONE HALF DAYS. PEOPLE WANTED TO MEET THE HERO, DR. DOLITTLE.
THE MAYOR GAVE ME A SOLID GOLD COLLAR.
INSIDE THE COLLAR IT SAID "TO JIP, THE WORLD'S CLEVEREST DOG."

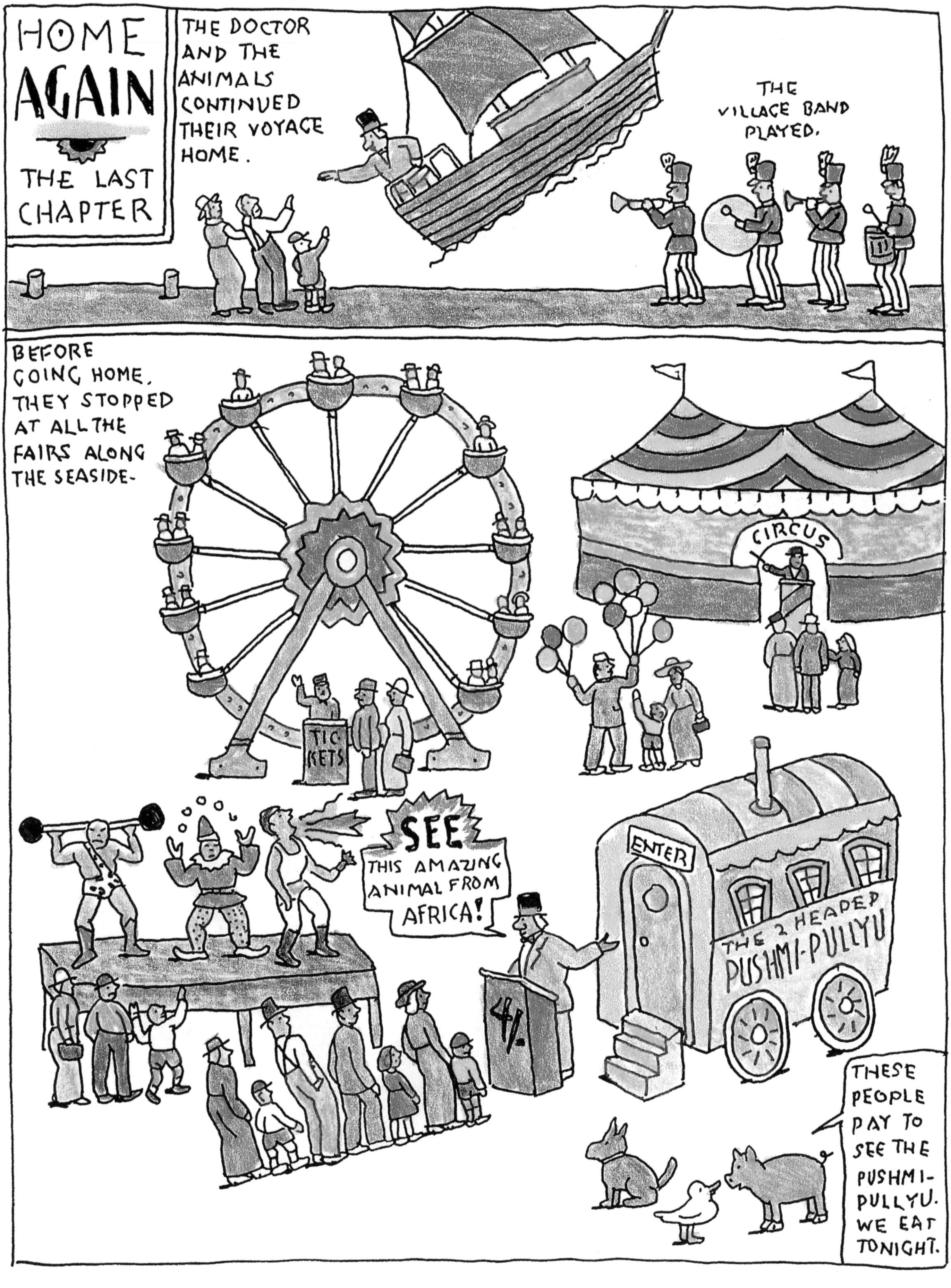

HOME AGAIN
THE LAST CHAPTER
THE DOCTOR AND THE ANIMALS CONTINUED THEIR VOYAGE HOME.
THE VILLAGE BAND PLAYED.
BEFORE GOING HOME, THEY STOPPED AT ALL THE FAIRS ALONG THE SEASIDE-
CIRCUS
TIC KETS
SEE THIS AMAZING ANIMAL FROM AFRICA!
ENTER
THE 2 HEADED PUSHMI-PULLYU
4/-
THESE PEOPLE PAY TO SEE THE PUSHMI-PULLYU. WE EAT TONIGHT.

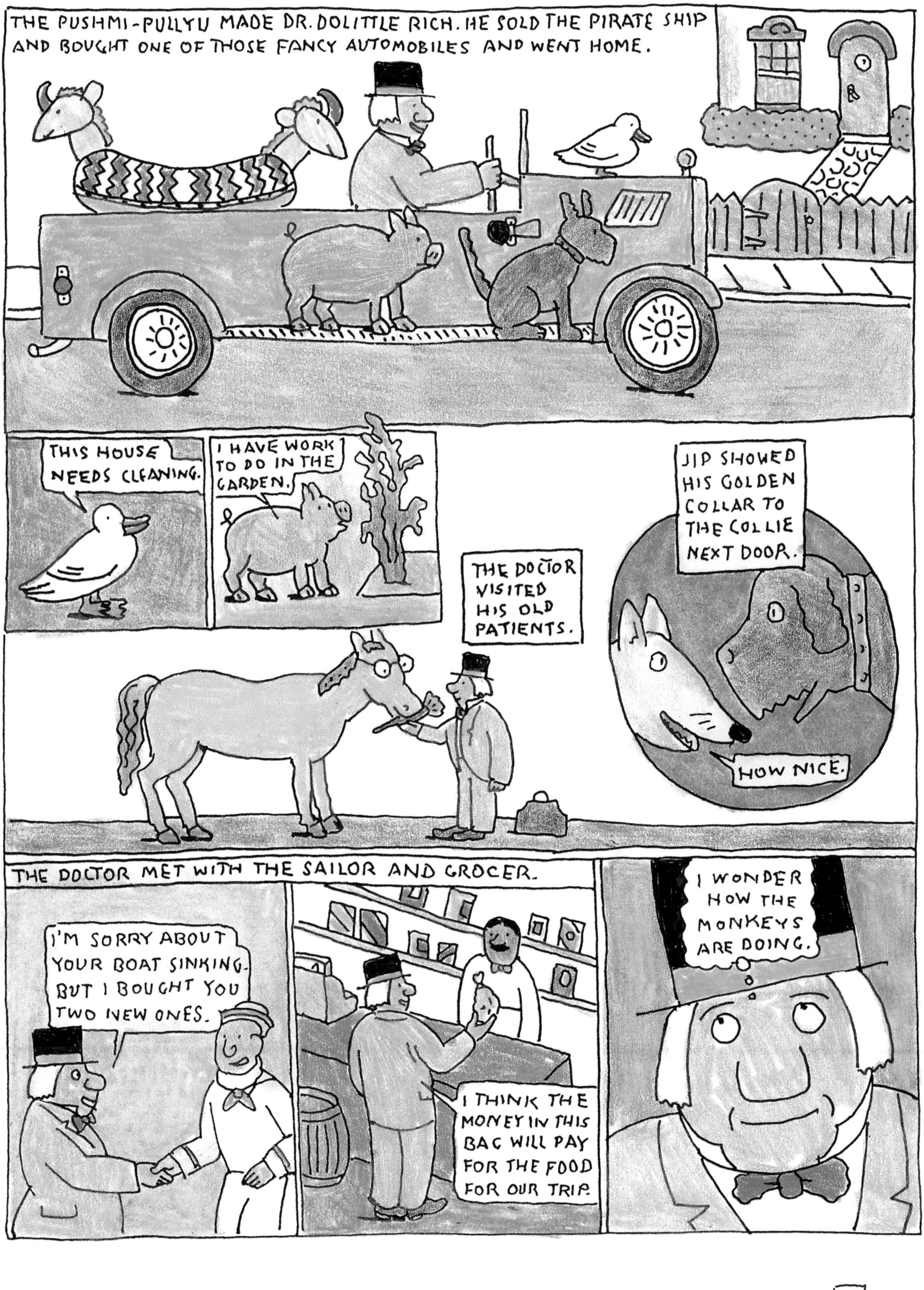
THE PUSHMI-PULLYU MADE DR. DOLITTLE RICH. HE SOLD THE PIRATE SHIP AND BOUGHT ONE OF THOSE FANCY AUTOMOBILES AND WENT HOME.
THIS HOUSE NEEDS CLEANING.
I HAVE WORK TO DO IN THE GARDEN.
THE DOCTOR VISITED HIS OLD PATIENTS.
JIP SHOWED HIS GOLDEN COLLAR TO THE COLLIE NEXT DOOR.
HOW NICE.
THE DOCTOR MET WITH THE SAILOR AND GROCER.
I'M SORRY ABOUT YOUR BOAT SINKING. BUT I BOUGHT YOU TWO NEW ONES.
I THINK THE MONEY IN THIS BAG WILL PAY FOR THE FOOD FOR OUR TRIP.
I WONDER HOW THE MONKEYS ARE DOING.

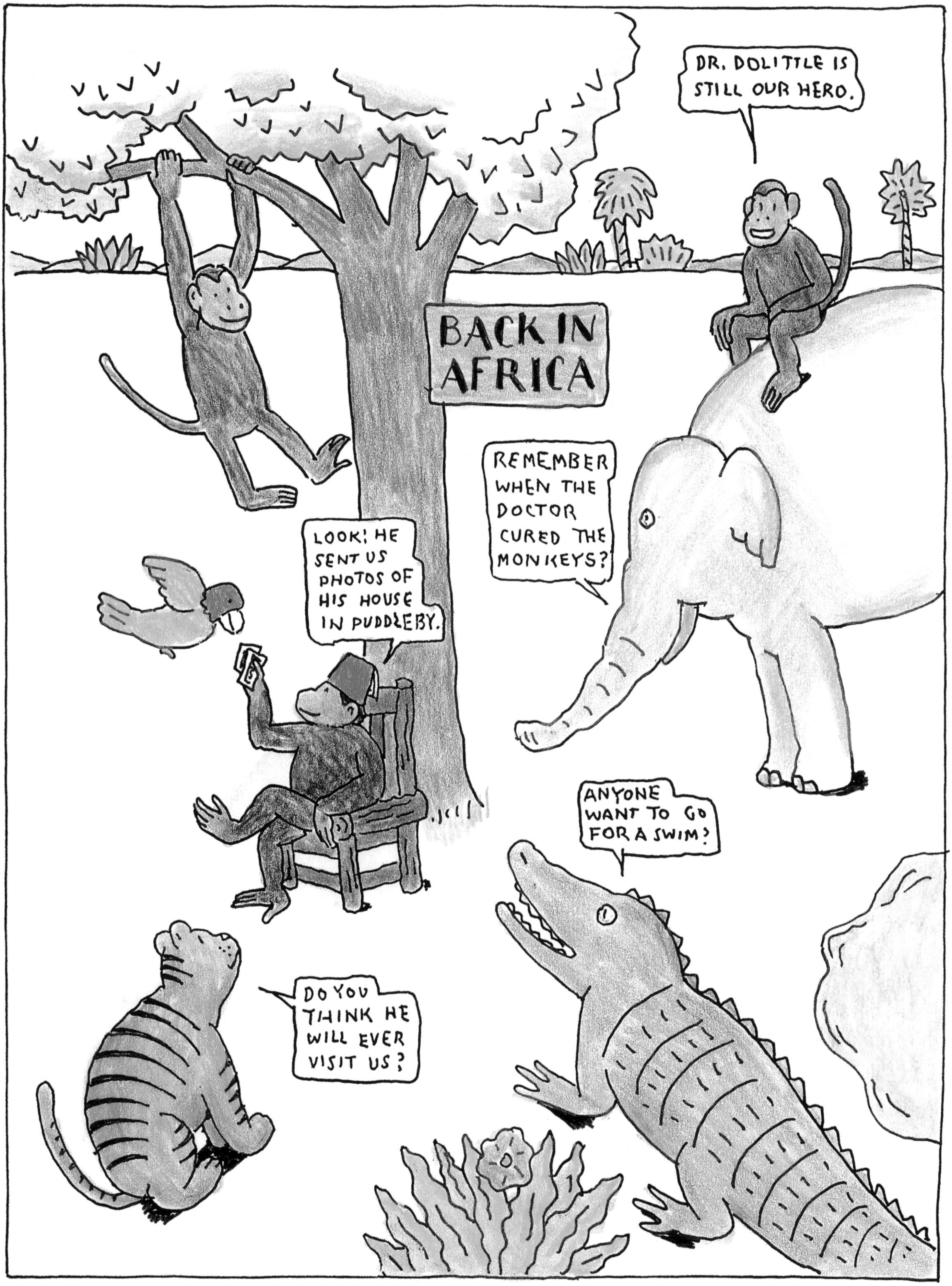

BACK IN AFRICA
DR. DOLITTLE IS STILL OUR HERO.
LOOK! HE SENT US PHOTOS OF HIS HOUSE IN PUDDLEBY.
REMEMBER WHEN THE DOCTOR CURED THE MONKEYS?
ANYONE WANT TO GO FOR A SWIM?
DO YOU THINK HE WILL EVER VISIT US?

SUPERCARS

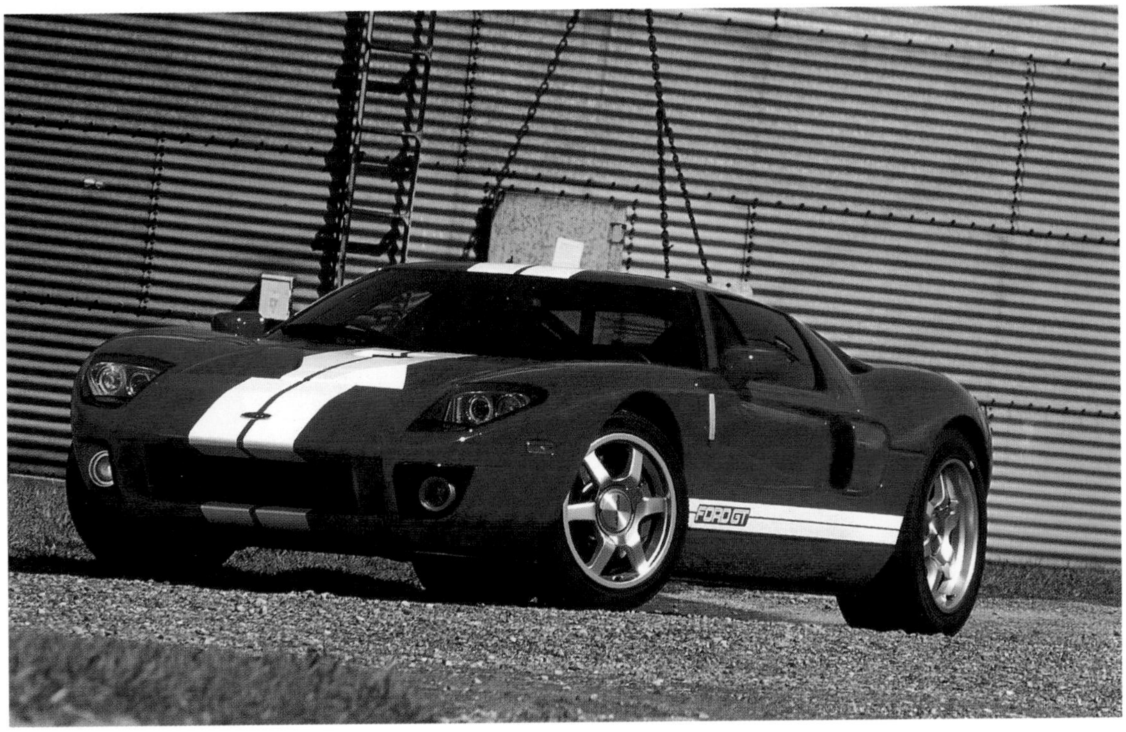
FORD GT

SUPER

THE ROAD & TRACK GUIDE TO CARS OF EXCEPTIONAL SPEED, POWER AND BEAUTY

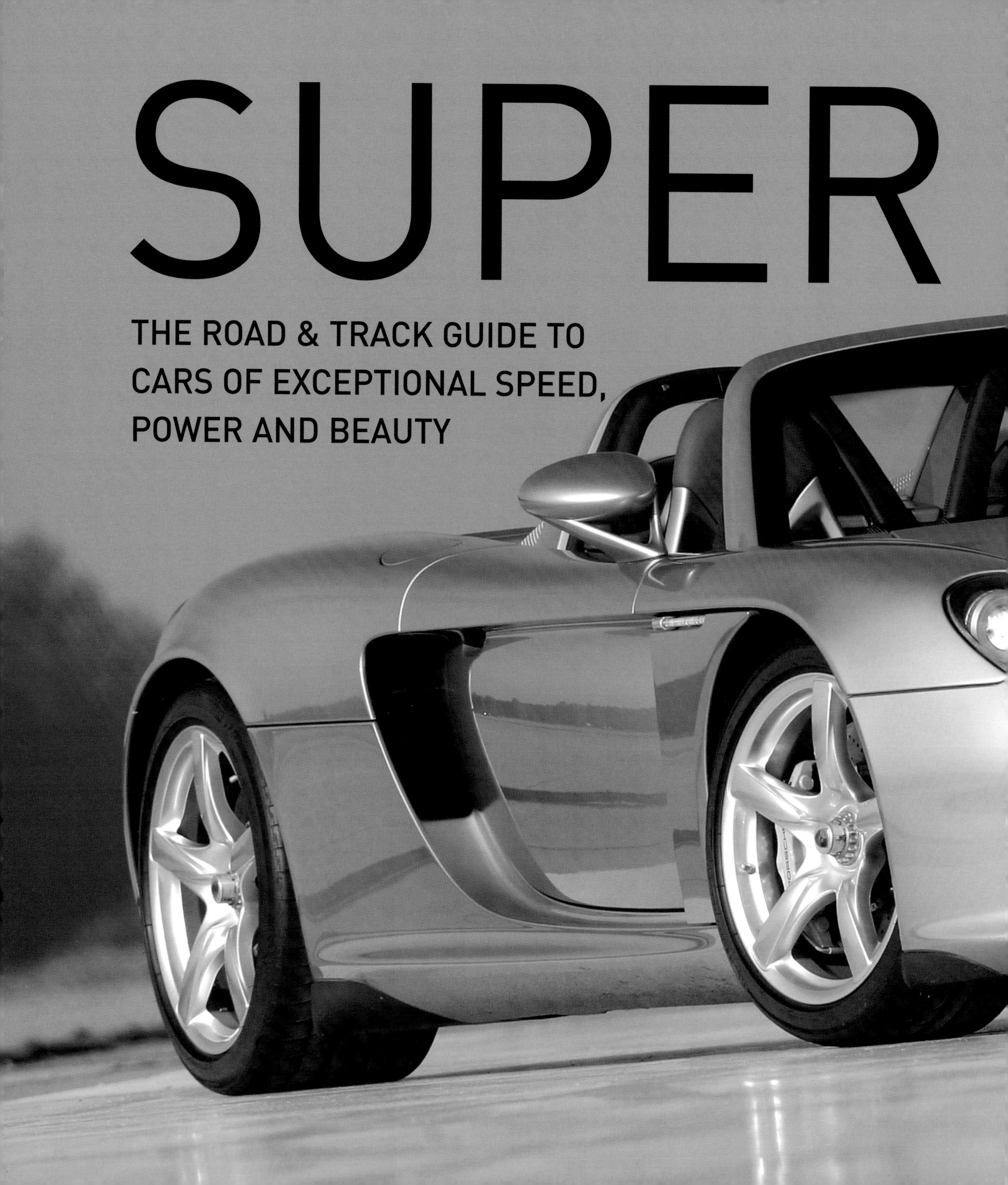

CARS

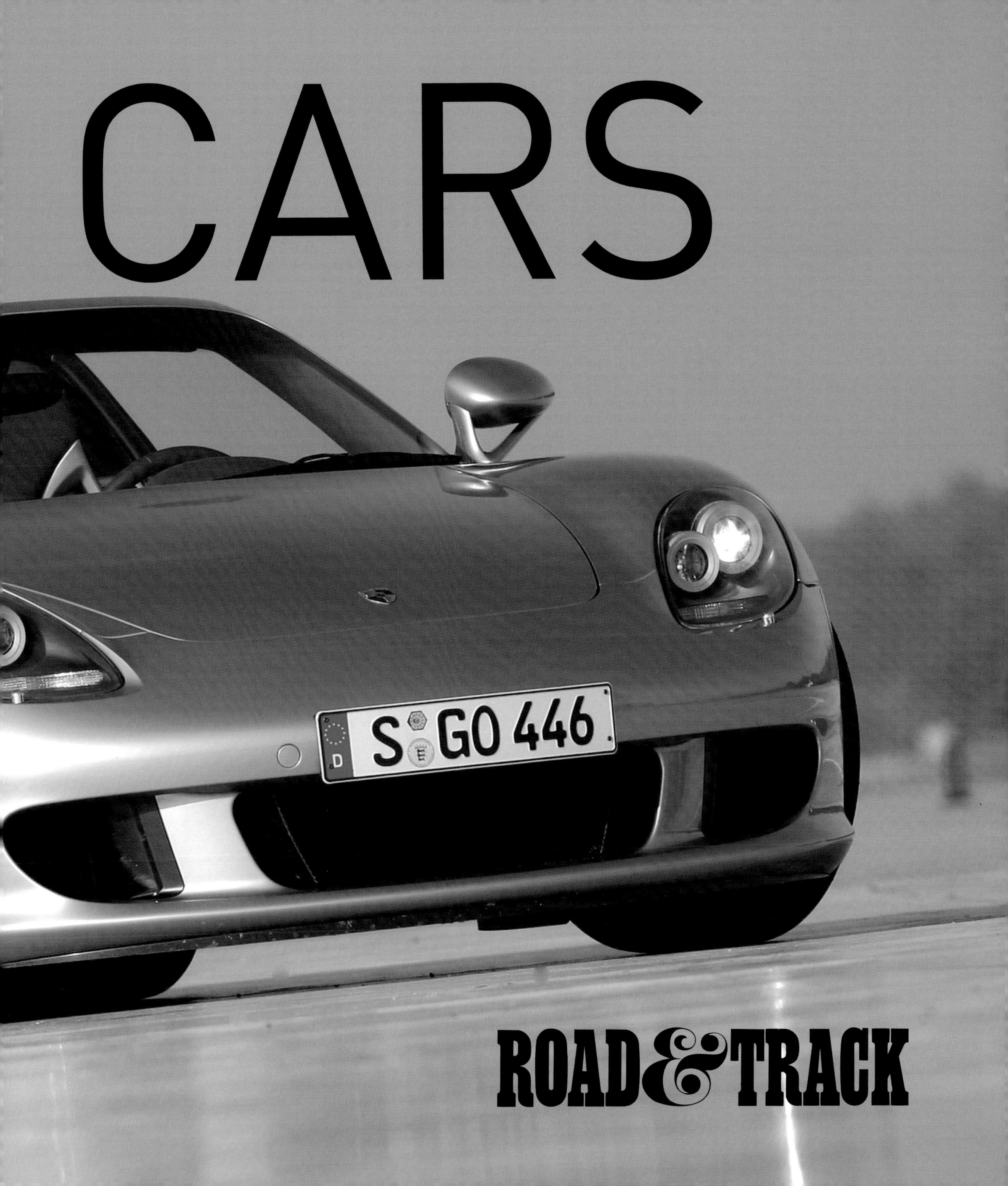
S GO 446
D

ROAD&TRACK

Designer, Patricia Fabricant
Editor, Doug Kott

Copyright © 2004 Filipacchi Publishing, Inc.
First published in the United States of America
by Filipacchi Publishing
1633 Broadway
New York, NY 10019

ISBN 2-85018-816-6

Printed in France by Clerc s.a.s.
18200 Saint-Amand-Montrond

CONTENTS

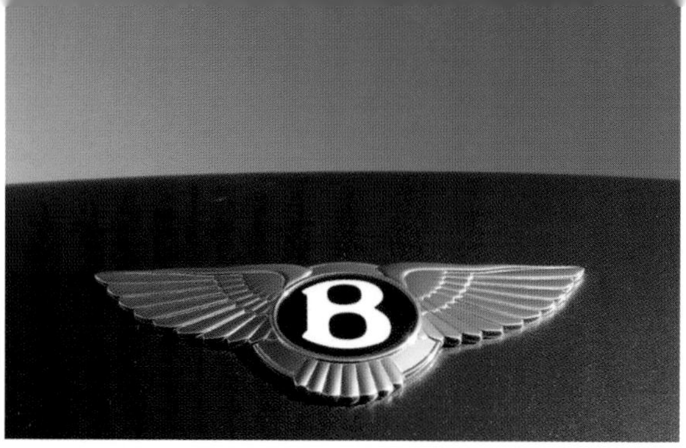

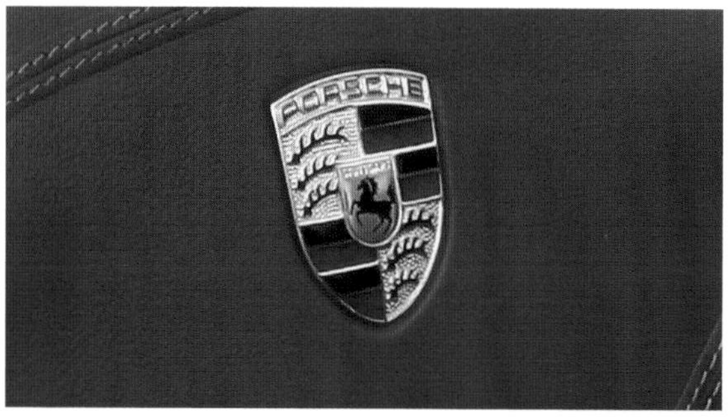
PORSCHE

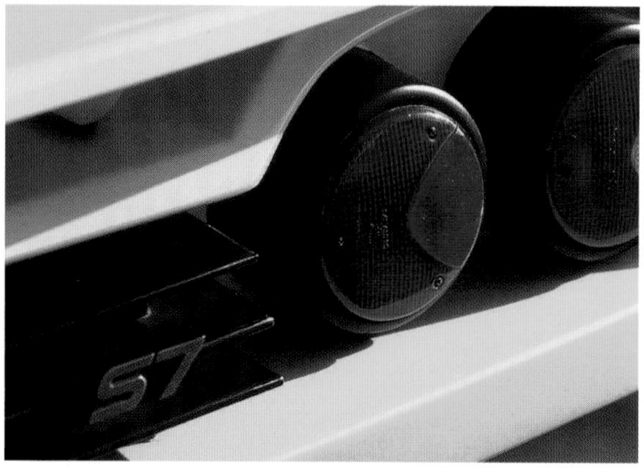
ST

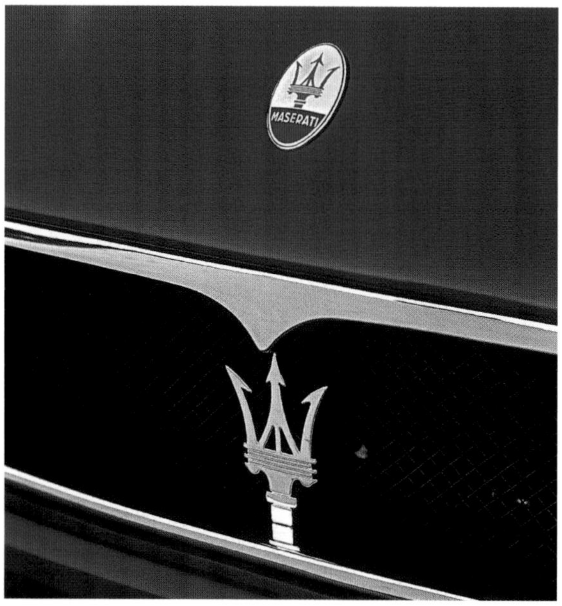
MASERATI

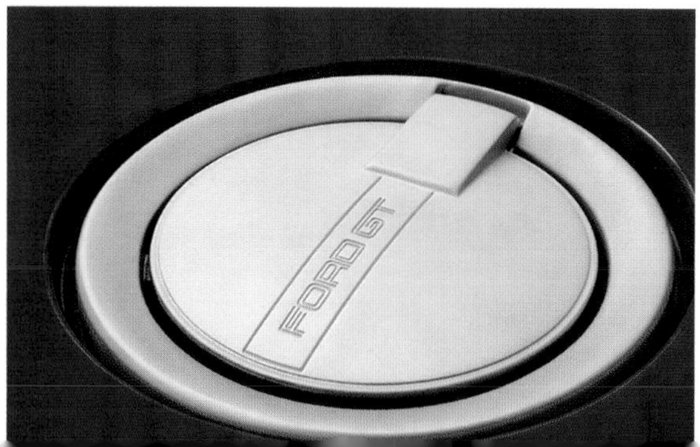
FORD GT

INTRODUCTION

SUPERCARS, DREAM CARS, EXOTIC CARS... each of these terms has been used to describe those fabulous automobiles that soar beyond mere transportation. Some 20 years ago, we created a series of special magazines devoted to (and titled) "Exotic Cars" because we wanted to bring readers into the inner circle. You see, these cars are so rare and high-priced that few of us ever get an opportunity to drive them. And depending on where you live, you might never see one on the road. But here, in the pages of "Road & Track"'s "Supercars," you can examine and enjoy them to your heart's content.

My first experience with a Supercar happened just about 30 years ago when I was given the assignment to help drive the first Lamborghini Countach in America from Los Angeles, California, to Phoenix, Arizona. It was an astonishing adventure, complete with two speeding citations (one each for me and my co-driver, the Lamborghini importer), questions from other motorists about how much it cost and how fast would it go, and a lifetime of memories of being behind the wheel of this incredible car that seemed more spaceship than automobile at the time. My fascination with Supercars was cemented by this experience, and my job at "Road & Track" provided many opportunities to enjoy driving other Lamborghinis, Ferraris, Maseratis, Porsches, Bentleys, and other cars that qualify as Supercars.

In every arena of human endeavor, there is a category that is well above the norm, and that is certainly the case in the automotive world. Supercars take us from the humdrum world of mundane transportation to an adventure in driving that is like no other.

When you slip into the driver's seat of a Ferrari at the factory in Maranello, Italy, for example, and set off into the Apennine Mountains, you know immediately that you are in for a thrill. The road curves back and forth as you make your way to the summit, changing gears through the gated shifter and listening to the rumble of the exhaust. The car's balance and powerful performance prove addictive.

Or think about taking a 600-horsepower Lamborghini out onto the narrow highway that runs in front of the factory near Sant'Agata, Italy. The unbelievable thrust of the V-12 engine sends chills up and down your spine, while the noise of the 12 cylinders makes you wish there was a volume switch so you could turn it up even louder. I was in this situation a few years ago and came up behind a long string of cars and trucks. The road ahead was open and my friend, Valentino Balboni, motioned for me to make the pass. With my right foot planted on the throttle, the Lamborghini shot forward like a rocket and the traffic we were passing became merely a hazy blur. In an instant we were by them all and back in our lane—smiling.

But not all Supercars come from Italy. I've also enjoyed similar thrills driving cars like the Bentley Continental GT in the northern reaches of Scotland. Or the Aston Martin DB7 Volante convertible across France, returning to England from the 24 Hours of Le Mans racing classic.

And in Germany, when the rapeseed oil crops are flowering with their electric-yellow blossoms, the Supercars from Porsche, Mercedes-Benz, BMW and other makers are stunningly beautiful to photograph against the brilliant background color. And, of course, then there are the German Autobahnen, those super-high-speed highways that allow drivers to revel in testing the limits of their cars' handling and performance.

Let's not forget that there are Supercars designed and engineered here in America, too. Believe me, when you engage 1st gear in a Dodge Viper and mash the throttle, the word "Super" will pop into your mind. The headlong rush toward triple-digit speeds seems to take no time at all, and the feeling of brute power is eminently rewarding.

I very much hope that you enjoy this collection of Supercars. They are the ultimate expression of automotive performance and personality.

Thos L. Bryant

Editor-in-Chief, "Road & Track"

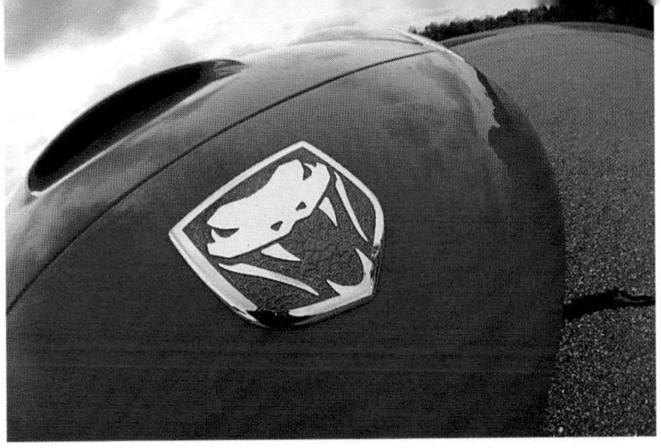

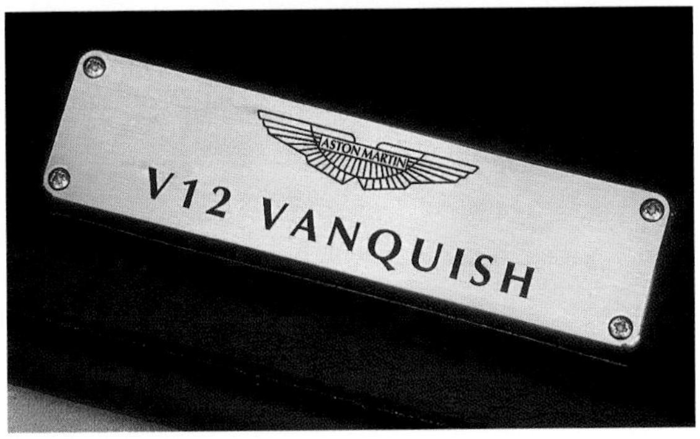
ASTON MARTIN
V12 VANQUISH

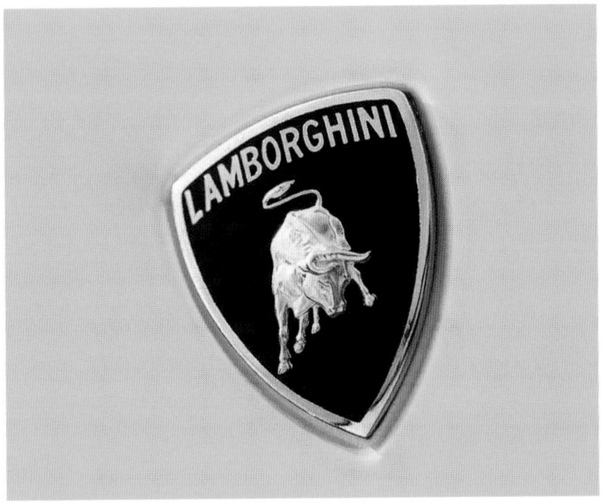
LAMBORGHINI

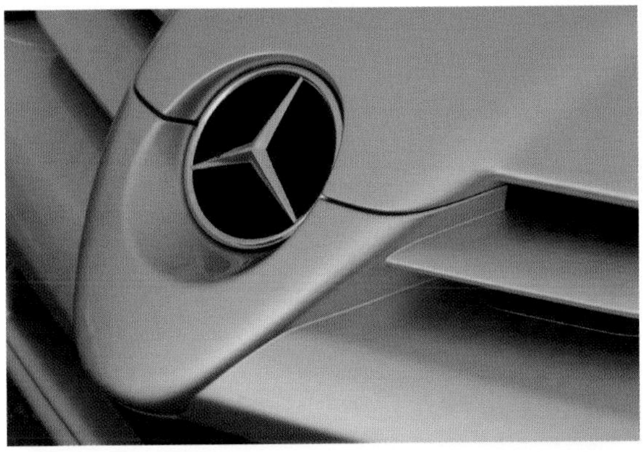

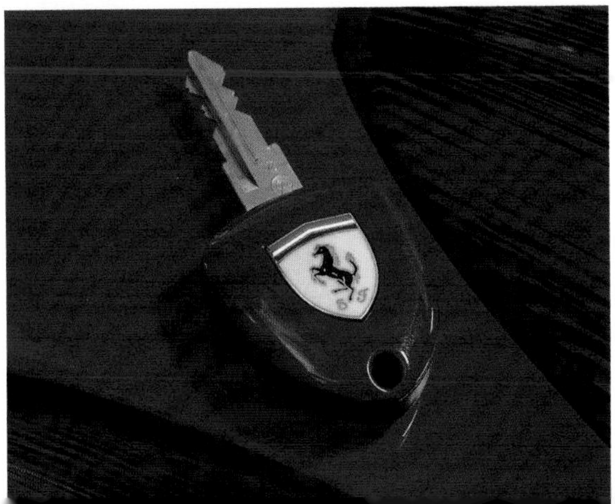

ASTON MARTIN VANQUISH

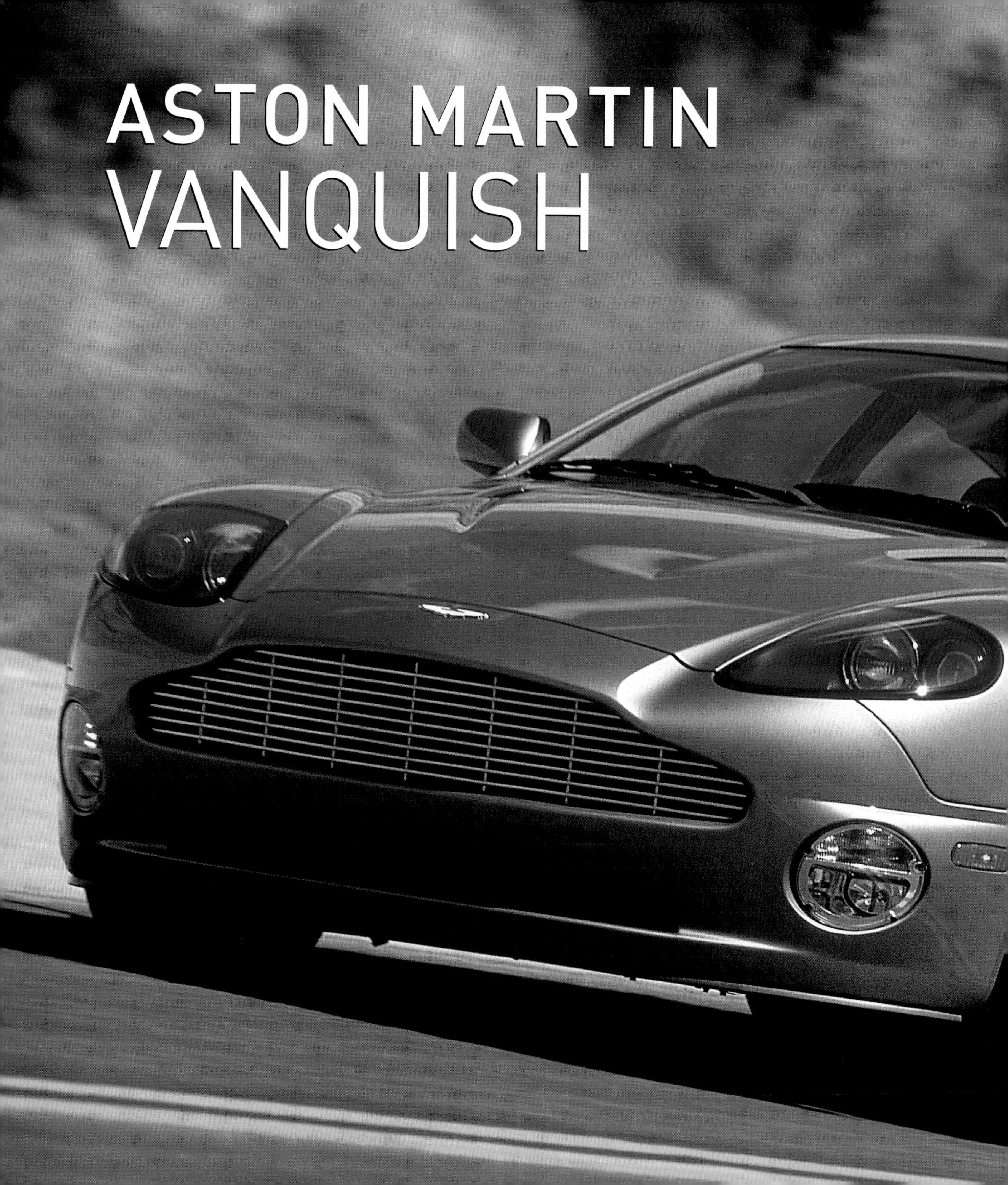

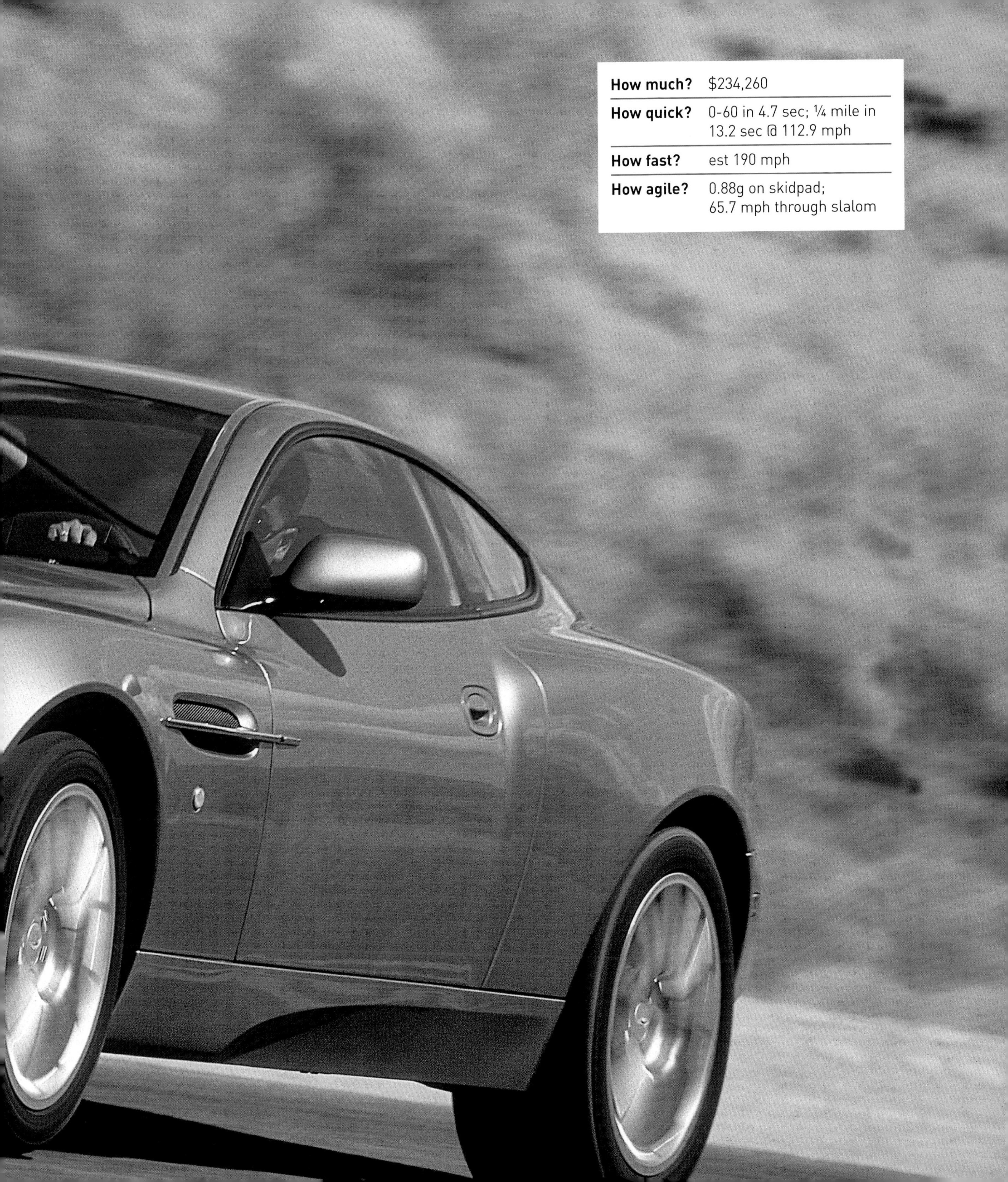

How much?	$234,260
How quick?	0-60 in 4.7 sec; ¼ mile in 13.2 sec @ 112.9 mph
How fast?	est 190 mph
How agile?	0.88g on skidpad; 65.7 mph through slalom

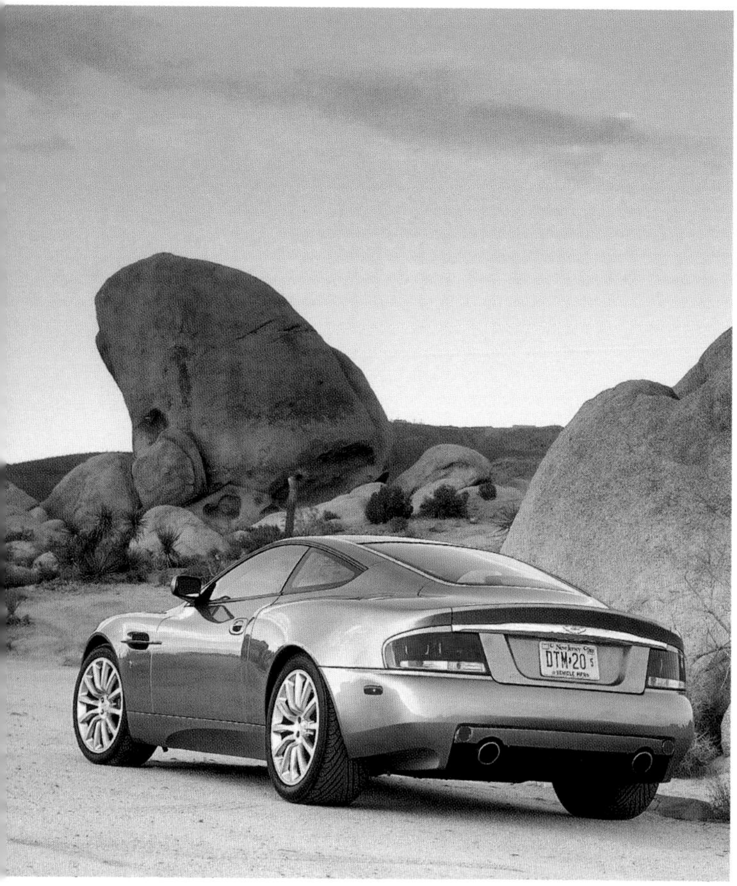
DTM•20

ABOVE: Its fastback roofline and basic proportions suggest the DB7, but there's more muscle and aggression here. Those stout dual tailpipes and the fat contact patches of the Yokohama AVS Sport tires signal that this is the ultimate Grand Touring Aston, the Vanquish.

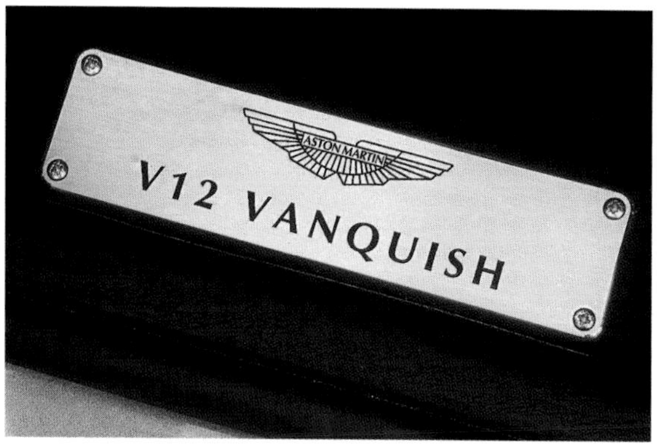
ASTON MARTIN
V12 VANQUISH

THE ULTIMATE GRAND TOURER

ALTHOUGH BICYCLES WERE HIS FIRST PASSION, Lionel Walker Birch Martin will be remembered for his second—in 1915 he officially registered the first Aston Martin automobile, his dark gray 2-seat hillclimb special. Had he lived past 1945, he would have seen the DB series, forever associated with James Bond; the Vantage and V8 models; the svelte DB7 and ultimately the Vanquish, the pinnacle of the firm's Grand Touring cars. Aston Martin has been characterized as the Englishman's Ferrari, and the Vanquish fits the mold neatly, with outstanding roadholding and power blended with Connolly leather and Wilton wool carpeting. It also points to the future...beneath its formed aluminum body panels lies a composite chassis utilizing carbon fiber, steel and aluminum.

As enthusiasts, we marvel at the history, the styling, the machinery and the technology that are infused into a performance car's DNA. However, what ultimately wins our affection is the thrilling driving experience that stimulates our human senses: an engine's bold and authoritative bark and a well-balanced, confidence-inspiring chassis.

In the world of $100,000-plus automobiles, most manufacturers focus on what they do best. Climb aboard a Porsche 911 Turbo and you immediately recognize its purpose: to speed through a corner with utmost grip and confidence. The BMW Z8 and Mercedes-Benz CL and SL are Teutonic engineering masterpieces. The Lamborghini Murciélago's road presence is intimidating, and various Ferraris tempt with beautiful styling and race-bred engines.

Steeped in history, Aston Martin has the rich racing heritage and reputation for handcrafting high-performance sports cars. Now adding to that impressive résumé is the Vanquish. It is the ultimate Gran Turismo that not only delivers top-notch styling, performance and luxury, but most important, an exhilarating driving experience that excites our senses of sight, hearing, smell and touch, all at the same time.

Inspired by the Aston Martin DB4GT Zagato, designer Ian Callum has taken the elegant and classic lines of the past and penned a bold and chiseled look for the Vanquish. Up front, a large, signature Aston Martin grille is incorporated into the single-piece bumper. Below it are two auxiliary driving lights/turn indicators and an air intake. A pair of twin-lamp projector headlights confidently focus on the road ahead. Just behind them is a wide, upward-sloping bonnet interrupted by a center hump that's flanked by a pair of engine-bay cooling vents.

In profile, the Aston's long hood complements the steeply raked windshield. The elegant roofline picks up where the windshield leaves off and gradually finishes at the rear with a gentle lip acting as a spoiler. Aft of the large front wheel wells are side air vents, highlighted by slender chrome trim, that blend nicely into the door panels. And with the cockpit's narrow greenhouse design, Callum is able to sculpt a tall beltline that balances nicely with the forceful and broad contours of the rear fenders. Around the back, large taillights smoothly merge into

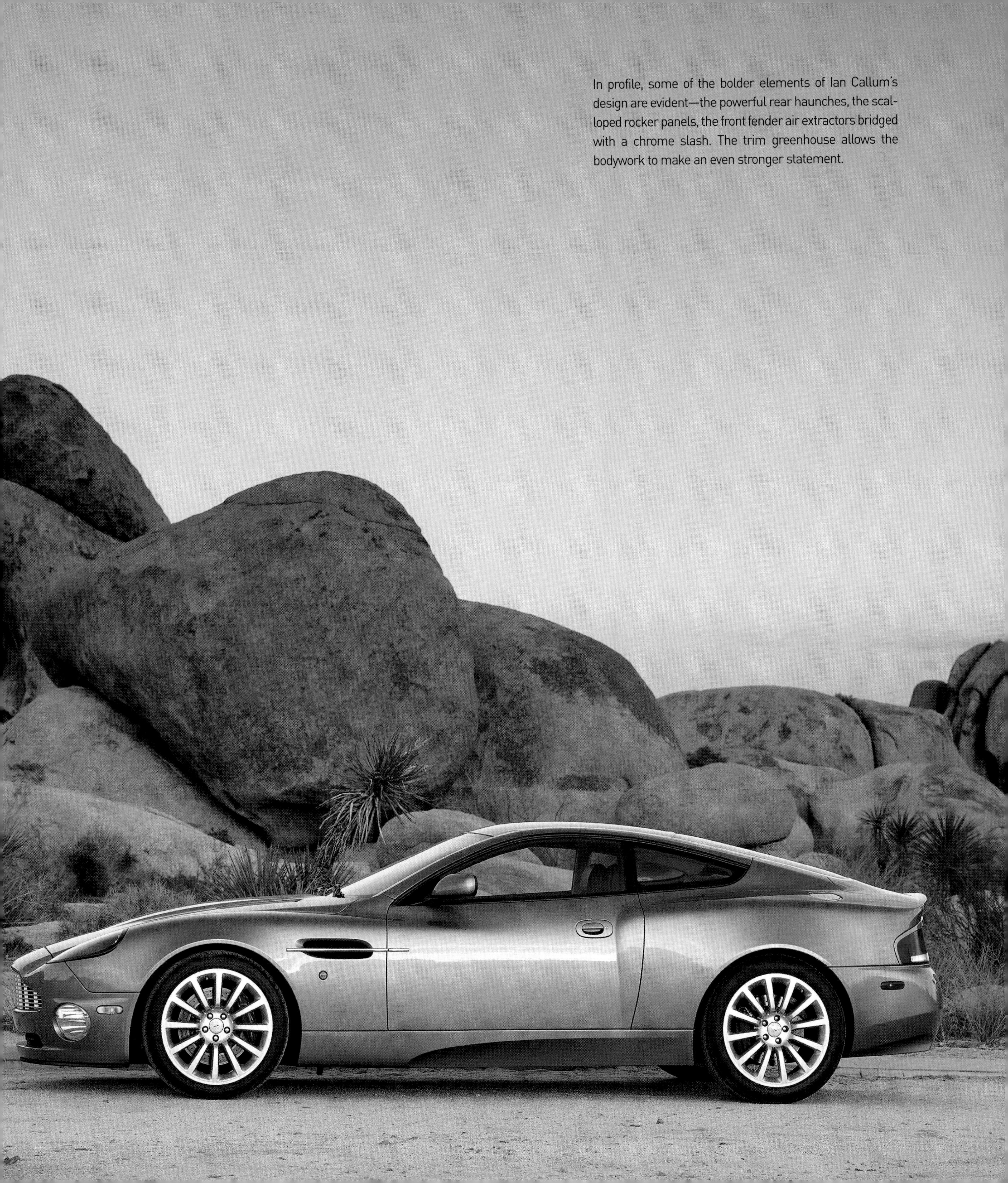

In profile, some of the bolder elements of Ian Callum's design are evident—the powerful rear haunches, the scalloped rocker panels, the front fender air extractors bridged with a chrome slash. The trim greenhouse allows the bodywork to make an even stronger statement.

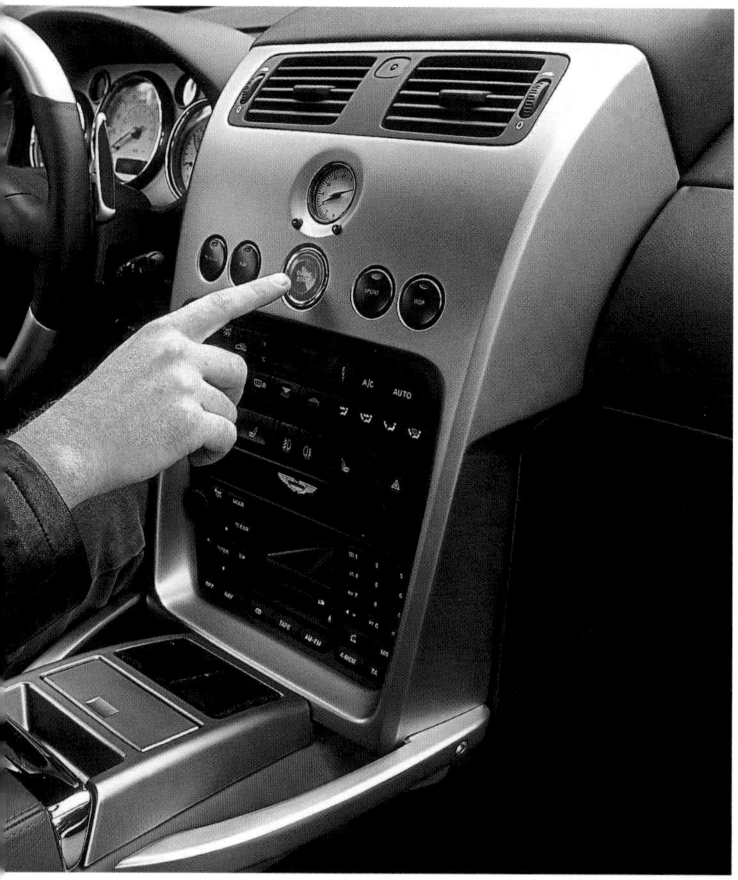
A/C
AUTO

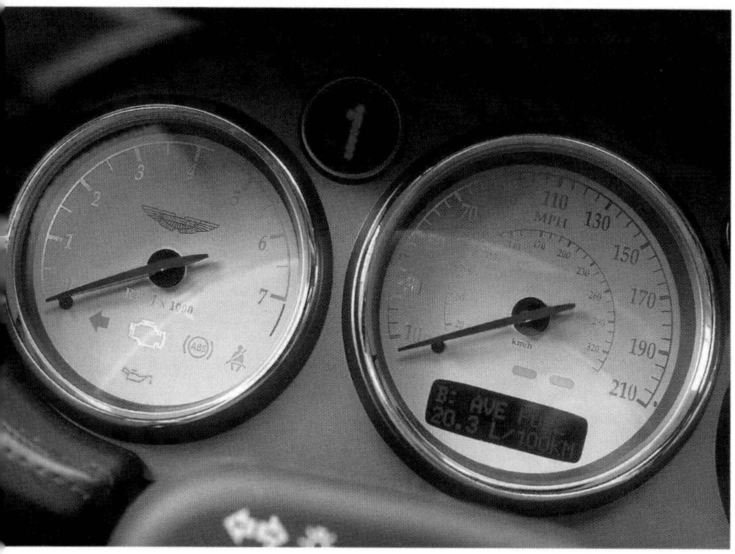
MPH
130
150
170
190
210

ABOVE: Press the large red button beneath the petite analog clock, and you summon the wrath of the 5.9-liter, 460-bhp V-12. It's actually very quiet at idle, but as the tach needle spins toward its 7000-rpm redline, guttural, glorious sounds are released, with acceleration to match.

OPPOSITE: Despite its low roofline, the Vanquish is surprisingly roomy inside, and exquisitely trimmed with handcrafted materials.

the bumper, with a pair of tailpipes sandwiching a functional lower-body diffuser. A quick look underneath the car reveals the Aston Martin's aerodynamically efficient flat underbody design.

Open the door to see the high-tech interior styling and smell the traditional rich aroma of Connolly hides. Abundant leather wraps around the entire cockpit and is carefully stitched into the Alcantara-quilted seats. A suede headliner and more than 129 sq. ft. of Wilton carpeting complete the interior furnishings. The aluminum door handles and the engraved "Aston Martin" aluminum doorsill trim pieces are modern design cues. At the center, the sculpted console begins at the base of the windshield, then flows smoothly down to the center armrest outlined by a pair of brushed aluminum struts. On the console are buttons for the engine start (in red), reverse, traction control and Sport mode (allowing the engine revs to reach redline before upshifting in Automatic mode). A minor gripe: the door handles, window switches, climate and sound system controls are taken directly out of Ford's Jaguar parts bin.

Slide into the driver's seat. From the supportive side bolsters hugging you in place and the sight and the smell of the cockpit, to your fingers wrapping around the padded leather steering wheel, everything conveys sportiness and luxury. The aluminum paddle shifters (upshift on the right and downshift on the left) are accented by more strips of leather. On the instrument panel, a small round display indicating the current gear selection separates the ivory-faced, chrome-ringed 7500-rpm tach and the 210-mph speedometer. Fuel level and coolant temperature gauges can also be found and monitored inside the binnacle. Surprisingly, the low-profile roofline does not translate to a lack of head room inside the Vanquish. In fact, our over-6-foot staffers find the Aston Martin to be very roomy. However, we all agree that the two rear seats are there purely for looks.

Insert the key and turn on the ignition. Pull both paddle shifters back, and the Magneti Marelli 6-speed manual transmission goes into Neutral. Push the starter button and the 5.9-liter V-12 quietly comes to life. At idle, this dohc powerplant is docile compared with most other super-performance sports cars. A quick pull on the right paddle shifter puts the car into 1st gear. Stomp on the gas pedal. The electronic drive-by-wire throttle immediately snaps open, releasing the might of all 12 pistons. Delivery of 460 bhp and 400 lb.-ft. of torque is linear and buttery-smooth, and the accompanying engine growl is simply mesmerizing. The rumble through the twin exhaust resonates in the cabin and it ensures that occupants can hear and feel the car's awesome power.

On the drag strip, too much initial throttle input and the Vanquish's generous 19-in. rear tires can't find enough grip for proper standing-start acceleration runs. Only about 70-percent throttle is needed for the Aston Martin to rocket away with modest wheelspin. Once on its way, a slight lifting of the throttle helps the Magneti Marelli electronics change gears in less than 250 milliseconds (less than the blink of an eye). According to the owner's manual, throttle lifts are not necessary to upshift. But this causes a longer pause between gears as the computer slows the engine rpm to match vehicle speed.

Our radar clocked the Vanquish's 0-to-60-mph acceleration time at 4.7 seconds, and the quarter mile at 13.2 sec. with 112.9 mph showing on the speedo.

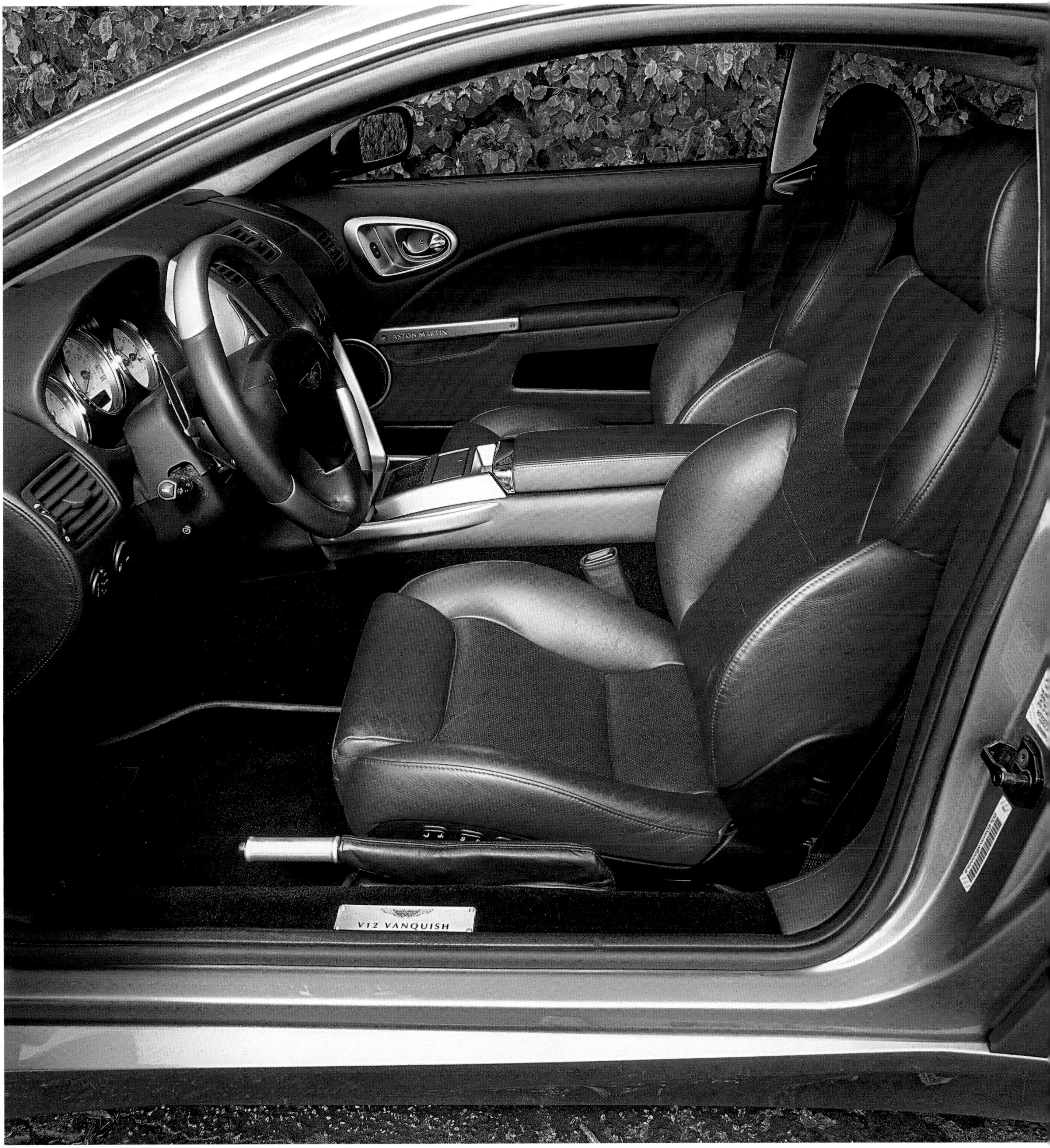
ASTON MARTIN
V12 VANQUISH

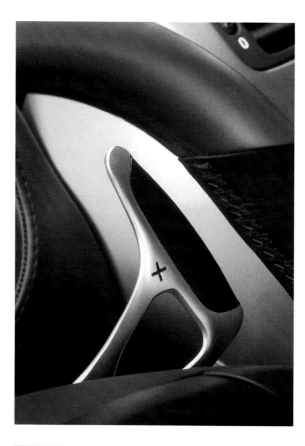

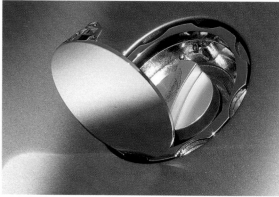

Although these numbers do not beat times turned in by pure sports cars like the Porsche 911 Turbo, they are still close and extremely competitive when compared with the BMW Z8 and the Ferrari 550 Maranello.

When it comes to slowing the Aston Martin's massive 4110-lb. curb weight, its vented front 14.0-in. and rear 13.0-in. Brembo disc brakes provide tremendous power. With full ABS application, the Vanquish stops in 125 ft. from 60 mph, and 228 ft. from 80 mph. There is no hint of fade during the braking exercises, though some front wheel hop is detected.

On the road, if the Vanquish's endless pulling power and captivating engine rumble don't impress you, its solid and competent chassis surely will. At the core of the super-rigid body structure is the transmission tunnel made entirely from carbon fiber. This serves as the base to which the extruded aluminum floor and the front and rear bulkheads are bonded and riveted. Single-piece composite body side sections with carbon-fiber windscreen pillars are also bonded to the central tunnel to create a high-strength safety cell. Ahead of the cockpit, a subframe constructed with steel, aluminum and carbon fiber carries the engine, transmission and front suspension. Along the sides and at the rear, the deformable extruded aluminum rails, composite floor and parcel shelf provide extra crash protection. On the outside, all the body panels are made of super-plastic-formed and pressed aluminum, and then bonded to the chassis by hand by the craftsmen at Newport Pagnell.

On the Interstate, the Vanquish's ride is firm but comfortable, with little unwanted road noise transmitted through the cabin, making it easy to exceed the speed limit without much effort. And with the engine's exhaust deepening as the tach sweeps past 3500 rpm, the Aston Martin lures you into dipping deeper into the throttle. One editor noted that "it is mandatory to drive with the windows open to get the full effect" of the V-12's throaty snarl.

FROM TOP: A wealth of details—a leather-trimmed shift paddle; an aluminum fuel cap fit for an exotic; enormous 19-in. alloy wheels housing Brembo brakes; and the grille shape that's been an Aston trademark for decades.

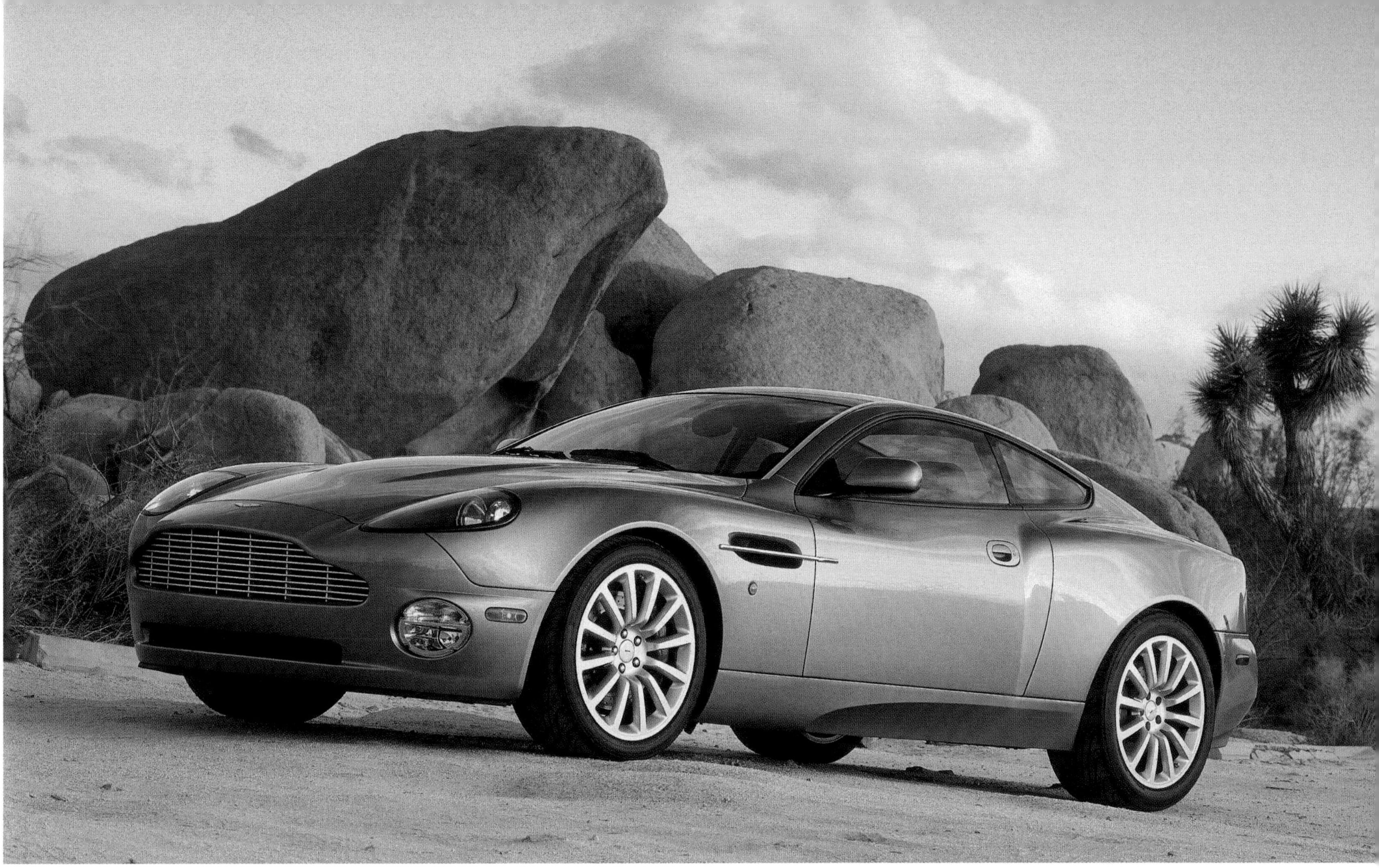

Winding along mountain roads, the Vanquish is the perfect companion. Thanks to its suspension design of coil springs, tube shocks, anti-roll bars and aluminum upper and lower A-arms at all four corners, this Grand Tourer grips the asphalt with poise. The variable power-assisted, rack-and-pinion steering is nicely weighted, and it directs the front 255/40ZR-19 tires with immediacy. At the rear there are a limited-slip differential and massive 285/40ZR-19 tires.

As the pace quickens, the Vanquish rolls a bit through the turns. The progressive manner in which the car leans to one side and generates lateral grip actually helps the driver sense its handling limit. There are no surprises; the Aston Martin stays composed all the way to the apex. And with judicious application, the car's awesome power can be unleashed with full throttle onto the straight. On the test track, the Vanquish generates a respectable 0.88g of lateral acceleration on the skidpad, and averages 65.7 mph through the slalom—outstanding for such a wide car. Overall, the Aston Martin exhibits moderate understeer, then transitions to mild understeer thanks to a chassis that responds well to throttle modulation.

At a list price of $234,260 and an annual production rate approaching 600 cars (with 200 per year allotted for North America), the Aston Martin Vanquish is a very exclusive Grand Tourer. But for those fortunate few enthusiasts—and that would include James Bond in 2002's "Die Another Day"—the rewards of piloting such a super GT are tremendous. The Vanquish's powerful presence, its first-rate handling dynamics and fabulously furnished cockpit make for a driving experience unlike any other.

BELOW: Aluminum and carbon-fiber chassis elements frame the 460-bhp, 4-cam V-12. Note the foil "chimneys" that route heat upward.

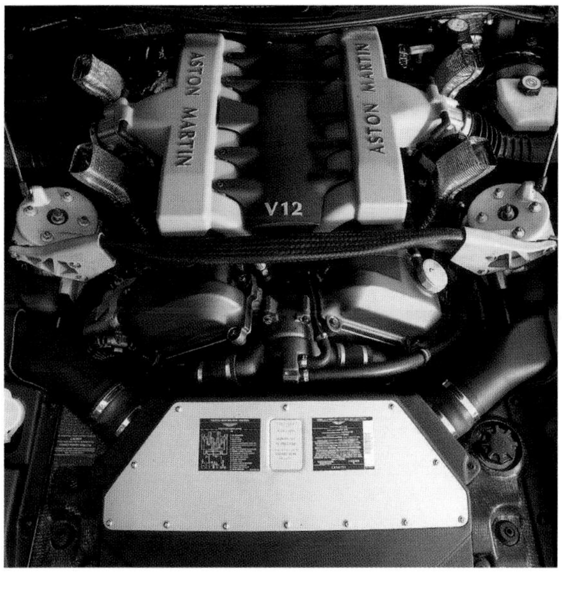
ASTON MARTIN
ASTON MARTIN
V12

BENTLEY
CONTINENTAL GT

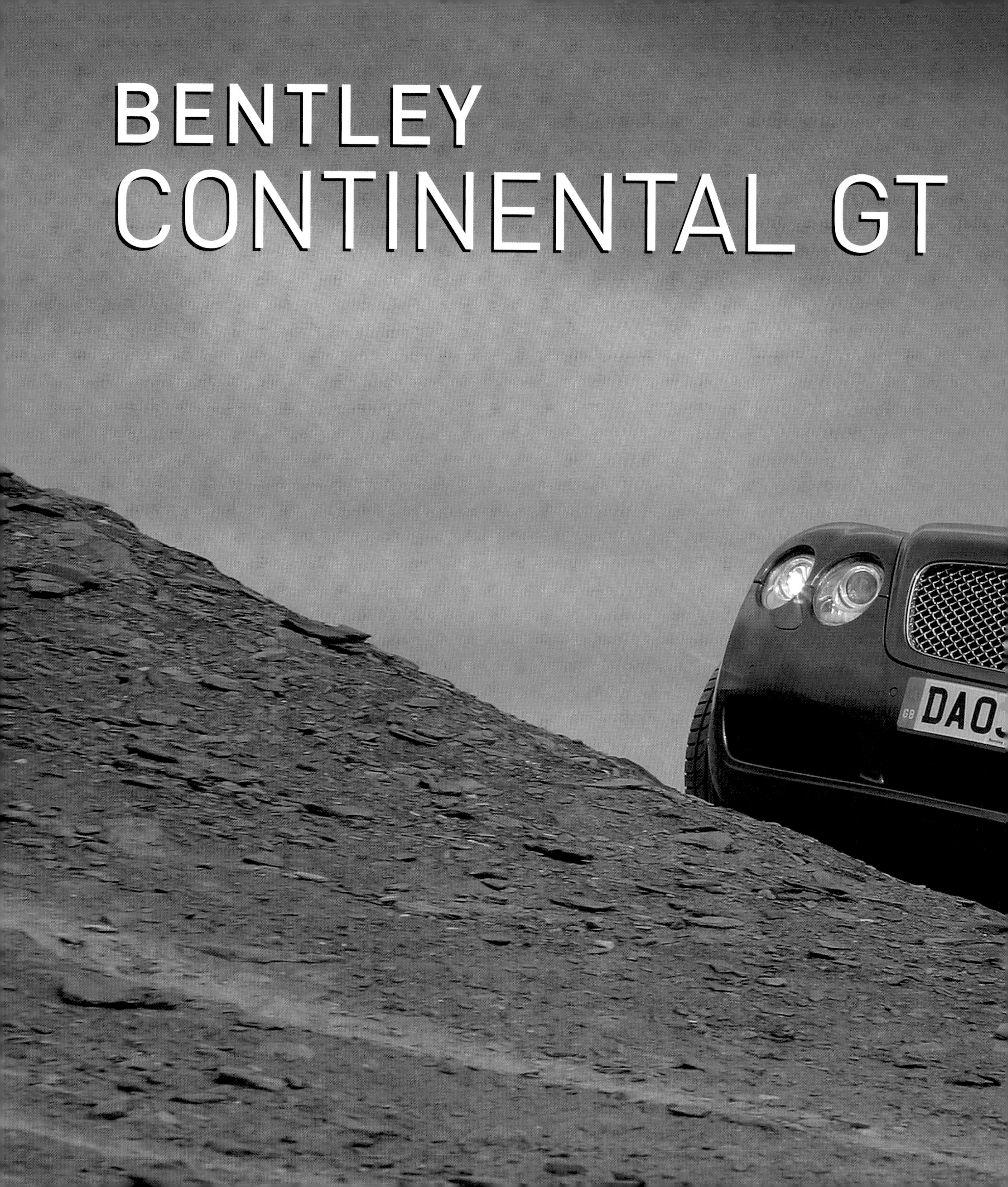

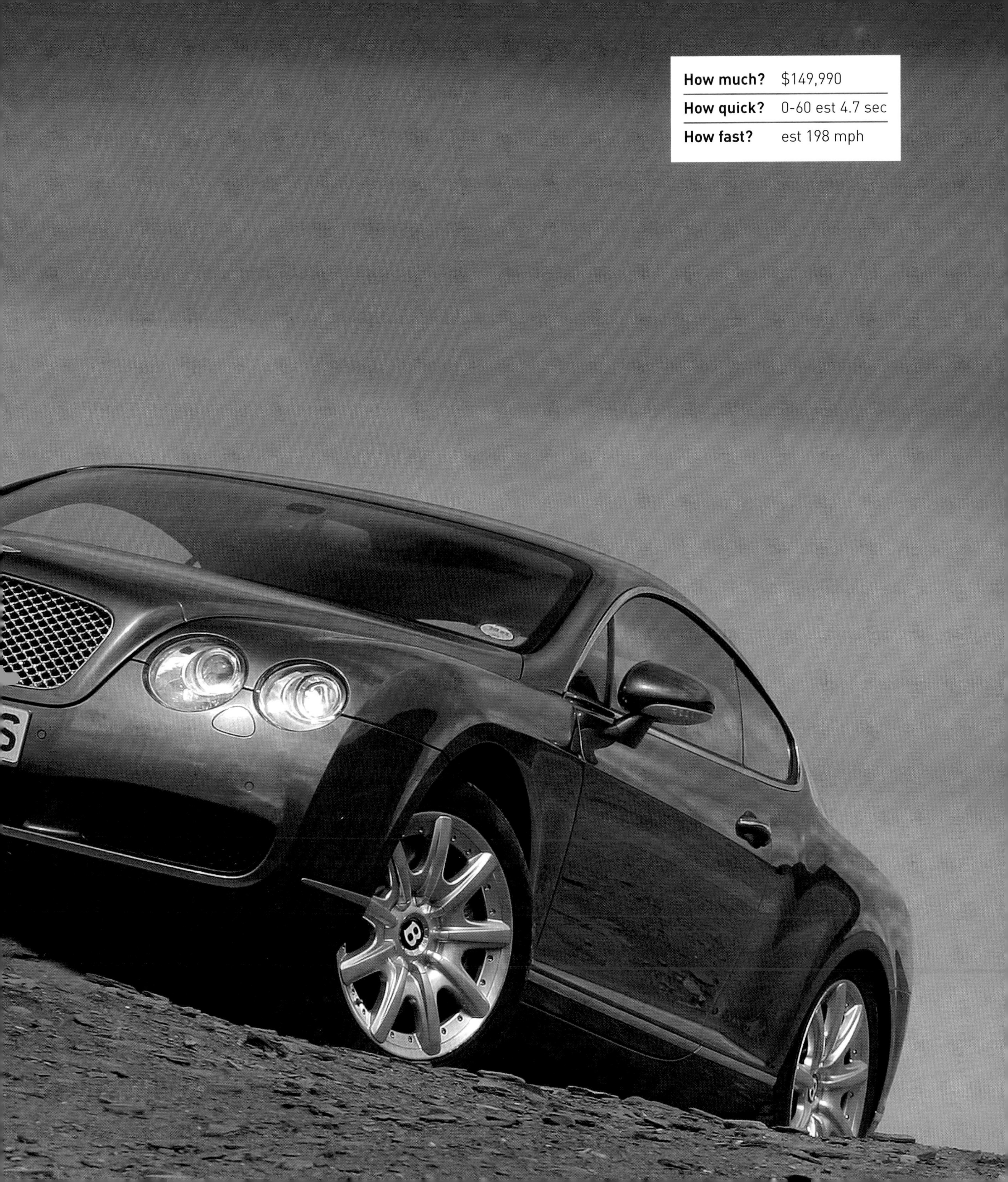

How much?	$149,990
How quick?	0-60 est 4.7 sec
How fast?	est 198 mph

ABOVE: The look is unmistakably Bentley as you peer over the Continental GT's shapely haunches. Yet beneath the skin lurks technology not heretofore seen from the Crewe factory, like all-wheel drive and a twin-turbo W-12 engine.

BELOW: Bentley's winged B logo has never flown so fast as on the nose of this exotic, whose top speed is estimated at 198 mph.

LOVE AT FIRST SIGHT, CONFIRMED

HISTORY CAME FULL CIRCLE IN 2003 as the Bentley Speed 8 claimed the overall victory at the epic Le Mans 24-hour enduro, recapturing the glory of the 1920s and 1930s when Bentley was the car to beat. Now owned by Volkswagen-Audi (the Speed 8 was essentially the dominating Audi R8 race car underneath), Bentley has been separated from its age-old sister marque, Rolls-Royce, now owned by BMW. But even in new hands, Bentley continues to build road cars that are far more driver-oriented than those with the Spirit of Ecstasy hood ornament. Case in point: the Continental GT, with its twin-turbocharged W-12, all-wheel drive and scintillating performance that would have put a broad smile on W.O. Bentley's face.

When I walked up onto the Bentley show stand at Detroit's North American International Auto Show, my intent was to open the door of the very handsome coupe and sit in the driver's seat. This was my first exposure to the Continental GT in finished form and I was determined to try it on for size. Fortunately, my friend John Crawford, director of Bentley public relations in America, was on hand and quickly swung the driver's door wide open for me.

There are some cars that just get it right, and the Bentley design staff did an excellent job with this car. The interior materials and fitments are everything you would expect in a Grand Touring car from the legendary Bentley marque. The leather upholstery is the model of supple texture and rich color. The wool carpeting is cozy and the abundant use of aluminum makes the interior look like—forgive me, ladies—a gentleman's den.

I turned to Mr. Crawford and said, "I can't wait to drive it. The interior is everything I expected it would be." John smiled and replied that he was certain I would find the car's dynamics equally impressive.

Six months later I had my opportunity to drive the Bentley Continental GT around the northern reaches of Scotland, from Wick to Inverness via a circuitous and beautiful route. But first there was a visit to the factory at Crewe, near Manchester in the Midlands of England, to see what changes had been wrought with the takeover of Bentley by Volkswagen.

First and foremost, VW committed to investing more than $750 million in Bentley, and the first car out of the box is the Continental GT. Bentley executives see this car as the rebirth of the Grand Touring car in the finest tradition, with lots of horsepower, excellent road manners, exemplary accommodations and beautiful styling. And, at a price of $149,990, it's a veritable bargain in the world of Bentley automobiles.

The Continental GT fills this bill quite nicely, thank you. The power comes from a 6.0-liter W-12 engine with 552 bhp and 479 lb.-ft. of torque. This powerplant is built and tested in a new facility at the Crewe factory, and each engine is hand assembled with matched parts to ensure balance and performance are

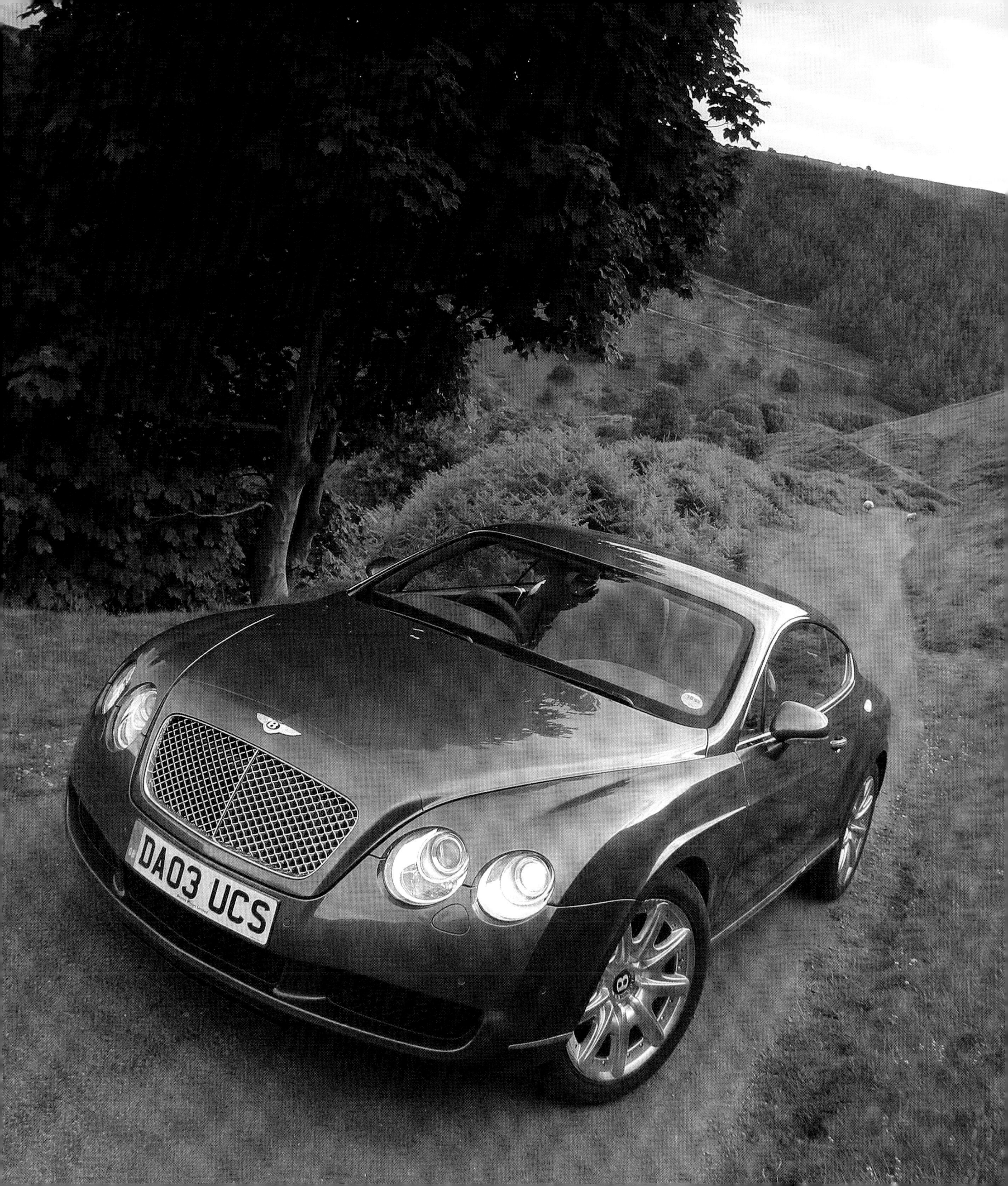
DA03 UCS

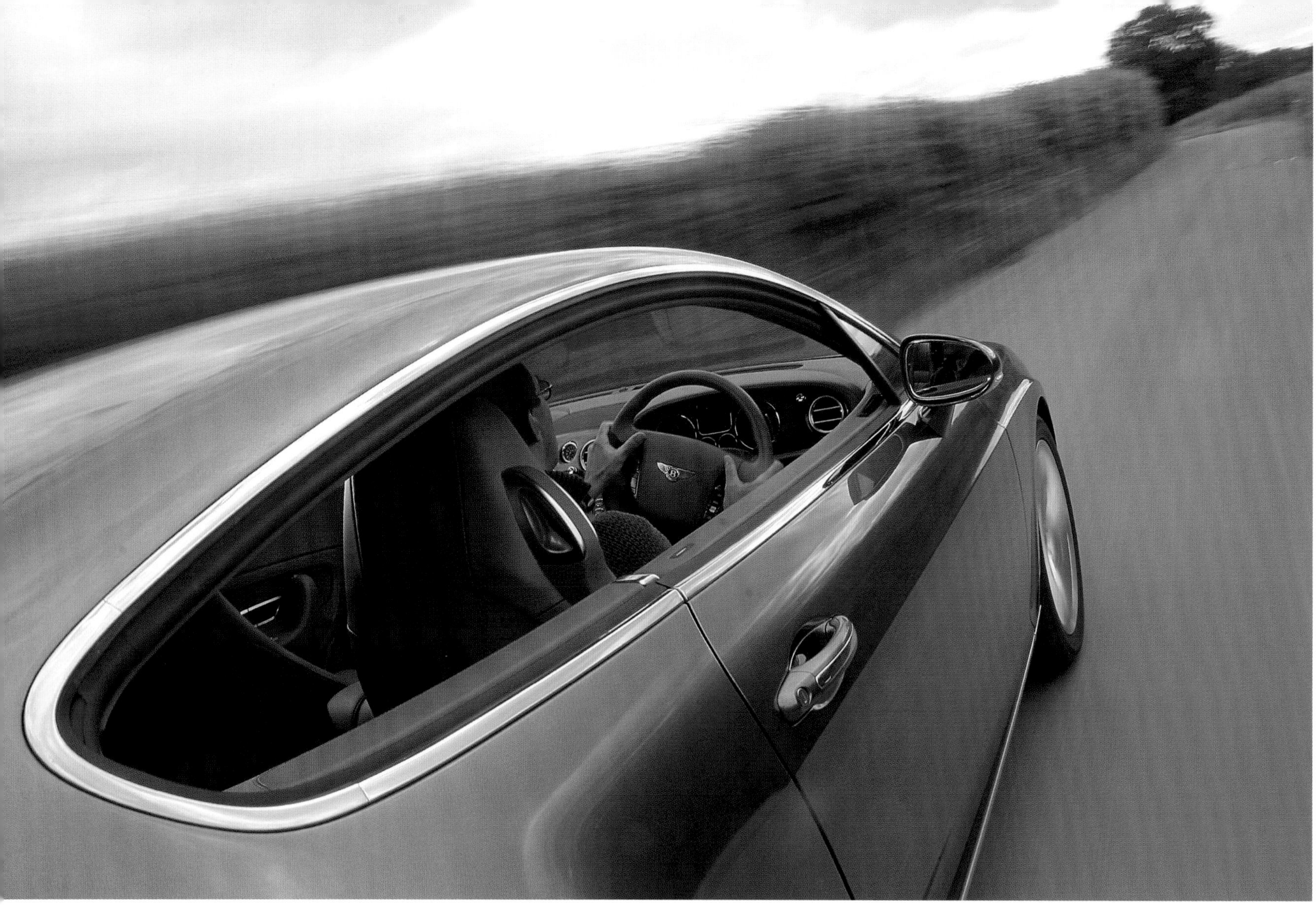

ABOVE: The Continental GT is a true pillarless coupe, and what better way to see the British countryside, with windows down and the hedge rows blurring by.

OPPOSITE, FROM TOP: There's artistry everywhere—projector headlamps set within subtly scalloped recesses; the underside of a rearview mirror, with its turn-signal repeater and "puddle lamps" that illuminate when you open the door; handsome 19-in. alloy wheels carrying 275/40R-19 tires.

at their peaks. The W-12 design, essentially two 15-degree narrow-angle V-6s joined by a common crankshaft, results in a 12-cylinder powerplant that takes up much less space than a conventional V-12 would. Other unusual features of the Bentley engine are the specially developed pistons designed to deliver the 9.5:1 compression ratio, which is unusually high for a turbocharged engine. The W-12 benefits from seven main bearings, pent-roof combustion chambers and variable valve timing for both intake and exhaust valves.

Twin KKK turbochargers provide the additional oomph Bentley demanded of the GT. And the torque curve is nearly flat from 1600 rpm up to 6000 rpm. When you drive the car, all of this becomes readily apparent, as the Continental GT accelerates briskly and with the sure-footedness only all-wheel drive can provide. The power comes up quickly and in a linear fashion that belies the twin turbos. Bentley claims 0–60 mph takes a mere 4.7 seconds, and I have no reason to doubt this. Top speed is claimed to be a stupendous 198 mph.

The power is delivered to the wheels through a 6-speed automatic transmission built by ZF. Bentley engineers specified an automatic with the ability to lock its torque converter in normal driving so that it would provide the immediate response of a manual gearbox. At the same time, shift quality was required to be so smooth that the driver might not even notice that a gear change had taken place. As with most current premium-price cars, Tiptronic actuation is in the system, so the driver can opt for fully automatic mode, or shift with the gear lever or with the paddles behind the steering wheel.

Despite the Bentley's weight of 5250 lb., it drives with scarcely a hint of heftiness. The engine ramps up with enthusiasm and loves to run straight up to the redline without a pause. The Continental GT benefits from a dedicated exhaust system that uses two six-into-one manifolds for utmost efficiency. In addition, special tuning was done to ensure that the exhaust note and the induction noise are just right, lending a decided sporting sound to the driving experience of Bentley's fastest road car.

Changing gears is delightful with the 6-speed transmission, and the paddle shifters work with a minimum of fuss and a maximum of smoothness. Even in the fully automatic mode, the Continental GT steps out in a lively fashion and makes passing other traffic a very quick event. The gearbox is exceptionally lightweight and compact, and despite its six speeds, it has almost 30 percent fewer components than a conventional 5-speed automatic transmission. Coupled with the security of all-wheel drive, this excellent gearbox makes the Bentley truly appropriate for long-distance touring at the highest levels of comfort, convenience and performance.

The Bentley engineering team believes it is imperative to have a chassis that is second to none in a GT that is capable of nearly 200 mph. The chassis specifications include double wishbones at the front end and a multilink system at the rear. Air springs are used all around and incorporate infinitely adjustable electronic dampers. This setup allows the driver to select different modes of sporting or touring suspension characteristics so that optimal handling performance and ride comfort are available.

Keeping the Bentley under control no matter the driving conditions is the responsibility of the electronic stability systems built into each Continental GT. ASR traction control and Bosch Electronic Stability Program (ESP) are part of the package, although the driver can disable them if desired. But for ensuring safety from pesky ice patches and inclement weather, they are great to have.

The Bentley steering is by rack and pinion, and I found it nicely linear and communicative throughout my driving experience, whether on high-speed motorways or the twisty little tracks around the tors and lochs of Scotland. The brakes are vented and slotted discs, with Bosch anti-lock enhanced by brake assist and electronic brake force distribution. Safe, sure stops are a breeze from any speed.

It comes as no surprise that the Bentley boffins place great emphasis on the Continental GT's body structure. After all, if you are going to have a car that is capable of great speed for covering long distances in an atmosphere of quiet comfort, the basic structure needs to be a rigid one. And with a stiffer body, the less the occupants will notice any vibrations and undue noise. Thanks to virtual engineering with computers and three-dimensional digital models of the car, Bentley was able to predict the car's structural integrity prior to the building of the first prototype. Then, turning to aerospace technologies, Bentley used adhesives for bonding, especially in areas where long seals were called for, such as around the door openings.

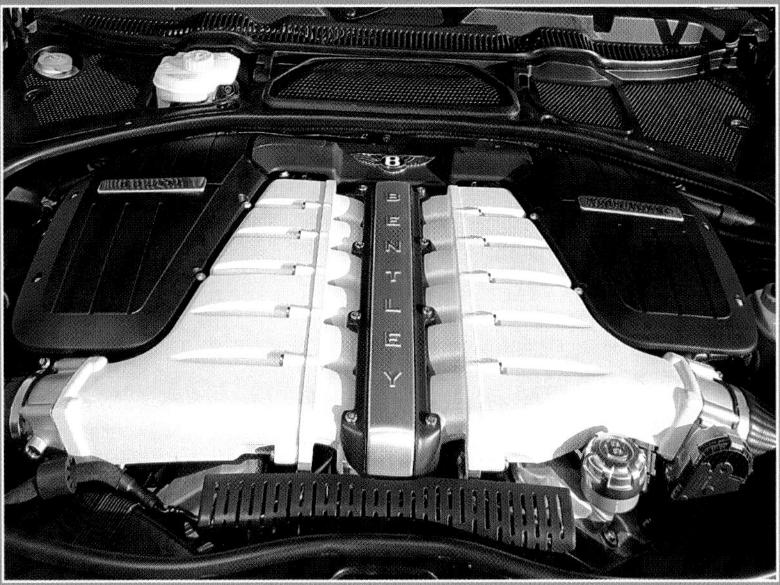
BENTLEY

LEFT: A marvel of packaging as well as power, the Continental GT's 6.0-liter W-12 engine is essentially two narrow-angle V-6 engines joined by a common crankshaft. With the help of twin turbochargers, it makes a prodigious 552 bhp.

BELOW: The GT's profile manages to convey substance, authority and elegance all at once.

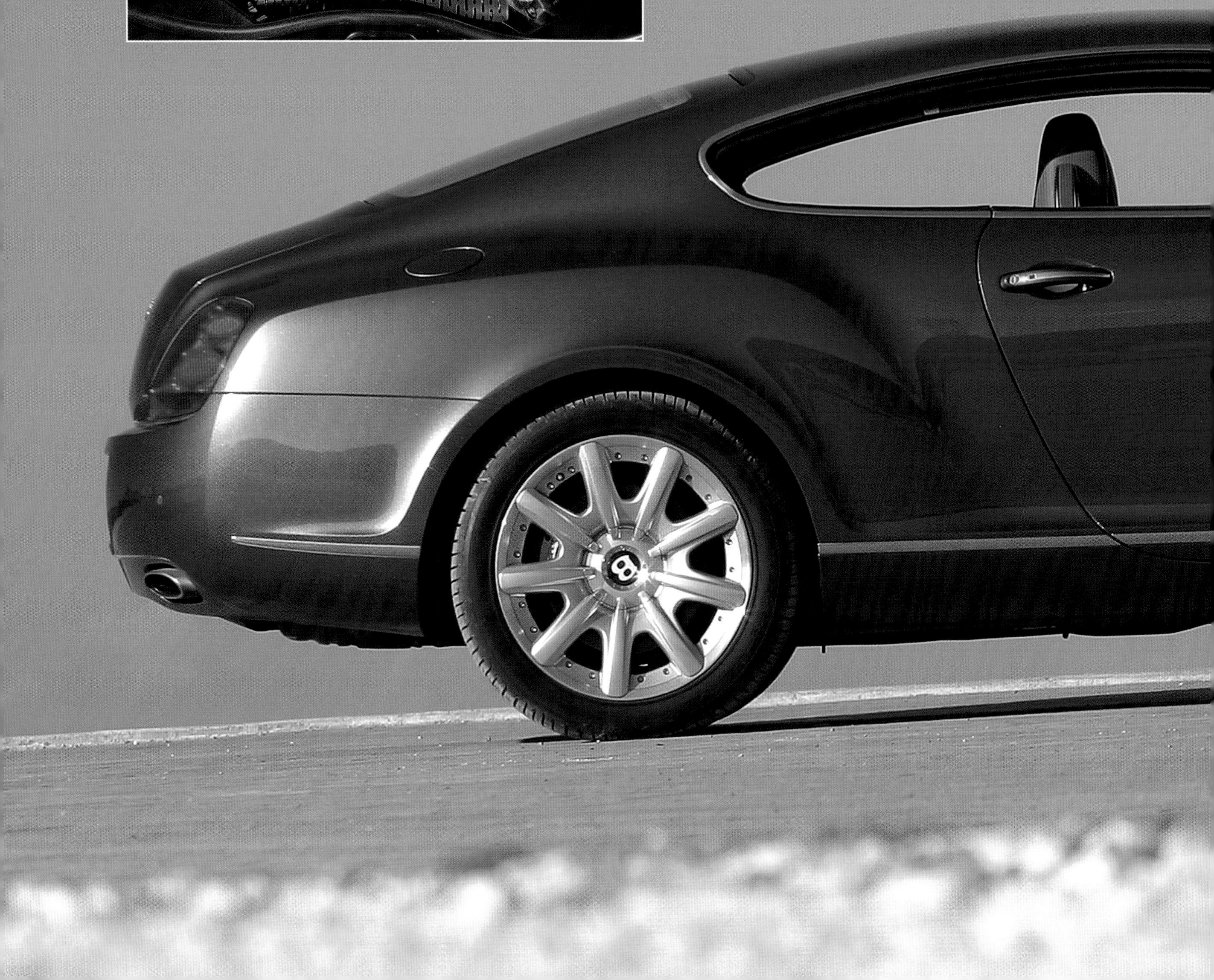

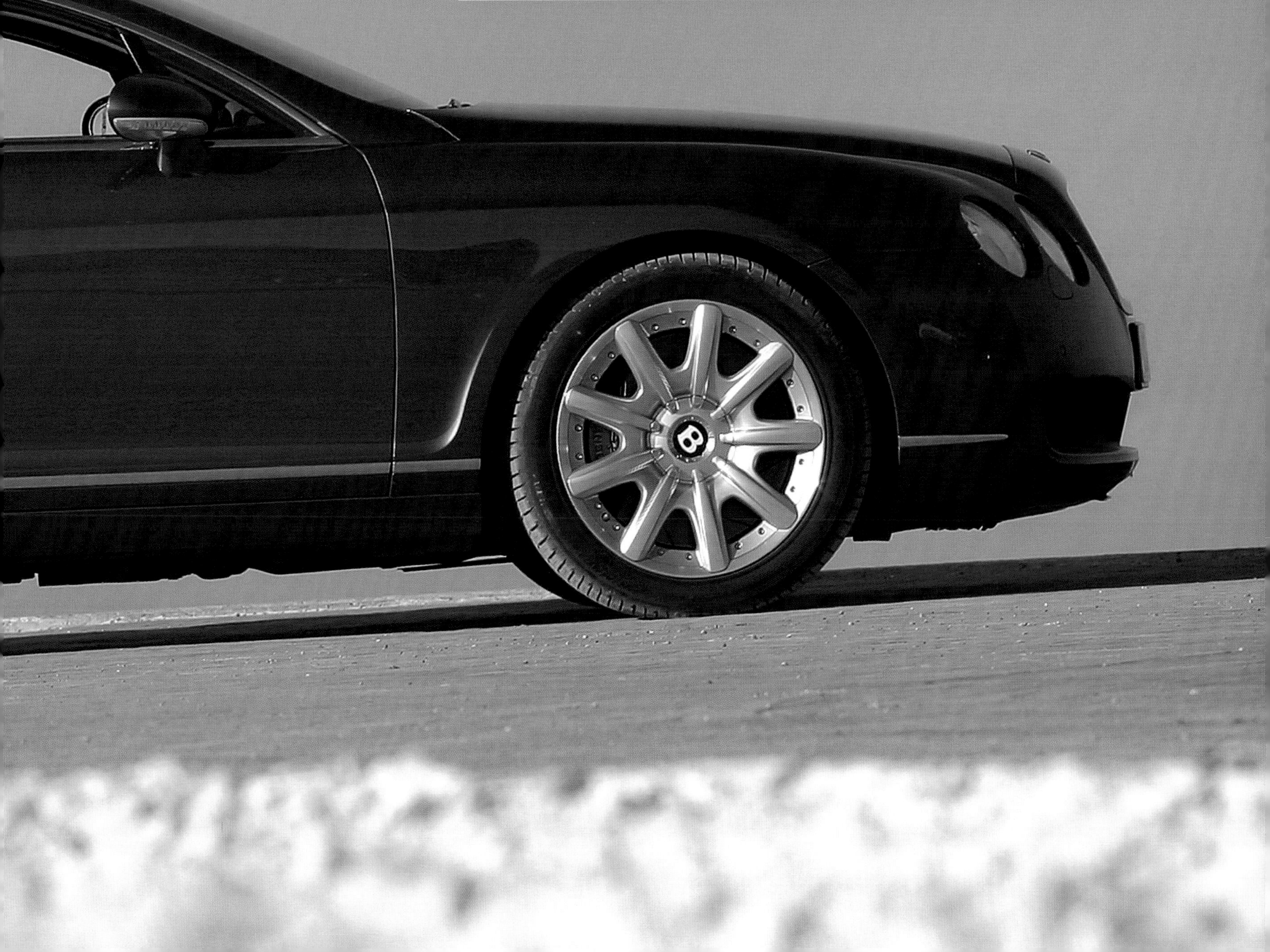

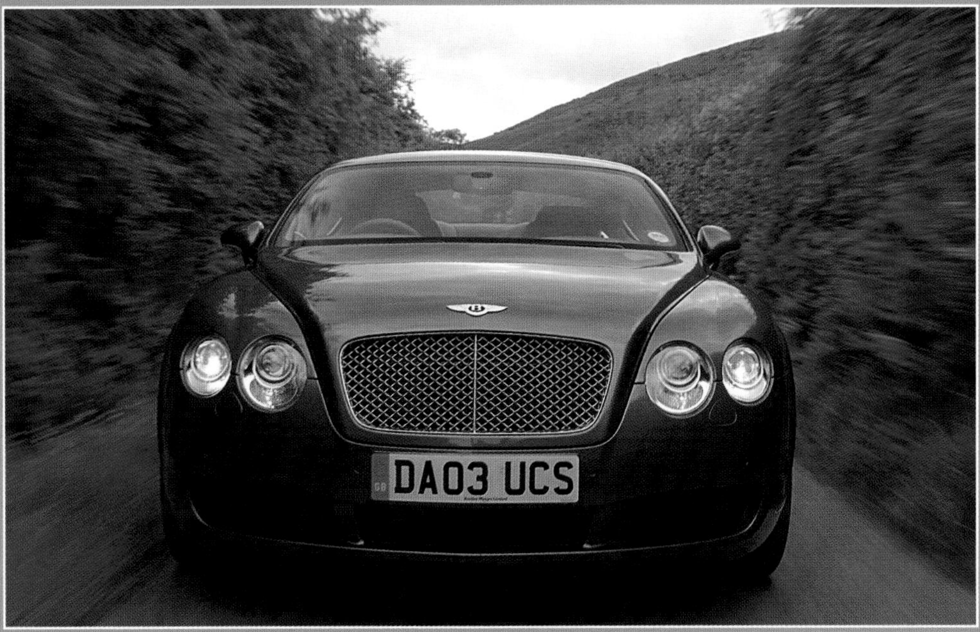
DA03 UCS

ON/OFF
A/C
NAVI
TRIP
RESET
AUDIO/TV
PHONE
HELP
VEHICLE
SET UP
BAND
CD
TV
START
STOP

rpm x1000
EPC
P
R
N
D
S
423.8km
18.0°C
2874km
mph

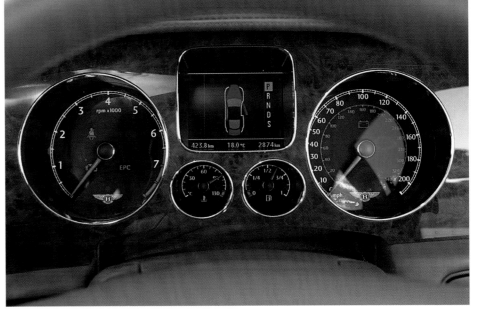

ABOVE: Old-world charm meets modern technology in an interior that conceals multiple microprocessors behind supple leather hides and veneers of polished wood. Gear lever taps the ZF transmission's six ratios; slipping it into the slot to its left enables the sequential shift mode.

OPPOSITE: You'll lose track of time after spending some of it behind the Continental GT's steering wheel. It's difficult to imagine a more lavishly appointed interior.

I find the overall styling of the car very pleasing, though the front end can be a bit heavy-looking from some angles. But overall, the Continental GT is handsome and purposeful, leaving no doubt that it is a car of substance for people of substance. The long hood is evocative of Bentleys of the 1920s that gained so much fame racing at the 24 Hours of Le Mans in the hands of the Bentley Boys. And the beautifully sculpted roofline that sweeps from front to rear is outstanding. Add to that the short rear deck's business-like aspect and you have a very tidy styling treatment. At the same time, the rear luggage space is quite large and there is a pass-through into the rear-seat area for long items such as snow skis.

Speaking of the interior, this may well be the best designed and outfitted interior I've seen. The materials are absolutely first-class and the fit and finish are excellent. Each leather hide is specially selected and then cut using a new digital process to minimize waste. The wood trim throughout the car is of the highest order, and the traditional Bentley chrome bull's-eye air vents with their organ-stop controls make certain you never forget what marque you're in.

Lest you think the Continental GT is all about old-world charm and craftsmanship, don't be surprised to learn that this car also carries some two miles of electrical cables in a wiring harness that weighs more than 100 lb. There are also 70 microprocessors, 35 control units and three control area networks to co-ordinate communications among all the electronic bits. Boy, times have most certainly changed.

When I arrived at the airfield near Wick, I was invited to ride to the hotel in a Blower Bentley from the 1920s. Taking the wheel of the big, powerful car was Sarah Perris, director of worldwide communications for Bentley and an enthusiastic driver of classic Bentleys. We set off toward the hotel Ackergill Tower on the coast. It was a thrilling ride through gorgeous countryside on a rare warm afternoon in the north of Scotland. Wearing leather caps and goggles, we were easily able to imagine ourselves within the period when the car was built, an era of fast cars, beautiful women and powerful men. Later, as I began to drive the Continental GT, I thought about the noise and power of the Blower Bentley, and what a handful it was to drive. By contrast, the new car is a dream—fast, sure-footed, comfortable, luxurious and quiet. And, yet, with all of that, it still carries the flavor and excitement of its 75-year-old predecessor. And for that, we should all offer thanks to the dedicated people at the new Bentley.

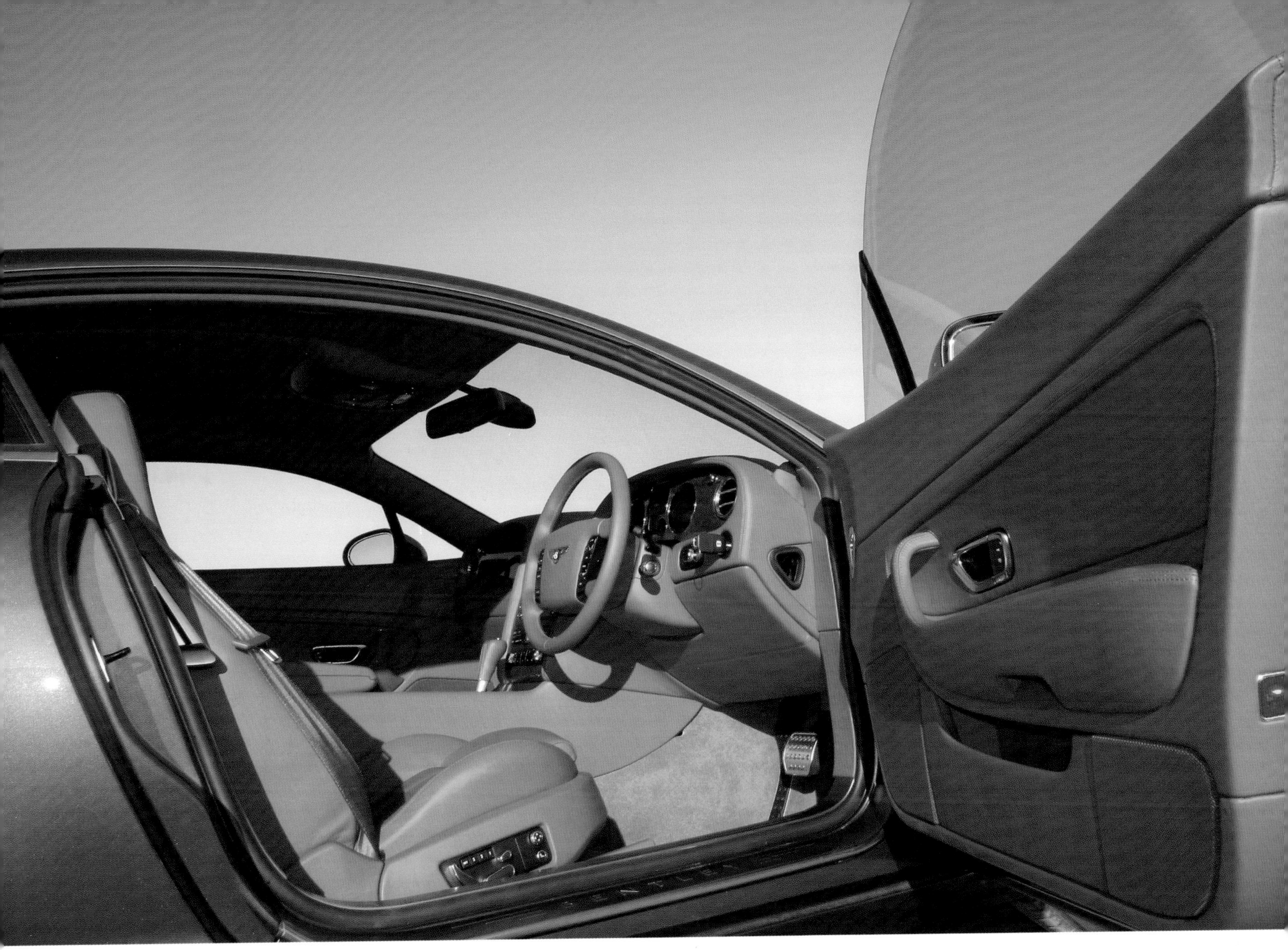

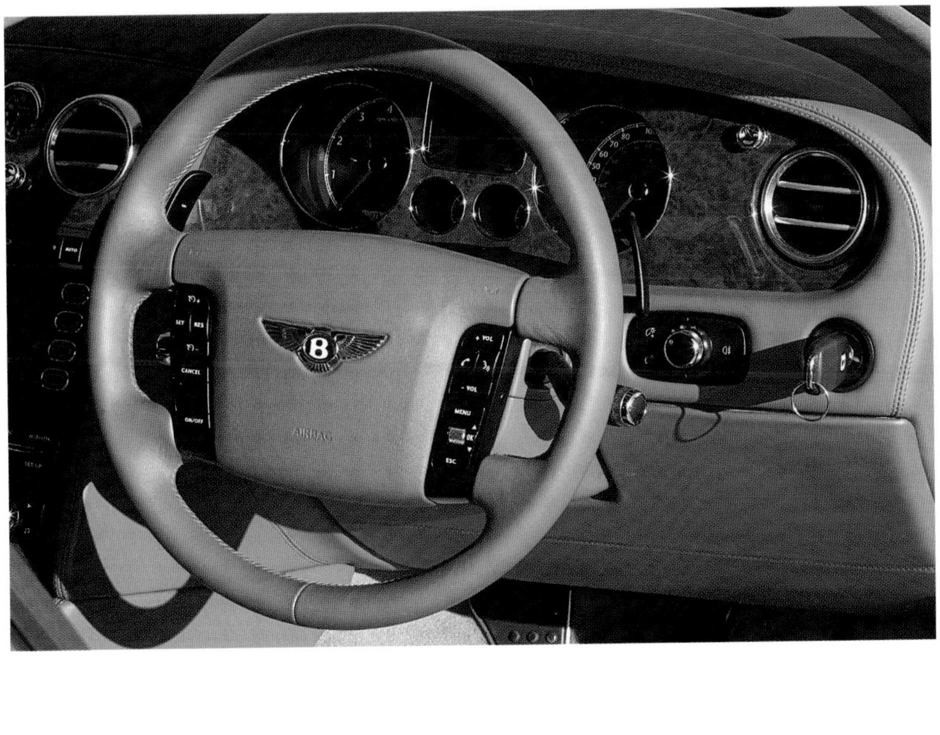

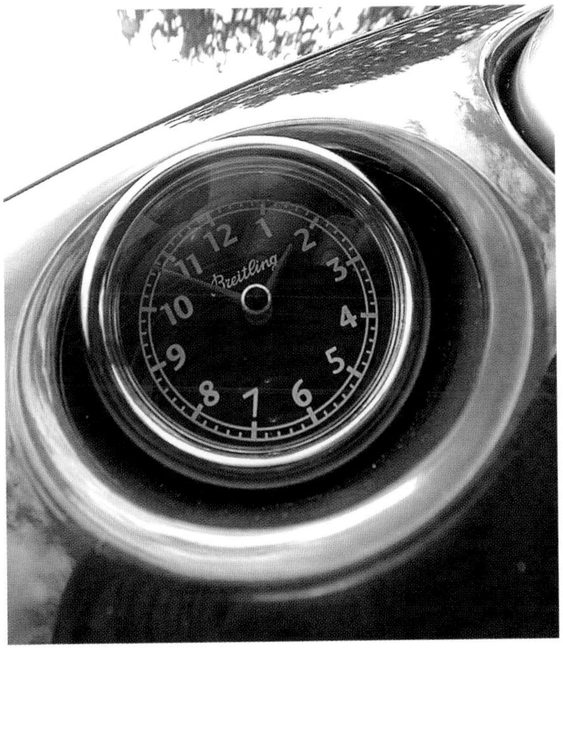
Breitling

DODGE
VIPER SRT-10

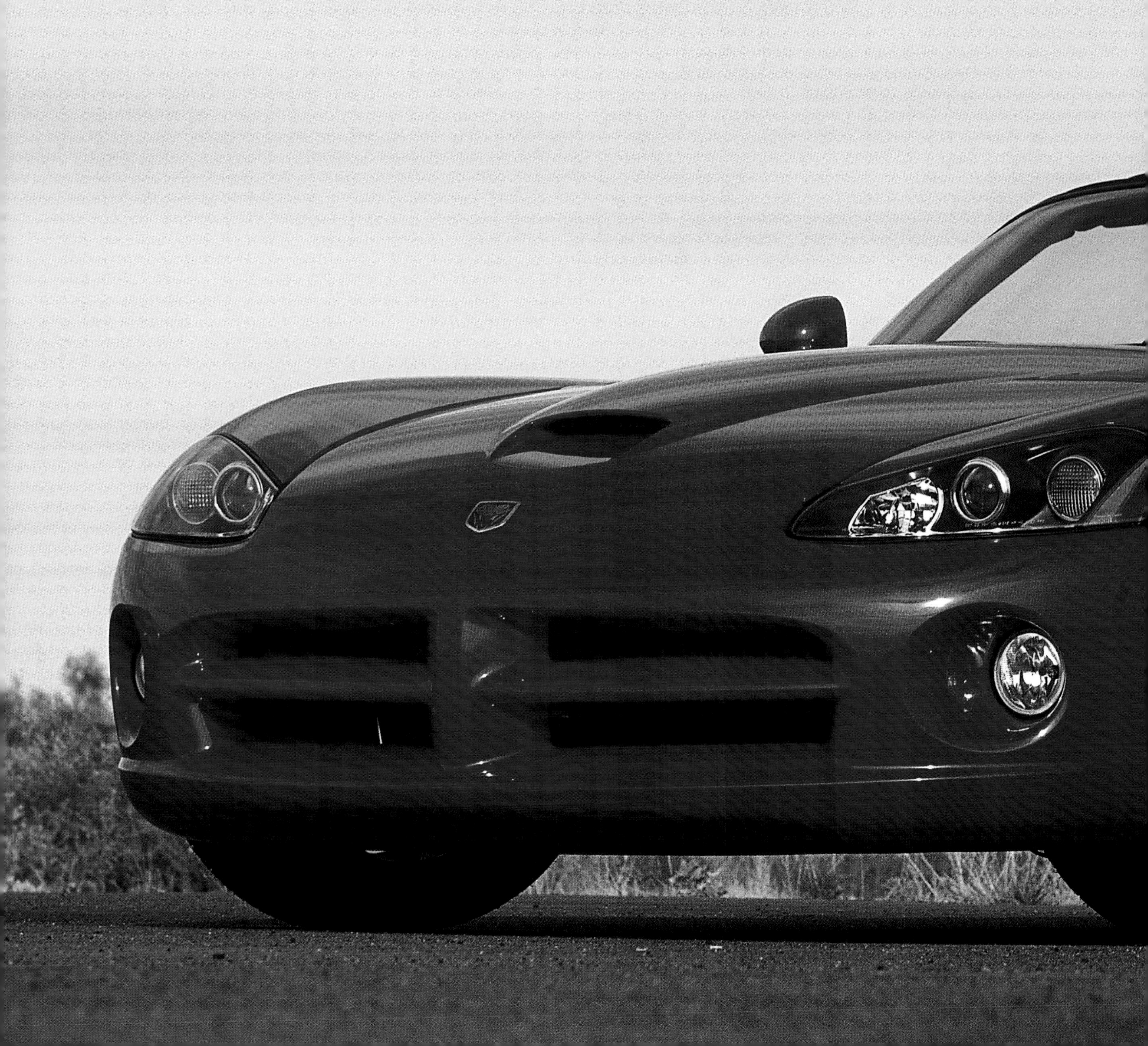

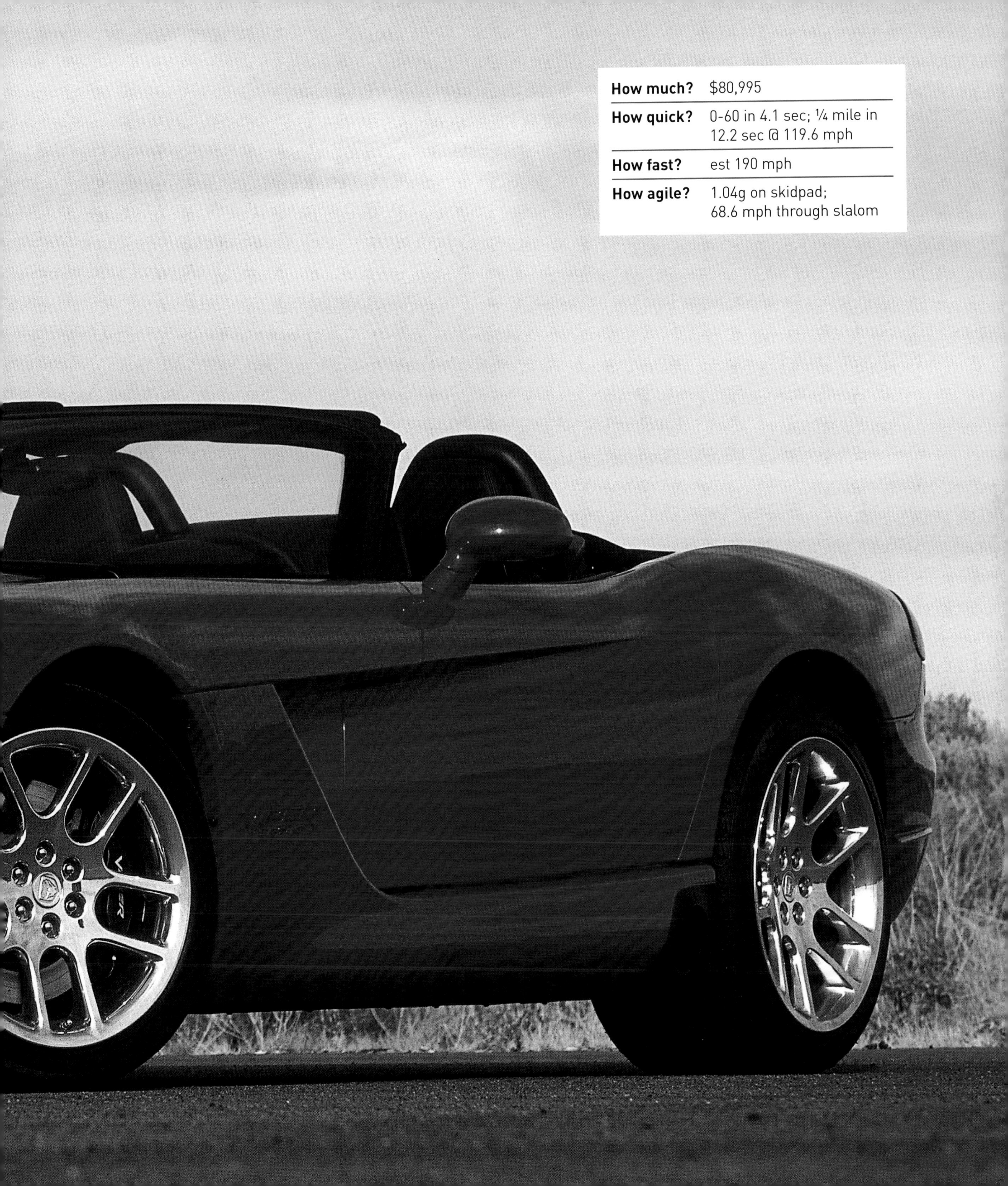

How much?	$80,995
How quick?	0-60 in 4.1 sec; ¼ mile in 12.2 sec @ 119.6 mph
How fast?	est 190 mph
How agile?	1.04g on skidpad; 68.6 mph through slalom

GOING TO EXTREMES

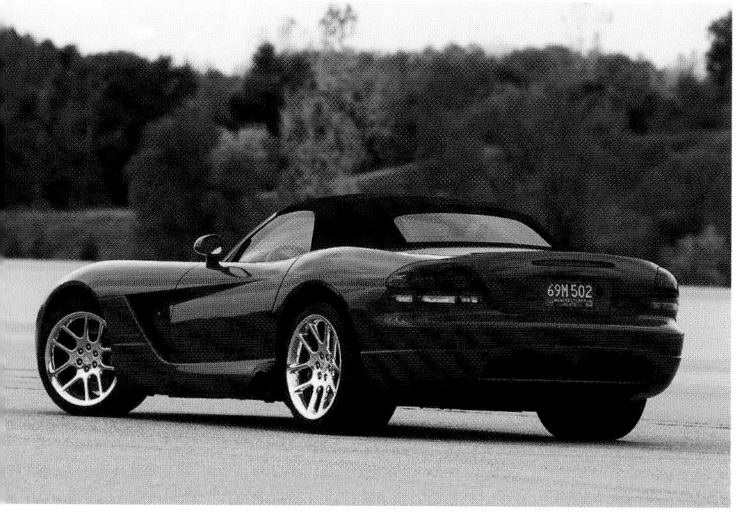
69M502

ABOVE: Now in its second generation, the more user-friendly Viper has a conventional folding soft-top, a huge improvement over the original's Byzantine contraption of fabric and bows.

IN THE LATE 1980s, no doubt weary of Chevrolet's Corvette claiming the uncontested title of "America's Sports Car," Dodge set out to do something about it. In just three short years, the Viper metamorphosed from auto-show darling to production-car reality, complete with its truck-derived 400-bhp V-10, steam-roller-width tires and a muscle-bound 2-seat roadster body that seemed larger than life. Explosive, raw and somewhat crude, the original Viper was perhaps too elemental for even hard-core sports-car fans, so its redesign for 2003 incorporated a more conventional folding soft-top, improved heat insulation for the engine and exhaust, and tamer bodywork...but not before bumping the V-10's output to 500 bhp for the quickest-accelerating Viper ever. Make a little room, Corvette, for two at the top.

Ever the bad boy among performance cars, the original Dodge Viper is admired for both brute power and rough edges. As such, it's not for everyone.

The same holds true on the track. Club racers and time-trial warriors alike flock to the Viper like moths to a flame. And let's not overlook the purpose-built GTS-R, a car that delivered three successive class wins at Le Mans and an overall win at the Rolex 24 Hours of Daytona.

Now there's an all-new production Viper, the SRT-10, and Dodge is seeking to broaden the appeal of its V-10-powered icon while adding even more performance. The new Viper is still a bad boy, albeit with a bit more polish. To see how the SRT-10 performs, Road Test Editor Patrick Hong and I arranged a test session at Chrysler's Chelsea Proving Grounds in Michigan.

In 2002, I was exposed to the Viper on four different occasions, driving it three of those times. When I first saw it at the 2001 North American International Auto Show, I thought Osamu Shikado's design was too pretty to be a Viper. There's no mistaking the face with its snake-eye headlamps and cross-hair grille treatment, and the sides definitely have a bold look thanks to the deep, angular vents and side pipes. But the look softens considerably through the rear haunches, which curve gently into a tapered rear end topped by a small ducktail spoiler.

BELOW: With fangs bared, the Viper is more than capable of striking at its prime competitor, the Chevrolet Corvette.

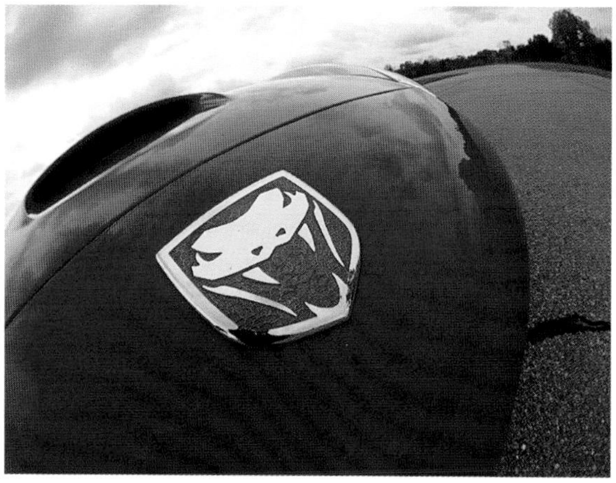

The more I see the new Viper, the better I like it. It seems familiarity with this design breeds contentment. The Viper has the classic proportioning and detailing that will wear well on a car that should be able to last five years or more without a facelift.

Equally satisfying are the improvements to the car's ergonomics. The larger footprint, which includes a 2.6-in.-longer wheelbase, at 98.8 in., allows for much better packaging. The pedals are now directly in front of the driver, and the manual adjustment for the cluster has been supplanted by a power control. The new bucket seats are firmly bolstered. The steering wheel is thick and grippy, and the Tremec 6-speed has a firm feel to its short and precise throws.

The instrument cluster is new, with a large center tachometer flanked on the right by a smaller speedometer and on the left by an even smaller fuel gauge. To the right of the steering wheel in the center console are four auxiliary gauges

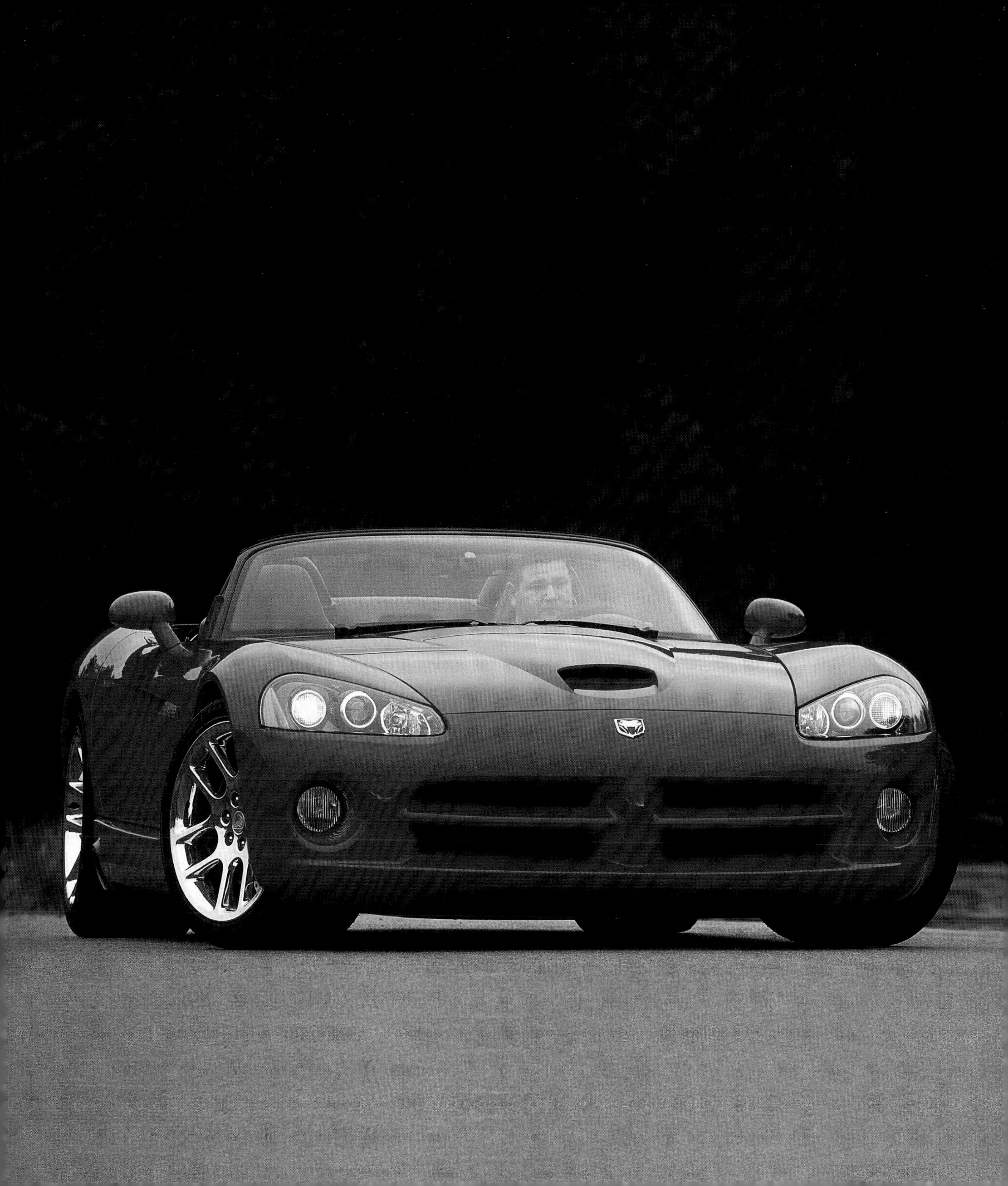

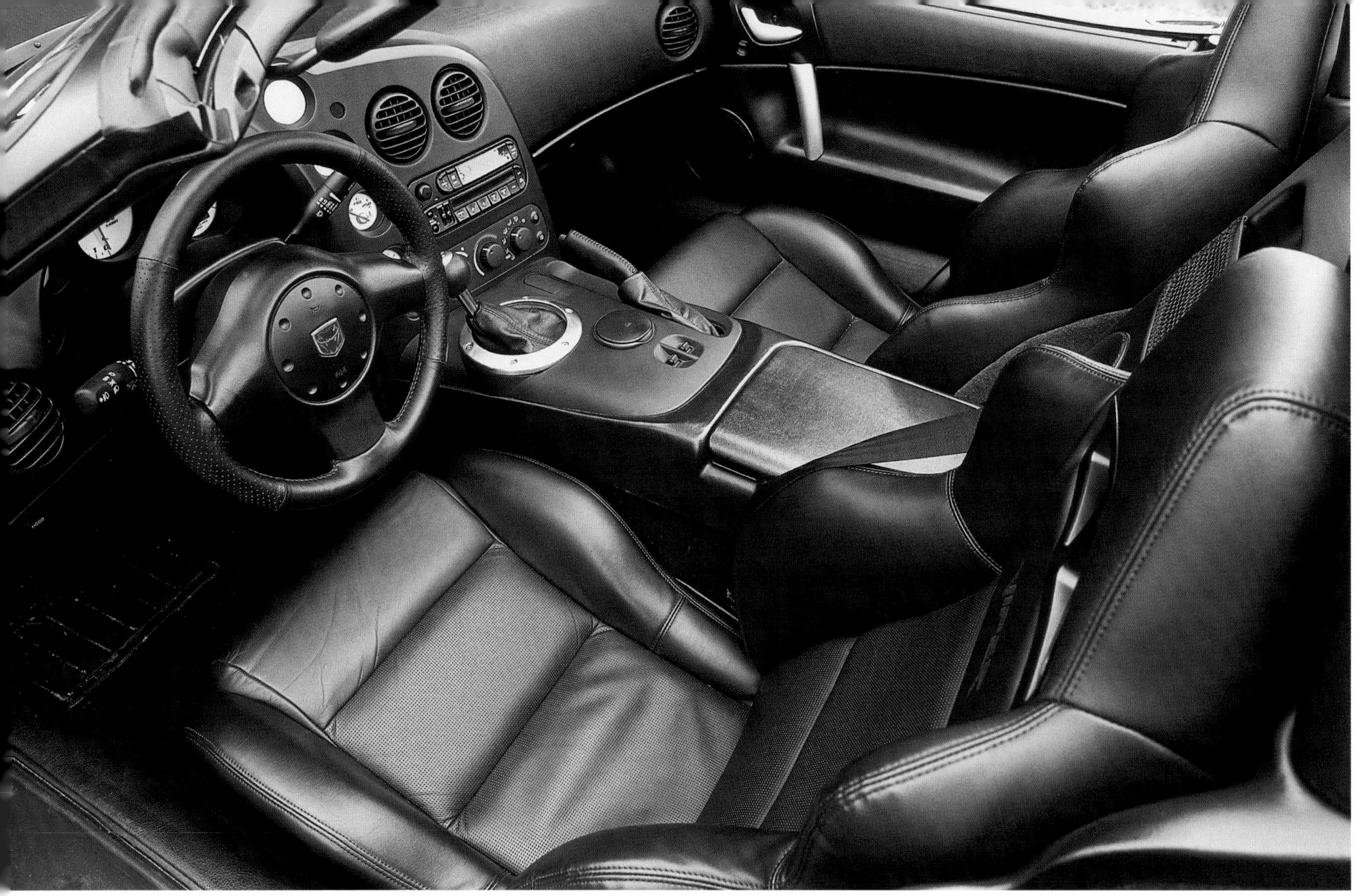

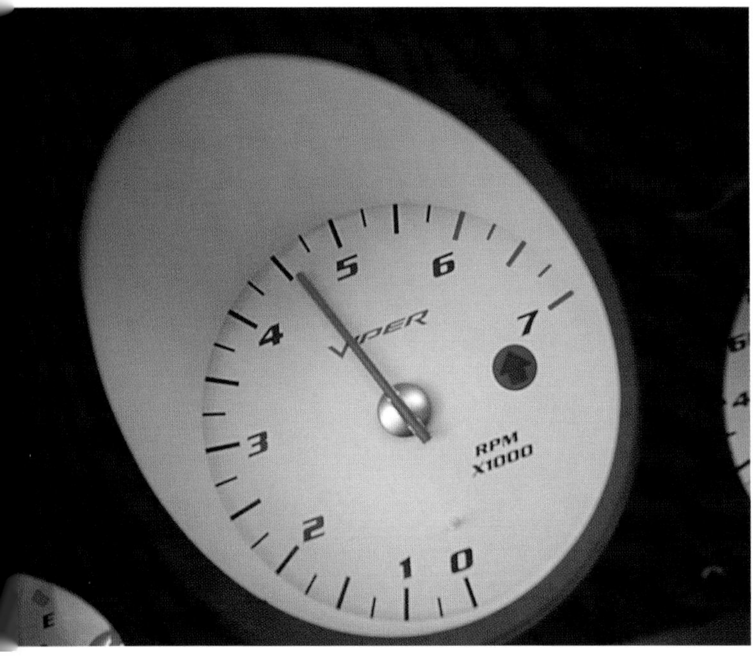
VIPER
RPM
X1000

for oil and water temperature, oil pressure and voltage. And just below the instruments is the engine-start button.

A gentle push of the red button and the 8.3-liter V-10 rumbles to life, each throaty side pipe sounding off from all 10 cylinders, thanks to the way the exhaust is routed and interconnected. The pipes pass through the rocker sills but then, behind the driver, they cross and exit on the opposite side of the car. A small section links the two pipes where they run parallel, enabling the sound from both banks of cylinders to mix. The ghosts of the UPS truck exhaust note have been exorcised and now the Viper has the snarl to match the drivetrain's bite.

The 0.3-liter increase in displacement to 8.3 has boosted the pushrod V-10's output to the magic 500-bhp level at 5600 rpm. Likewise, torque is up to 525 lb.-ft. at 4200 rpm. And that increased performance is for a car that has a curb weight of 3390 lb., some 115 lb. lighter than the 2000 460-bhp Viper GTS ACR we tested previously. This infusion of extra muscle is apparent in the numbers—the new SRT-10 accelerates to 60 mph in 4.1 seconds and covers the quarter mile in 12.2 sec. at a speed of 119.6 mph. The ACR was good for a 0–60 time of 4.4 sec. and a quarter of 12.6 sec. at 114.4 mph.

Even more telling are the skidpad and slalom numbers resulting from the revised suspension and tire package. In addition to the longer wheelbase, the Viper has a 1.8-in.-narrower 57.8-in. front track and 0.3-in.-wider 60.9-in. rear track coupled with 18 x 10-in. front and 19 x 13-in. rear wheels shod with Michelin Pilot Sport tires. As a result, the SRT-10 recorded 1.04g around the skidpad and 68.6 mph in the 700-ft. slalom (versus the ACR's 0.98g and 63.6 mph). Keep in mind, this is the stock Viper compared to the last-generation GTS ACR, which not only had a stiffer suspension but also an extra 10 bhp over the base model.

These numbers reflect not only higher grip, but also the more refined and settled nature of the Viper's chassis. The steering has a more linear action and improved on-center feel. The body motions are well controlled and the transitions in handling are much more progressive.

The braking on the SRT-10 is most impressive of all. The Brembo package features 14.0-in. vented discs all around, equipped with 4-piston calipers. In addition to gaining an inch in rotor size, the Viper also is equipped with ABS. The 60–0 stop took just 114 ft. compared with the GTS ACR's non-ABS 156 ft. From 80 mph, the SRT-10 used just 196 ft. while the previous car required 258.

Several quick tours around the 1.7-mile handling track at Chelsea reinforced my earlier impressions of the car as being much more civilized in both ride and handling. And yet, when pushed hard, it could deliver the kind of straight-line thrills that have been a Viper trademark. With the top stowed, cockpit wind management is quite good, with minimal intrusion even at speeds of 90 mph or higher. Cockpit heat has been a problem. In the few cars I've been exposed to, the driver's side in particular gets as hot as a sauna. Contrary to suggestions that they address the problem with a new cedar planking trim insert, the Viper team is using more material to better seal the cabin, and increased the airflow around the exhaust system with a new air dam mounted behind the front wheels.

The changes beg the question: Is a "more civilized Viper" an oxymoron? Not at all. With its extra power and torque, a truly usable convertible top, improved ergonomics and a lower center of gravity, the Viper SRT-10 improves on the hairy-chested, smoke-churning performance of the original while sanding down the thorns that made the original car such a prickly beast.

ABOVE: The center dash houses no-nonsense controls and a curved stack of white-faced ancillary gauges.

OPPOSITE: Thickly bolstered seats are an absolute necessity, as the Viper corners like no other exotic—at 1.04g around the *Road & Track* skidpad, it's the current record-holder for production cars.

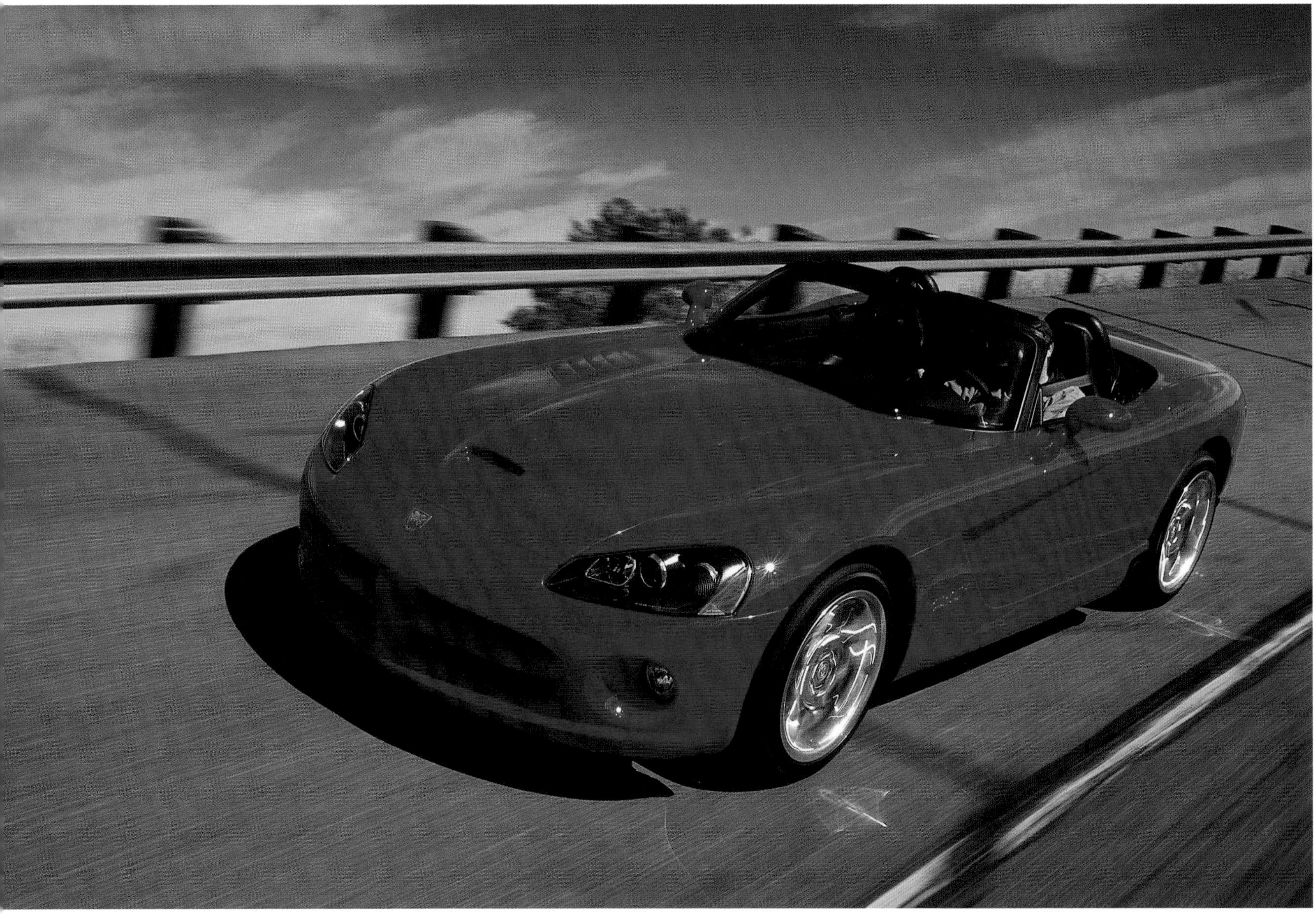

RIGHT: Fire up the 8.3-liter pushrod V-10, and it's an engine that is felt as much as it's heard, through both vibration and the way you're pushed back in the seat when all 500 bhp are unleashed. Exhaust sound is much improved over the original car's, thanks to its interconnected, crisscrossing system.

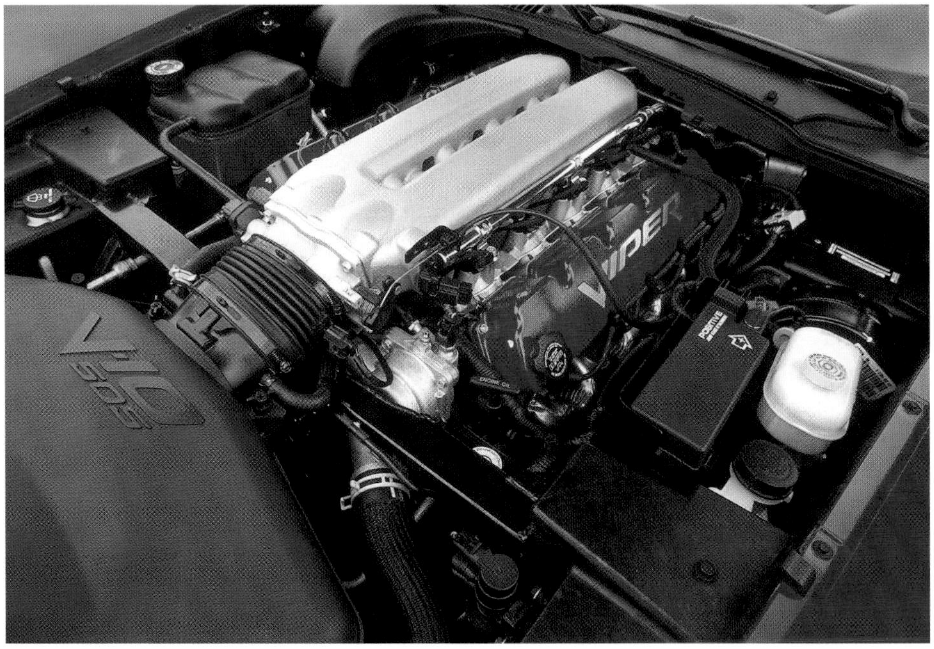
VIPER
V-10

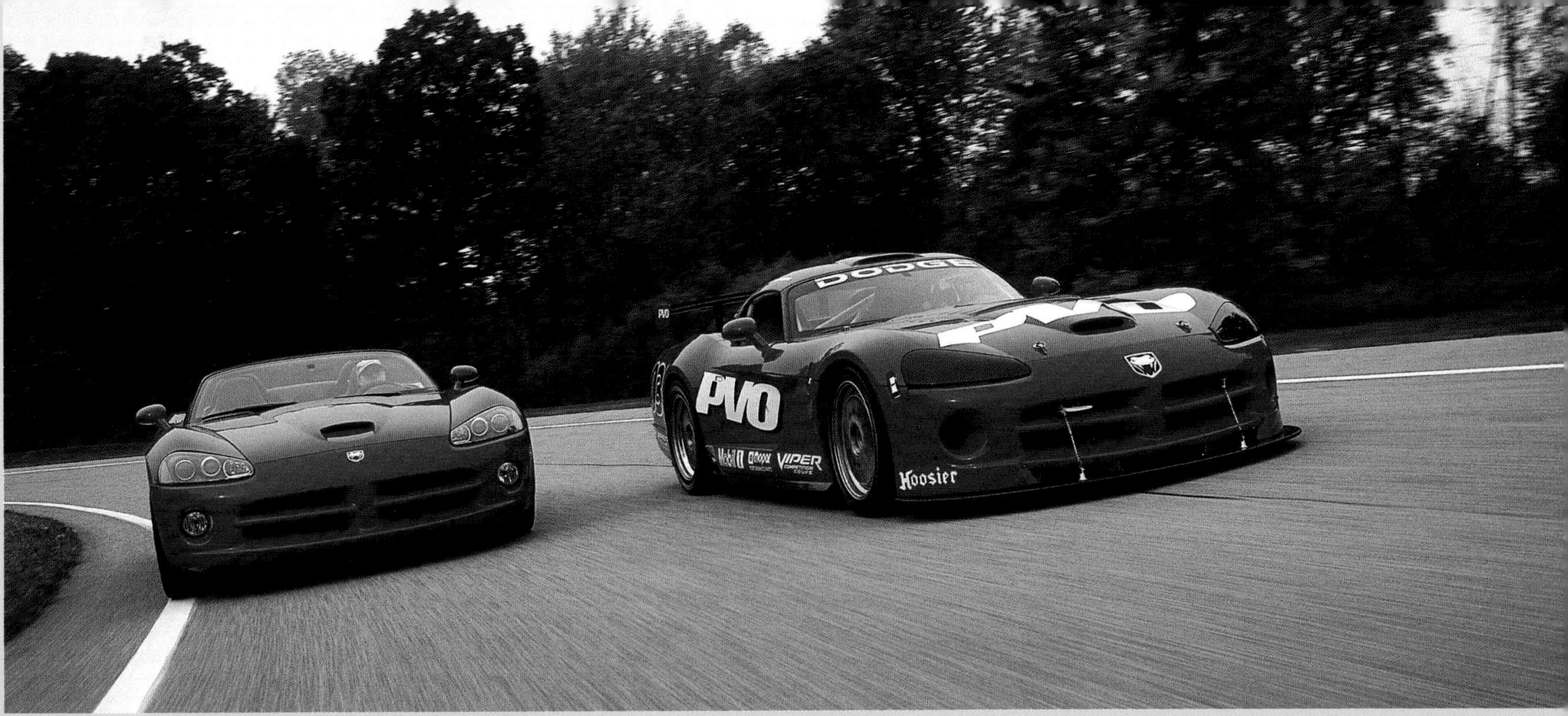
DODGE
PVO
PVO
VIPER
Hoosier

RACE READY: THE VIPER COMPETITION COUPE

For now, all road-going versions of the Viper will be convertibles. But when designers first toyed with the idea of what the new car would look like, they started with the baddest Viper of all, the GTS-R coupe. It was this shape the public saw first when the concept was unveiled at the Detroit auto show in January 2000.

Performance Vehicle Operations (PVO) decided to use the coupe body from the show car to do a replacement for the FIA-certified GTS-R. Management rejected the project as too costly, so PVO came back with the idea of doing the Competition Coupe based on a more-or-less stock SRT-10 rolling chassis. Rather than creating a vehicle for an all-out assault on Le Mans, this new approach would provide track-ready race cars for Dodge Viper enthusiasts at a much lower cost and in much higher volumes.

The Competition Coupe is intended for use in the Viper Racing League, SCCA World Challenge and Grand-Am Cup events, according to Eric Petersen, the car's development engineer. As of late 2003, 60 Competition Coupes had been sold, and Chrysler will continue to build them based on demand at the current list price of $129,000.

In Competition Coupe form, the Viper has a much more aggressive overall shape than the stock roadster's, with a front splitter, air extractors in the hood and a roof-mounted scoop to direct airflow to the driver. At the rear, the bodywork has been lengthened to create a cowl-like effect over the taillamps, topped with a sizable spoiler.

Beneath the skin is a stock Viper frame to which an FIA-spec cage has been added. There is a large X-shape crossmember that fits over the engine and a full cage in the cockpit. The Competition Coupe retains the SRT-10's suspension, but replaces all the rubber bushings with bearings, and the rack-and-pinion steering is mounted directly to the framework. While Michelin is working on a tire for the Competition Coupe, the model we drove was shod with specially developed Hoosier slicks mounted to 18 x 11-in. front and 19 x 14-in. rear three-piece BBS wheels, which are an inch wider than stock.

The engine modifications are minimal. There's a new cam, a reduced-backpressure exhaust system with no catalytic converters and a modified oilpan to increase oil pressure (the system remains a wet sump). The engine produces 520 bhp and 540 lb.-ft. of torque. The transmission is fitted with a larger cooler and has a shorter-throw shift linkage, and the stock electronically controlled limited-slip differential has been replaced by the viscous-coupled racing diff from the GTS-R.

The one area that the PVO group left alone was the stock car's Brembo brake package with its ABS. "The brake system is one of the areas that really keeps this car cost-competitive," Petersen says. "We'll be able to sell stock one-piece rotors relatively cheap compared to the two-piece race rotors, which can get quite expensive."

It's this relative affordability that is key. The epic battles between Corvettes and Vipers at Le Mans may be over, but in the meantime, this new Competition Coupe will provide plenty of thrills for drivers and spectators alike at tracks much closer to home.

FERRARI ENZO

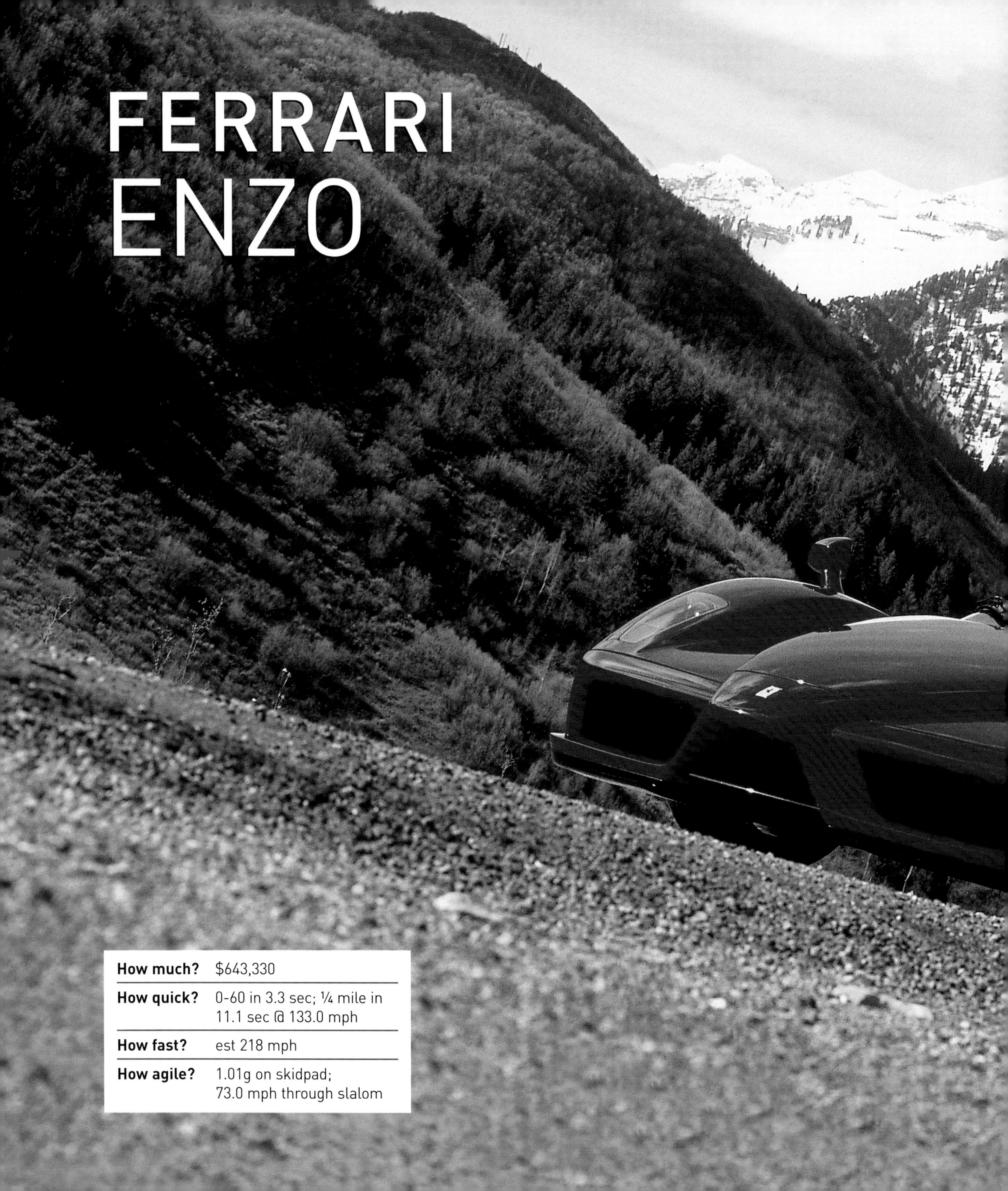

How much?	$643,330
How quick?	0-60 in 3.3 sec; ¼ mile in 11.1 sec @ 133.0 mph
How fast?	est 218 mph
How agile?	1.01g on skidpad; 73.0 mph through slalom

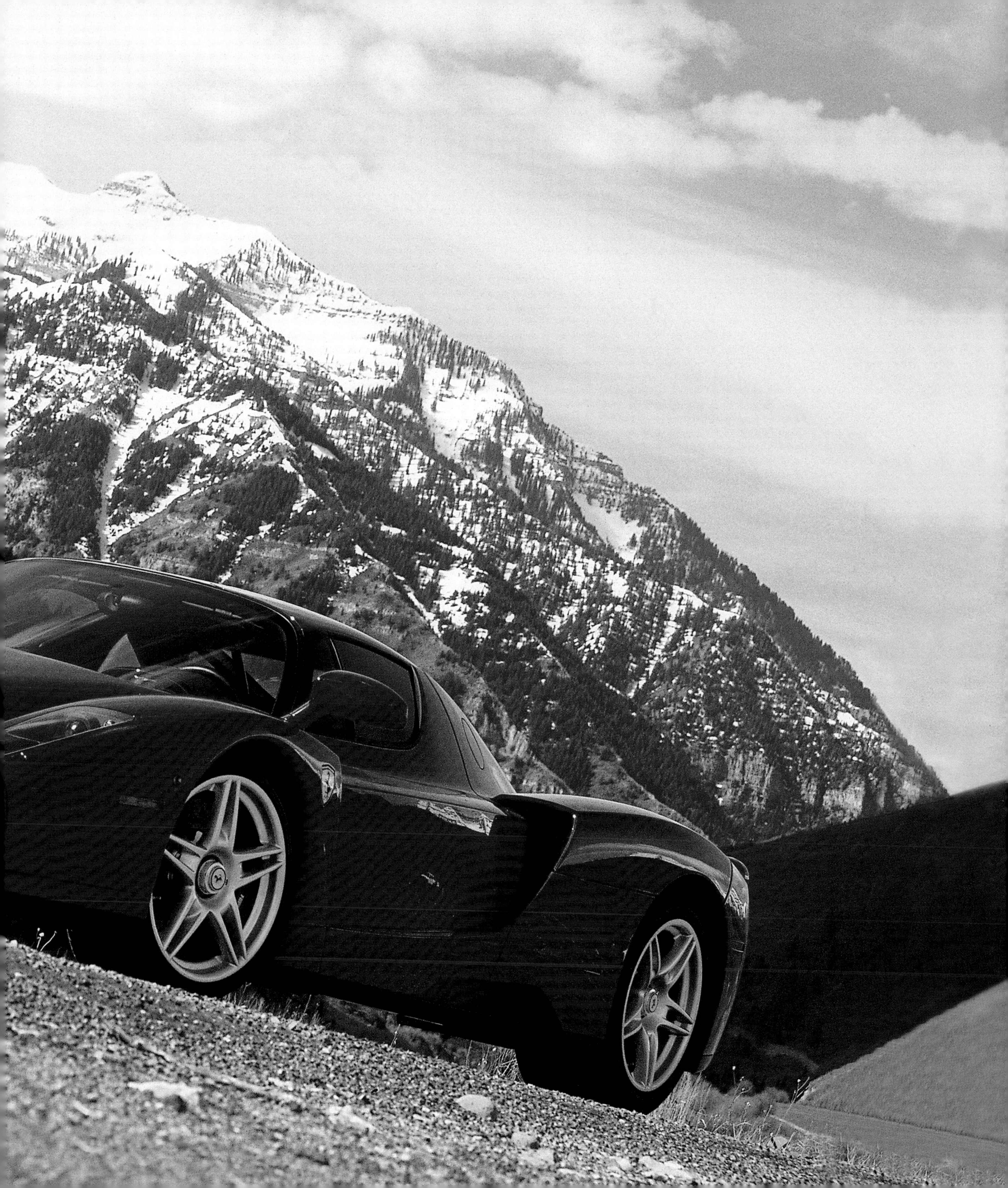

MARANELLO'S WINGLESS WONDER SETS THE NEW STANDARD

FERRARI HAS HAD A LONG AND STORIED COMPETITION HISTORY since its founding in 1947. It's been said that the man himself, Enzo Ferrari, was far more interested in racing than manufacturing road cars, and the still-growing list of victories in Formula 1 and sports-car racing speaks to this. It seems only natural, then, to build a road car that approaches the performance and handling of a Formula 1 machine, using the same technologies and exotic materials The first embodiment of this was the shovel-nosed, high-winged F40 of 1987. The less angular though more potent F50 of 1997 followed. And today, there is the Enzo, the quickest road car "Road & Track" has ever tested, with a name posthumously honoring the man who inspired it.

Extraordinary places bring together extraordinary events. The Bonneville Salt Flats was a lake that covered one-third of the state of Utah some 15,000 years ago. Now it is a vast plain against the backdrop of mountains that spans 30,000 acres, covered with a snow-white, hard-packed crust of salt. It is a setting best described as an alien world that has seen many land speed records set by the likes of Sir Malcolm Campbell, Craig Breedlove and Gary Gabelich's rocket car, the "Blue Flame."

Today, with the wind gusts almost finishing their yearly task of drying the lake bed after the winter rainfalls, the Bonneville Salt Flats again plays the role of another unusual meeting point. After months of searching and waiting, R&T Design Director Richard M. Baron, photographer John Lamm, racing legend and Contributing Editor Phil Hill and I are finally here tiptoeing around on the salty earth for a sunset photo shoot. Standing just a few feet away is a brand-new, sparkling red Ferrari Enzo that appears almost as alien as the salt flats itself. Needless to say, we are looking forward to our drive in the incredible Enzo in the next few days. And all this is made possible by its generous owner, Richard Losee.

In person, the Enzo's front angles and flowing rear that once seemed at odds with each other in photos now blend nicely. Just as aerodynamics dominates the Formula 1 cars, the newest super Ferrari's form follows the same function: to pierce through the atmosphere with minimum disturbance. Pininfarina and Maranello engineers designed the Enzo to be aerodynamically stable without the pronounced wings like the ones seen on the F40 and the F50.

Walk up to the front of the Enzo and note how its low stance is accentuated by its width. Leading the carefully sculpted body is a pointed nose that slopes downward, but keeps a high profile at the very tip. Get as close to the ground as possible and stare directly into the narrow headlights. The broad fenders begin at the top edges of two lower rectangular radiator air intakes, then grow strongly upward and outward to the rest of the car. Center stage, just below the high nose, is another inlet with an all-black carbon-fiber wing mounted below. Squint and

ABOVE: The Ferrari Enzo in its natural milieu—on a sinuous canyon road, the driver taking full advantage of its extraordinary engine, suspension and brakes.

BELOW: A special car needs an equally special key, one that proudly wears the prancing horse emblem of Scuderia Ferrari.

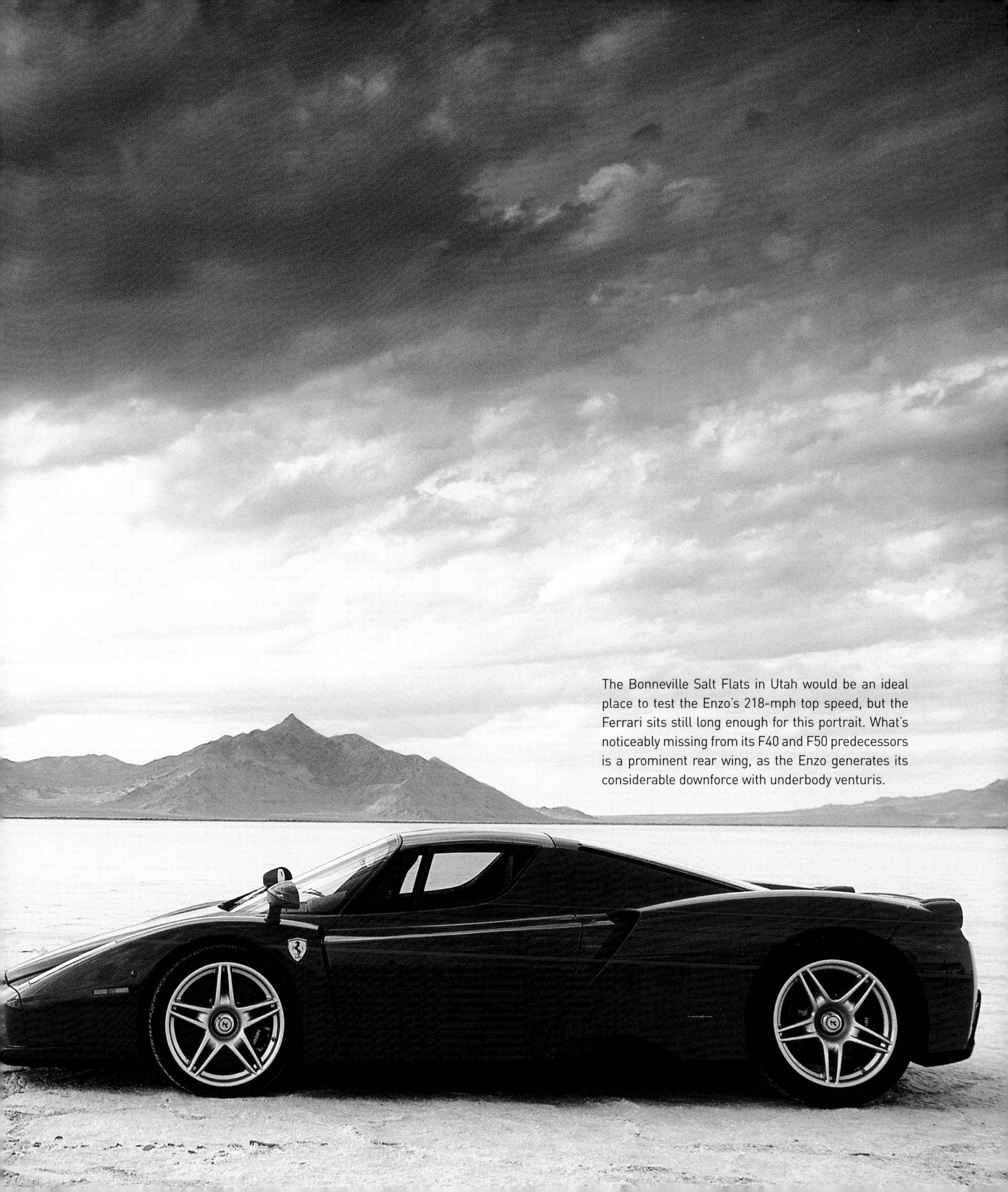

The Bonneville Salt Flats in Utah would be an ideal place to test the Enzo's 218-mph top speed, but the Ferrari sits still long enough for this portrait. What's noticeably missing from its F40 and F50 predecessors is a prominent rear wing, as the Enzo generates its considerable downforce with underbody venturis.

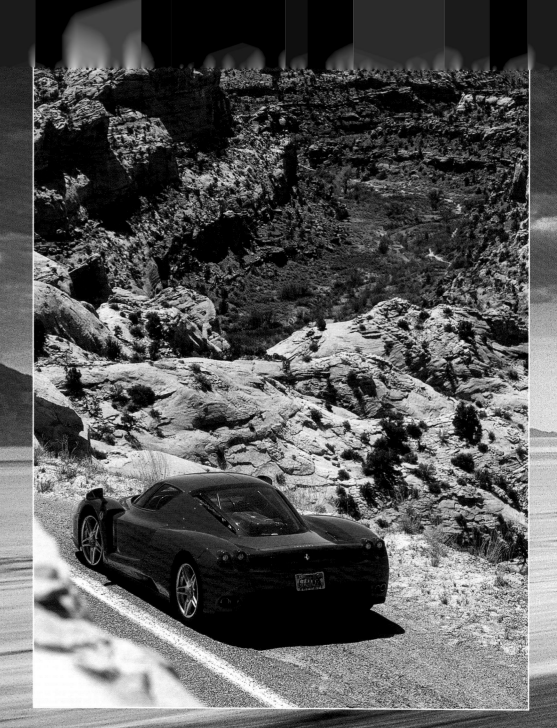

LEFT: Seen from the rear, it's obvious the Enzo is an aerodynamicist's dream. The exhaust system is moved to the corners to allow for an even larger rear diffuser.

RIGHT: At any speed, the Enzo is an impressive sight, a head-turner of the highest order. Despite its exotic construction and immense power, it remains a very usable road car.

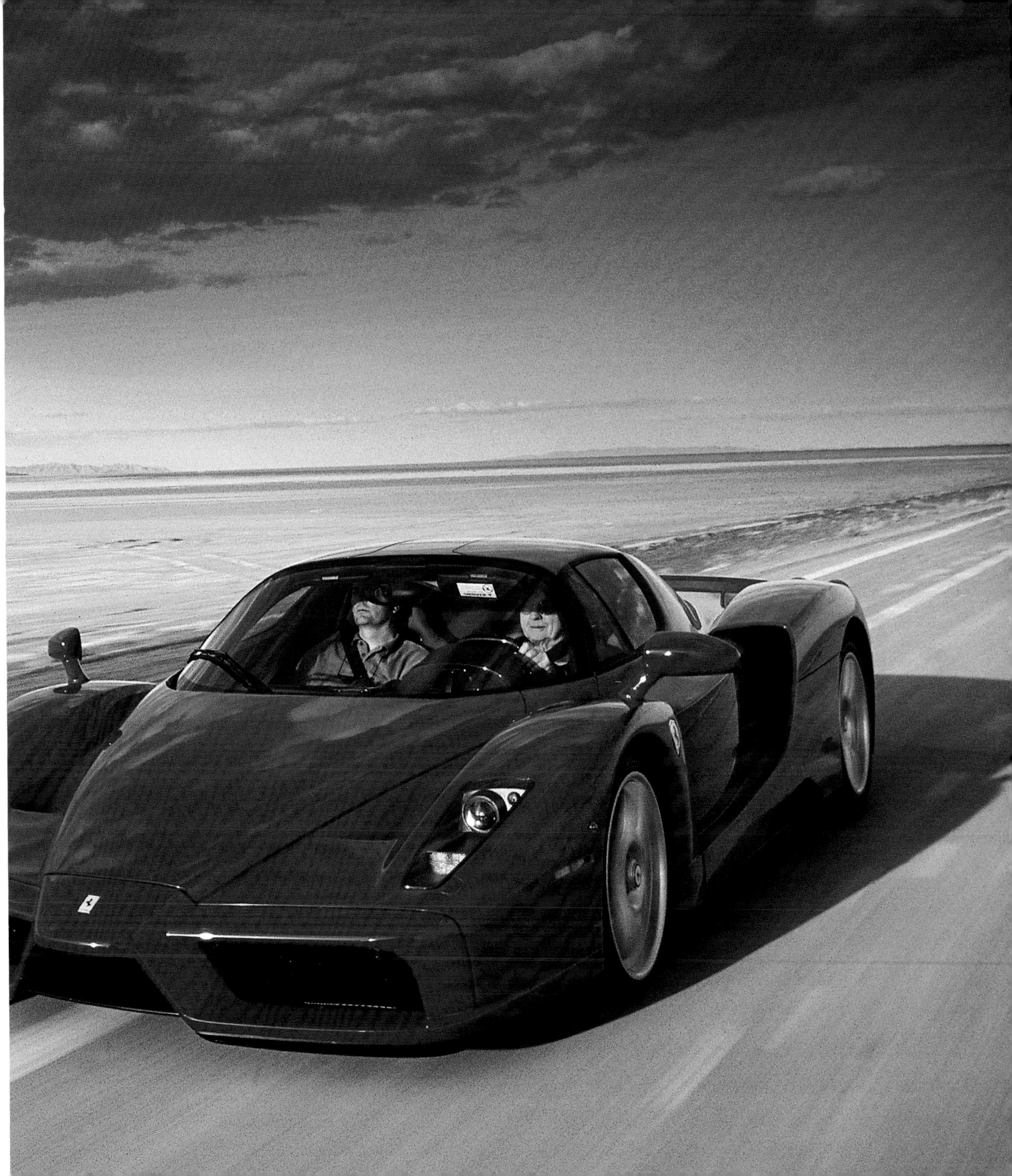

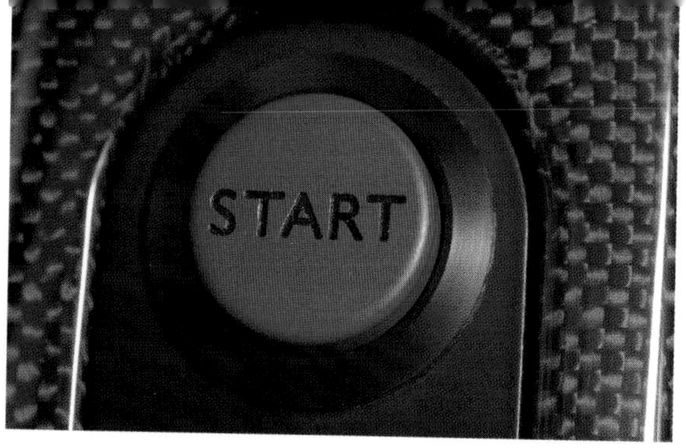
START

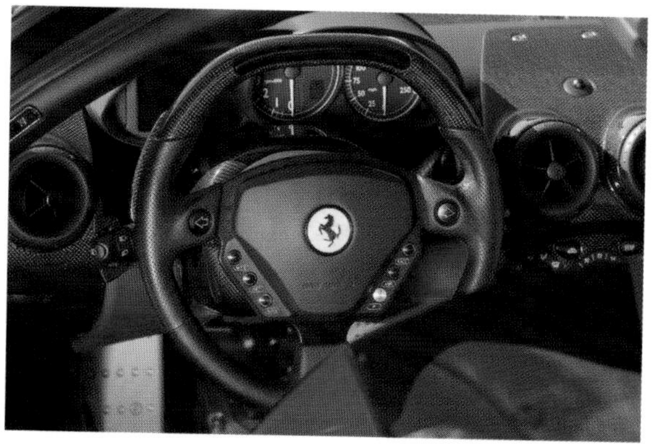

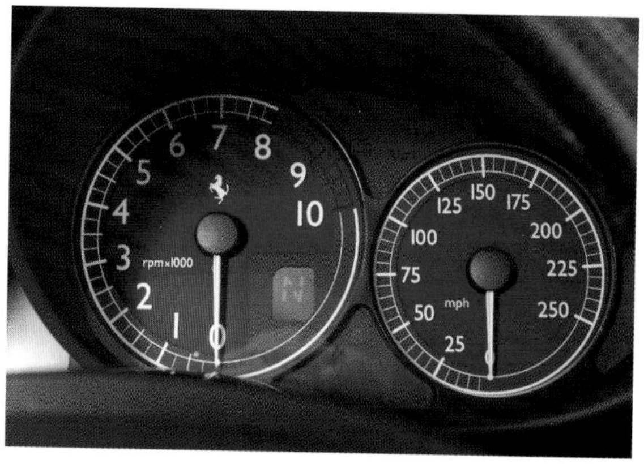
1
2
3
4
5
6
7
8
9
10
rpm×1000
25
50
75
100
125
150
175
200
225
250
mph

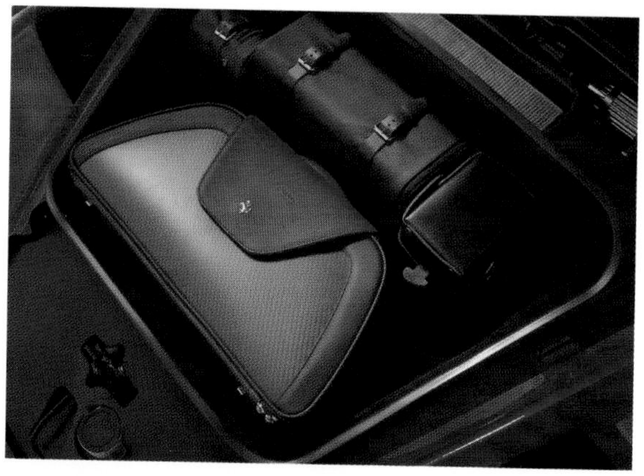

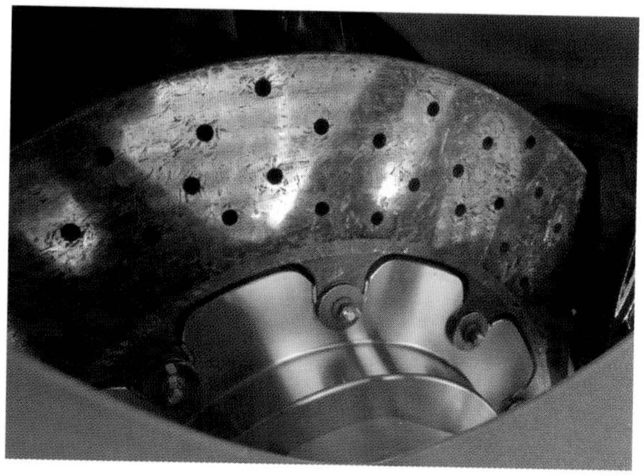

goes into a launch-control mode. Slowly dip into the throttle. Watch the engine revs build. And as soon as the tach needle sweeps past 2100 rpm, let go of the brake pedal and the clutch snaps into place.

Immediately the muted idling rumble from the V-12 opens up fully and emits a snarl that grows to a higher-pitched thumping note. The engine gulps in as much air as possible, adds fuel and churns out a sobering 650 bhp and 485 lb.-ft. of torque. The rear tires spin momentarily, and fight to bite into the asphalt. Easy and smooth on the throttle here because too much wheelspin slows the car down and loses precious time on the clock. Just before the first shift at 44 mph, get to full throttle. In Race Mode, the F1 transmission will swap gears in as little as 150 milliseconds.

Zero to 60 mph: 3.3 seconds.

Quarter-mile run: 11.1 sec. at 133.0 mph.

Unbelievable.

The Enzo has just recorded the best "Road & Track" acceleration run ever for a road car. Its 0–60-mph run equals the fastest time logged recently by the all-American Saleen S7. And its quarter-mile time and speed pulverize the mighty McLaren F1's numbers of 11.6 sec. traveling at a mere 125 mph past the quarter-mile mark.

When the time comes to stop—by the end of the acceleration run the Enzo is racing down the track at about 150 mph—the ample 15.0-in. vented carbon-ceramic discs slow the car with authority. There is never any hint of fade. The brake pedal travel is confidently short and actuation effort is firm. Panic stops from 60 and 80 mph show the Enzo needing only an excellent 109 and 188 ft., respectively, to come to a complete halt. Of note, the 188 ft. is another record, shared with the 360 Modena.

In the handling tests, the new Ferrari supercar's status is once again validated by "Road & Track"'s best-ever run of 73.0 mph through the slalom. The steering is quick and smooth, as though responding telepathically. The Enzo reacts to driver input instantly with mild understeer. Through the cones, it likes to be pushed a bit, but never loses composure. The rear stays firmly planted on the asphalt. With just a light dip of the throttle, the car can be lured to step out a bit and help turn in. And around our 200-ft.-diameter skidpad, little effort is needed to generate an amazing 1.01g of lateral acceleration. Remember, the Enzo is a road car, not a race car!

The myth that a super sports car with exceptional performance cannot be civilized at the same time has been broken. The Ferrari Enzo is both an ultra-high-performance car and a capable grand tourer. Just as when each speed record set at the Bonneville Salt Flats invites another challenger to go even faster, Maranello has entered the Enzo into another supercar realm where the rest of the world has to catch up.

LEFT, FROM TOP: It all starts here; Enzo's 3-spoke steering wheel has Formula-1 style ancillary buttons; yes, the speedometer reads to 250 mph; fitted leather luggage is standard; carbon-ceramic brake rotors are cross-drilled.

OPPOSITE: Hugely bolstered seats swathed in the brightest of red leathers dominate the Enzo's interior. Aluminum pedals are bottom-hinged, and the shift paddles behind the steering wheel show off the carbon fiber's texture.

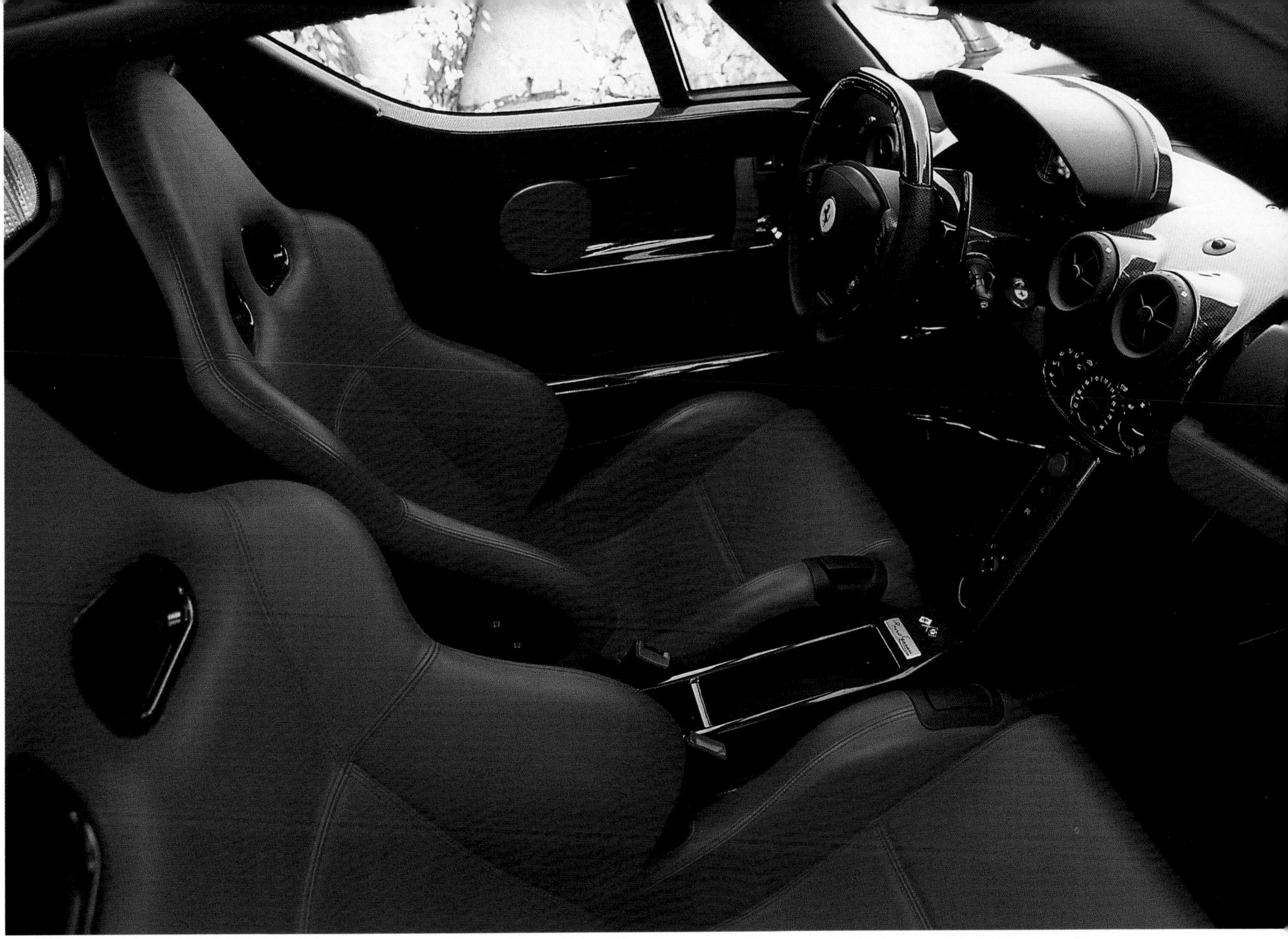

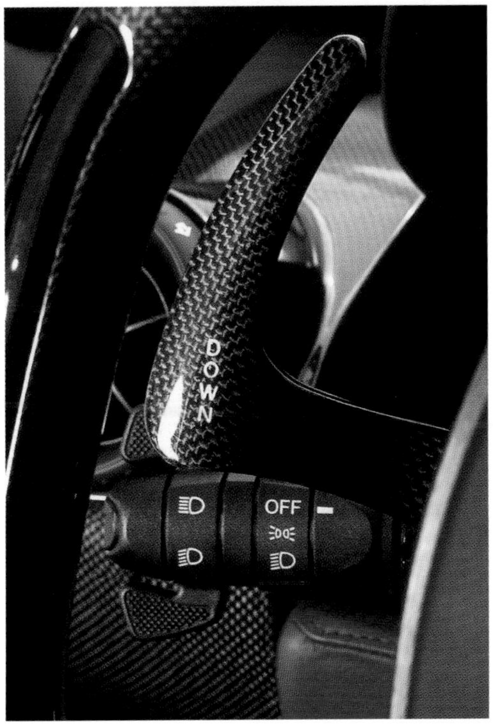
DOWN
OFF

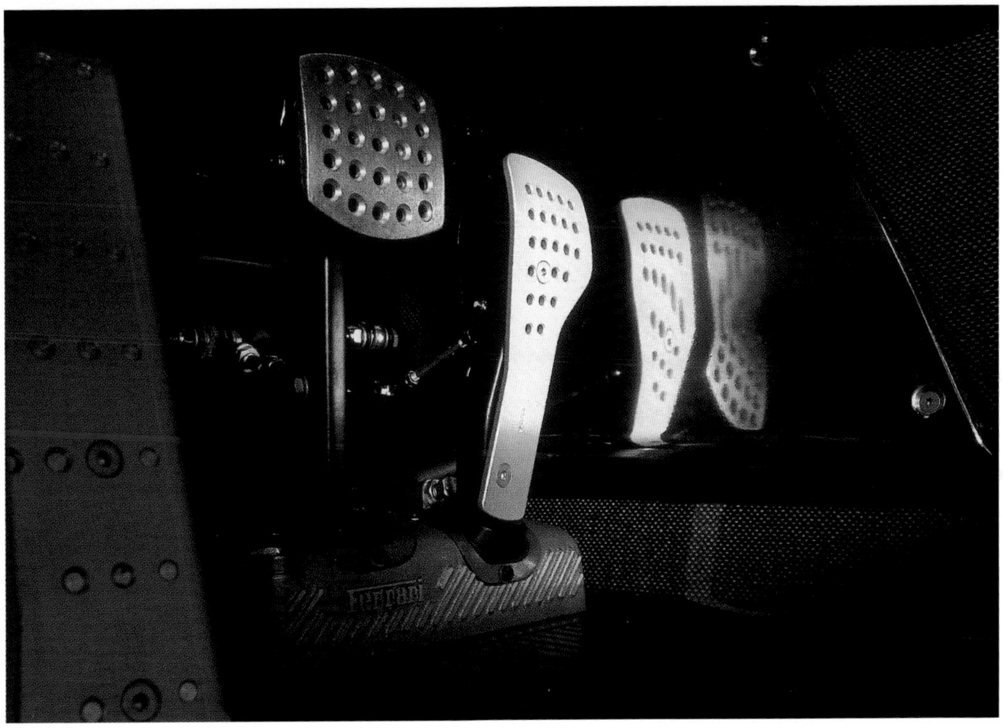

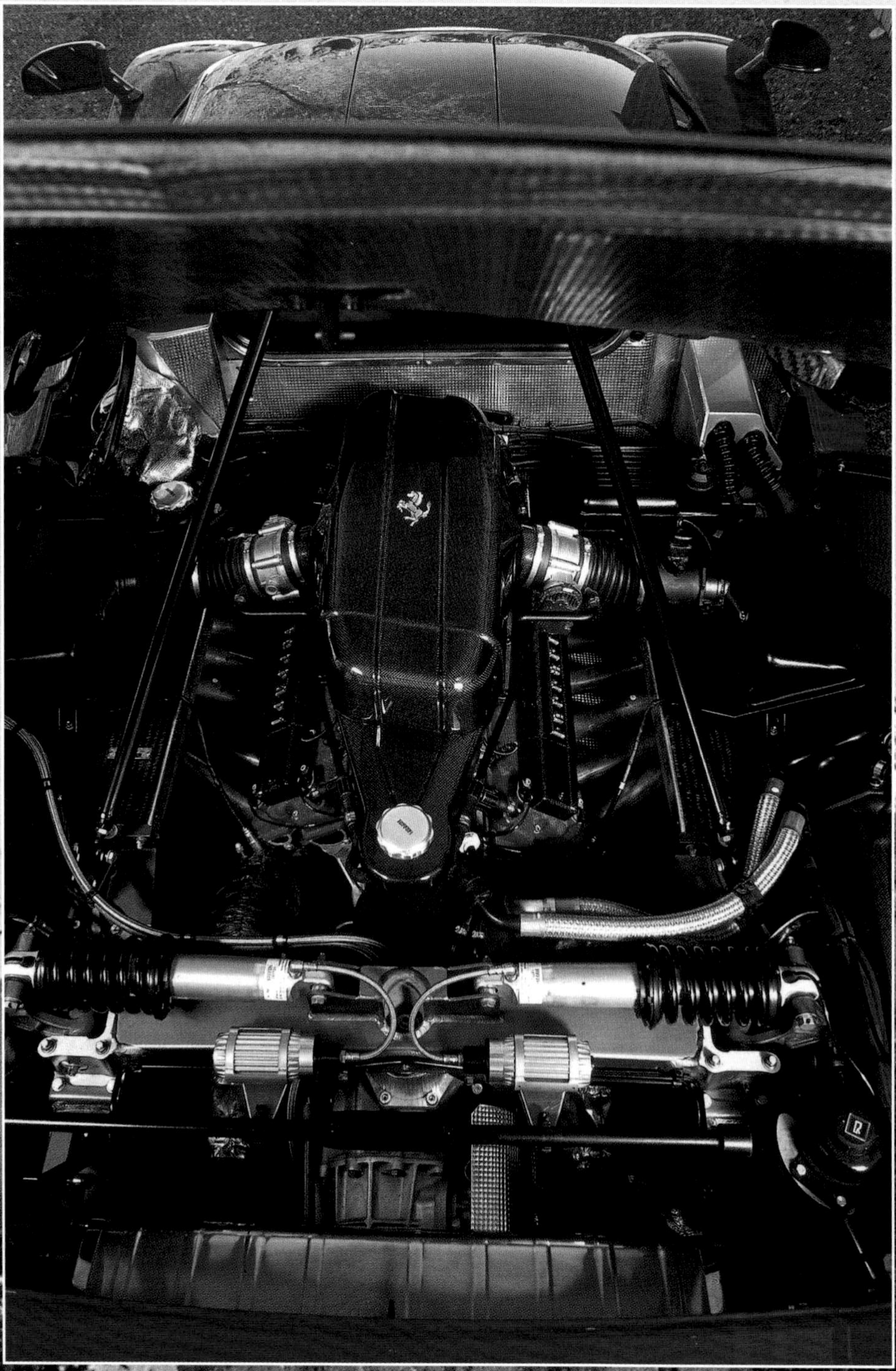

LEFT: The Enzo's business end, with 6.0 liters' worth of screaming Italian V-12, pumping out 650 bhp—more than four times the power of a 4-cylinder Honda Accord. Note the rear suspension's horizontally aligned coil-over shocks, with remote reservoirs.

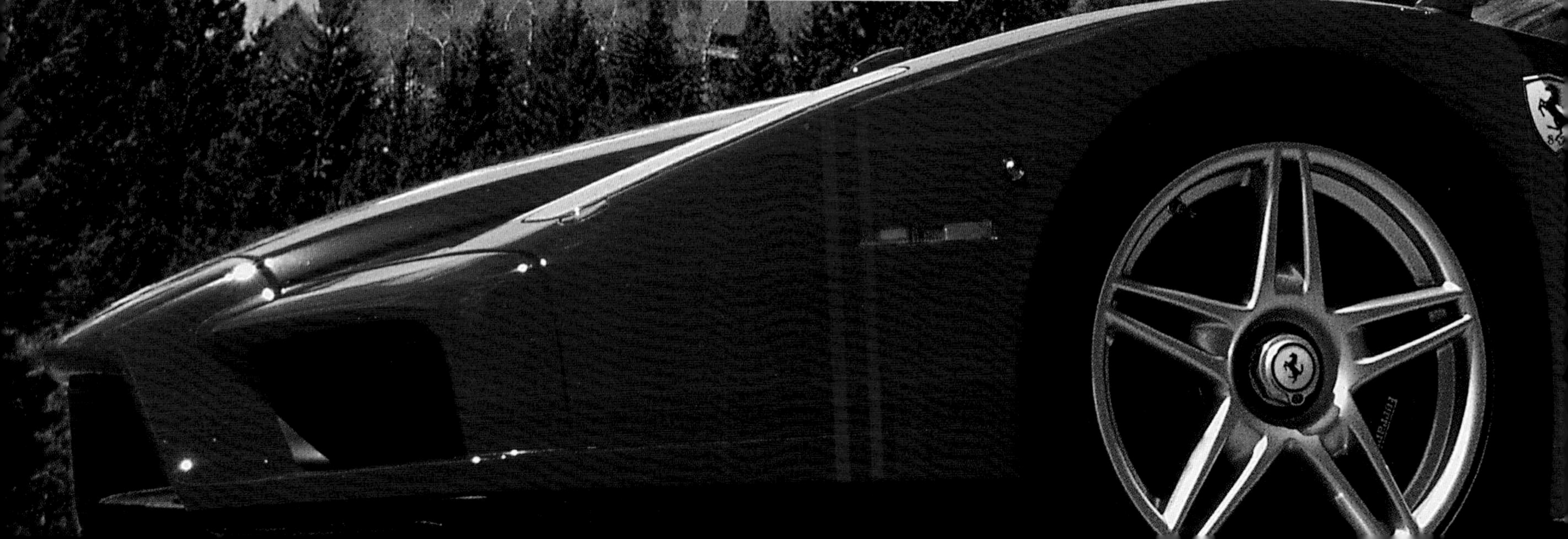

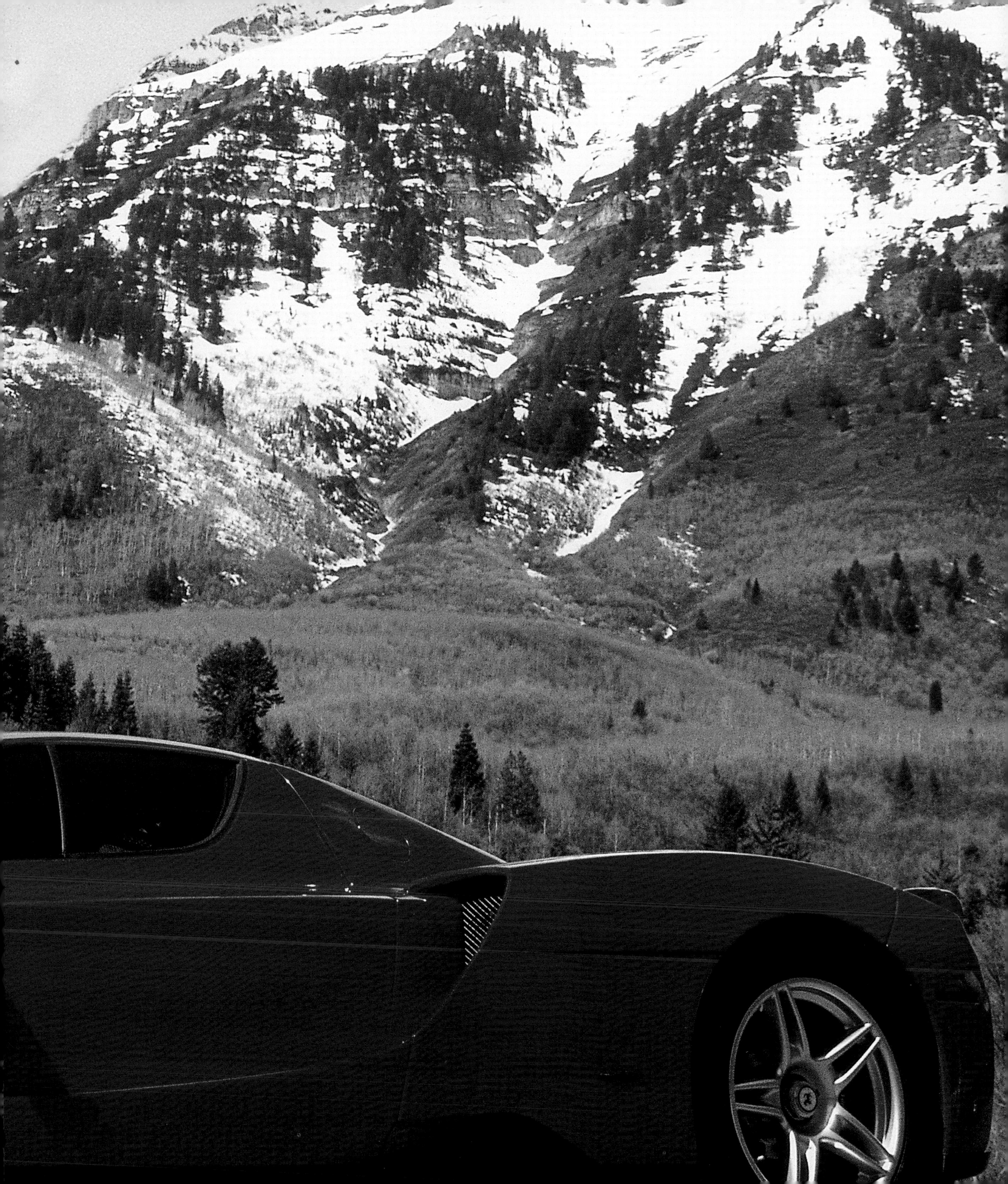

FORD
GT

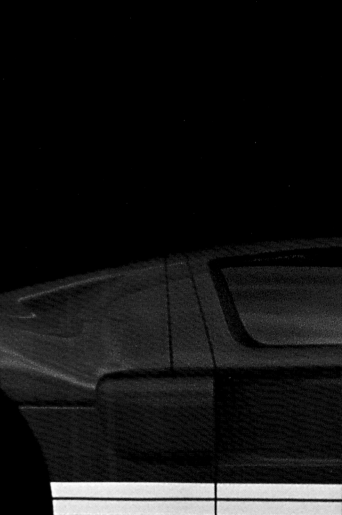

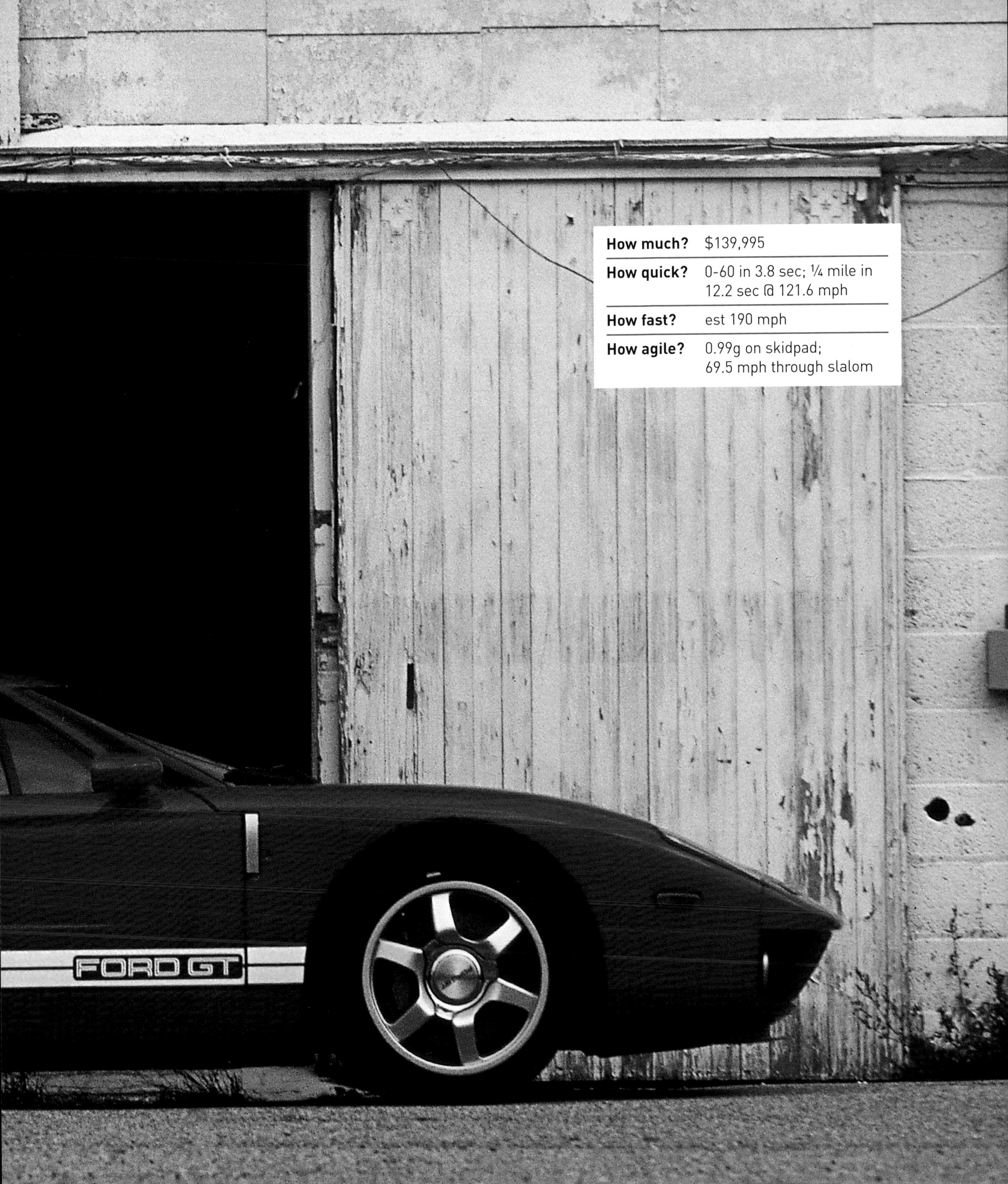
FORD GT

How much?	$139,995
How quick?	0-60 in 3.8 sec; ¼ mile in 12.2 sec @ 121.6 mph
How fast?	est 190 mph
How agile?	0.99g on skidpad; 69.5 mph through slalom

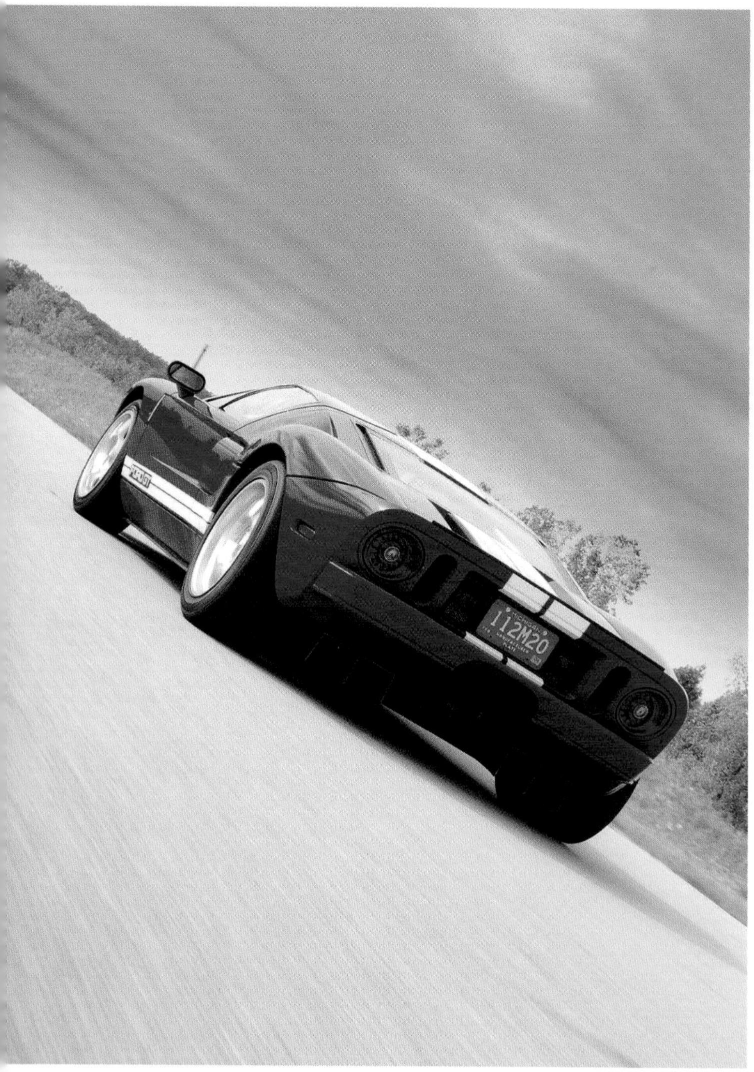
112M20

ABOVE: In 18 short months, the Ford GT went from auto-show turntable to living, breathing exotic, eclipsing the SVT Mustang Cobra as Ford's quickest-accelerating production car—by a good margin.

BELOW: Ford has sweat the details, right down to the lettering on the GT's fuel cap.

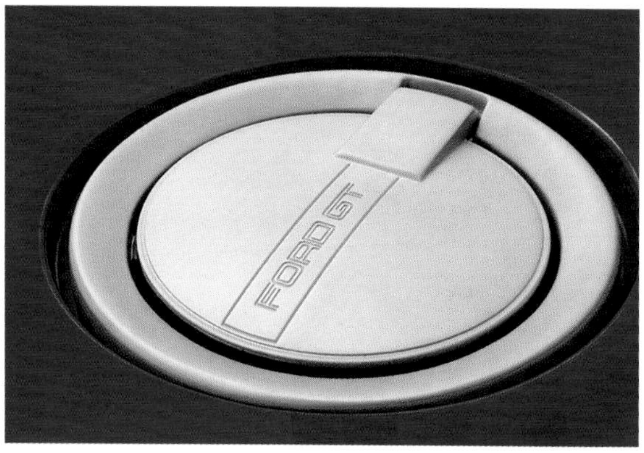
FORD GT

AMERICAN THUNDER ROARS BACK TO THE TOP

FIVE YEARS AGO, the idea of Ford creating a mid-engine exotic to compete with Ferrari's 360 Modena might have seemed preposterous. Today, if you've secured a place on the waiting list and have $139,995 burning a hole in your pocket, you can buy just such a car at your Ford dealership. If you grew up with a passion for racing, the GT's shape will be instantly recognizable, as it's a slightly scaled-up version of the 1960s' world-beating Ford GT40s so dominant in international endurance racing. Yet the GT trades an aluminum space frame for the race car's stamped-steel monocoque and is thoroughly domesticated, with effective air conditioning, power-assisted steering and a supercharged 550-bhp 5.4-liter V-8 that's miles removed from the original's carbureted 427.

It was an awesome sight at the 1966 24 Hours of Le Mans. Under a rain-soaked afternoon sky, the first three cars crossing the finish line all wore the Ford GT40 name. It was a proud moment for Henry Ford II, seeing his team break the European carmakers' stronghold on sports-car racing and end Ferrari's streak of supremacy over the famed endurance race. Following that incredible feat were three more consecutive wins at the same race in La Sarthe, making the GT40 one of the most dominant race cars in motorsports history.

While Ford's success on the racetrack has continued in various forms of motor racing since those victories at Le Mans, somehow that enthusiasm never completely made its way into the Blue Oval's production cars. In the current class of road-going exotics, the European manufacturers, especially Ferrari, continue to lead in the marketplace. Sure, there are the Ford Mustang, the Chevrolet Corvette and the Dodge Viper, but fair or not, none of these has ever reached supercar status in the eyes of many enthusiasts.

Enter the 2005 Ford GT.

Since the introduction of the Ford GT concept car at the 2002 North American International Auto Show, it had been an amazingly short 18 months and already the first three production versions were finished in time to celebrate Ford's 100th anniversary in June 2003. Instead of taking the usual four to five years of development time, the extremely enthusiastic Ford GT team compressed the entire schedule to build this high-performance sports car—not only the finest in America, but one to challenge the class benchmark, the Ferrari 360 Modena.

At first glance, the Ford GT looks like an exact copy of the original GT40. Up front, the characteristic large projecting headlights ride forward on the tips of broad fenders. Below, two round foglights at the outer edges add to the car's menacing look. And in between, a wide center opening serves to scoop up cool ambient air for the radiators before being extracted upward through two openings carved out of the hood. Walk around to the side and follow the racing stripes rearward; the GT's low and wide body stance is apparent. Like the road-going

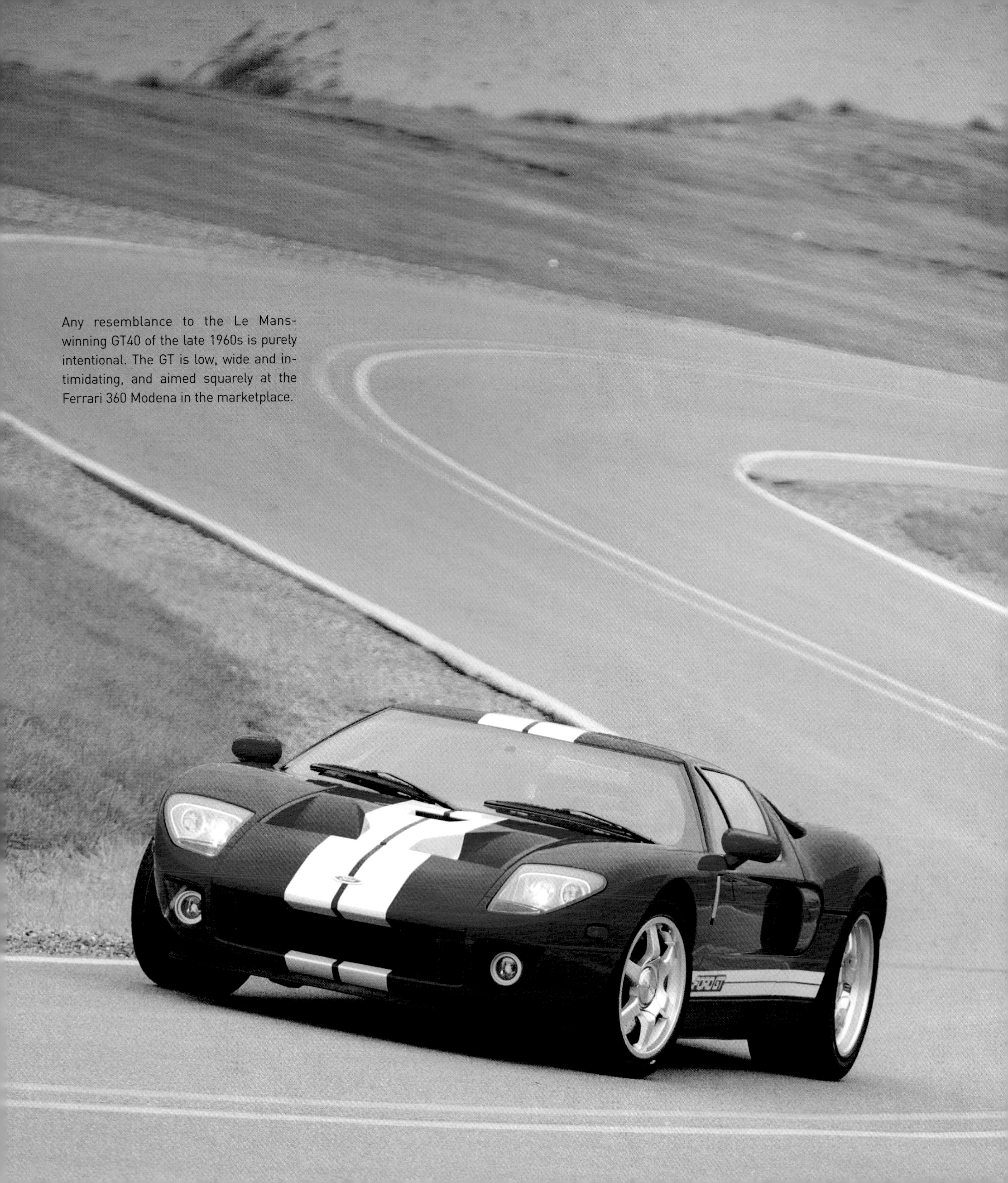

Any resemblance to the Le Mans-winning GT40 of the late 1960s is purely intentional. The GT is low, wide and intimidating, and aimed squarely at the Ferrari 360 Modena in the marketplace.

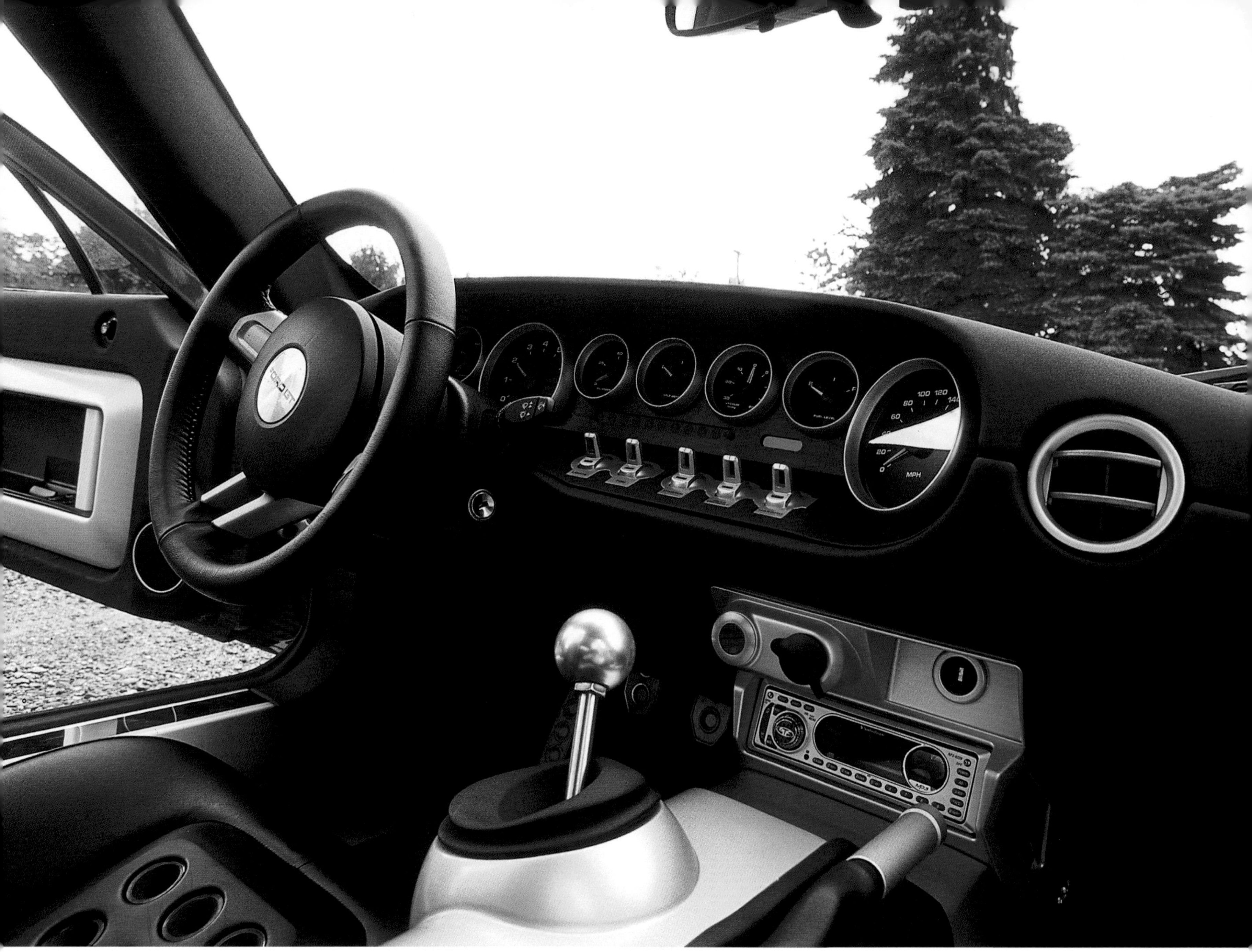

ABOVE: The dash design, too, is an homage to the race car's, with its row of gauges positioned in an oval recess with a strip of stylized toggle switches. With the lights on, it's easy to imagine a nighttime blast down the rain-slick Mulsanne Straight at Le Mans.

OPPOSITE, FROM TOP: Like any proper sports machine, the tachometer gets a prominent spot in the instrument panel; soothing lighting for the climate controls on the center console, which houses the fuel tank; and carbon-fiber detailing on the knob that adjusts seatback rake.

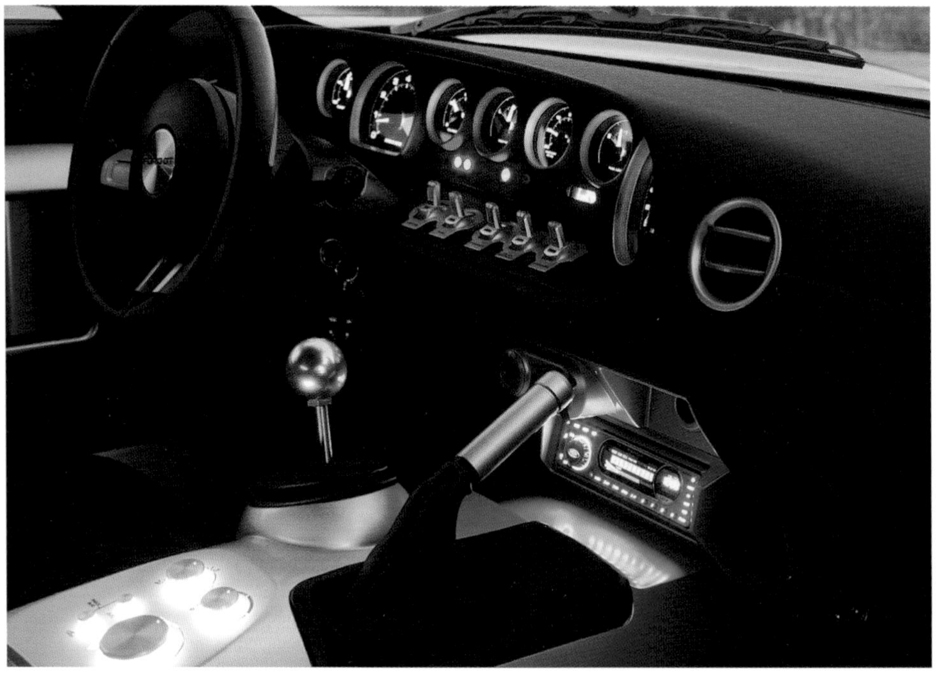

GT40 Mark II, the modern car sports a low ride height of only 44.3 in. (compared with the race car's 40.5 in.), a full 3.5 in. lower than the 360 Modena. To accommodate a roomier cockpit, the wheelbase is extended to 106.7 in., nearly 12 in. longer than the Le Mans winner.

At the back, just aft of the cockpit, are a number of air intakes that feed into the engine compartment. The top ones behind the window supply the thirsty powerplant, and the large rectangular inlets cut partly into the doors allow cooling of the engine bay (the left one) and of the transaxle radiator (right). Put your hand on the engine cover, and you'll notice how flat the expansive lid is. It continues all the way to the end, finishing in a ducktail. Capping the rear are two large circular taillights and a bumper that houses the double tailpipes at the center.

To preserve the silhouette of the original GT40 but achieve high-speed stability, Ford engineers put a lot of effort into the GT's underside aerodynamics. At the front splitters create downforce and limit the amount of air traveling underneath the vehicle. Side splitters are also present below the doorsills. They ensure as little disturbance as possible to the air that is being accelerated through the smooth and enclosed bellypan before being expelled by rear venturi tunnels.

To keep the GT40's trademark cut-into-the-roof doors on the Ford GT meant compromising a bit on the ease of entry. The door has to be swung all the way out so the top that makes up part of the roof will not interfere as you step into the cockpit. And before closing, much care is needed so the roof will not graze your head. Once inside, the simple yet functional themes of the Le Mans-winning race car are retained but updated with modern materials. Matte-black Azdel SuperLite plastic composite makes up the dash, the door panels and the bottom of the center console. The sweeping instrument panel has a cutout that houses all the important analog gauges. The aluminum-bezel-wrapped tachometer is centered just behind the steering wheel, and the speedometer is positioned at the farthest right and canted toward the driver. Below the gauges is a row of vintage-style switches that operate the car's other functions such as headlights and foglamps. Underneath the dash in the middle are a red starter button and the 260-watt McIntosh stereo system. The brushed-magnesium center tunnel not only holds the shift lever and the climate-control dials, but also covers the center-mounted fuel tank underneath.

The Ford GT's chassis is constructed with an all-aluminum space frame using 35 extrusions, several complex castings and various stamped aluminum panels. Detail engineering such as strategically placed lightening holes on castings and optimized thickness of the primary frame rails at different locations help to maximize strength and to minimize weight. For safety and ease of repair, replaceable extruded aluminum crush rails connect the front and rear bumpers to the chassis and serve to absorb most of the energy during a collision. According to factory engineers, the Ford GT's chassis is 40 percent stiffer than that of the Ferrari 360 Modena.

On the outside, the Ford GT uses the super plastic forming (SPF) method to mold its aluminum body panels into shape. Rather than using a costly two-sided metal die to stamp out the panels, aluminum sheets are heated to 950 degrees Fahrenheit and are formed over the single-sided die with high-pressure air. SPF allows for complicated shapes to be made in one piece, such as the rear

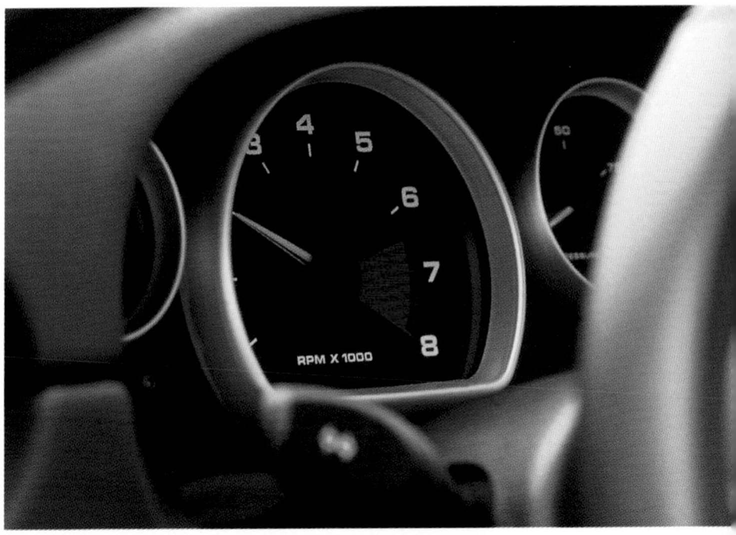
RPM X 1000

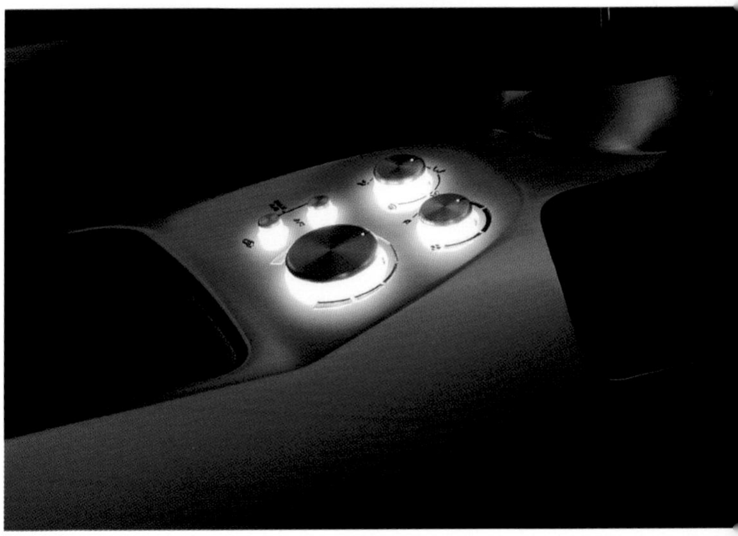

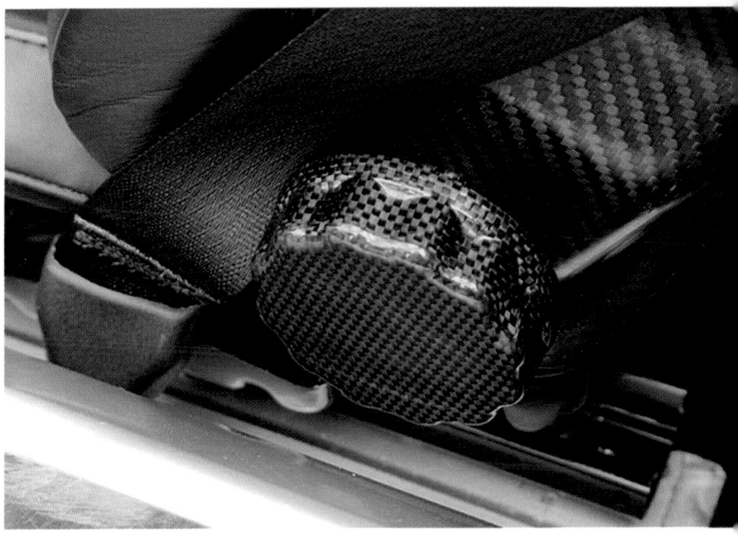

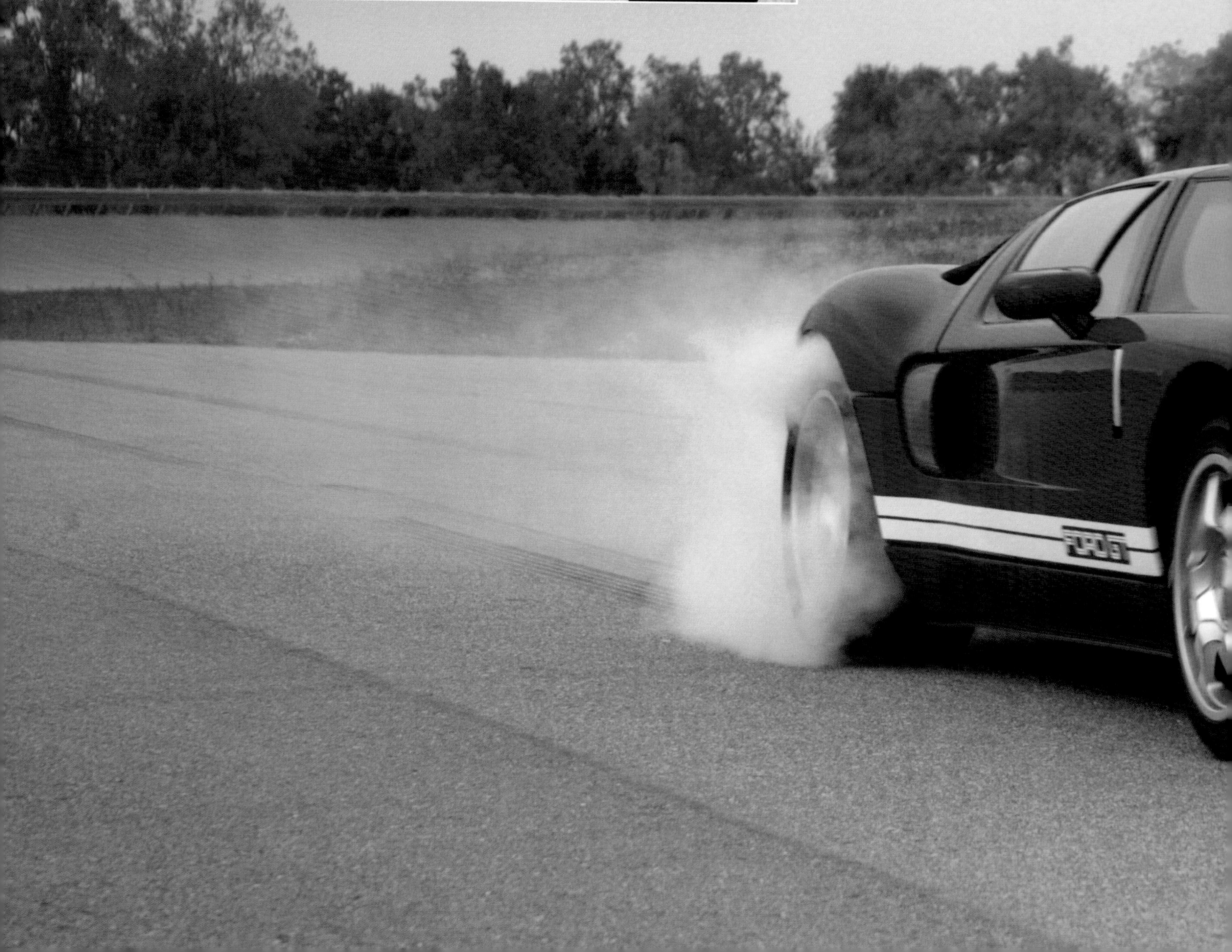

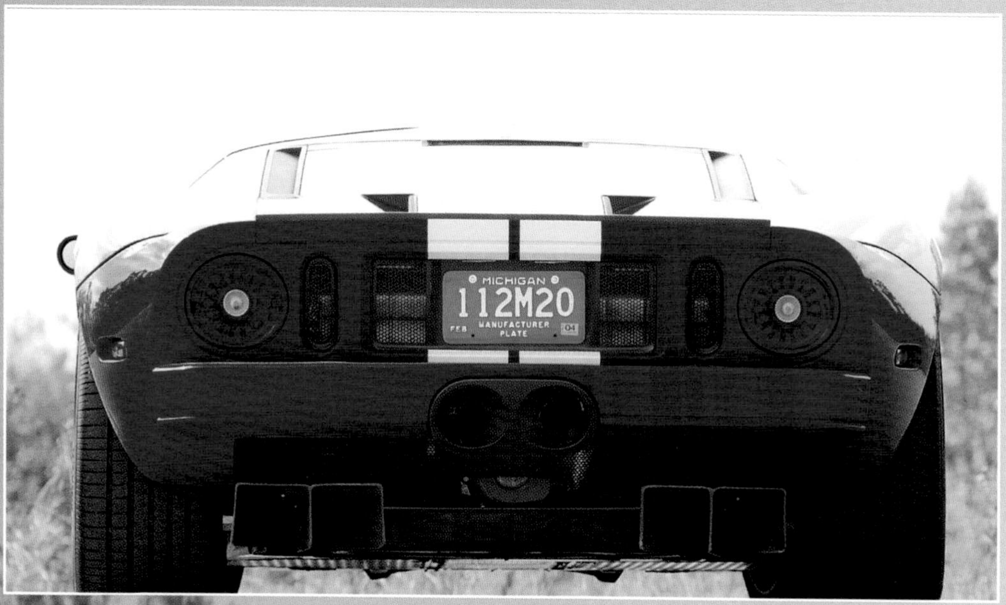
MICHIGAN
112M20
MANUFACTURER PLATE

LEFT: The GT profits from an understanding of aerodynamics unfathomable in the 1960s. Case in point: the downforce-producing diffuser positioned beneath the rear bumper.

BELOW: Go ahead, lay down two thick black stripes of rubber; the deep well of torque served up by the supercharged 5.4-liter V-8 makes it easy. Driver aids such as traction control and stability control are absent here for purity's sake.

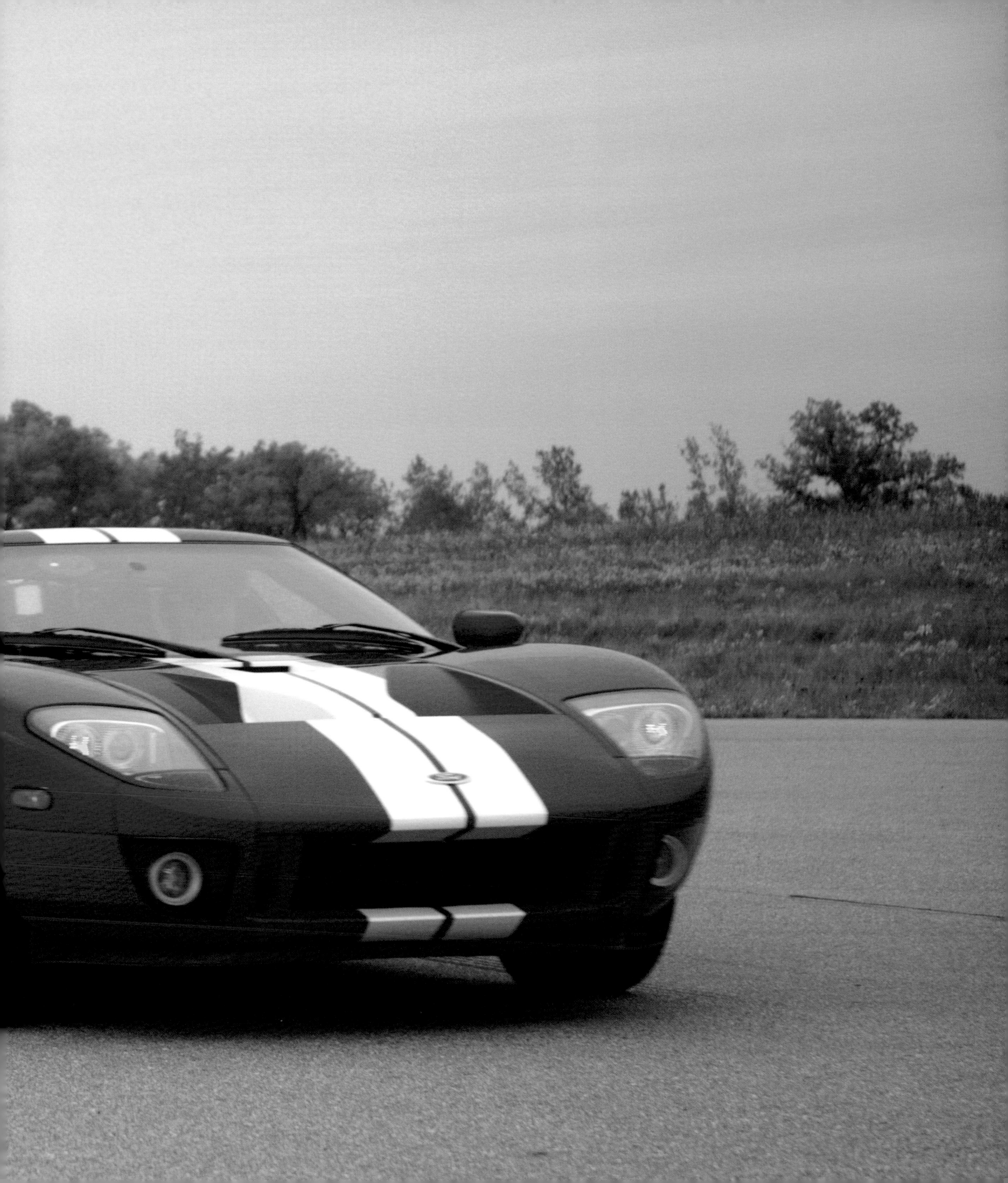

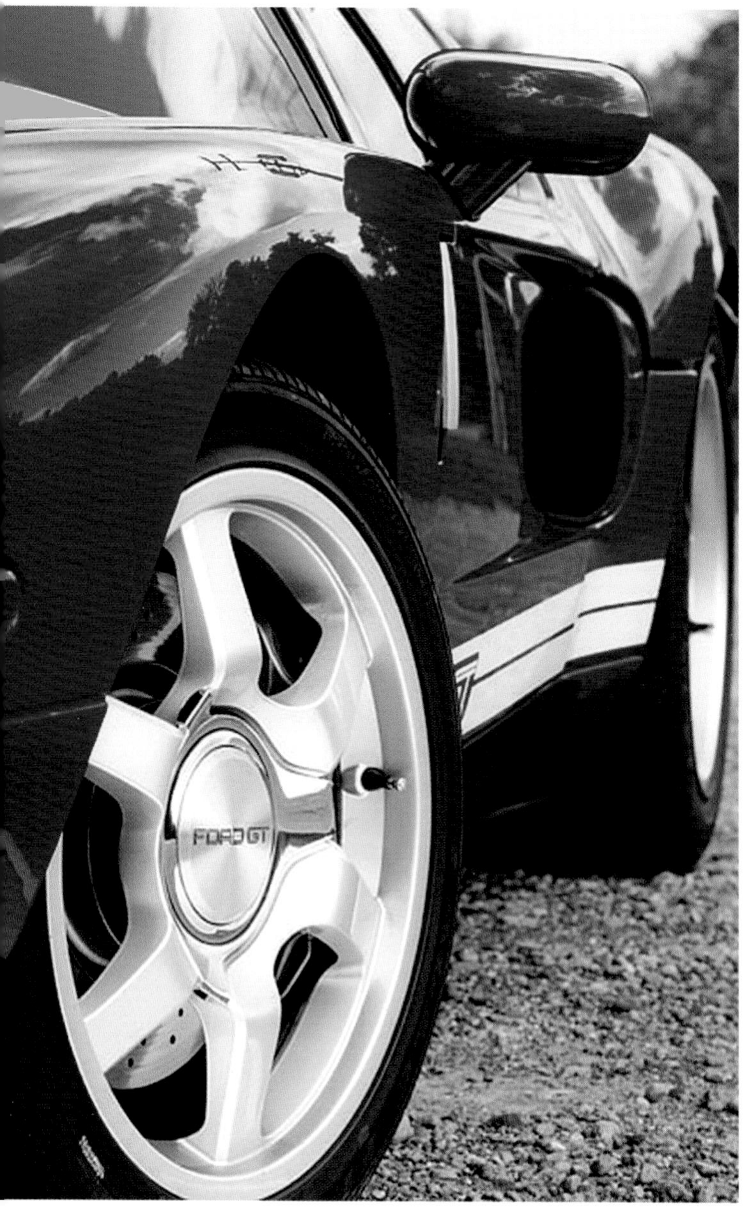
FORD GT

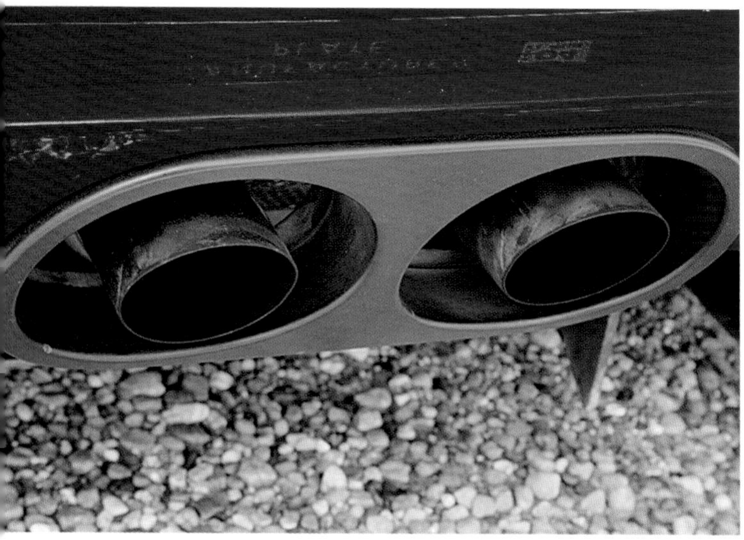

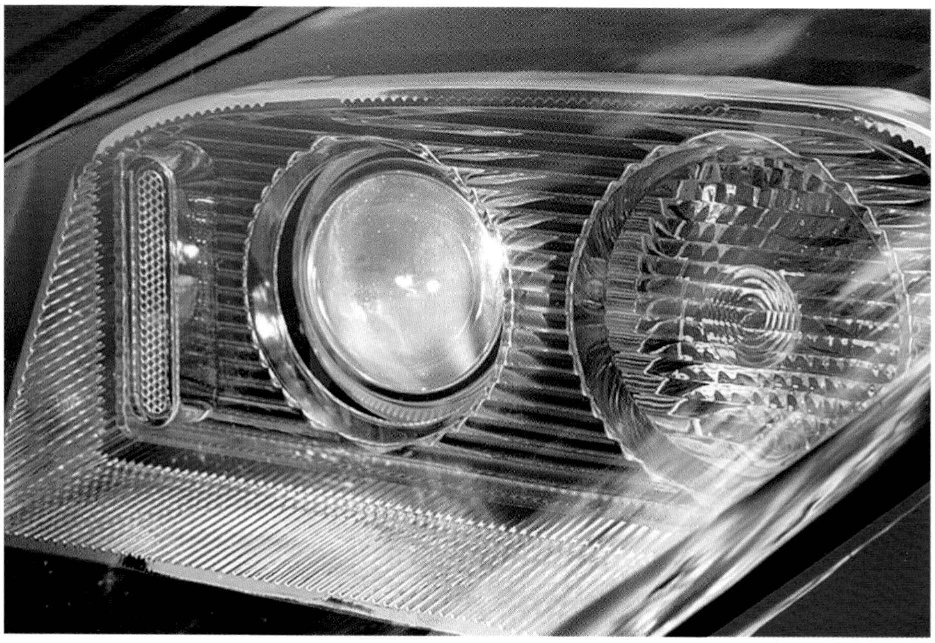

clamshell engine cover on the GT. Of note, the rear clamshell is hemmed to a carbon-fiber inner lining for added rigidity, an industry first.

Turn the ignition key and press the starter button. The massive powerplant sitting midships in the Ford GT idles smoothly. A quick tap on the throttle, and the engine belts out a roaring note. There is no doubt that the 5.4-liter V-8's throaty rumble is American-born. The all-aluminum dohc power unit is fitted with an Eaton Model 2300 screw-type supercharger, and it is capable of serving up 550 bhp at 6500 rpm and 500 lb.-ft. of torque at 3750 rpm.

The Lysholm supercharger breathes through a water-to-air intercooler and adds up to 12.0 psi of boost to give the engine that extra punch. Dual fuel injectors feed each cylinder. Forged aluminum pistons atop shot-peened H-beam connecting rods transmit power through the forged-steel crankshaft. From there, a low-effort twin-plate clutch connects the Ricardo 6-speed transaxle to the power unit. A torque-sensing limited-slip differential makes certain all 550 bhp and 500 lb.-ft. of torque are put to the ground properly on acceleration. To keep the GT's powerplant well lubricated under all driving conditions, a dry-sump oil system is utilized.

A standing-start acceleration run at the drag strip is at the heart of every American sports car. And the Ford GT takes up the challenge with ease. Hold the engine rpm at 2800 and drop the clutch. Too anxious on the gas pedal and the rear tires light up instantly and plumes of white smoke billow out from the wheel wells. Best starts are accomplished with progressive throttle input. And once off the line, there is no need to change gears before reaching 60 mph. After that, shifting through the gears requires modest effort, especially from 2nd to 3rd where the gearbox feels notchy and a bit harder to engage.

Our radar gun clocks the Ford GT's 0–60-mph time at 3.8 seconds, and the

CLOCKWISE FROM LEFT: Unfinished exhaust tips give race-car edge; faux knock-offs are well integrated into the cast-aluminum BBS wheels and conceal conventional lug nuts; projector-beam headlamps blend nicely into the overall design .

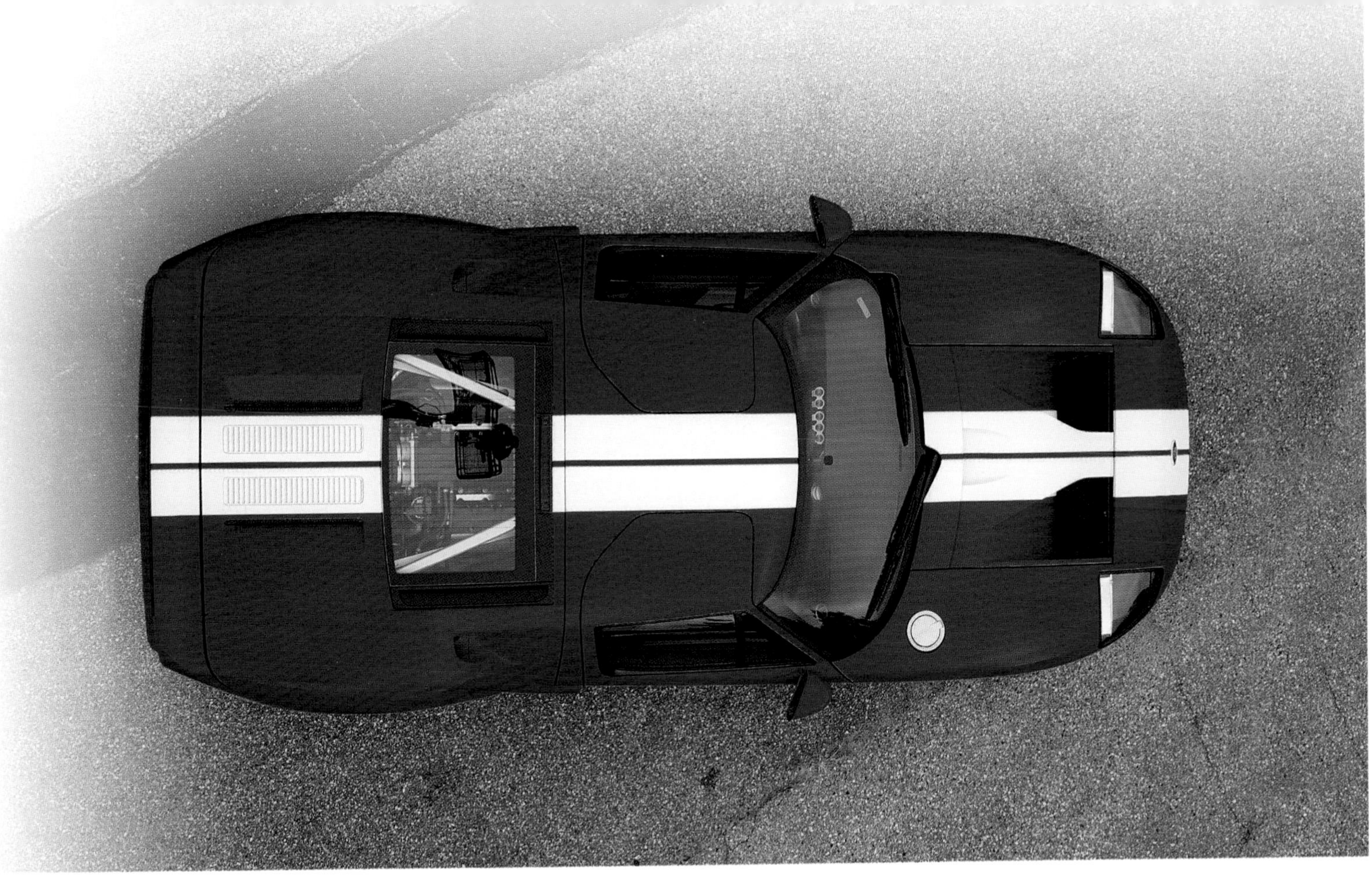

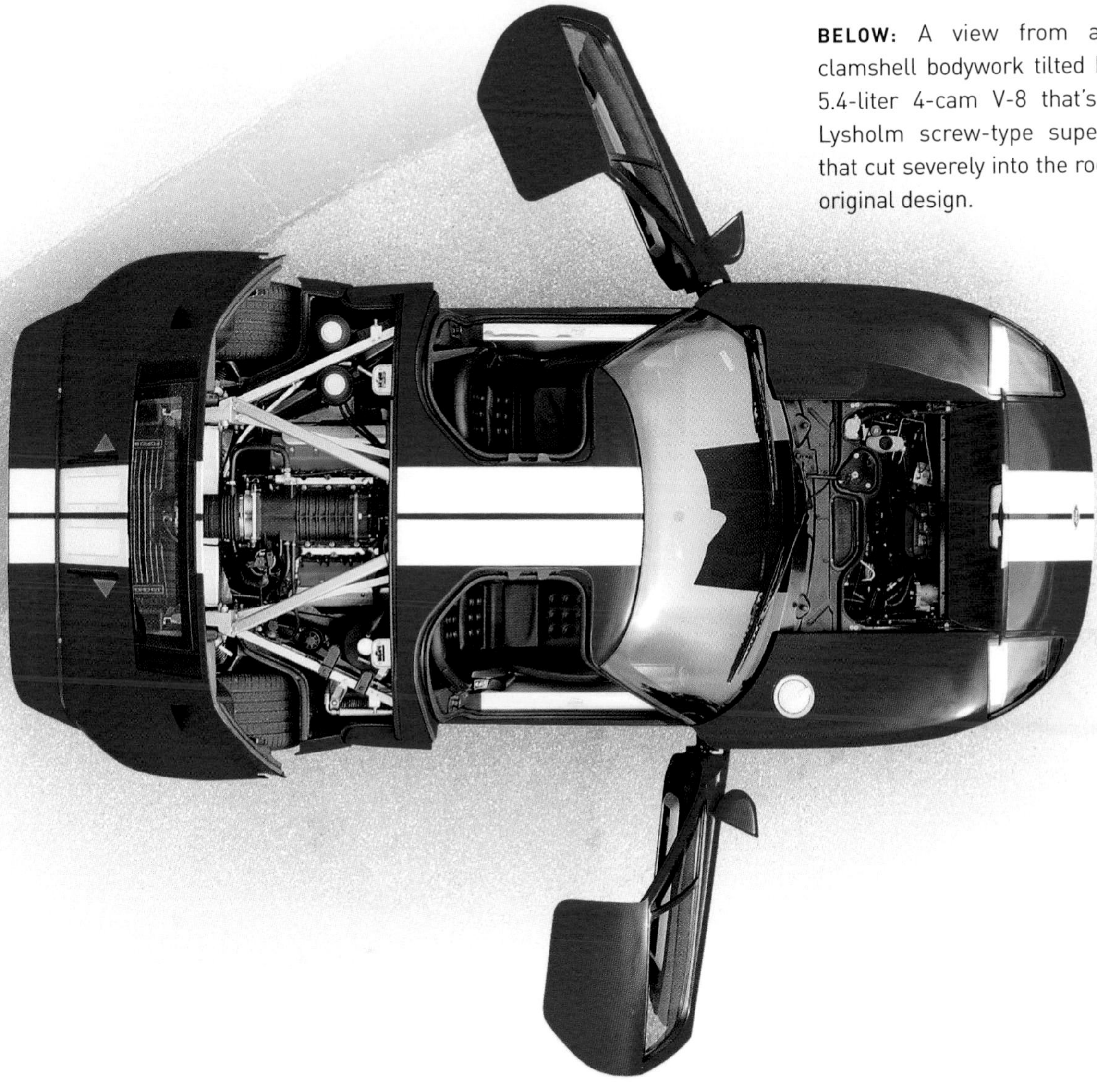

BELOW: A view from above with the clamshell bodywork tilted back reveals the 5.4-liter 4-cam V-8 that's capped with a Lysholm screw-type supercharger. Doors that cut severely into the roof are true to the original design.

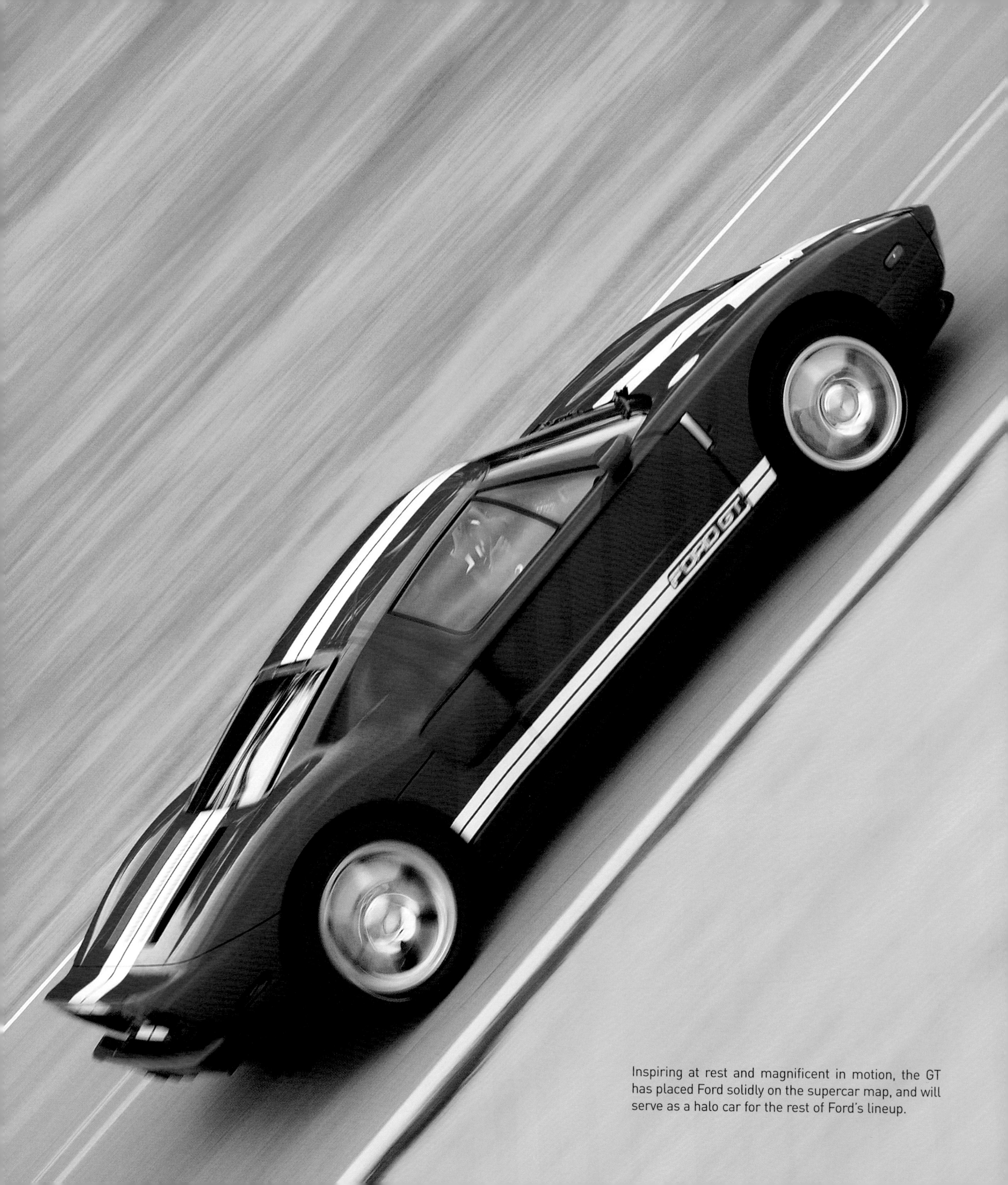
FORD GT

Inspiring at rest and magnificent in motion, the GT has placed Ford solidly on the supercar map, and will serve as a halo car for the rest of Ford's lineup.

quarter-mile sprint at 12.2 sec. with the speedometer indicating 121.6 mph. This emphatically beats the Ferrari 360 Modena's acceleration time of 4.3 sec. from zero to 60 mph, and its quarter-mile posting of 12.8 sec. at 112.5 mph.

Employing a suspension setup of unequal upper A-arms and lower L-arms, coil-over monotube shocks and anti-roll bars all around, the Ford GT is tuned to soak up road imperfections with ease at cruise and also grip the asphalt with confidence while cornering. Helping to plant all four corners firmly on the ground are one-piece cast-aluminum BBS wheels wrapped in Goodyear Eagle F1 Supercar tires: 235/45ZR-18s up front and 315/40ZR-19s at the rear. The job of slowing the 3400-lb. GT relies on 4-piston Brembo calipers clamping down on front 14.0-in. and rear 13.2-in. cross-drilled and vented discs.

On the street, the Ford GT is extremely easy to drive. Stop-and-go traffic is not a problem thanks to the low-effort clutch actuation and the broad torque band that comes on progressively. However, the clutch take-up does require some getting used to because of the long pedal travel. Over the concrete gaps on the Interstate, the ride is taut but comfortable. And when the time comes for passing, simply dip into the throttle and the generous torque available from the 5.4-liter engine will wind up quickly and push you past slower traffic without breaking a sweat.

Pick a winding road through the mountains and the GT's handling prowess will truly shine. Initially, the car may feel big and wide on the twisties because of the low seating position, plus the view forward and around the car is somewhat limited by the thick A-pillars and the high nose and tail. But as soon as you dial in some steering, the responsiveness of the GT to your inputs suddenly shrinks its perceived size. There is some lightness off-center as you turn the steering wheel, but after that the effort increases in a nice, linear fashion. After a while, you can feel your confidence build because the GT tracks the turns with poise and never exhibits any hint of swapping ends.

Driving around Mazda Raceway Laguna Seca, the Ford GT's race-car heritage is apparent. Like the original GT40 Mark II, there can be no substitute for cubic inches. The power from the supercharged 5.4-liter V-8 is tremendous, especially when accelerating off a corner onto a straightaway. The loud rumble emitting from the GT at full throttle is not unlike the ear-piercing growl of the GT40. Compared with the Ferrari 360 Modena, the Ford GT's horsepower advantage wins the acceleration contest hands down. And through various chicanes, the GT's roadholding ability also exceeds the Ferrari's. This is also shown in our slalom test. The Ford supercar can thread its way through the cones at an amazing average speed of 69.5 mph, more than 2 mph faster than the Modena's 67.4-mph pace. In the Ford GT, the driver can lap the racetrack close to its limits quickly but after that, less margin for error is permitted. This contrasts to the Ferrari's character of always involving the driver (more work needed) no matter if the car is asked to go half-pace or full-out.

It is about time that a U.S. automaker enters the supercar ranks. Riding on the Blue Oval's rich motorsport heritage, the Ford GT serves as the perfect car to bring the kind of spirit and excitement craved by all enthusiasts back into its production cars. And why not challenge the best in class the first time out? Watch out. America is roaring back to the top.

ABOVE: Doesn't the Ford GT somehow look "right," photographed on the banking with the guardrail in the background? It's no coincidence.

LAMBORGHINI GALLARDO

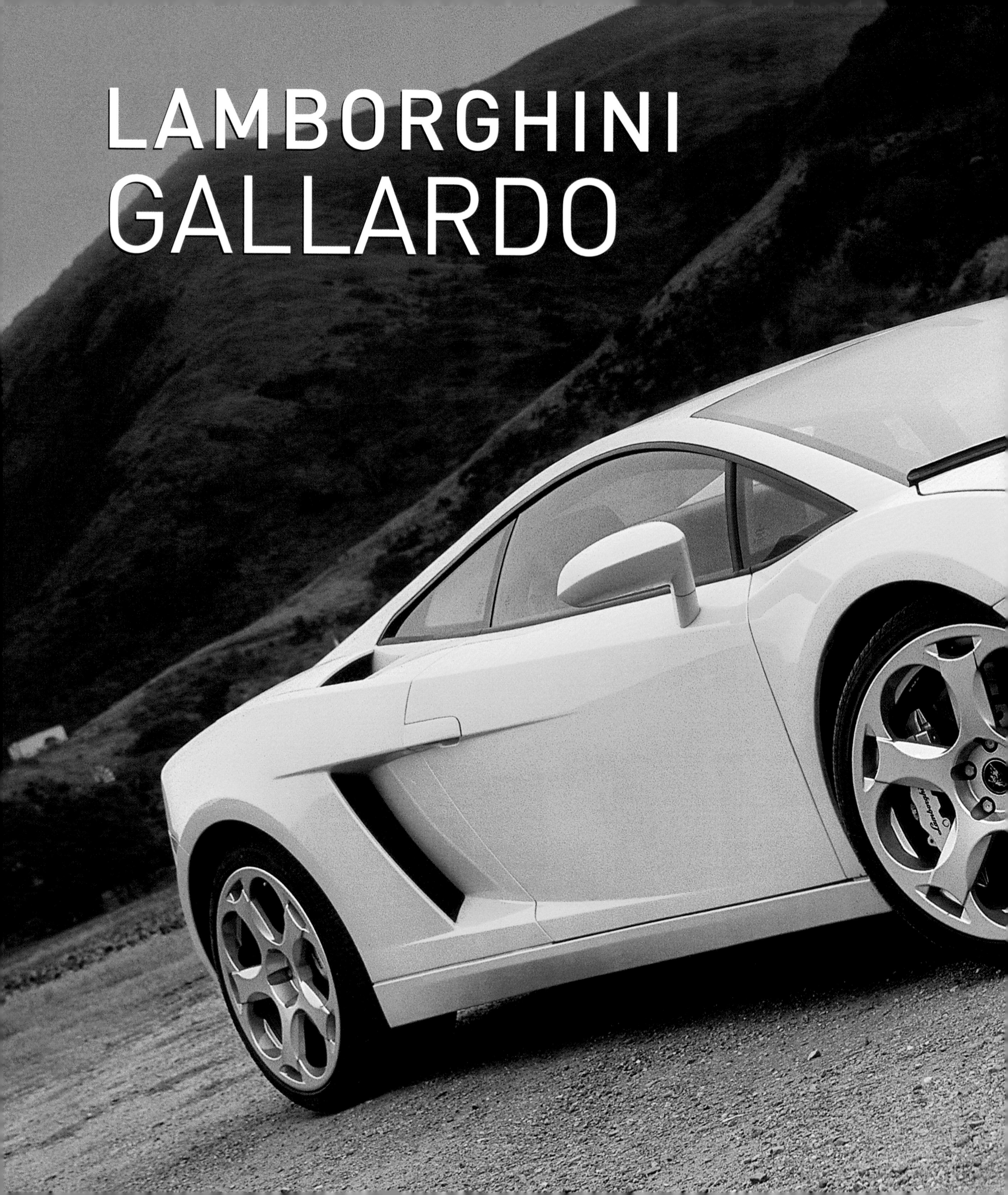

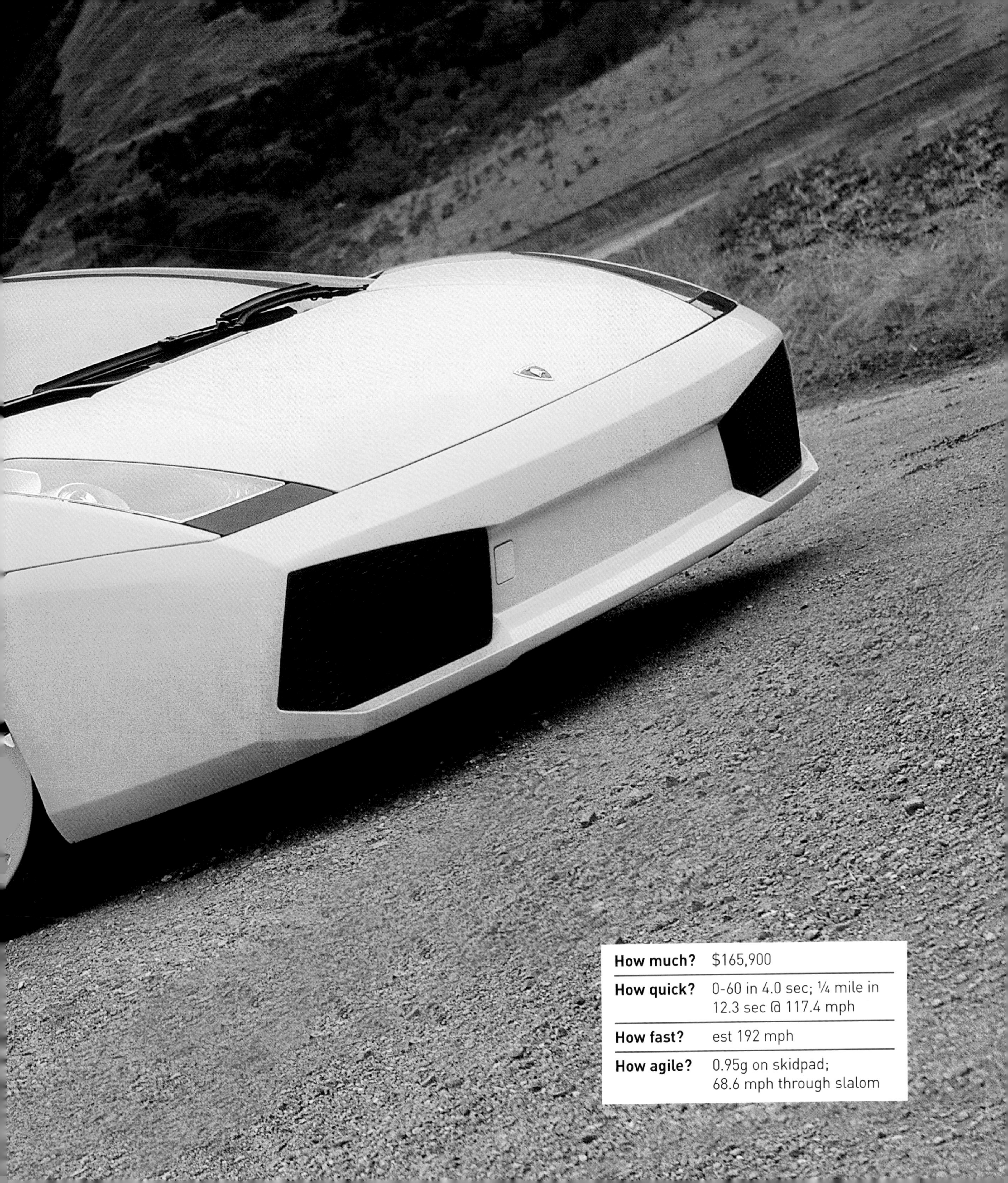

How much?	$165,900
How quick?	0-60 in 4.0 sec; ¼ mile in 12.3 sec @ 117.4 mph
How fast?	est 192 mph
How agile?	0.95g on skidpad; 68.6 mph through slalom

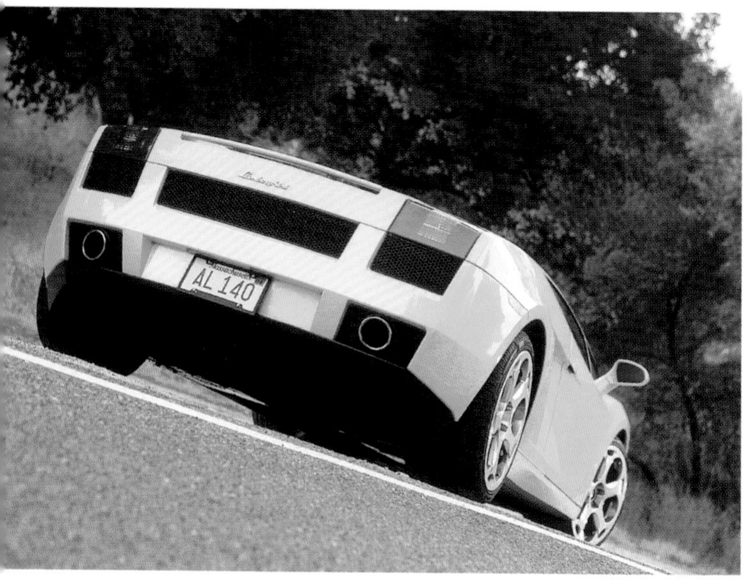

ABOVE: Quick things come in small packages and the Gallardo is proof, as fully capable of blurring the scenery as its big brother, the Murciélago. Although their noses are similar, the Gallardo's squared-off tail sets it apart.

BELOW: The fighting bull on Lamborghini's emblem embodies the spirit of all the cars that roll off the assembly line in Sant'Agata Bolognese.

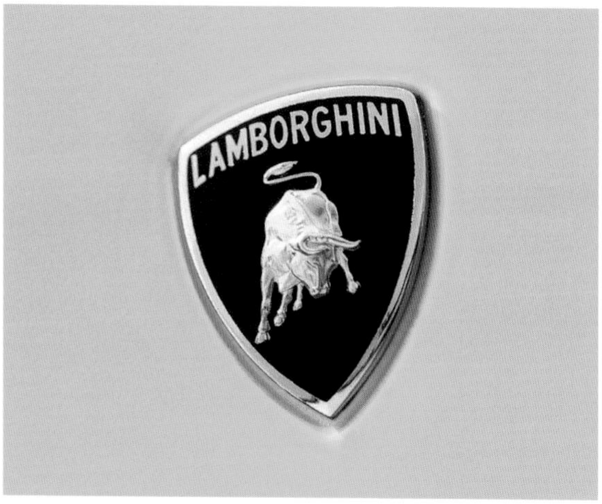
LAMBORGHINI

SMALLER AND MORE AGILE, BUT NO LESS FURIOUS

WHILE CARS SUCH AS THE MIURA AND COUNTACH put Lamborghini on the map (or at least on the bedroom walls of most adolescent boys), a series of smaller mid-engine Lamborghinis—the Urraco, Silhouette and Jalpa—emerged around 1970 as adversaries to the Porsche 911, a car that founder Ferruccio Lamborghini himself much admired. In recent times, Lamborghini's second tier went away, allowing the firm from Sant'Agata Bolognese to channel its resources into the Countach's successors, the Diablo and Murciélago. Well, the small Lamborghini is back in the form of the mid-engine, all-wheel-drive Gallardo, whose 500-bhp V-10 offers performance to rival....you guessed it...the Porsche 911 GT2. Yes, it's smaller than its Murciélago stablemate, but the Gallardo is no less fierce.

The bull on the Automobili Lamborghini insignia matches perfectly the company's reputation of building exotic sports cars. From the Miura, the Countach, to the Diablo, every automobile that rolled out of the Sant'Agata Bolognese factory was designed with the same forceful personality as the fighting bull shown on the emblem: Its head hunched over, nostrils flared, horns lowered and pointed forward, there is absolutely no uncertainty about its aim to intimidate.

After a flurry of ownership changes in the past decade, Lamborghini had lost a bit of the fighting bull's hard-charging attitude and badly trailed its cross-town prancing horse rival. But out of chaos came renewed focus and determination. Now under Audi's ownership, Lamborghini is poised to get back on track. Following the successful launch of the Murciélago just a few years ago, the Italian sports-car maker is adding another member to its family: the Gallardo (pronounced "ga-yardo"). It's sexy, it's fast and it's agile. And, of course, intimidating.

In photographs where the larger Murciélago and the new Gallardo are staged together, the relative size difference seems minimal to the eye. However, in person, the new Lamborghini's smaller footprint is apparent. While the Murciélago sports an overall length of 180.3 in. and width of 80.5 in., the Gallardo is considerably shorter and narrower—169.3 in. long and 74.8 in. wide.

There is a lot of family resemblance between the overall design themes of the Murciélago and the Gallardo. The lower front bumper on both cars is capped at the edge with blacked-out mesh screens that lead into air intakes for the two split radiators. Also, both have the expansive front hood with two cutlines that run all the way to the large and almost flat windscreen. But that's where the similarities end. While the Murciélago takes a flowing and smooth approach to its exterior lines, the Gallardo wears a more straight-cut and boy-racer-type skin.

Up front, leading the way, is a pair of stacked circular headlights in narrow, rectangular housings aligned on the outer edges of the nose. This gives the Gallardo a menacing squint. Walk around to the side, and the first thing you'll

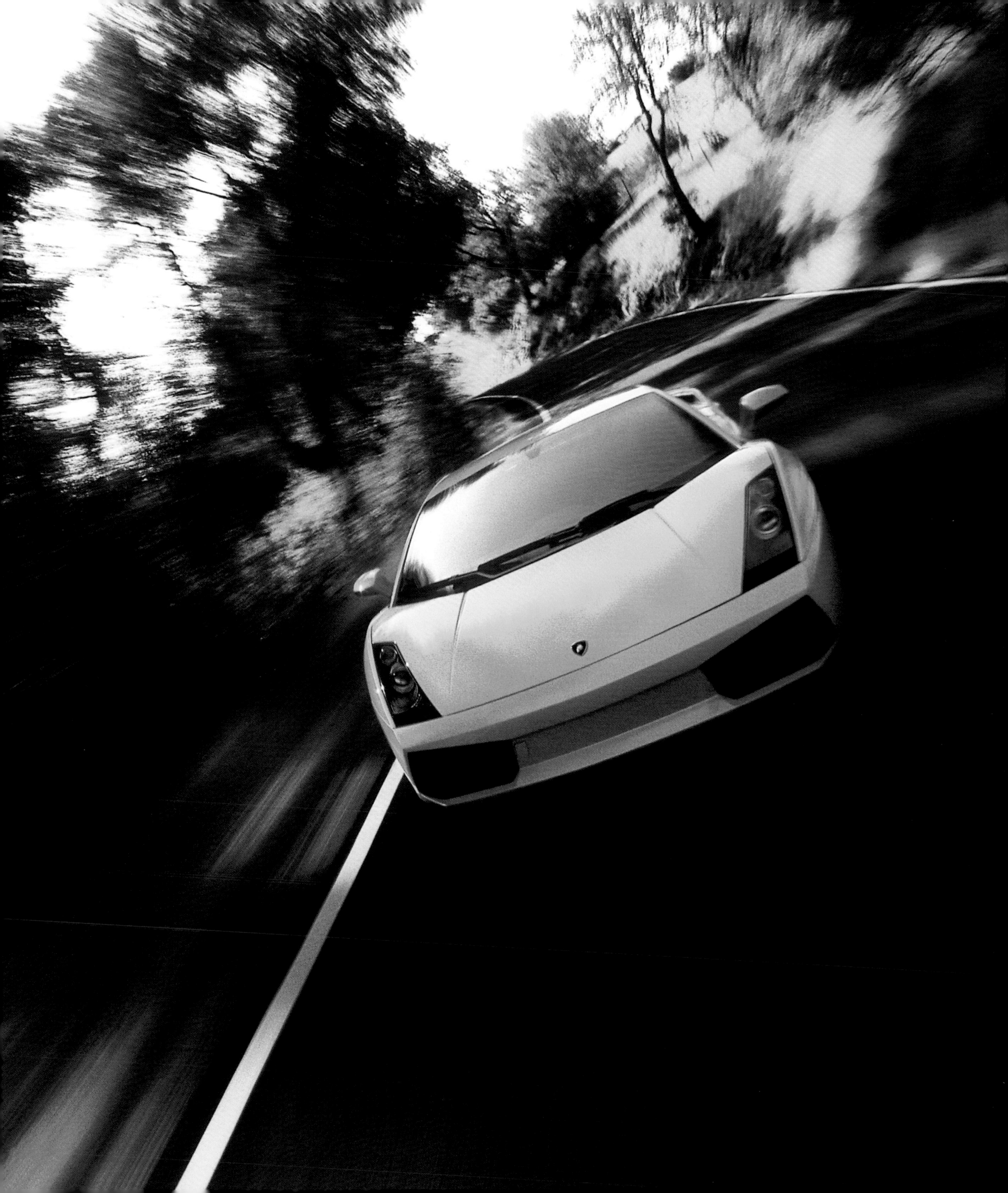

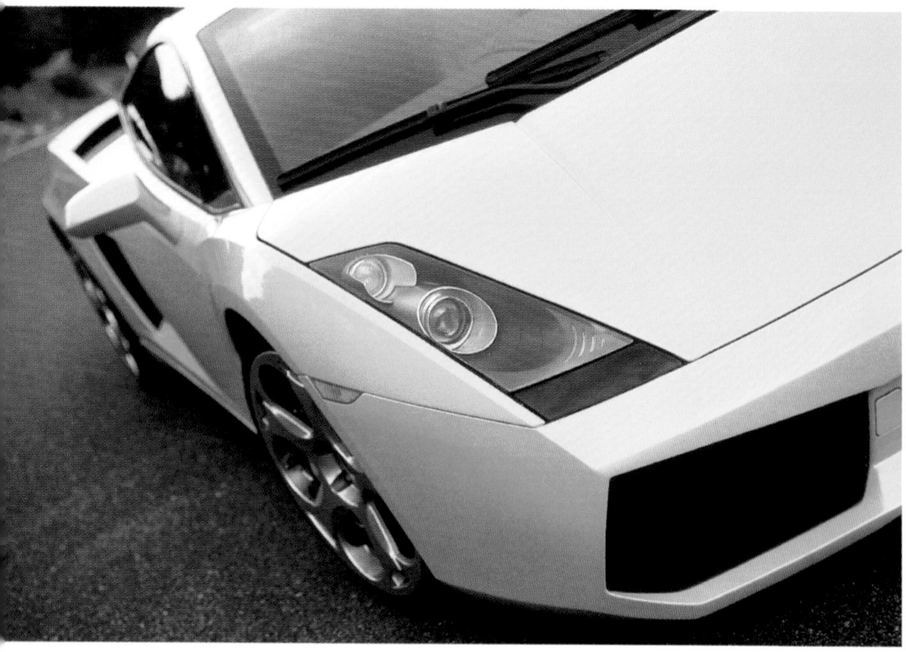

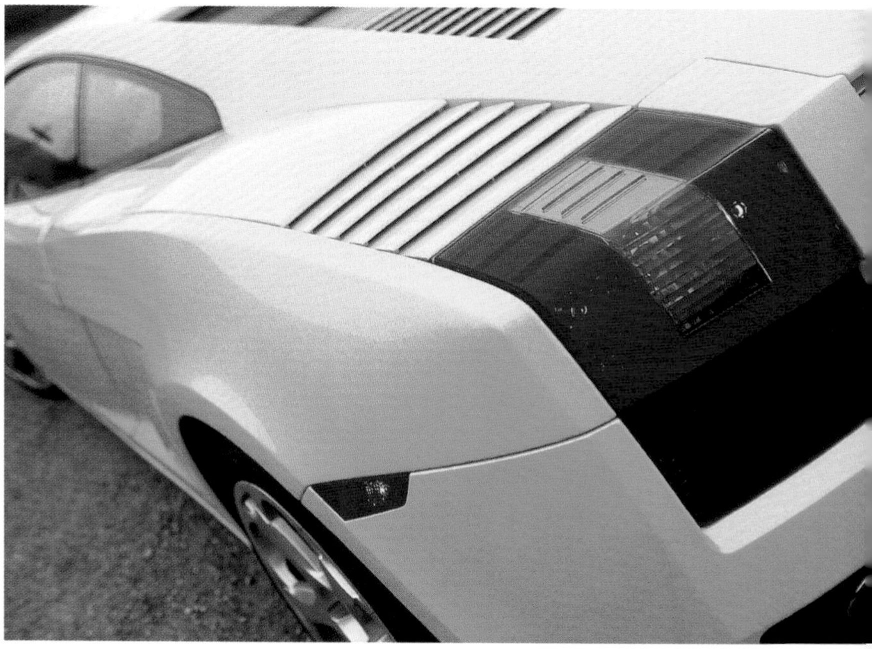

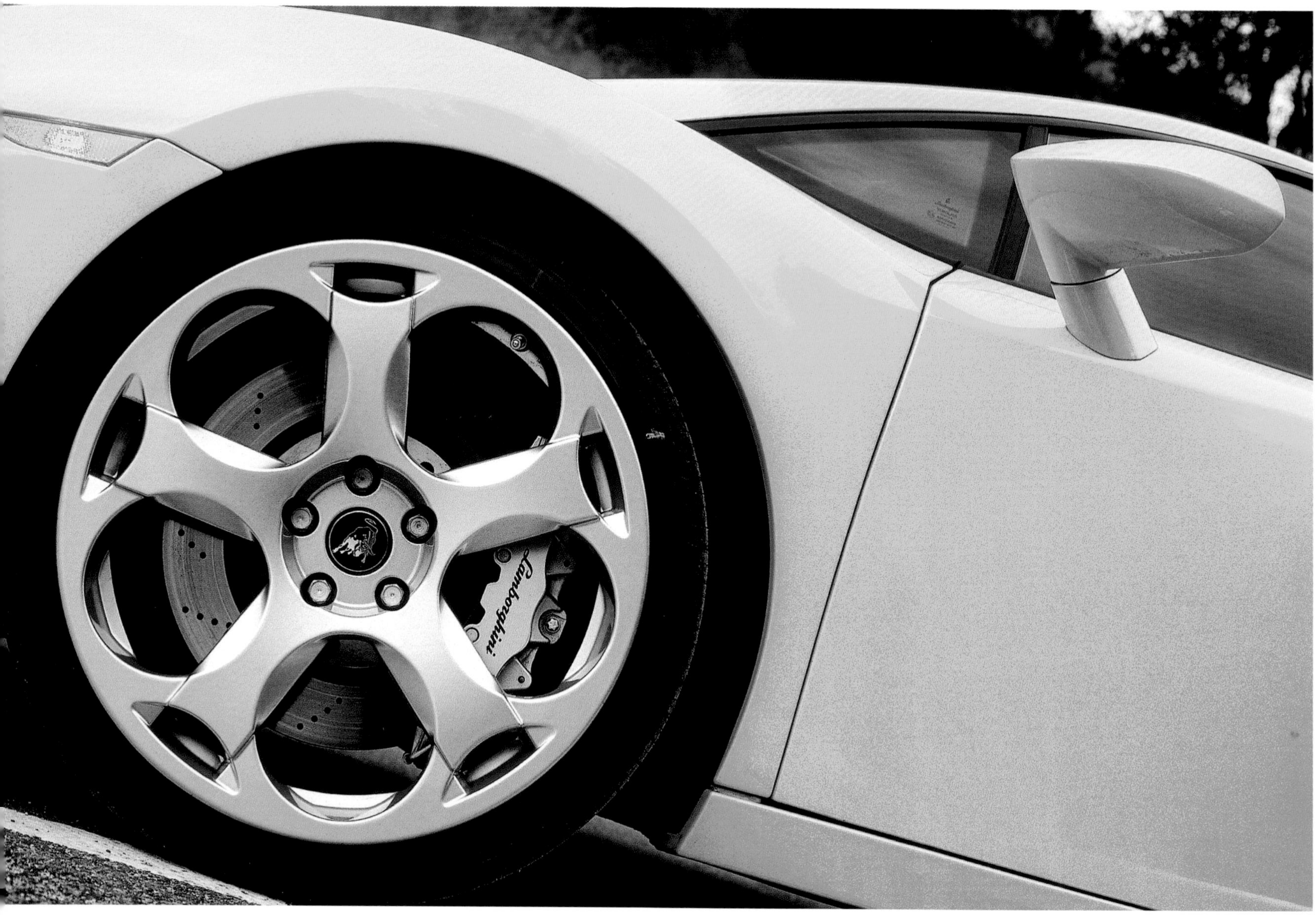
Lamborghini

notice about the car's profile is how steeply the nose dives toward the pavement, and how little overhang there is at the front and the rear. The flowing roofline is complemented by a series of crisp shoulder lines that clearly define the chiseled rear fenders. Just forward of the rear wheels, tall and thin air intakes molded into the bodywork serve to cool the engine oil on the left and the transmission oil on the right. Openings atop the rear fenders are where the mid-mounted engine breathes in fresh air.

Around the back, simple vertical and horizontal lines define the taillights, blacked-out cooling mesh and the lower bumper. On top of the rear deck, there is a small wing that raises automatically when the car is traveling more than 90 mph. The straight-edge look continues on the engine cover and forward of the taillights where louvers provide additional cooling for the engine compartment.

Open the door, and the Gallardo welcomes you with its handsome interior furnished in rich leather. As with any low-slung sports car, first plant your bottom onto the driver's seat, then swing your legs inside to complete a graceful entrance. Once in, you can feel how the aggressive seat bolsters hold you in place. The steering wheel telescopes and tilts, and there is plenty of head room and seat adjustments so that even a 6-foot-tall person will feel comfortable.

The instrument panel is low and gracefully slopes away from the base of the windshield. In front of the driver is the instrument cluster. The 10,000-rpm tachometer and the 210-mph speedometer are prominent, flanked by the coolant temperature and fuel-level gauges. On the center dash, the oil-pressure, oil-temperature and voltage gauges are placed at the top, followed by three large circular air vents. A row of toggle switches between the radio and climate controls is a nice detail. But with everything else about the car designed with such an Italian flair, some of our staff complained about the Audi-sourced (yet quite functional) climate controls.

Just as a fighting bull's tremendous power is its foremost character trait, a Lamborghini's extreme horsepower output has always helped it pull away from its competitors. This new Gallardo is no exception. Even though the baby Lambo is smaller, Sant'Agata engineers still are able to fit the biggest engine possible into a tight package. The result is an all-aluminum V-10 dohc 5.0-liter powerplant that produces 500 bhp (DIN) at 7800 rpm and serves up 376 lb.-ft. of torque at 4500 rpm. With variable intake- and exhaust-valve timing working together with variable-length runners for channeling fresh air into the combustion chambers, the Gallardo's torque output is optimized over a broad rpm range. In fact, 80 percent of maximum torque is delivered at a very low 1500 rpm.

Instead of adopting the more conventional 72-degree angle between the cylinders for a V-10, the Lamborghini engineers decided to go with the 90-degree split to lower the engine height. Even-firing intervals for smoothness are achieved with 18-degree offset crankpins. A dry-sump lubrication system and a small-diameter twin-plate clutch are additional features that help to lower the car's center of gravity.

Power from the V-10 is transmitted to the wheels via Lamborghini's permanent all-wheel-drive system. Torque is distributed to the front and the rear axles through a center differential positioned between the engine and the rear-overhanging gearbox. A viscous coupling up front controls how much power

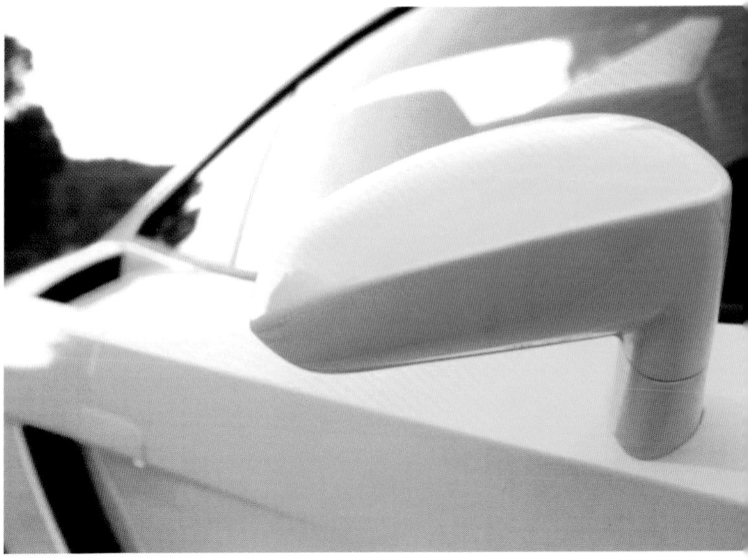

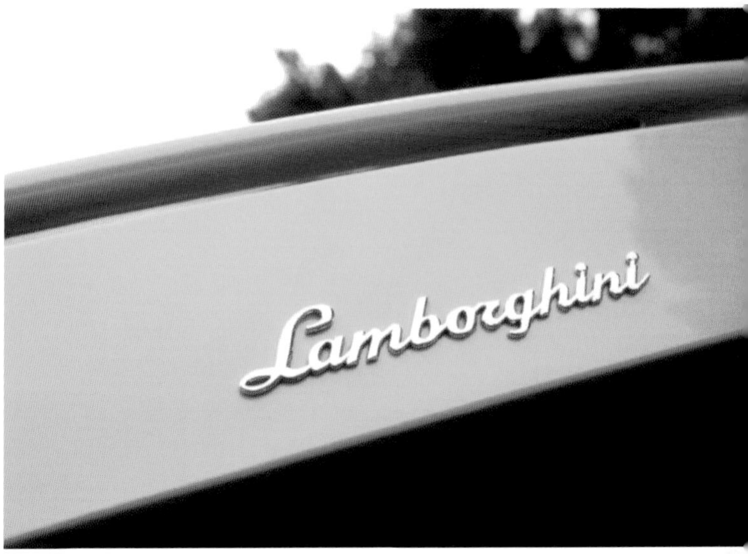
Lamborghini

ABOVE AND OPPOSITE: There's an exciting tension created by the angular, geometric shapes of the Gallardo's headlights, taillights, mirrors, vents and ducts, all drawn together in a cohesive shape that's more about hard-edged muscle and less about voluptuous curves. Oversized discs and 8-piston Brembo calipers are framed by ornate alloy wheels that provide a nice counterpoint to the sheet metal.

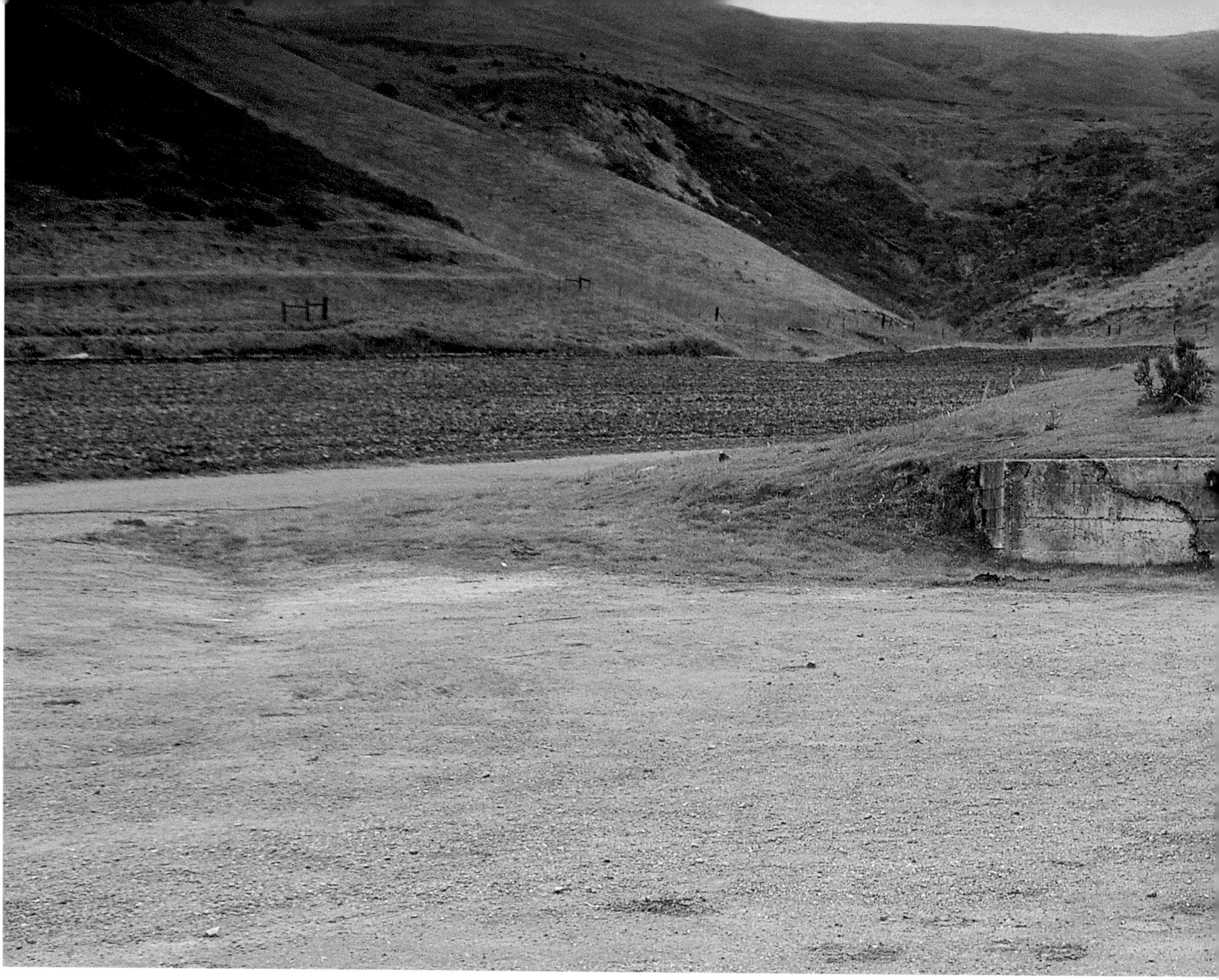

OPPOSITE: Unlike the Murciélago's unconventional "backward" engine mounting, where power is routed forward to the transmission, then back to a differential beneath the engine, the Gallardo's 500-bhp V-10 follows standard mid-engine practice. Shifting is anything but conventional, as the 6-speed transmission is equipped with "e-gear," an electrohydraulic paddle-shift system.

passes through to the front wheels. On dry pavement, torque is split 30/70 in favor of the rear. But if traction is limited, power can be reapportioned up to a 50/50 split. For better off-the-corner acceleration, computer-controlled brakes (Automatic Brake Differential, ABD) are used to regulate front-end slip while the rear retains a 45-percent limited-slip differential. Standard on the Gallardo are ABS, yaw and traction control (ESP), which work with throttle-by-wire and awd to ensure maximum safety and traction under adverse weather conditions.

Our test car came equipped with Lamborghini's "e-gear." It is the optional electrohydraulically actuated 6-speed manual gearbox. In the cockpit, the upshift paddle is on the right of the steering wheel, its downshift counterpart on the left. According to factory technicians, this much-improved F1-style transmission is the latest generation of the Magneti Marelli Selespeed, the same type of paddle-shift system used by Ferrari, Alfa Romeo and Aston Martin.

On the drag strip, launching the Gallardo from a standing start is easy. Put the e-gear into Sport mode. This changes the time required to swap gears from 0.22 second to 0.17. Turn off the traction/yaw control and take your foot off the brake pedal. With the car standing still, simply romp on the throttle until it hits

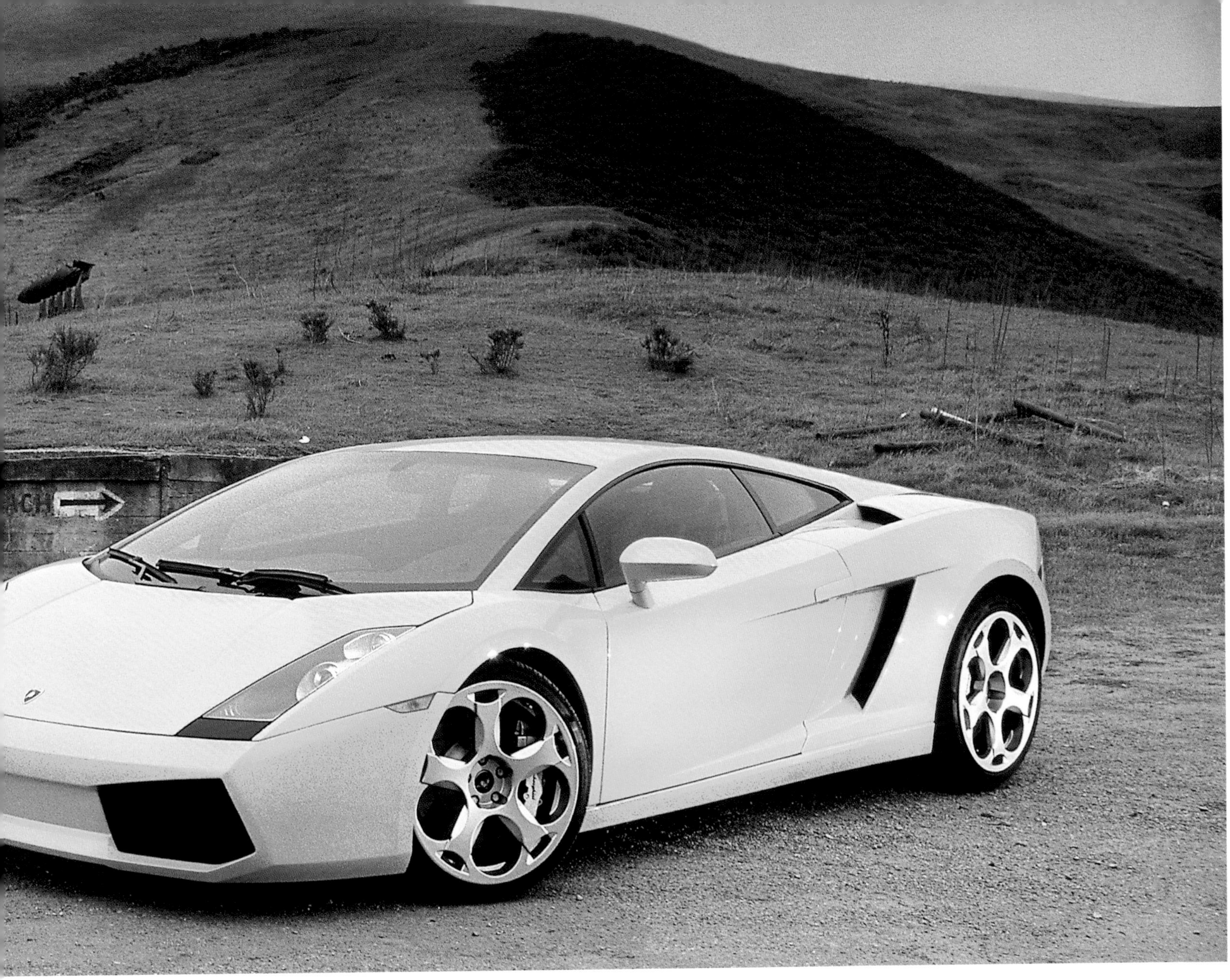

the floor. Just before the car takes off, the engine rpm jump to near 3500 and the clutch engages immediately. The rear wheels spin and momentarily break traction. But soon, the all-wheel drive kicks in and shifts power to the front wheels.

Once all four tires grab the asphalt, the Gallardo explodes forward with a ferocious growl. The deep-throated rumble through the exhaust is accompanied by hisses from the thirsty V-10 gulping as much fresh air as possible through the air intakes just over your shoulders. Your eyes focus on the tach needle racing toward the 8100-rpm redline. Once there, a simple pull of the upshift paddle, and the galloping bull catches a second breath and continues to thrust forward with all its might. Zero to 60 mph takes only 4.0 sec. The quarter mile is reached in 12.3 sec. with the speedometer registering 117.4 mph. These numbers are quick enough to jump ahead of the Ferrari 360 Modena and leave its cross-town adversary in the rearview mirror.

When the time comes to stop, the Brembo 8-piston front and 4-piston rear calipers take hold of the brake discs with confidence and authority. The front 14.4-in. and rear 13.2-in. vented discs slow the Gallardo from 60 mph in 110 ft., and from 80 mph in a very respectable 194 ft.

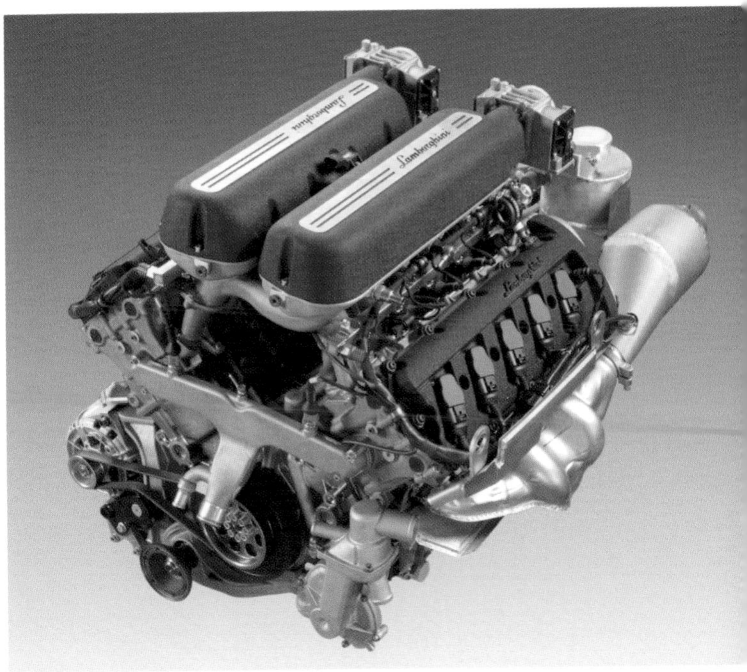

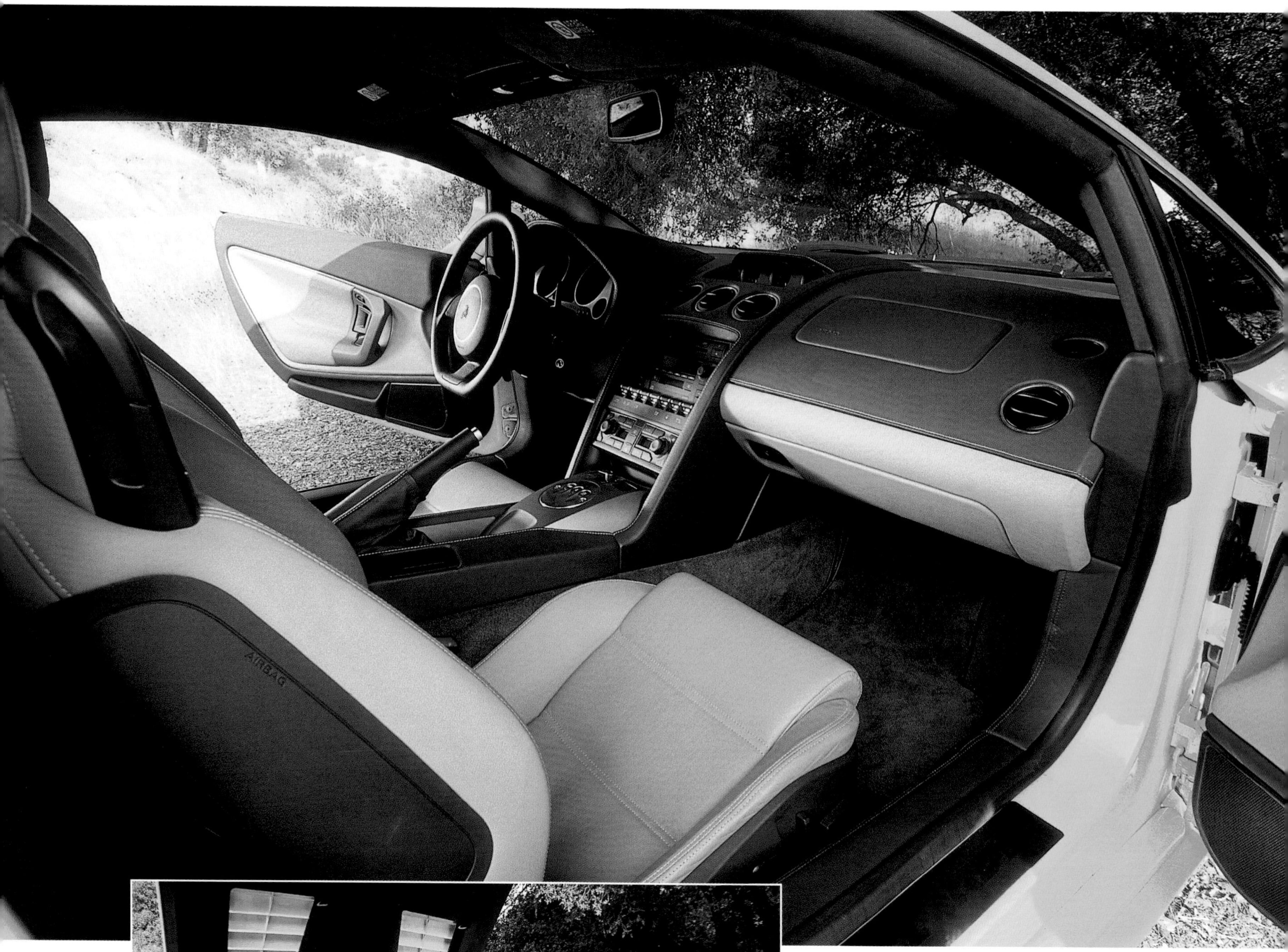
AIRBAG

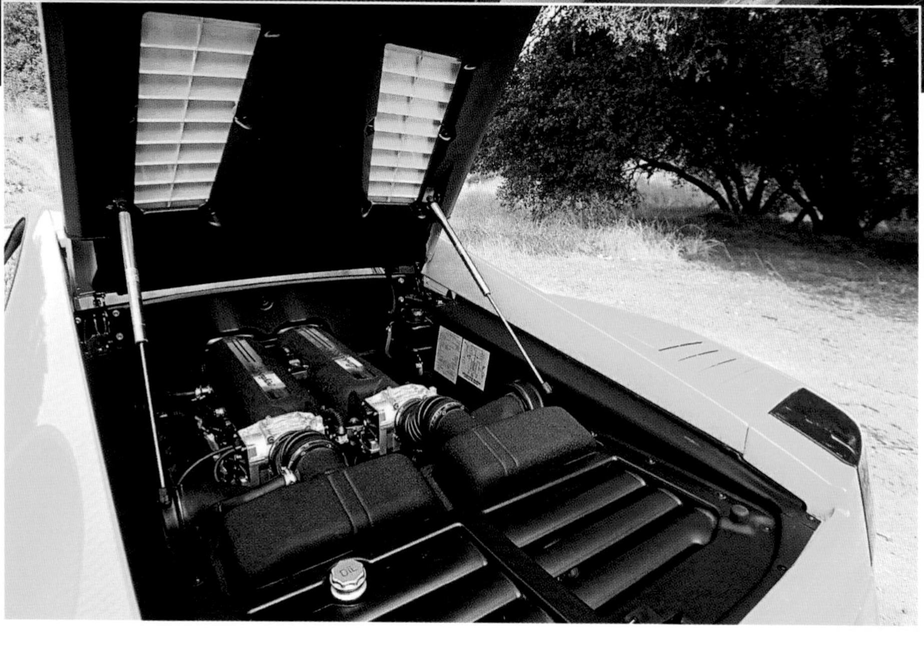

ABOVE AND LEFT: The rich smell of leather permeates the Gallardo's interior, which is not the ergonomic penalty box that Italian exotic cars used to be. Note the squared-off bottom of the steering wheel for extra thigh clearance. The engine bay is quite tidy too, with black wrinkle-finish paint dressing up the V-10's intake plenums and airboxes.

OPPOSITE, FROM TOP: The slender aluminum upshift stalk for the e-gear transmission; a dress plate where the standard shift lever usually resides; and special toggle switches, a counterpoint to familiar Audi-sourced buttons and knobs.

With high horsepower comes high demand for a proper chassis and a suspension setup to match. To save weight, Lamborghini engineers borrowed aluminum space-frame technology from Audi to design and build the Gallardo's chassis. The space frame is constructed of aluminum extrusions and joined together at various castings. The exterior aluminum body panels are mounted to the frame using rivets, screws or welds. And holding up the Gallardo's chassis at all four corners is the double wishbone suspension setup with springs and Koni dampers all around, with anti-roll bars front and rear. The Pirelli P Zero Rosso tires are size 235/35ZR-19 in front and 295/30ZR-19 at the rear.

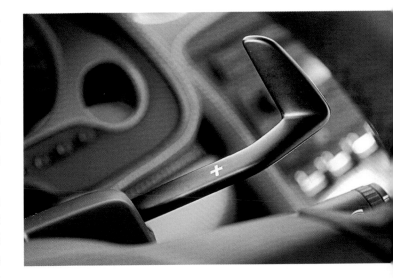

Around town, the Gallardo's manners are docile. The car never feels on edge despite all that power on tap. The view forward is excellent, thanks in part to the split window toward the base of the A-pillar allowing for an unobstructed view when rounding corners. Surprisingly, the vision to the rear through the outside mirrors and the rear window is fairly good. This helps define the car's corners for the driver and allows for ease of maneuvering in parking lots or through heavy traffic. On the road, the ride over the highway concrete slabs is acceptable. However, any long-distance road trip of three hours or so can be taxing on the lower back since the seats are firm and the suspension is tuned for sporty handling.

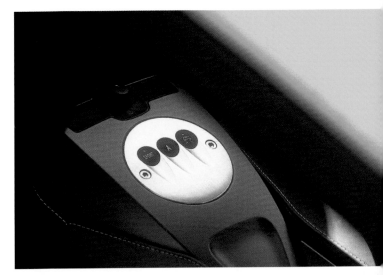

And sporty handling is where the Gallardo excels. Find a winding country road and the baby Lambo rewards with its buttery-smooth sense of balance as it dances through the corners. The car feels light but hunkered down, thanks to its all-wheel-drive grip. The nicely weighted steering directs it precisely through an apex with just a slight hint of understeer for safety. And as the turn straightens out, the V-10 is eager to serve up gobs of power. The Gallardo explodes off the corner with an immense acceleration force. With ESP turned on, there is no way the rear will step out even with an overly aggressive hit on the gas pedal. With the computer aids off, you can kick its tail out with such a progressive motion that there is plenty of time to countersteer, adjust throttle input and hold the slide.

At the test track, the Gallardo circled our 200-ft.-diameter skidpad averaging an excellent 0.95g and showing moderate understeer. And on our slalom course, the car's ability to thread through the cones with ease was impressive. None of the bulkiness and sluggishness in sudden directional changes normally associated with all-wheel-drive vehicles is there. The smaller and more agile Lamborghini responds to every steering input quickly and progressively so there are no surprises. The Gallardo's 68.6-mph average through the slalom places it ahead of the Murciélago and the Ferrari 360 Modena. It even outpaces most production Porsches, with the 911 GT2 ahead by only 0.1 mph.

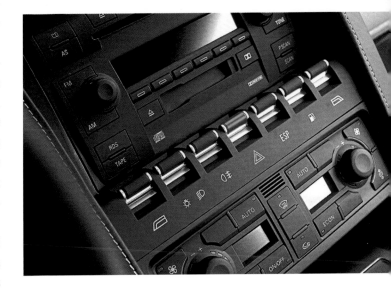

Fighting bulls are usually associated with muscular builds, brute force and speed. They usually are not known for agility. And previous Lamborghini sports cars have stayed true to the marque's emblem and focused on exotic good looks and awe-inspiring power. To run with the best of the exotic sports-car players, the new Gallardo has been bred to inherit all of the brand's strongest DNA along with newfound agility. Surely, that will make others pause and think: Yes, the Lamborghini is fast in a straight line, but can its adversaries still run and hide from its horns in the corners? I don't think so.

CD
AS
FM
AM
RDS
TAPE
TONE
ESP
AUTO
AUTO
ECON
ON/OFF

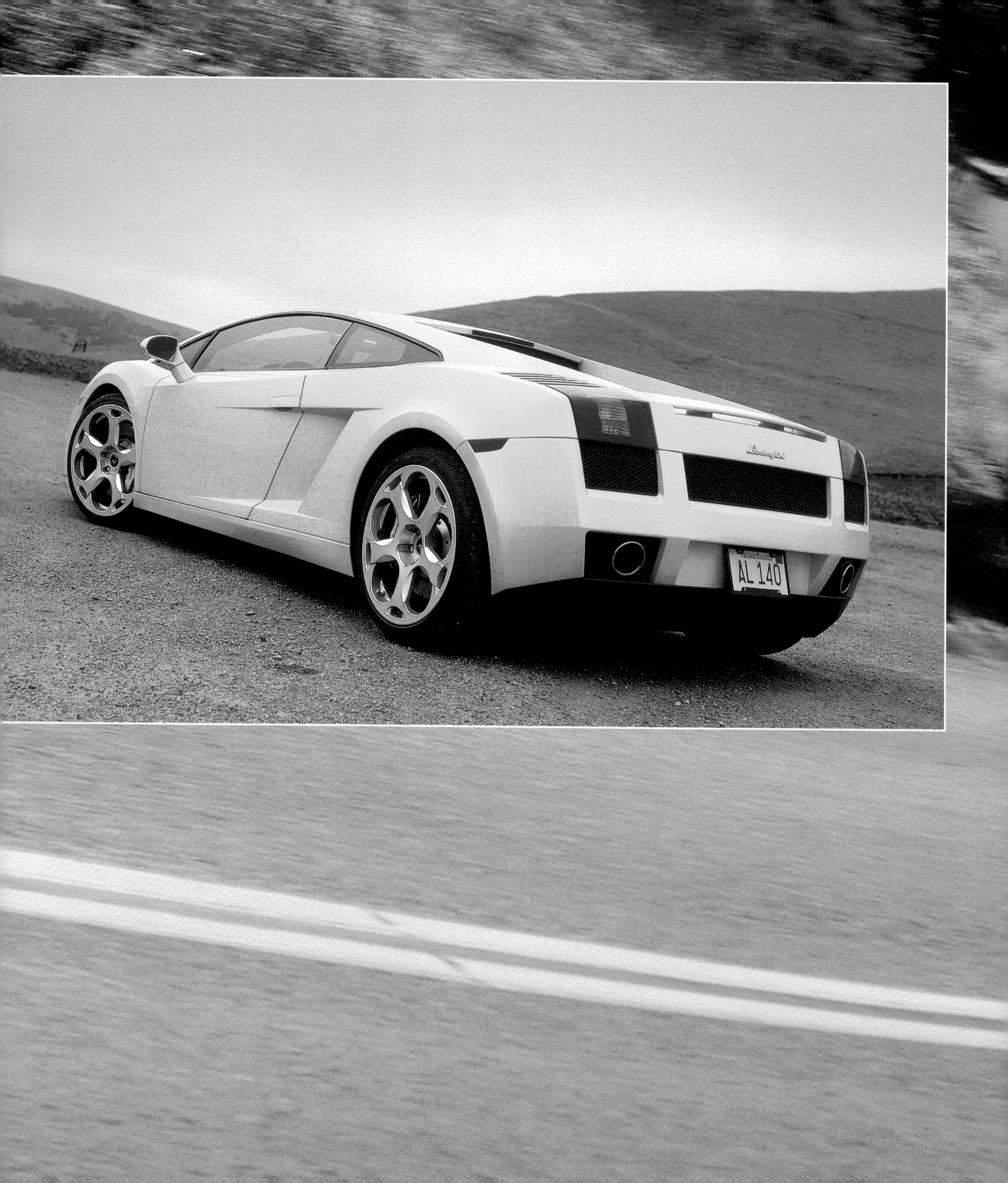
Lamborghini
Massachusetts
AL 140

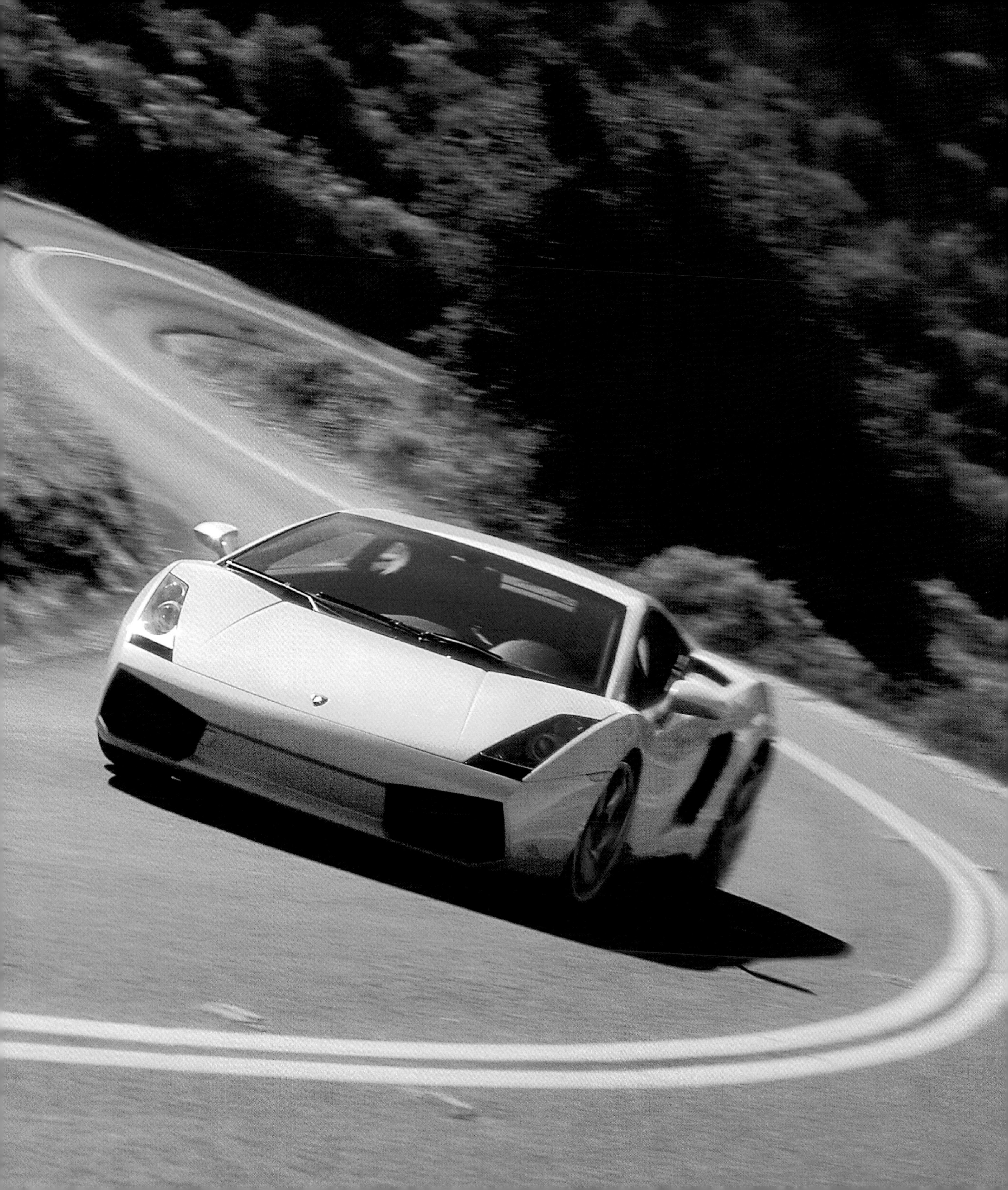

LAMBORGHINI MURCIELAGO

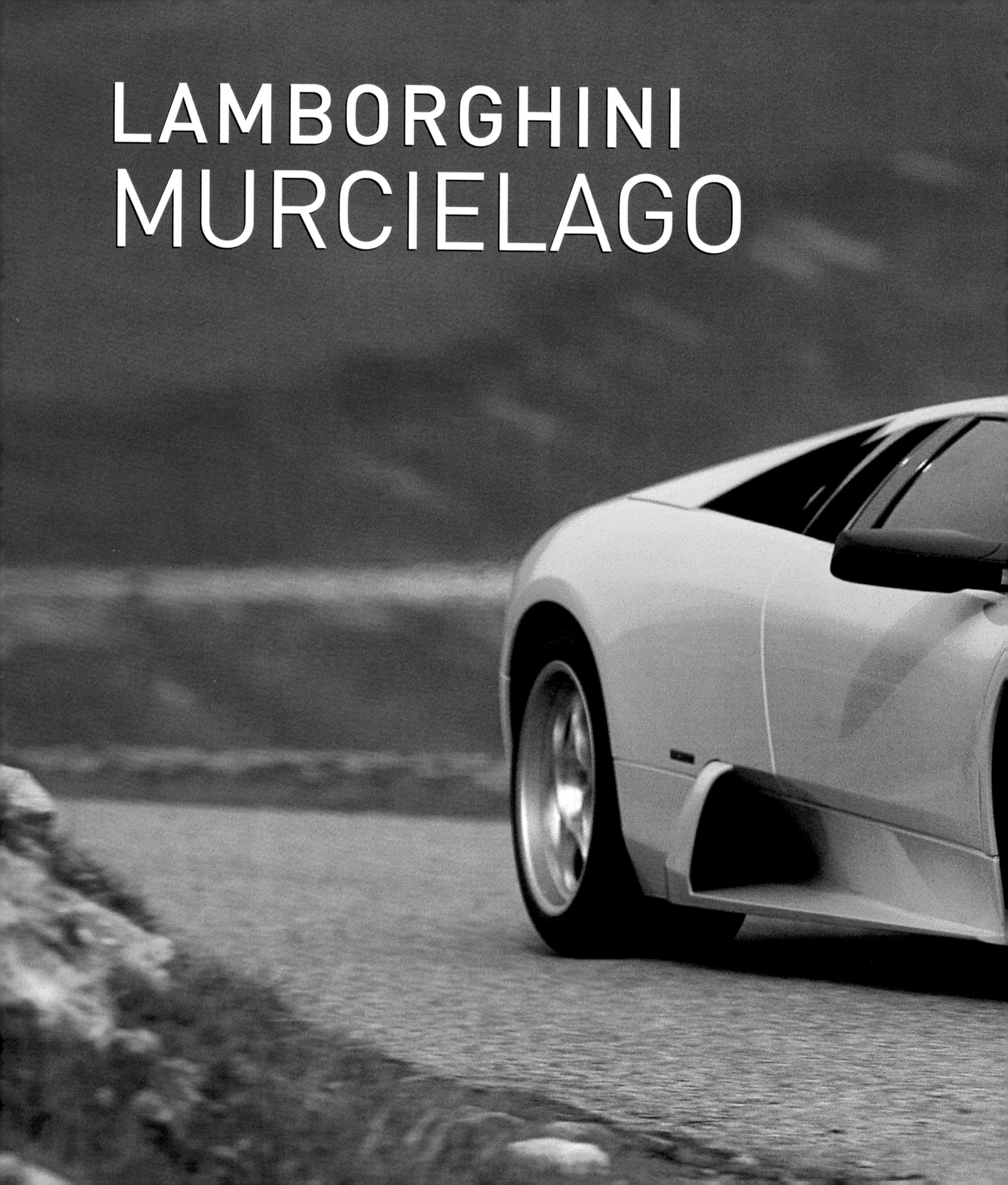

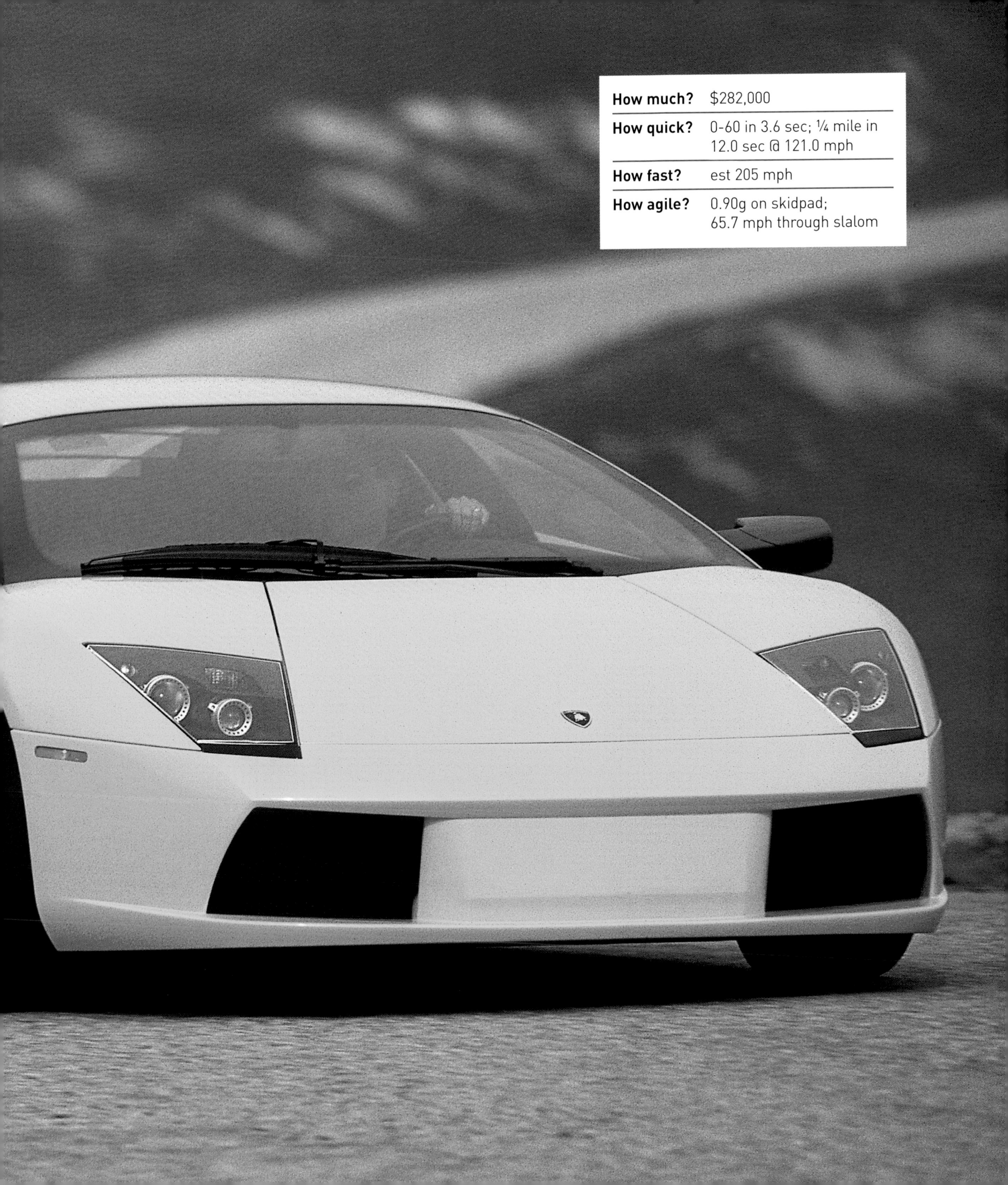

How much?	$282,000
How quick?	0-60 in 3.6 sec; ¼ mile in 12.0 sec @ 121.0 mph
How fast?	est 205 mph
How agile?	0.90g on skidpad; 65.7 mph through slalom

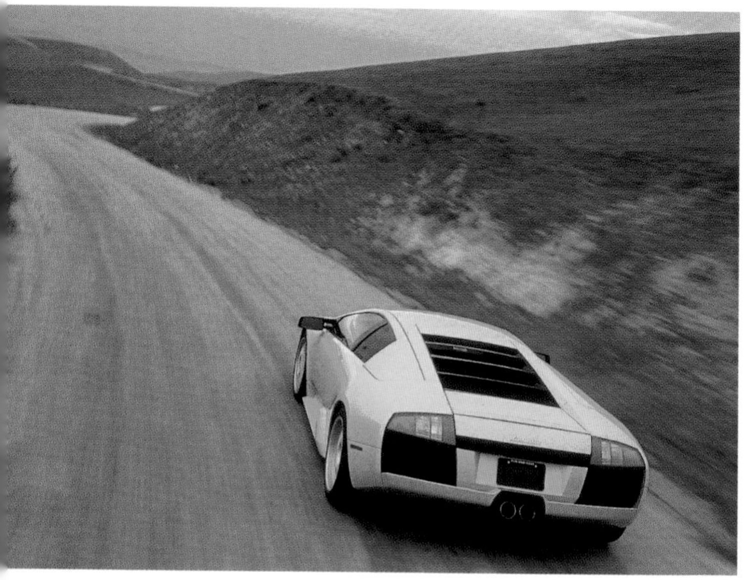

ABOVE: A little slice of heaven—a Lamborghini Murciélago, a Southern California sunset, and a challenging stretch of road ahead.

BELOW: No bull, just raw speed from the worthy successor to the Countach and Diablo.

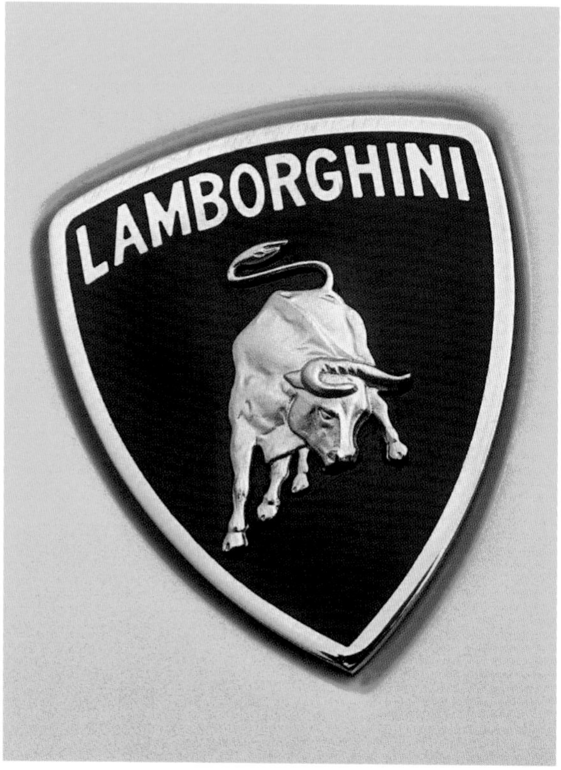
LAMBORGHINI

BEAUTY AND THE BEAST

TO FULLY UNDERSTAND THE MURCIELAGO, you must first understand its progenitor, the Countach. Its very name—"a hard-to-define Piemontese expletive, and let's leave it at that as this is a family magazine," we said in "Road & Track"'s November 1973 issue—no doubt expressed the astonishment people must have felt, first laying eyes on this wicked mid-engine wedge penned by famous Italian stylist Nuccio Bertone. Its modern-day successor, the Murciélago, walks a little more softly (with less angular but still mesmerizing lines penned by Belgian stylist Luc Donckerwolke) but carries an even bigger stick: a mid-mounted, aluminum 4-cam V-12 producing 580 bhp served up to all four wheels. Experience one, as we did, and you might just coin an expletive all your own.

The afternoon sun must have been shining with extraordinary brilliance on October 5, 1879. A beautiful but ferocious bull named Murciélago ("Mur-see-á-lah-go") entered the bullring in Cordoba, Spain, and was met by matador Rafael Molina, nicknamed "Lagartijo," or "Lounge Lizard." And instead of delivering death during "suerte suprema," the third and final stage of "La Corrida," Molina chose not to plunge his sword into Murciélago's heart and spared the bull's life. A rare occurrence indeed, one that is reserved for a bull that has shown exceptional spirit and strength in the arena.

This imposing Lamborghini from Sant'Agata Bolognese is also a bull specially bred for beauty and strength. It is the successor to the legendary Countach and the famous Diablo. It also takes the name of Murciélago and captures the same aura, one that lures with its muscular looks but intimidates with a forceful presence.

So it is fitting that under a Southern California sun of extraordinary brilliance and warmth, the Murciélago arrives at our offices in Newport Beach, California. Its pearl-toned yellow skin reflects a glistening gold along its broad shoulders; we have never seen a yellow as striking as this. Up front, staring right into your eyes, is a pair of trapezoidal exposed xenon headlights above two air scoops. What follows is a wide and steeply raked windscreen that opens up to a mighty torso with chiseled-in upper and lower body air-intake channels that suggest a powerful force lurking beneath the sleek lines. Around the back, two huge heat vents reside beneath the angular taillights: one on each side flanking the large, center-mounted twin tailpipes on the bottom. There are no subtleties here—just a bold statement about potential power.

Open up the trademark Lamborghini scissor door (which swings up 5 degrees higher than the Diablo's) and the rich smell of Italian leather immediately rushes out. The easiest and most graceful way to climb aboard still means falling backward into the sport seat, then maneuvering your legs into the footwell. However, our taller staff members appreciate the roomier footbox, the lower doorsills and the redesigned roof that allow easier ingress and egress and better comfort inside the car.

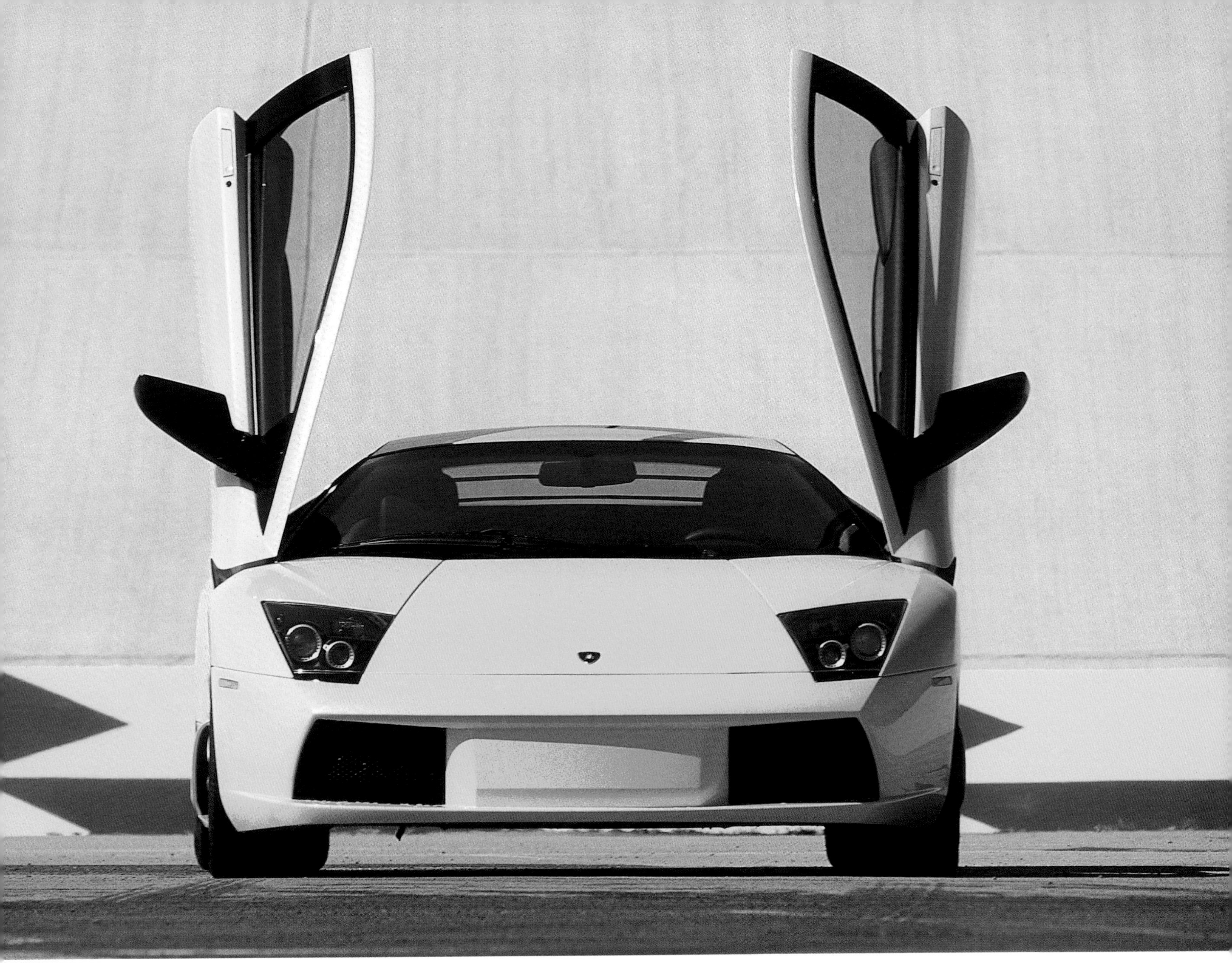

ABOVE: Viewed head-on, the Murciélago exudes an intimidating presence. It can back it up on the test track—at Nardo in Italy, it set several FIA world speed records for a production car, one of which was averaging 189.548 mph for one hour.

The interior is updated with a neatly packaged instrument cluster set within a handsome, sweeping dash. All of the Murciélago's important vital signs are positioned right in front of the driver, and the automated climate and radio controls are within easy reach. Round air vents outlined by polished aluminum fit the modern look carried throughout the rest of the cockpit. The steering wheel is well padded for a sporty feel. The shiny, round shifter now operates within a gate that has a straight 1-2 shift rather than the dogleg pattern on the Diablo. The seats are very supportive, with aggressive side bolsters to firmly hold you in place as the Murciélago flexes its muscles on the road and through the turns.

Strap in with the center-mounted seatbelts. Insert and turn the ignition key. Give the gas pedal a quick tap. The massive 6.2-liter V-12 engine roars with a husky growl, clears its throat with a few crackles through the exhaust pipes and then settles into a low rumble. The Murciélago V-12 idles much more smoothly than the Diablo's lumpier 6.0-liter powerplant.

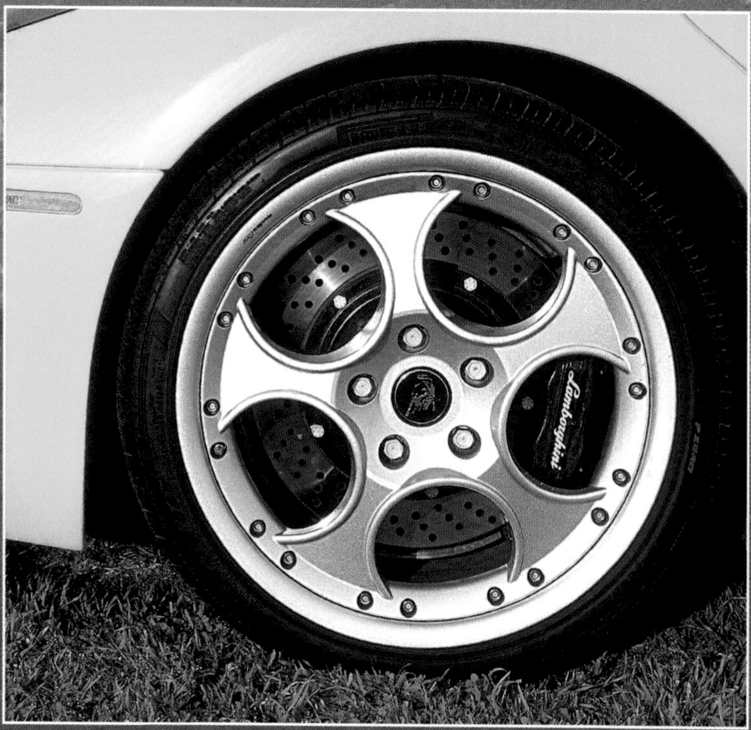
Lamborghini

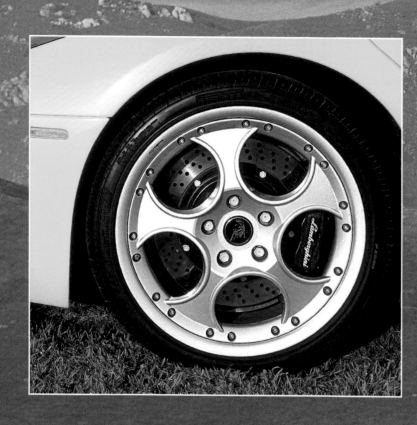

LEFT: All four of the Murciélago's wheels are driven, and all are braked with generously-sized alloy calipers clamping down on cross-drilled, vented rotors.

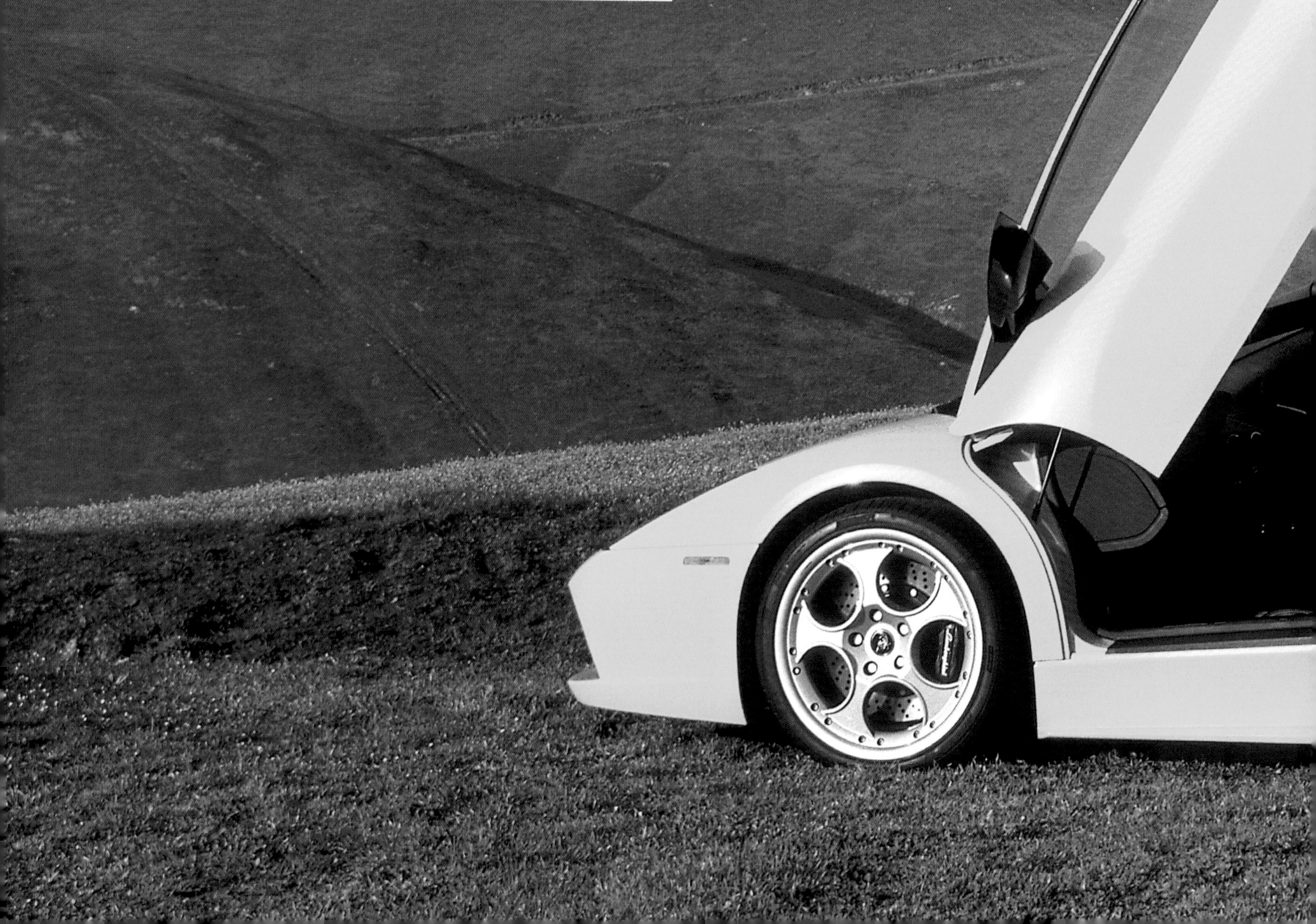

BELOW: In the manner of its Countach and Diablo predecessors, the Murciélago's doors pivot upward, scissor style.

RIGHT: "Bat wing" intakes can swing open as much as 20 degrees to cool the V-12 engine, at the cost of extra aerodynamic drag. Spent gases exit through twin pipes that are neatly countersunk into the middle of the rear bumper.

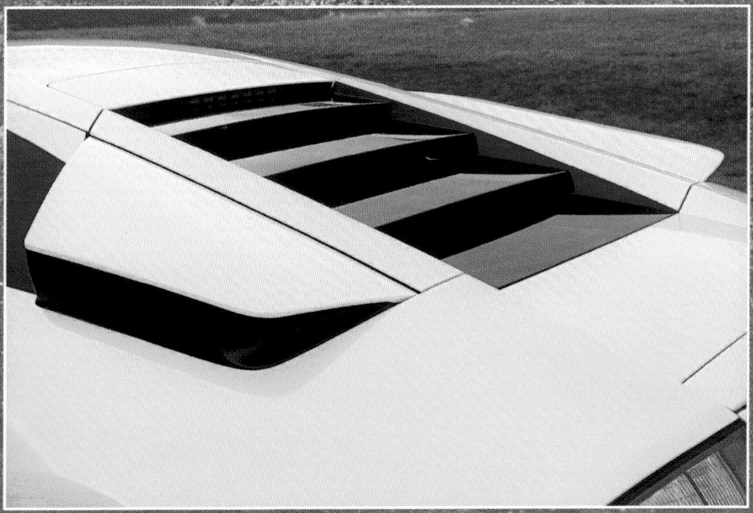

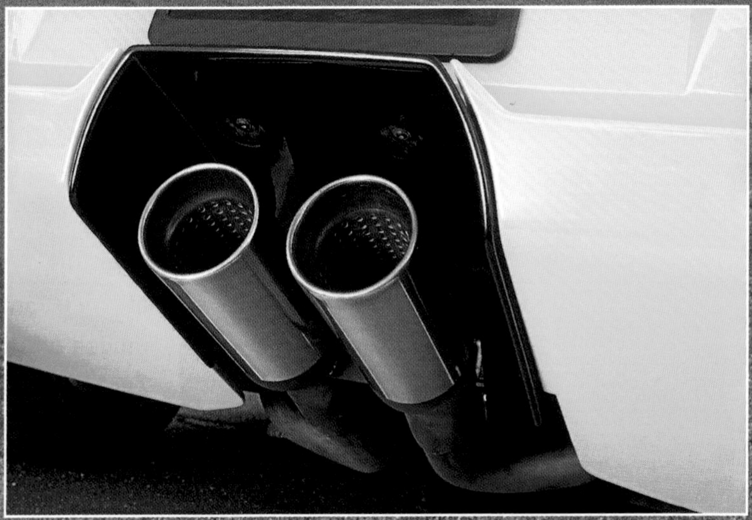

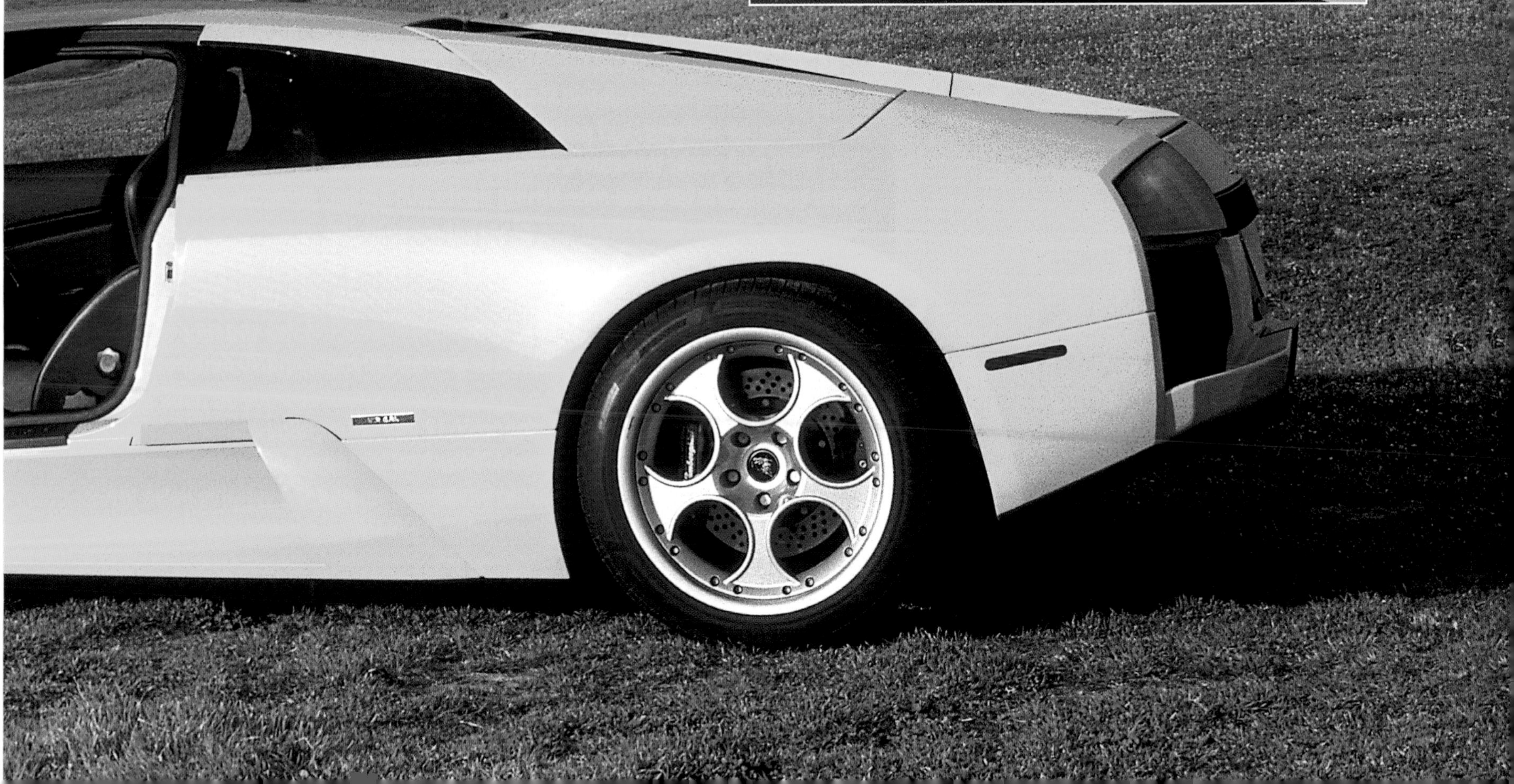

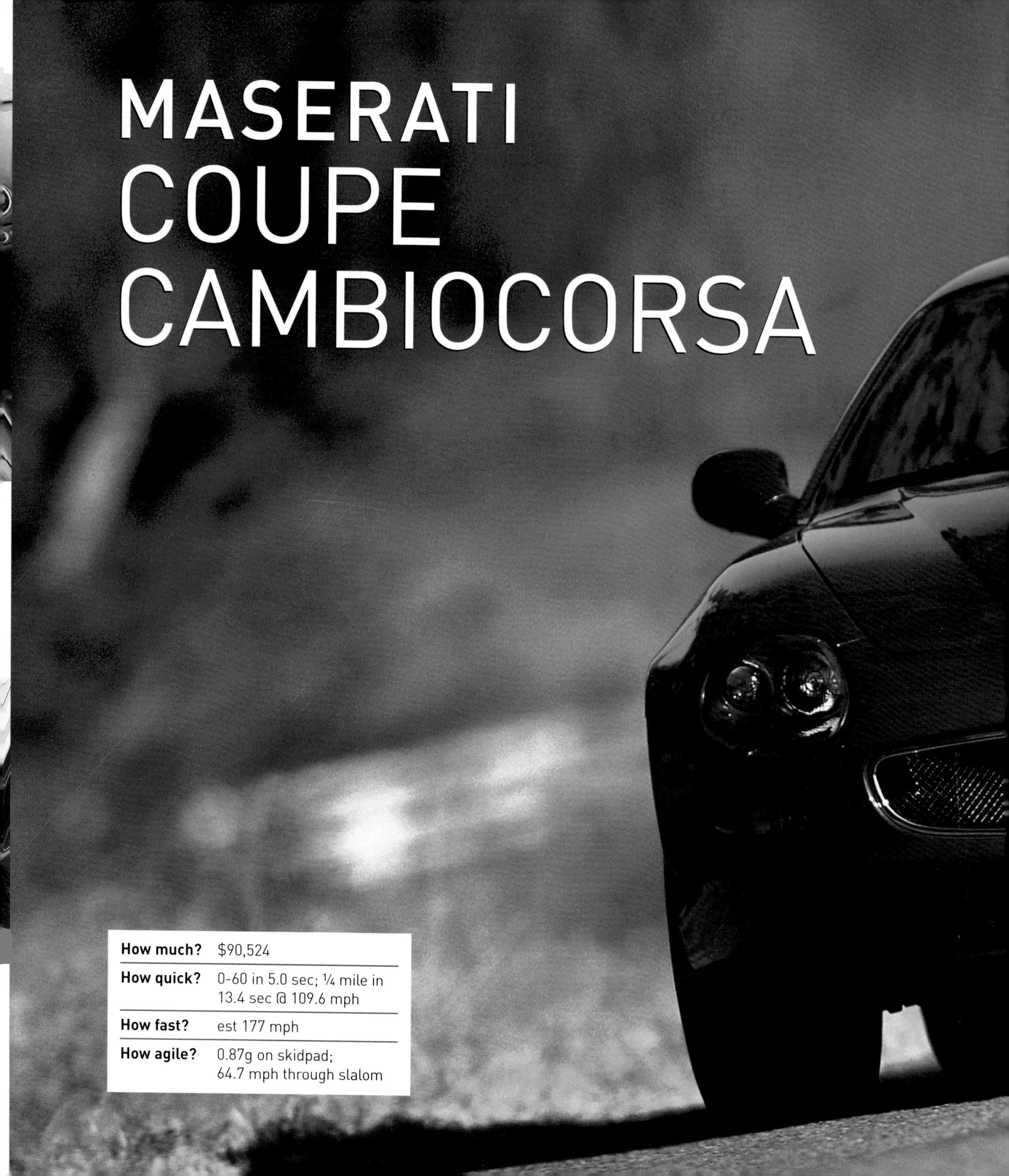

MASERATI COUPE CAMBIOCORSA

How much?	$90,524
How quick?	0-60 in 5.0 sec; ¼ mile in 13.4 sec @ 109.6 mph
How fast?	est 177 mph
How agile?	0.87g on skidpad; 64.7 mph through slalom

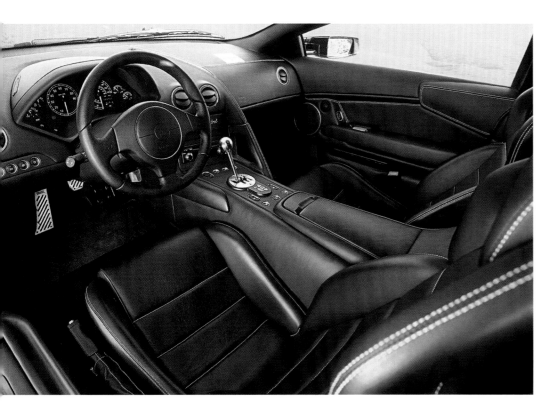

Slide the shifter forward. The 1st gear slots in positively and the clutch pedal requires little effort to engage. The new 6-speed transmission is the first of its kind for Lamborghini. The primary and secondary layshafts ride on three bearings to ensure proper rigidity and steadiness during operation. Lubrication is forced. Double- and triple-cone synchronizers provide precise gear changes with considerably lower effort.

Like the Diablo, the Murciélago is equipped with a permanent all-wheel-drive system via a central viscous coupling. When needed, 28 to 80 percent of the torque can be delivered to the front. Limited-slip differentials are installed at the front and rear, with the former allowing 25-percent slip side to side, the latter 45 percent. When necessary, traction is also controlled by limiting the amount of driving torque available, thanks to the electronic management system modulating the drive-by-wire throttle and retarding the fuel injection/ignition.

ABOVE: Hand-sewn leather interior is far more ergonomically sound than the Diablo's, but no less exotic. Note the console-mounted grab-handle for the passenger, a Lamborghini hallmark.

BELOW: Four throttle bodies feed the 580-bhp, 6.2-liter V-12, a brute capable of rocketing the Murciélago to 60 mph in just 3.6 seconds.

Lamborghini
Lamborghini

On the test track with the traction control turned off, hold the engine revs at 5000 rpm. Drop the clutch and squeeze the throttle. The Murciélago explodes off the line. There is very little wheelspin before the generous Pirelli P Zero Rosso 245/35ZR-18 front and 335/30ZR-18 rear tires bite down on the asphalt. In fact, the lack of tire squeal off the line can be mistaken for clutch slip after a standing start.

Once on its way, the Murciélago's V-12 is irrepressible. The immense acceleration is accompanied by a thunderous roar, which can be heard and felt in the cockpit. Did you ever stand at a railroad crossing and feel the ground shake as a train rushed past? Being in the Lamborghini produces the same sensation, except now the shaking is in your fingertips as you upshift through the gears.

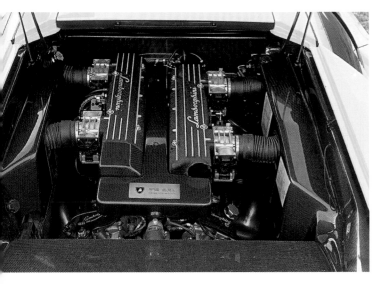

Even on a dusty test track, the Murciélago can rocket to 60 mph in 3.6 seconds, and trip the quarter-mile timing lights at 12.0 sec. with the speedometer registering 121.0 mph. This alone places the car in the super-exclusive exotic sports car club that includes the Ferrari Enzo and Porsche Carrera GT. Keep your foot in the throttle and the car continues to accelerate up to 145 mph before we run out of room at the track. A small spoiler aft of the engine cover ensures high-speed stability. It tilts up 50 degrees at 80 mph, and 70 degrees when speeds exceed 137.

The Murciélago's 6192-cc 60-degree V-12 aluminum-alloy engine is capable of serving up 580 bhp at 7500 rpm and 479 lb.-ft. of torque at 5400 rpm. The drive-by-wire electronic throttle, the variable intake system and the variable valve timing on both the inlet and exhaust camshafts are features designed to make sure the engine is flexible enough to meet the driver's power demand at any speed. In fact, a full 369 lb.-ft. of torque is available as low as 2000 rpm. And unlike the Diablo, the new Lamborghini uses a dry sump that allows the engine to be mounted almost 2 in. lower in the chassis, further lowering the car's center of gravity.

Stand behind the Murciélago at idle and you can appreciate the enormous heat generated by the V-12 powerplant. Keeping the engine cool is a Variable Airflow Cooling System (VACS). Two large radiators reside at the back end of the engine compartment and draw in cool air through two deep channels hidden beneath a pair of flaps. When needed, the flap just aft of the cockpit can pivot open 20 degrees to take in more fresh air, although the drag coefficient is then increased from 0.33 to 0.36. With the flap fully open, the Murciélago takes on the appearance of a bat, which is exactly what the car's Spanish name translates to in English.

The new Lamborghini's chassis is a steel tubular design, with the rest of the structure supplemented by carbon-fiber/honeycomb elements attached with rivets and adhesives. The roof and the body panels are made of steel, and the floorpan is fabricated out of carbon fiber. Overall, an impressive 14,747 lb.-ft. per degree of torsional rigidity is achieved with the car.

Upper and lower A-arms are found at each corner, teamed with coil springs and shock absorbers with electronic damping. Up front, the mounting points for the suspension have been moved forward by 0.6 in. to make room for the footbox. The rear springs—two per side—feed their wheel loads to a stiffer, removable crossmember.

On the same dusty test track, the Murciélago exhibited moderate understeer, and managed only 0.90g of lateral acceleration around the 200-ft.-diameter skidpad. However, the Lamborghini came alive through our 700-ft. slalom. It turned in a respectable 65.7-mph average speed, responding well to quick steering inputs and throttle modulation while threading through the cones.

On the road, the Lamborghini's ride is firm and borders on harsh for extended trips. The driver-selectable electronic damper settings can make only slight improvements to ride quality. However, the Murciélago is a sports car, not exactly intended for luxury cruises on the Interstate.

Just as matadors carefully study their fighting bulls' behavior during the first of three stages in "La Corrida," the Murciélago deserves just as much attention before you take it to its limits. At first, the Lamborghini feels big and sluggish, especially with a slower-than-expected steering ratio. But once you get comfortable with its driving dynamics, its massive girth feels less imposing.

On winding roads, there's a confident brake pedal feel and the quick-reacting 4-channel ABS with Dynamic Rear Proportioning (DRP) slows the car with authority before an approaching corner. DRP guarantees optimum distribution of braking force between front and rear wheels. Through the turn, the firmness of the suspension holds the car rock-steady with slight understeer. And as soon as you clip the apex and find that the road opens up to a straightaway, you can lean on the throttle and be rewarded with a thrill ride unlike any other. And even though there is 479 lb.-ft. of torque on tap from the Murciélago's V-12, there is never a tendency for the car to oversteer, unless you're aggressive with the throttle, of course.

While it is hard for us to fully comprehend the beauty of the bull named Murciélago who fought so valiantly more than a century ago, Lamborghini has taken and infused the same majesty into an awesome automobile for modern matadors to appreciate. Murciélago has returned to glory once again.

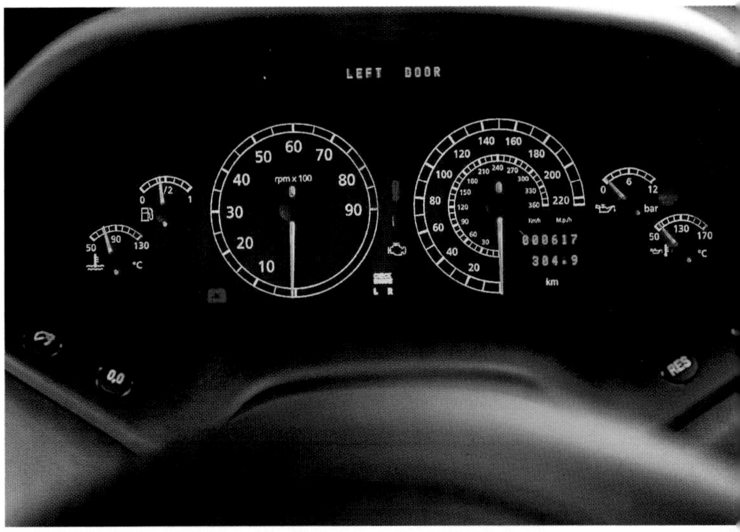
LEFT DOOR
50 60 70
40 80
30 90
20
10
rpm x 100
140 160
120 180
100 200
80 220
60
40
20
km/h
000617
304.9
km

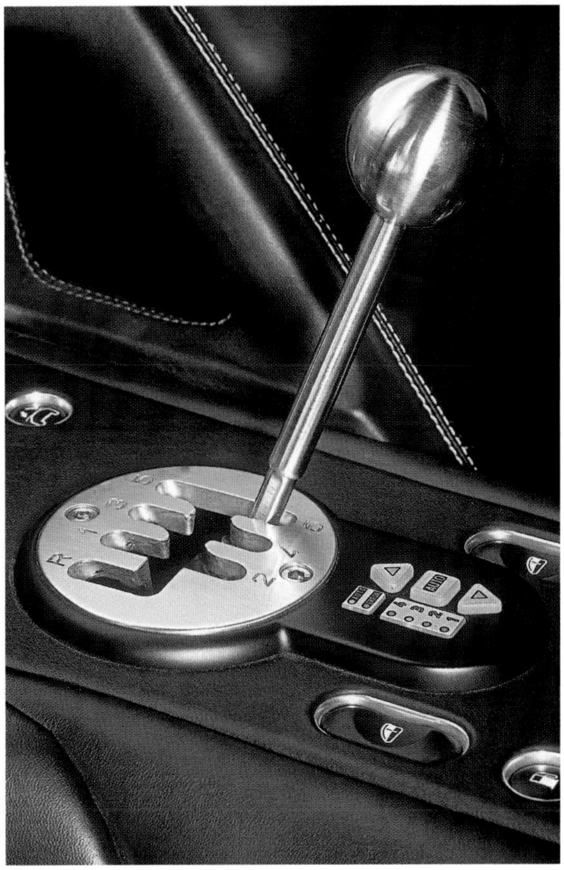

FROM TOP: Brightly illuminated dials keep tabs on the Murciélago's vital signs. The 6-speed's substantial aluminum gate eliminates uncertainty when shifting. Buttons aft of the gate allow selection of four different shock-absorber modes.

MASERATI COUPE CAMBIOCORSA

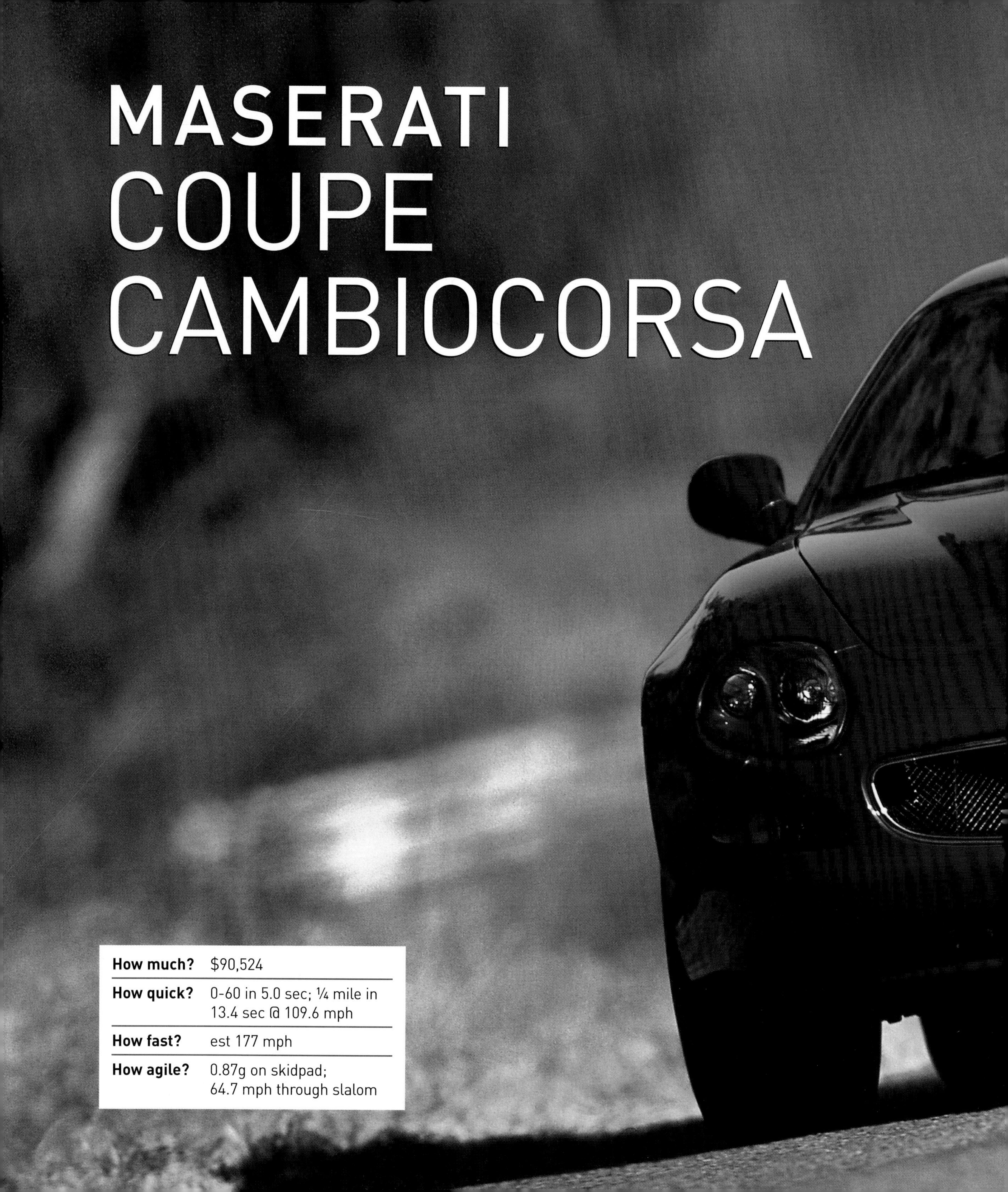

How much?	$90,524
How quick?	0-60 in 5.0 sec; ¼ mile in 13.4 sec @ 109.6 mph
How fast?	est 177 mph
How agile?	0.87g on skidpad; 64.7 mph through slalom

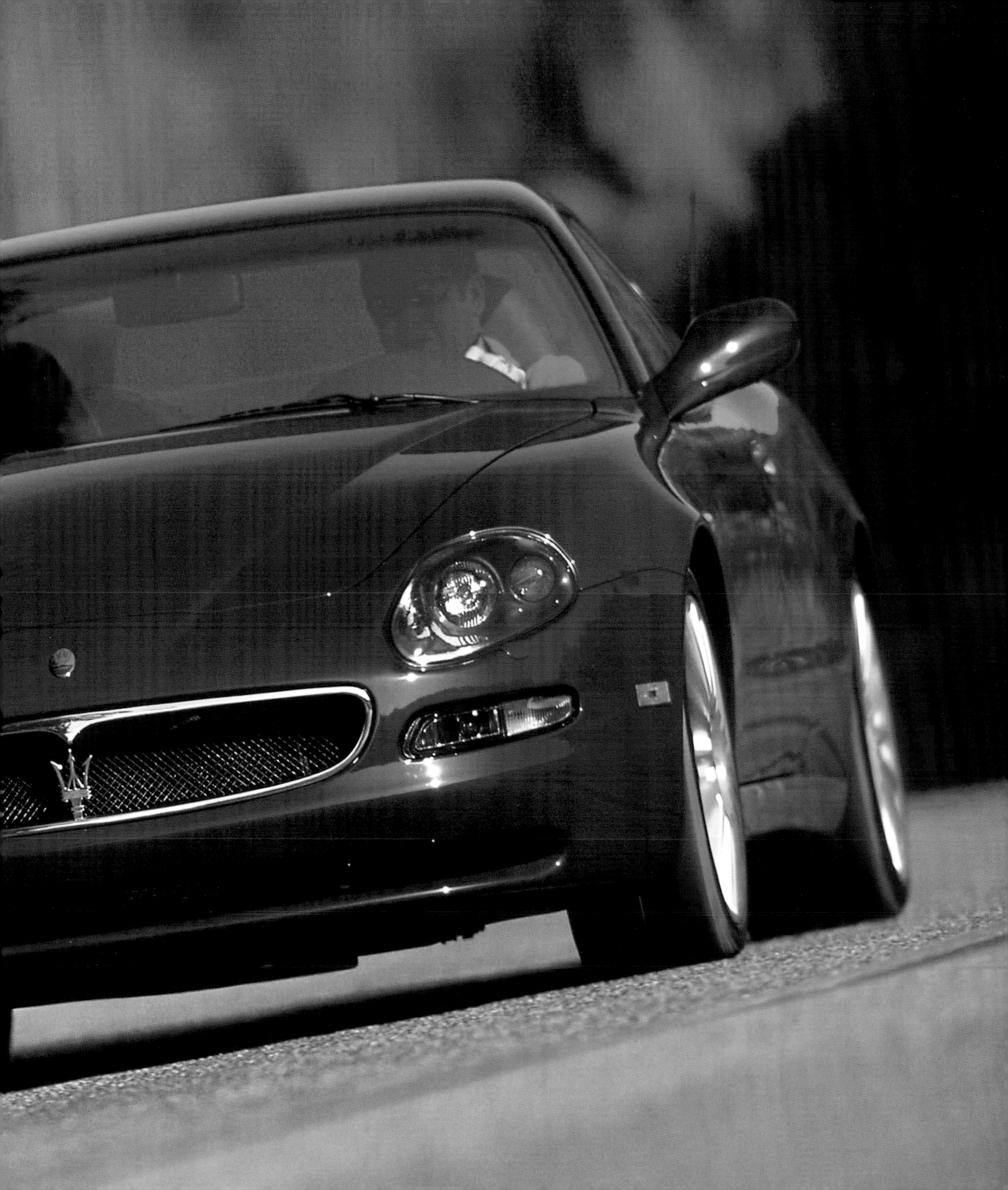

ABOVE: The Italian love of driving comes through unfiltered with Maserati's new Coupe. A rear-mounted transaxle helps optimize weight distribution, and it shows with crisp and balanced handling.

BELOW: The famed Trident logo lives on, revived by Ferrari's purchase of Maserati in 1997.

AN EVERYDAY EXOTIC

OLD RIVALS, HARDENED FROM DECADES OF BATTLE on the racetrack and in the marketplace, laid down their swords when Ferrari purchased Maserati in September of 1997. Profiting from Ferrari's engineering, production and distribution know-how, the revived marque so proudly bearing the trident symbol is thriving once again, offering up the Maserati Coupe as proof. According to Ferrari chairman Luca di Montezemolo, the buyer of an extreme sports car should look toward Ferrari, but if you want the same sort of Italian flair with the balance tilted slightly toward comfort, then a Maserati is the answer. If there's any doubt about the new Coupe's sporting side, one shrieking trip to the redline of its 390-bhp 4.2-liter V-8 should convince you otherwise.

Maserati is more than just a great name; it's a great marque with a storied racing history. Cars bearing Neptune's Trident have won the Mille Miglia, the Targa Florio, the Formula 1 World Championship, even the Indianapolis 500. Twice. And in the 1960s, the lightweight Birdcage Maserati left an indelible mark on the American sports-car racing scene.

In spite of these laurels, the Italian automaker has had a tumultuous history, dealing with, among other things, a succession of different owners. Further, its production cars haven't met with great success here in the U.S. Sure, the Ghibli, Khamsin, Merak and Bora qualified as exotics, but they never matched the stature or desirability of comparable Ferraris. Also, cars such as the large Quattroporte sedan of the early 1980s seemed a bit odd, whereas the Biturbo of the same era proved just plain unreliable. And then came a curious decision to build the TC by Maserati, a rebadged (and not particularly pretty) version of the front-drive Chrysler LeBaron.

But, as they might say in Florence, that's all "acqua" under the Ponte Vecchio now that Ferrari owns Maserati and is intent on making its longtime Modenese rival profitable.

The U.S. comeback, after an 11-year absence, started in 2002 with the Coupe and Spyder, a pair of Giugiaro-penned machines available through Ferrari dealers. Ferrari sees these Maseratis—which are built at the thoroughly modernized Maserati factory in Modena—as comfortable GT cars that aren't quite as extreme in performance, design and character as the steeds from Maranello.

And yes, after spending a couple of weeks with a Coupe fitted with the Cambiocorsa gearbox and optional Skyhook suspension system, we'd have to agree. This car isn't a 360 Modena. Nor is it a 575M. But it is a fine GT, a beautifully understated car that feels Italian not just in its driving position (which has the pedals a tad too close when the reach to the steering wheel is optimized) but also in the mechanical fury of its 4.2-liter V-8 heart, its sumptuous interior and its superb driving manners.

Those manners can be traced in part to the not-so-svelte 3640-lb. Coupe's

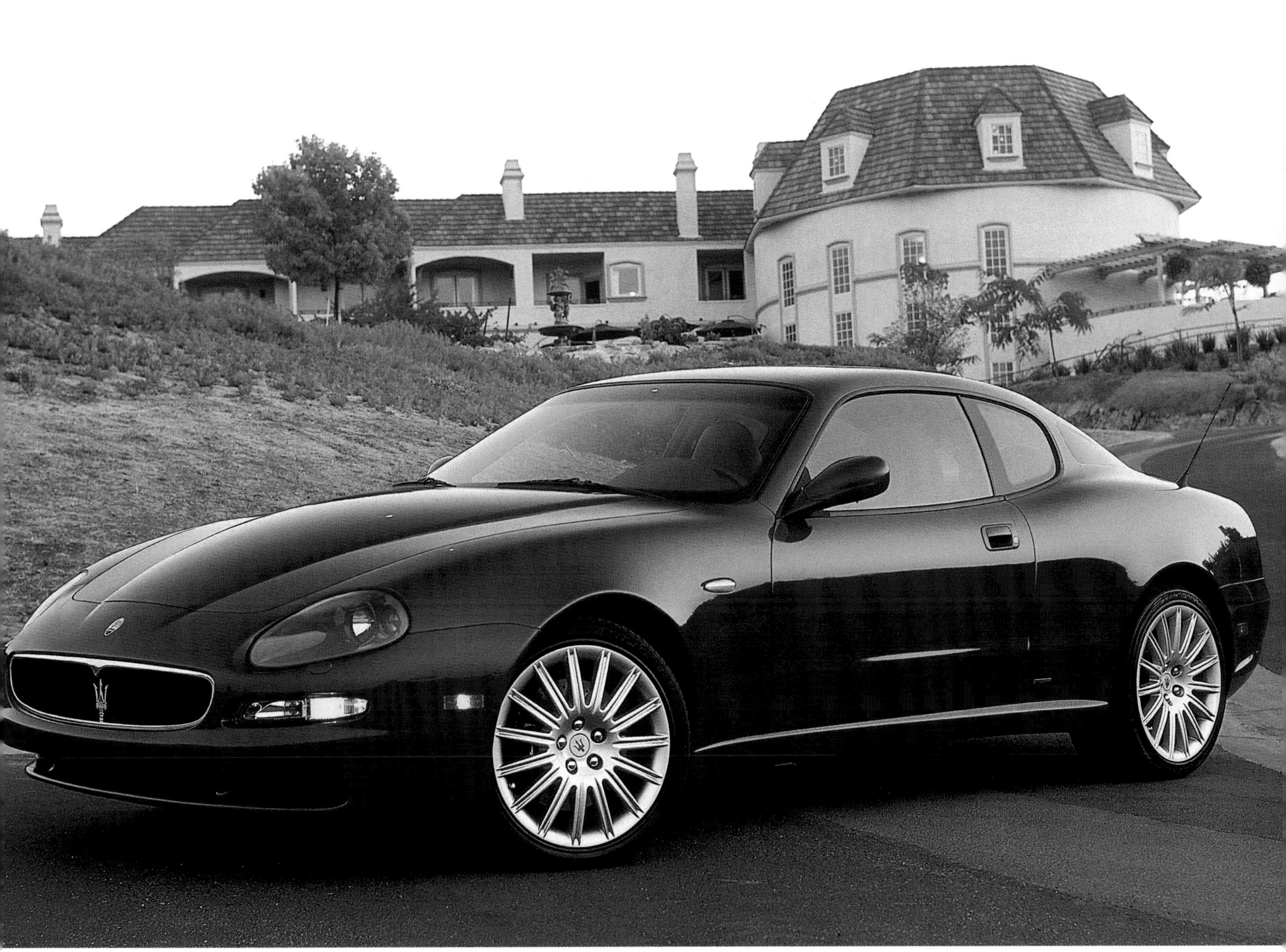

excellent 52/48 weight balance, made possible by having the 6-speed transaxle situated between the rear wheels and the battery in the trunk. Skyhook adjustable suspension damping also plays a role. Although we suspect a Coupe without the $2270 option would still work well, Skyhook does a commendable job of keeping the Coupe's ride relatively comfortable when traveling straight down the Interstate, and then automatically firming the damping when the road gets curvy. Six accelerometers (on the body, the front hubs and on the right rear) monitor the motions of the chassis and suspension and communicate with a computer that makes continuous real-time adjustments to the coil-over shock absorbers at each double-A-arm corner. The Sport mode, accessible via a push-button on the center console, is significantly firmer than the Normal setting, but not so stiff as to prevent body roll in the corners. What's more, the Sport mode provides for a more aggressive Cambiocorsa shift strategy.

The Cambiocorsa system, which shifts the 6-speed transaxle hydraulically via paddles mounted behind the steering wheel, is a mixed bag. On one hand, we love it, because full-throttle upshifts have never been so easy, so quick, so pre-

ABOVE: The Giugiaro-styled Coupe looks especially sweet in this shade of merlot. For a 2+2, it has a usable back seat, with decent head room afforded by its roofline.

cise. It would be great to have in a racing car because there's no danger of ever missing a shift. And the downshifts, particularly in the Sport mode, are accompanied by perfect blips of the throttle that make it sound like we are all better than we really are at heel-and-toeing.

Around town, however, at mild to medium throttle openings, the Cambiocorsa's shifts border on being too clunky, in either the fully automatic or manual modes. With every upshift there's a momentary loss of momentum that's slightly unsettling right in the middle of the shift. Although the driver can minimize this by lifting the throttle at each shift, such tricks shouldn't be necessary in such a fine touring car. Also on a critical note, the hydraulic linkage back at the transaxle makes what one editor called "a chorus of rattling thuds" as the car busily downshifts from one gear to the next while approaching stoplights. Not exactly confidence-inspiring, and it led one mechanically sympathetic editor to eliminate all that downshifting by pulling back on both paddles simultaneously to engage neutral every time he knew the car would be coming to a complete stop. One thing is for sure: The Coupe's vented and cross-drilled disc brakes—Brembos of more than one foot in diameter each—are more than up to the task of stopping the car without the help of engine braking.

In spite of the Cambiocorsa's good traits, and in spite of sales that show the public likes it more than we do, we'd still rather have the 6-speed manual transaxle found in the Coupe GT. The reason is simple: We know it may not be cutting-edge technology, but its shifts are always as smooth as its driver.

With either gear-change system, however, you get the same fantastic engine—a dry-sump 90-degree 4.2-liter V-8 with four chain-driven overhead camshafts and a row of auxiliary pumps on the side of the silicon-rich aluminum block that looks like it's from Ferrari's F1 program.

And you know what? The beautifully exposed engine is in fact from Ferrari, although it is dyno-tested (like all Maserati engines) at Maserati. Benefiting from variable-intake cam timing and a forged crankshaft that rides in an F1-style full saddle of bearings, this screaming V-8 puts out 390 bhp at 7000 rpm, and 333 lb.-ft. of torque at 4500.

This is a fantastic engine, with all the fury you'd expect and an entertaining ability to plant the driver in his seat. Each upshift is accompanied by just a hint of squat, and wheelspin in the first couple of gears is the norm if traction control is switched off. At the same time this engine is smooth and amazingly tractable, able to pull strongly from 2500 rpm in all gears yet still able to rev so quickly and ferociously that we could be fooled into believing it has a featherweight flywheel.

The numbers at the track verify the engine's potency. The Coupe Cambiocorsa, in Sport mode, hits 60 mph in 5.0 seconds, and then reaches the quarter mile in 13.4 sec. at an excellent trap speed of 109.6 mph. These results are not quite up to Maserati's claims, but it's worth mentioning that our test car, with only 1800 miles on its odometer, perhaps needed some more break-in miles.

No matter—this performance still puts the Maserati quicker than an Aston Martin DB7, and on a par with the Porsche 911 and Chevrolet Corvette. And neither of these last two cars can come close to matching the elegant atmosphere found inside this surprisingly spacious Maserati, which accommodates drivers as tall as 6 ft. 4 in.—and back-seat passengers no taller than 5 ft. 4 in.

Once inside, you'll see that leather is everywhere. On the exquisitely stitched seats. On the door panels. On the dash itself. On the steering wheel. And it's most appreciated on the shift paddles themselves, where the suede backing helps keep the driver's fingertips from slipping.

In traditional fashion, Maserati's trademark clock graces the padded leather center console, which in our test car is a monochromatic black that doesn't show the rich texture of the leather the way some lighter colors do. Nevertheless, it's still handsome, with attractive chrome-trimmed Jaeger gauges looming beneath a prominent leather-covered instrument hood. Most of the controls are straightforward and where you'd expect them to be, and we found it refreshing to see a steering wheel devoid of controls for the radio and the like.

None of us, however, was particularly fond of the Maserati Info Centre, which condenses the controls for the climate control, stereo, trip computer and navigation system into one simple screen but doesn't seem to facilitate the operation of any of those systems. On a positive note, the CD slot located between the seats is very convenient.

On the road, the Maserati is a fabulous Grand Tourer that effectively blends the stability and substance of—let's face it—a heavier car with manners more befitting a lighter sports car. It also doesn't need to be babied. It can go up driveways without scraping its nose; it can idle in stop-and-go traffic without overheating; its climate control works like a charm and there's nothing the least bit finicky about the car's operation. Although the low-profile Michelin Pilots do thump a bit over Botts dots and other sharp bumps, the Coupe has a well-damped suppleness to its suspension that's readily apparent when crossing dips at intersections.

Timeless and understated, the Maserati Coupe is an everyday exotic, an Italian DB7 for two-thirds the price. It's attractive, not flashy. And let it be known that we'd rather have our Coupe as a GT, the model with the 6-speed manual gearbox in place of the automatic shifting of the Coupe Cambiocorsa.

Let it also be known that the Maserati Coupe has proven itself on the racetracks of Europe. Race-prepped versions of the car, called the Trofeo, now compete in a single-marque championship that visits many Formula 1 tracks. Emanuele Smurra captured the inaugural championship, winning five races in 2003. The Roman, like the throng of Maserati enthusiasts worldwide, must be delighted to see the Trident competing again in the sport that is such an important part of its heritage.

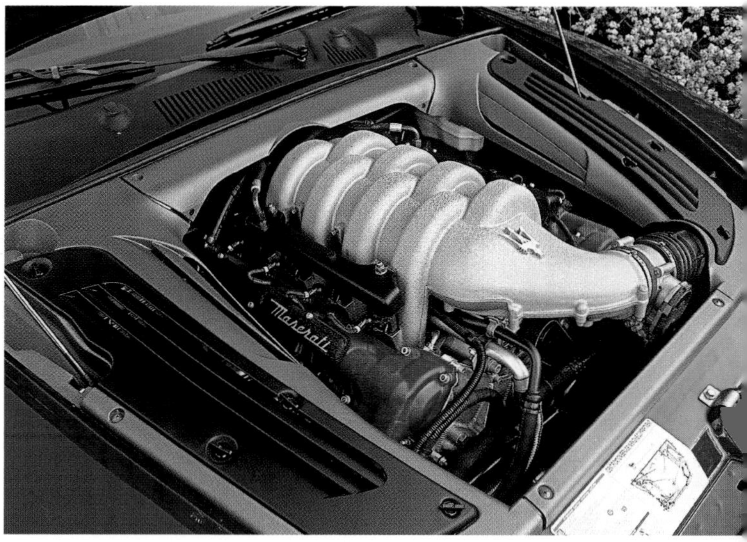

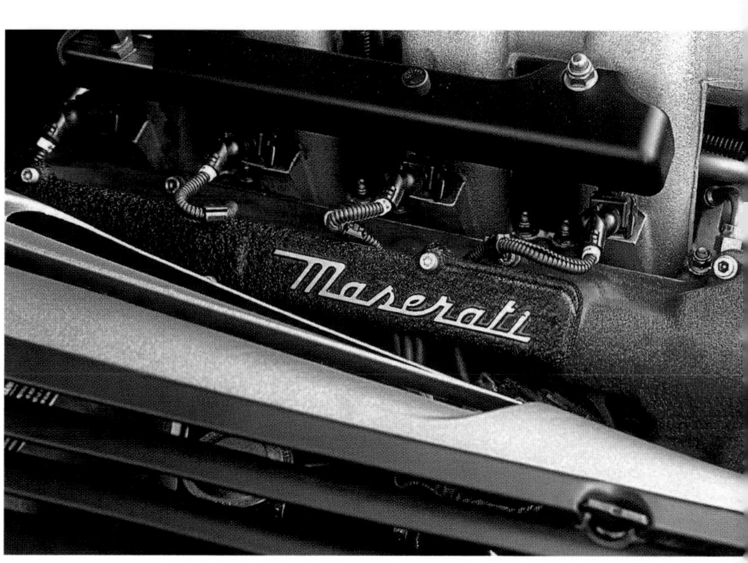
Maserati

ABOVE: The only things better than the 4.2-liter V-8's appearance—with lovely castings and wrinkle-finish paint—are its high-strung metallic sound and its easily summoned 390 bhp.

OPPOSITE: The Coupe's interior, with its dramatic double-arched dash, is Italian style at its finest, set off with leatherwork enhanced by contrasting piping. Note the Cambiocorsa system's gearchange paddles behind the steering wheel.

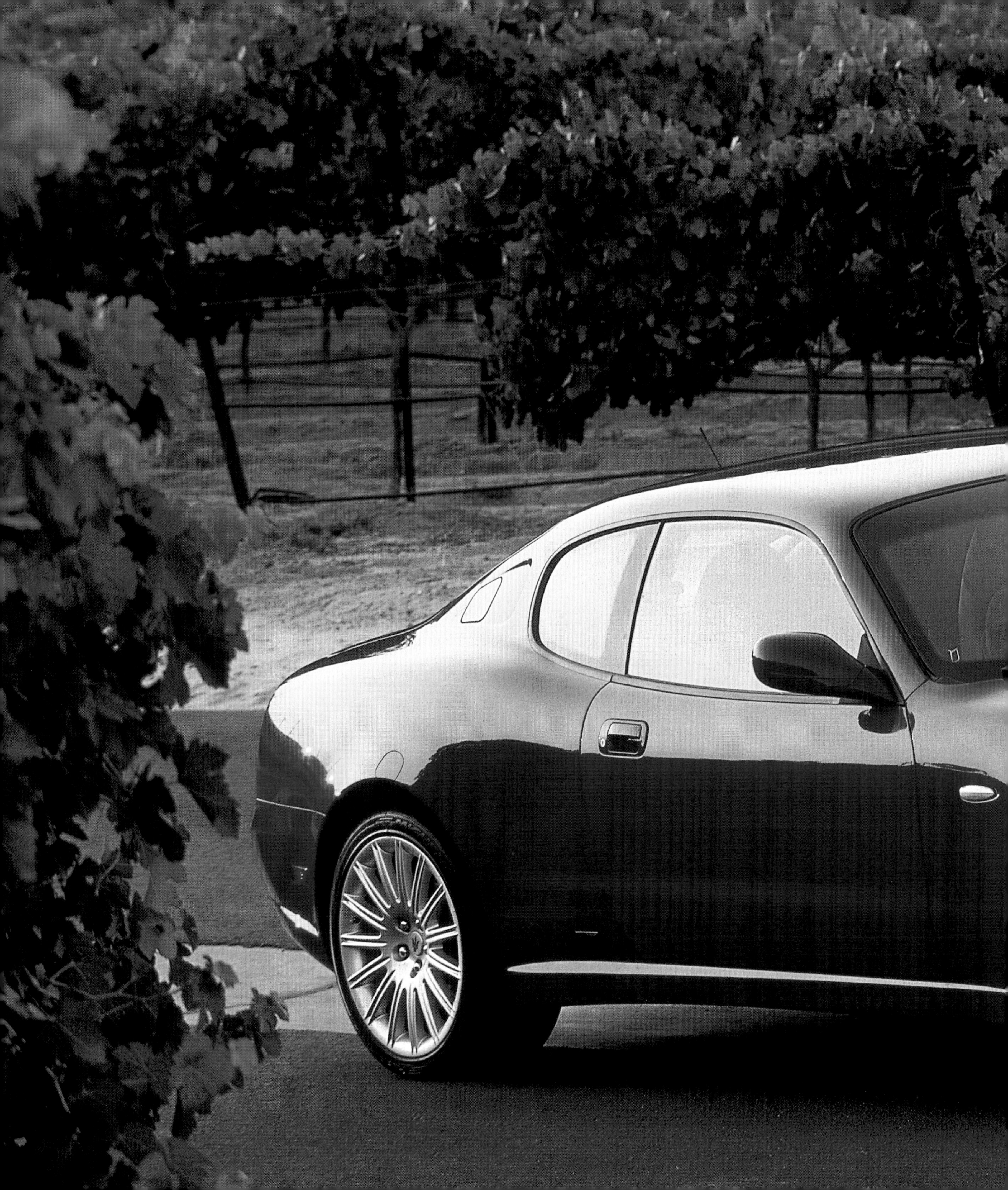

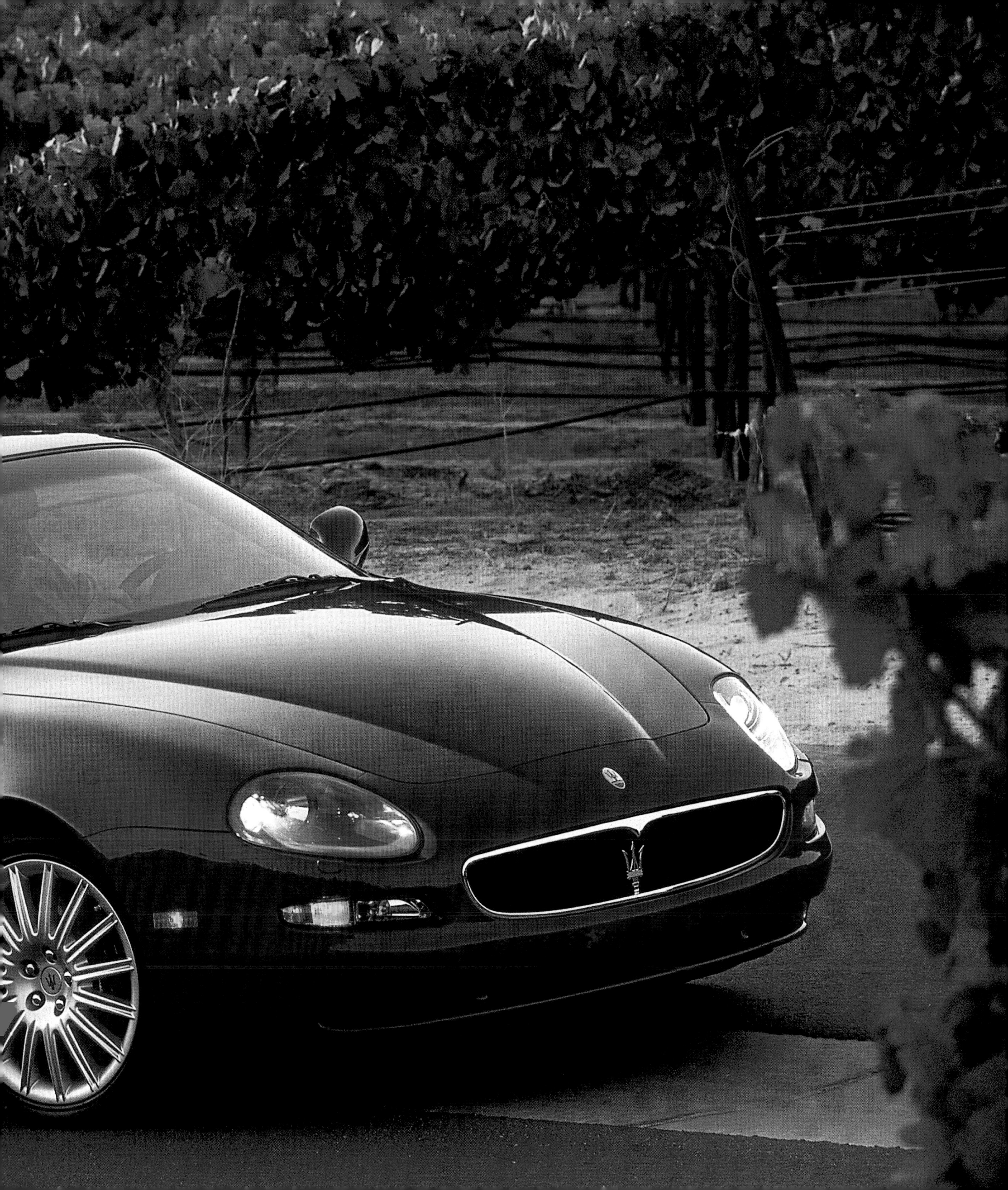

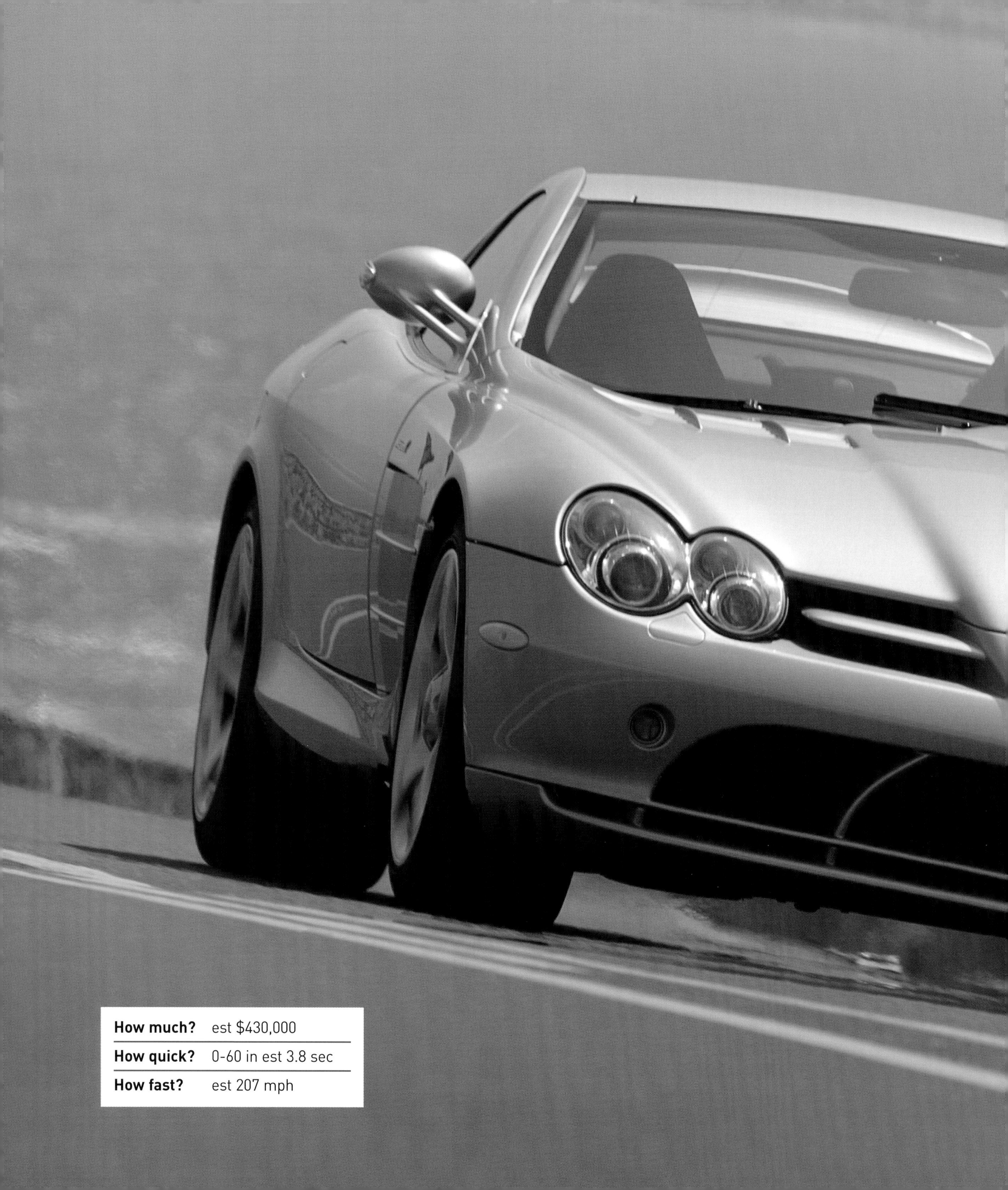

How much?	est $430,000
How quick?	0-60 in est 3.8 sec
How fast?	est 207 mph

MERCEDES-BENZ SLR McLAREN

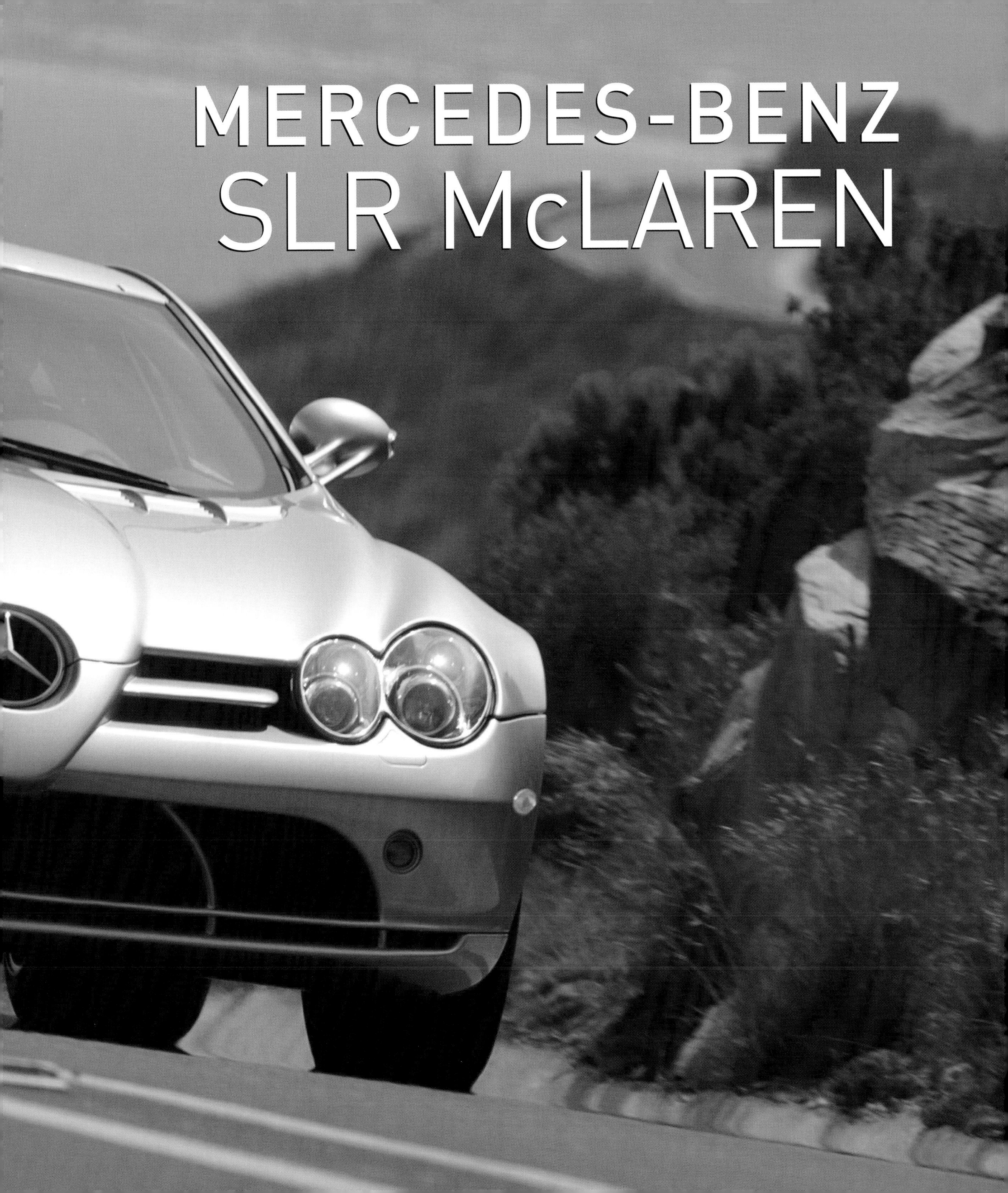

ABOVE: The words "Mercedes-Benz" and "exotic" don't necessarily roll off the tongue in one smooth elocution, but that's exactly what the SLR McLaren is. Gordon Murray of McLaren Formula 1 fame helped make it all possible.

BELOW: Short of an out-and-out competition car, the Mercedes emblem has never had so speedy a mount.

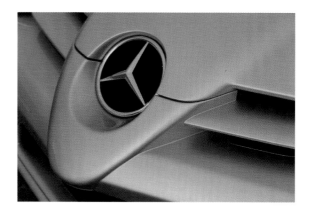

SUPERCAR WITH THE THREE-POINTED STAR

TO ANYONE FAMILIAR WITH THAT MEMORABLE PHOTO of Stirling Moss and Denis Jenkinson, their grime-coated goggle-faces beaming after winning the 1955 Mille Miglia, the legendary Mercedes-Benz 300SLR needs no introduction. Mercedes hopes to achieve that level of fame with its supercar homage to that Italian race winner—the SLR McLaren. Performance is the common denominator here, with 617 bhp generated by a supercharged 5.4-liter V-8 whose exhaust empties out aft of the front wheels, just like the original. But the new machine employs materials only dreamed of in the Eisenhower era, such as carbon fiber for its main structural cocoon. McLaren, which builds the car for Mercedes, is all too familiar with the material whose use it pioneered in Formula 1 cars.

How about a drive in Mercedes-Benz' carbon-fiber wonder, the SLR?

It's an easy step into the SLR before you settle into the carbon-fiber-shell driver's seat. Reach up and pull down the lightweight swing-up door, which snaps snugly shut.

Inside, the SLR is a tasty mélange of leather and aluminum with a hint of carbon fiber. If you know Mercedes you know some of the gauges, a bit of familiarity in a display nicely done that fits the mood and character of the SLR—most notably its prominent speedometer and tach. With Mercedes' penchant for safety, it's not surprising that six airbags are hidden but strategically placed around the interior. The seats are comfortable, with numerous replaceable pads and bolsters adapting it to various occupants' sizes.

Ignition on, you thumb up a little flap on the top of the SLR's shift lever, rather like knocking the "safe" cover off a trigger button. Press down on this button and the supercharged V-8 starts its rumble dance, 5.4 liters of V-8 supercharged and intercooled to 617 bhp and 575 lb.-ft. of torque, and sounding wonderfully threatening.

Twisting a dashboard rotary switch calls up any of three modes for the 5-speed automatic transmission: Comfort, Sport or Manual, the last with steering-wheel-mounted shift switches and three of its own shift programs: Sport, SuperSport and Race. We'll bet that if you just dial up Comfort, you'll get a thrill...we did.

Drag the shift lever to "D," point the car's long nose down the road and stomp. There's just a bit of tire squeal before traction control takes over—an amber warning light winking at you—and both wide rear tires dig in.

By Mercedes' numbers, you'd be at 60 mph in 3.8 seconds and as small as those digits might be, you get there with surprisingly little drama...great fun, but no need to hang on for dear life. With enough road and decent pavement, it's said you could get to 207 mph with the SLR, and we can attest to an easy-as-pie 120-plus.

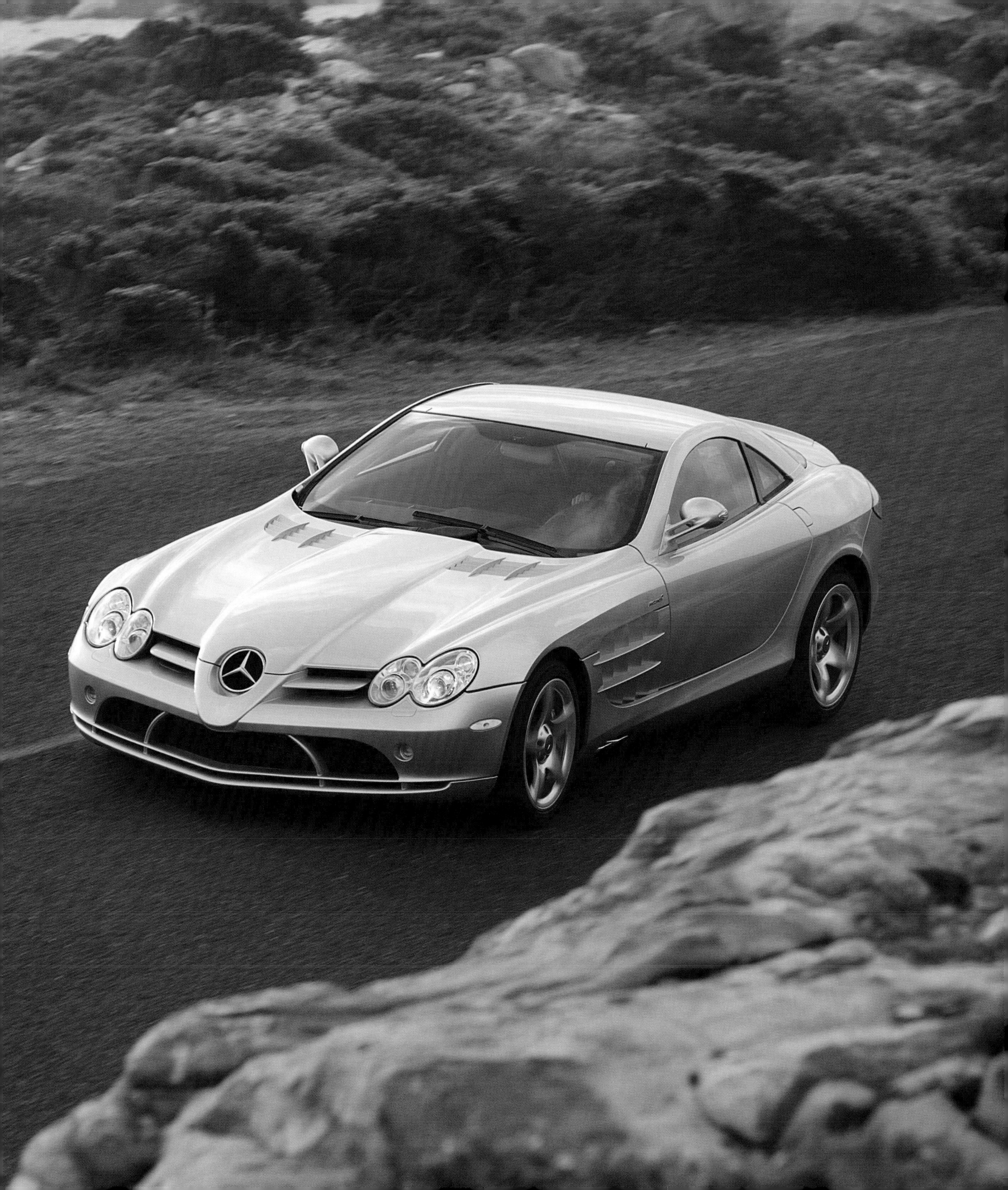

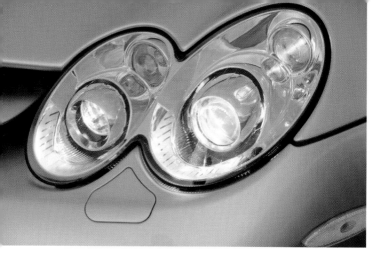

ABOVE: The peanut-shaped headlight clusters and wedgy Mercedes taillights are recognizable and, if you're a student of Mercedes racing history, so is the rear spoiler, **BELOW**. It can extend to an angle of 62 degrees under deceleration to serve as an air brake.

OPPOSITE: In an ode to the racing 300SLR of the mid-1950s, the new version also packages its exhaust directly behind the front wheels—no mean feat when dealing with modern noise restrictions, catalytic converters...and 617 bhp!

When the road strays from the straight and narrow, the SLR is just as accommodating, turning-in easily with an effort that belies the car's size and yet feels appropriate for its potential. It sounds odd to give a car human traits, but you feel a sense of confidence from the SLR.

The hardware? Cast aluminum upper and lower A-arm suspensions at both ends with gas shocks, coil springs and, up front, an anti-roll bar. Unsprung weight is kept to a minimum thanks to aluminum stub axles and wheels, plus—as on the Ferrari Enzo—hyper-expensive carbon-fiber/ceramic disc brakes. The rack-and-pinion steering has speed-sensitive assist, and while 19-in. wheels and tires (255/35ZR-19 front, 295/30ZR-19 rear) are standard, 18s (245/40ZR-18 and 295/35ZR-18) are a no-cost option. Standard on all SLRs is a tire pressure monitoring system.

Naturally, all the modern saviors are onboard, namely ESP electronic yaw control and electronic brake control, which mitigates the old dangers of dabbing the binders while cornering.

As the roads get twistier, or as city streets narrow, you get a sense of the SLR's size. At 183.3 in. long, 75.1 in. wide and 49.6 in. tall, the SLR is 4.8 in. longer, 3.2 in. wider and 1.5 in. lower than Mercedes' SL. Yet with a curb weight of about 3735 lb., it's roughly 310 lb. lighter. So the SLR is not a petite automobile and the seats slot you rather low in the car, a position that exaggerates the width and nose length. While you are aware of the Mercedes' size, it never feels too big.

At some point you'll need to slow the SLR and when you first try the exotic brakes, there is what feels like a slight hesitation before they begin to dramatically haul down the car. Nail the brakes hard and the deceleration moves you forward into your belts. If you were at 60 mph or more, you might notice movement in the rearview mirror. That would be the rear spoiler jumping to 62 degrees out back, its air brake angle providing as much as 300-plus lb. of added downforce. It's one of three deployment positions it can assume.

Normal fast driving will pop the spoiler up to a 10-degree driving stance, or you can manually set the angle of attack to 30 degrees for still more downforce. Incidentally, for all the force the spoiler must take at speed, it is finger safe when folding and will pop back up if it senses an obstruction.

That spoiler is just part of the SLR's aerodynamic package, which begins with a coefficient of drag of 0.37 and, thanks to the spoilers integrated into the Formula 1-emulating nose plus that active rear pop-up, provides significant downforce when needed. Included in the aero design is a flat underside for the SLR, broken up only by NACA ducts to cool the rear brakes and diff cooler, plus louvers that aid cooling the side-mounted engine exhaust system.

To help keep that underside smooth as a good skipping stone, Mercedes doesn't route the exhaust out back, but packs the catalytic converters and mufflers at the V-8's sides. This configuration is unique and offers a nice tie to the 1955 SLR, but made cooling the package tough—hence the big gills on the SLR's sides and chimneys that vent heated air up (and at some speeds down) and out. Just below the gills—and another link to the original SLR—exhaust pipes poke out from the sills.

The source of the SLR's heat and thunder is a sohc aluminum 90-degree

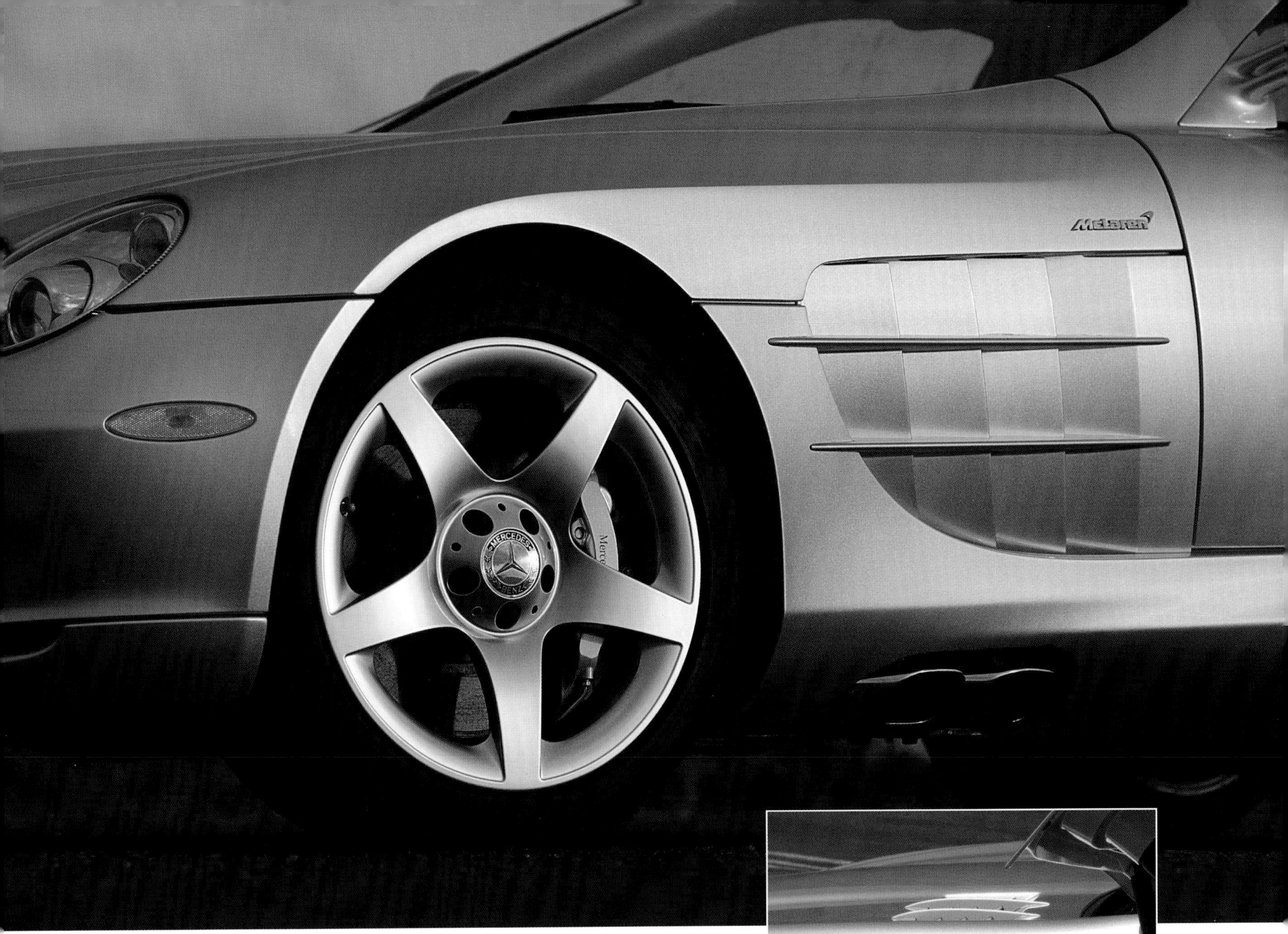

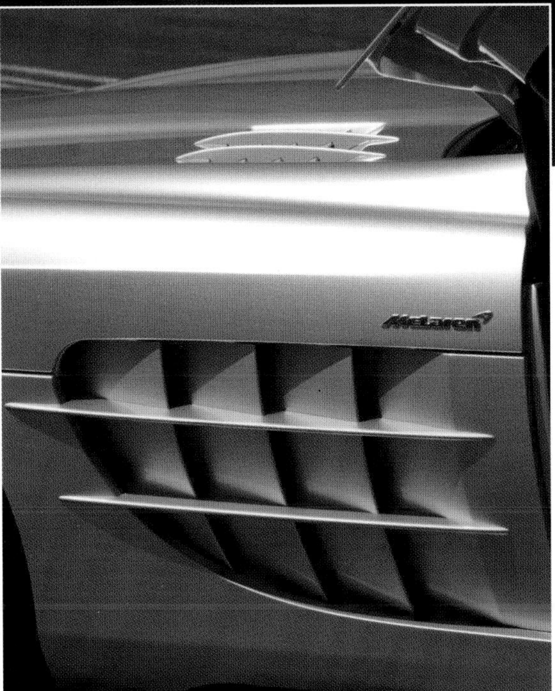

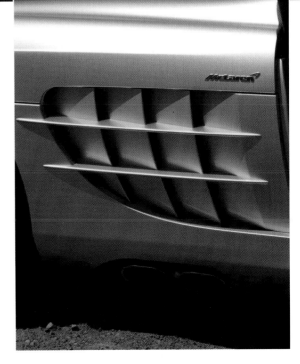

V-8 hand-built by AMG, fitted with a plaque displaying the engine builder's name, then shipped to England to be installed in the SLR in a factory McLaren built with Mercedes.

The V-8 has a dry sump so it sits low in the SLR, and is topped by a Lysholm-style screw-type supercharger settled between its banks. Spinning at up to 23,000 rpm, the blower huffs as much as 13 psi of charge through one water-cooled intercooler per bank and past each cylinder's two intake valves to be ignited by twin sparkplugs. The result? Come 6500 rpm the horsepower peaks at 617, while torque passes the 440-lb.-ft. mark by 1500 rpm, leveling off at 575 between 3250 and 5000 rpm.

This doesn't happen in silence. Off the line, the aural feedback is of a whopping great V-8, guttural stuff that reminds one more of—dare we say this?—a Hemi Cuda than a vintage 300SLR, more the Chrysler than the Daimler side of the heritage. When you're cruising with windows up and nail the gas, the prominent-but-not-excessive exhaust note is accompanied by a distant supercharger whine, like a vintage Mercedes SSK on the blower 30 feet

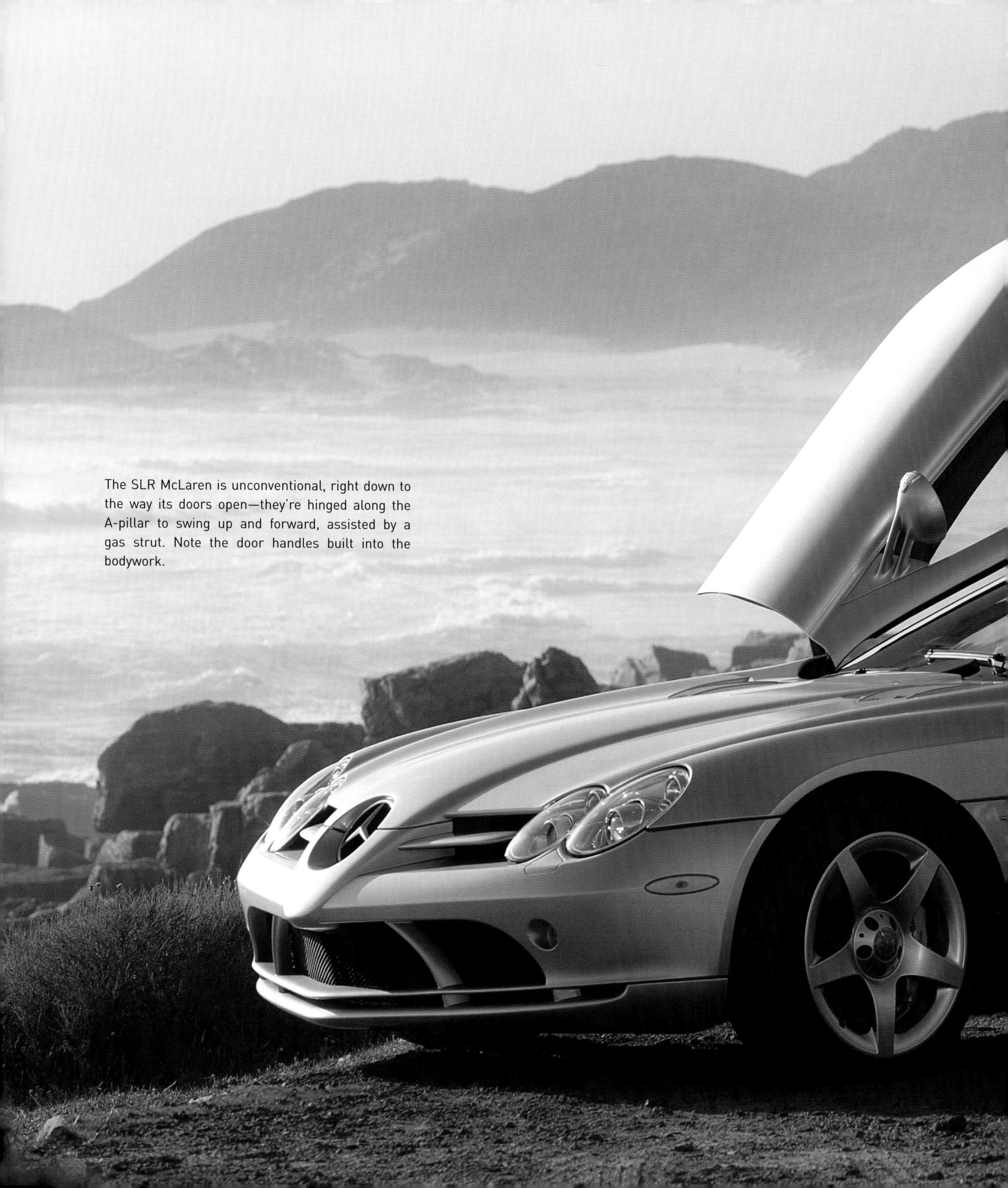

The SLR McLaren is unconventional, right down to the way its doors open—they're hinged along the A-pillar to swing up and forward, assisted by a gas strut. Note the door handles built into the bodywork.

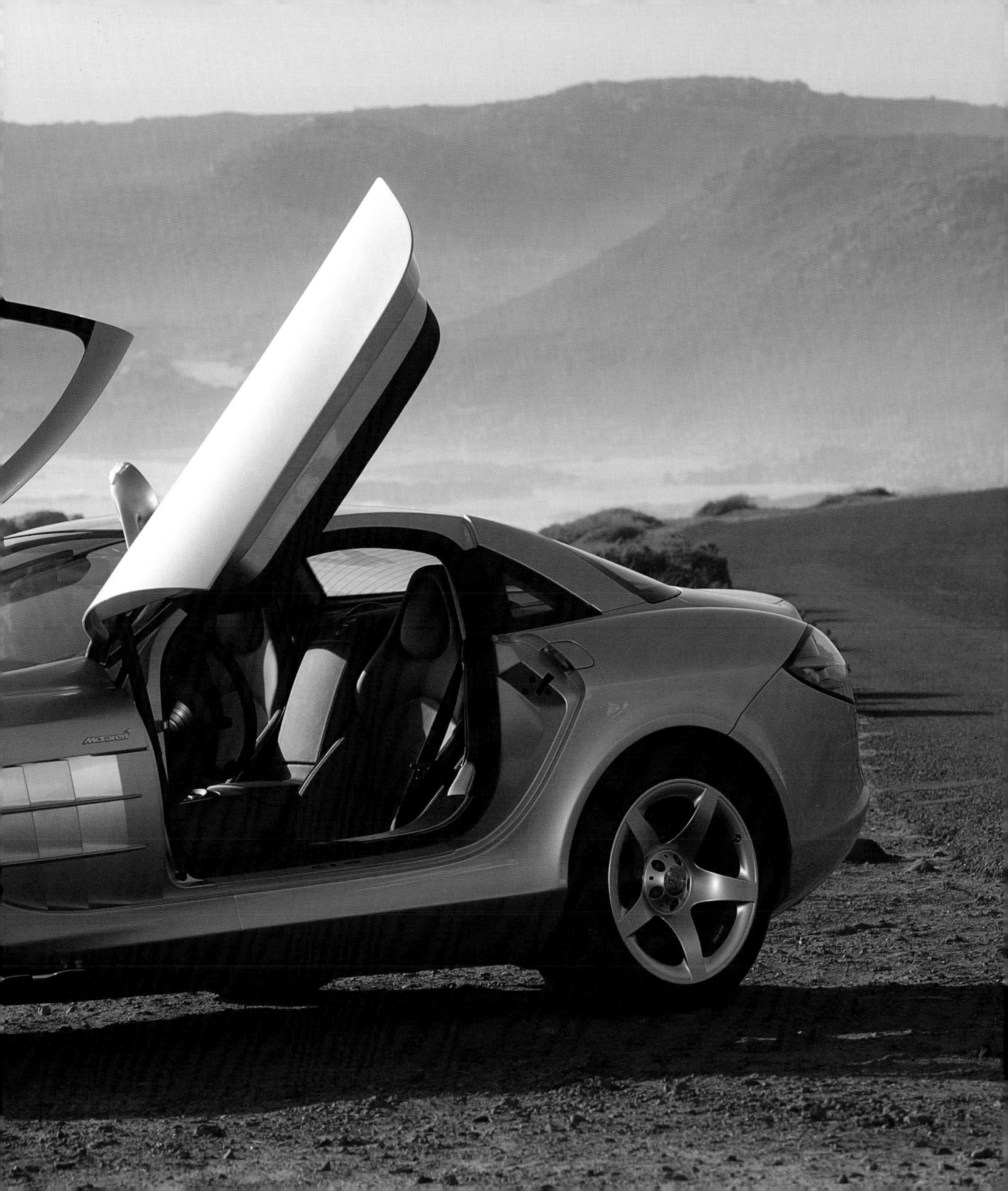

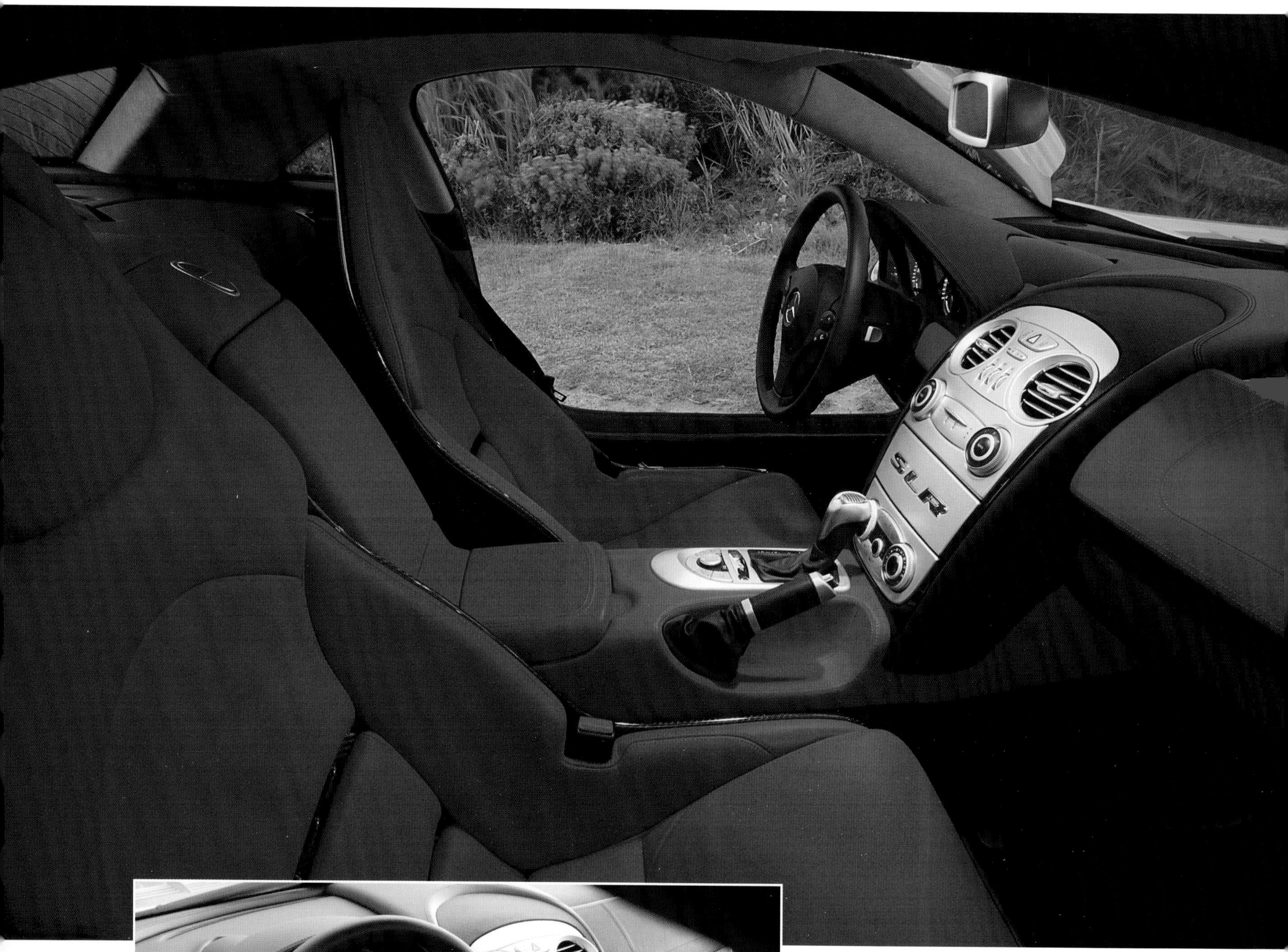
SLR

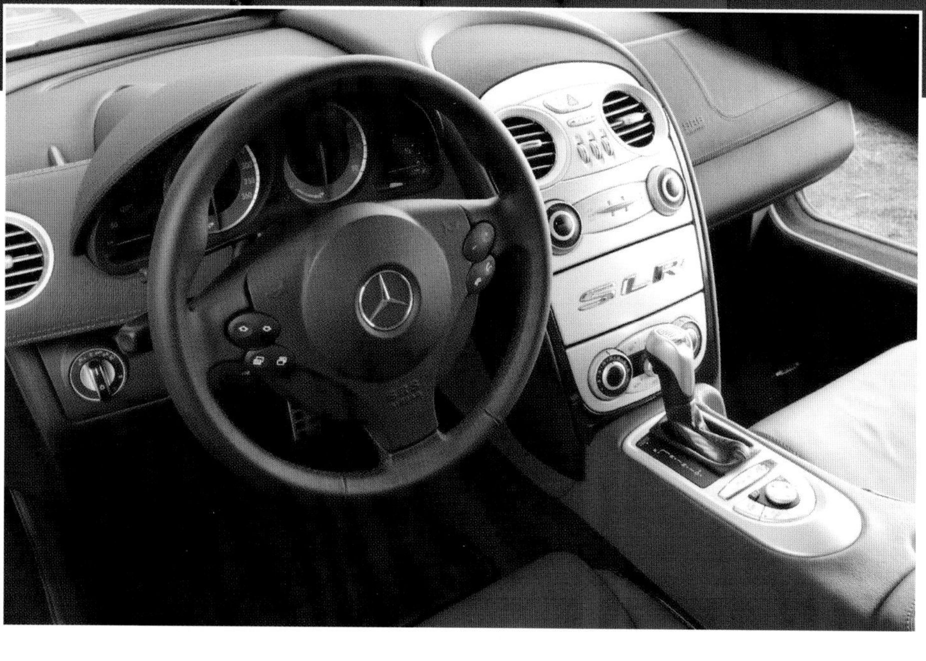
SLR

ABOVE: Familiar Mercedes design elements are intact inside, just exaggerated slightly for effect. Seats are thin carbon-fiber shells, lightly upholstered with leather, and the 3-spoke steering wheel is especially thick-rimmed.

OPPOSITE, FROM TOP: Deeply hooded dials are readable and to the point; center-stack controls are elegantly silver-trimmed and straightforward; sill incorporates seat controls, release for door.

off your bow. Lower your side window and do the same, particularly if you are alongside a rock wall or guardrail, and the echo bouncing back is of a huge, muffled 4-cylinder engine that loudly "pfuffs" at you.

Those cooling gills, a major element of the SLR's design, tend to attract attention. They're undeniably exciting and certainly make a statement, but are also controversial. The objective was to combine two important elements of the automaker's racing character, one being its current Formula 1 involvement with the SLR's maker McLaren, which explains the nose design. The other is Mercedes' racing history, specifically the 300SLRs, more specifically still the sole hardtop gullwing SLR named the Uhlenhaut coupe for the racing department's legendary engineer, Rudolf Uhlenhaut.

From some angles, the new SLR seems an entertaining rendering of classic long hood, personal cockpit, short deck proportions, but from other views several design elements seem an exaggeration, a bit bigger (too much bigger?) than life.

All you've read about thus far—design, engine, performance, driving experience—is about 60 percent of the SLR story. Tucked inside the shape is a technical tour de force, a great deal of it from the famed Formula 1 team of Gordon Murray and McLaren in England.

Much of the story revolves around the body, which is mainly carbon fiber, and how it is constructed in a way that minimizes the use of autoclaves, paving the way to more logical use of the strong, lightweight material in future production. Ninety-five percent of the SLR's major parts are made of various forms of carbon fiber, with more than 50 of the carbon-fiber and fiberglass pieces produced by McLaren, where both the floor assembly and the roof frame "spider" are formed in one piece.

Strip the SLR of its drivetrain, chassis parts, interior, glass and hood, and what you see is the heart of the SLR made up of three major components. At the back is the main body structure, a black cocoon for the passengers and trunk. Ahead of that in dull silver is a cast aluminum engine bay subframe, which also mounts the front suspension. At the very front is more black carbon fiber that is the first use of this material in a production car's crash structure, with lessons learned from McLaren's F1 experience.

This highly effective crash assembly is based on a pair of lightweight, 7.5-lb. cone-shaped pieces that point forward and crumple in an accident as they absorb impact in a consistent and predictable manner. These pieces are the first-ever carbon-fiber components for an automobile that are created in an automated system—woven, sewn, then transformed in a small mold—not laboriously made by hand.

Thanks to such innovative uses of carbon fiber, the SLR weighs in at some 30 percent less than an equivalent automobile made in the traditional manner with steel.

None of this comes cheaply, which is the reason the SLR wears a $400,000-plus price tag. At that, its cost is right up there with Porsche's Carrera GT, another major user of carbon fiber, though the Porsche is a mid-engine design with a rather different character than the SLR.

Compared with other limited-production cars like the Carrera GT or

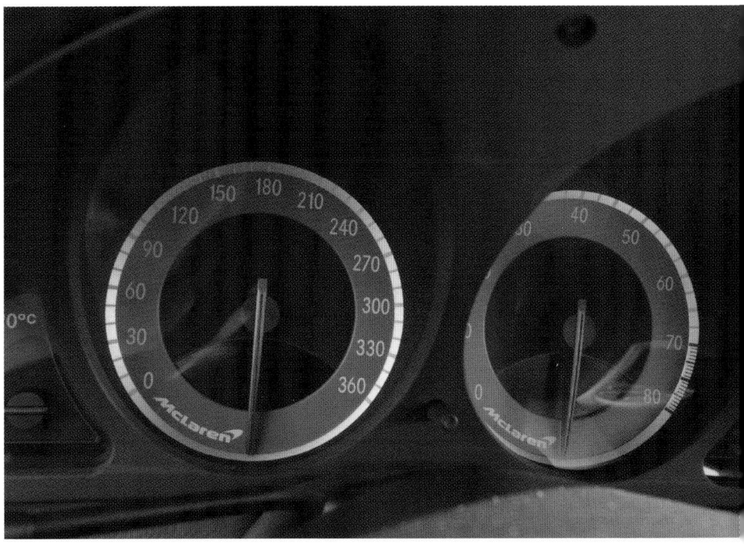
0 30 60 90 120 150 180 210 240 270 300 330 360
McLaren
0 40 50 60 70 80
McLaren

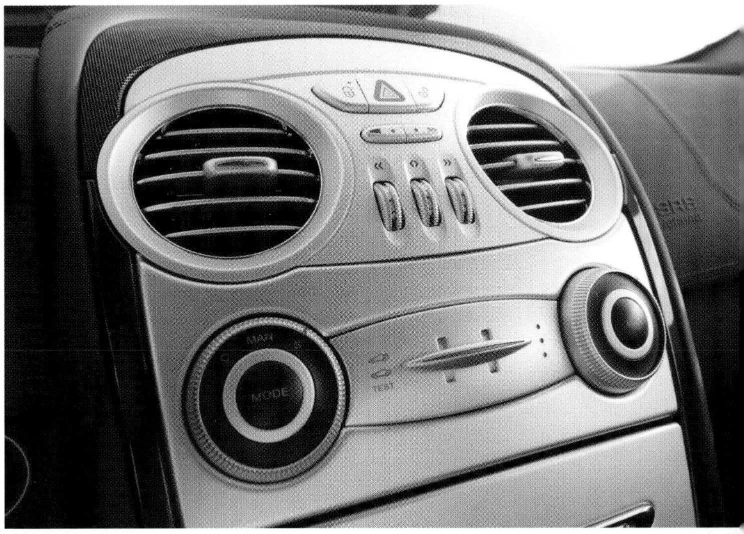
MAN
MODE
TEST

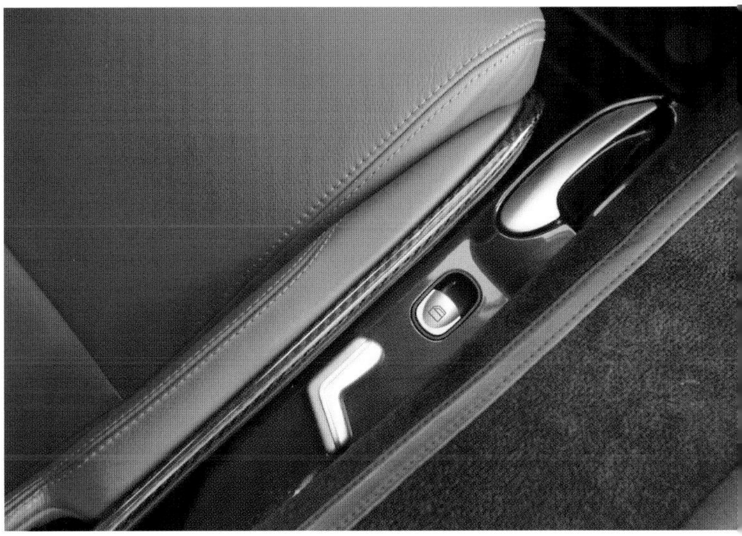

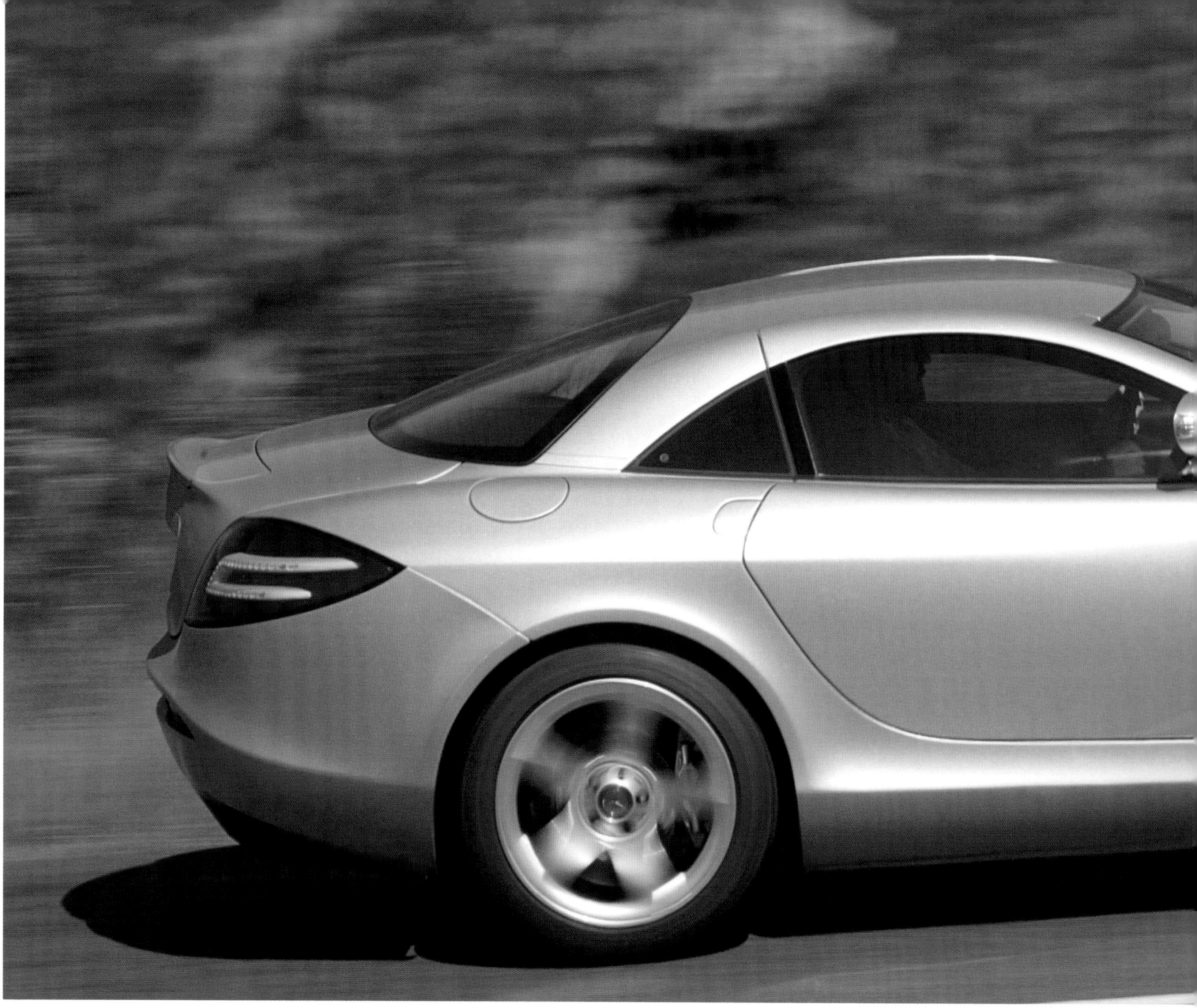

ABOVE: In profile, the SLR McLaren's long, tapered snout and rearward-pushed cockpit are evident, an effective form to punch a 207-mph hole in the air; head-on, its nose is meant to evoke the look of the McLaren-Mercedes Formula 1 car.

OPPOSITE: The SLR's mighty 5.4-liter V-8 sits low in the car, thanks to dry-sump lubrication, and pumps out an astonishing 617 bhp with help from a Lysholm screw-type supercharger.

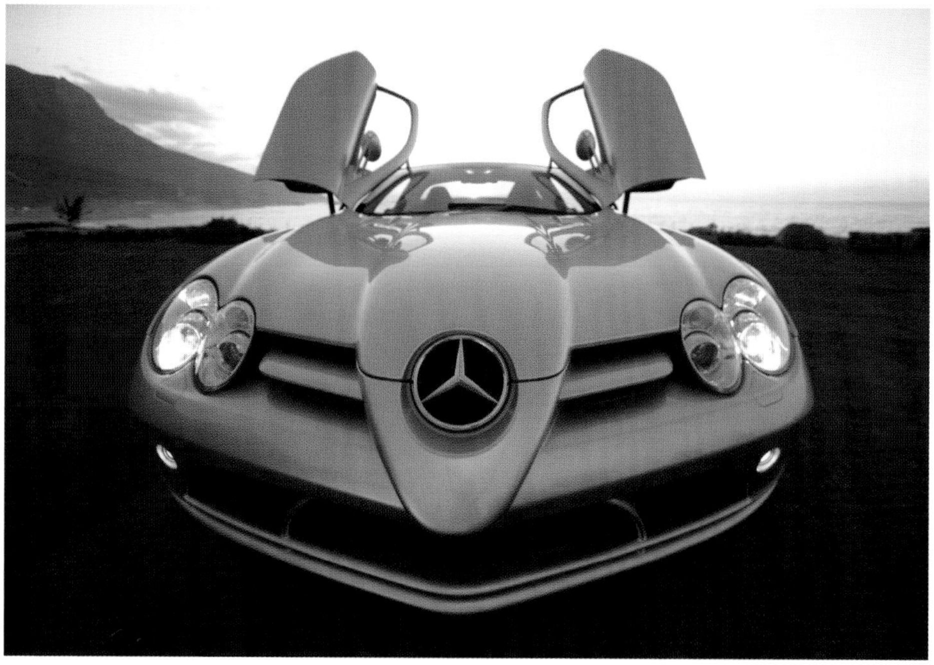

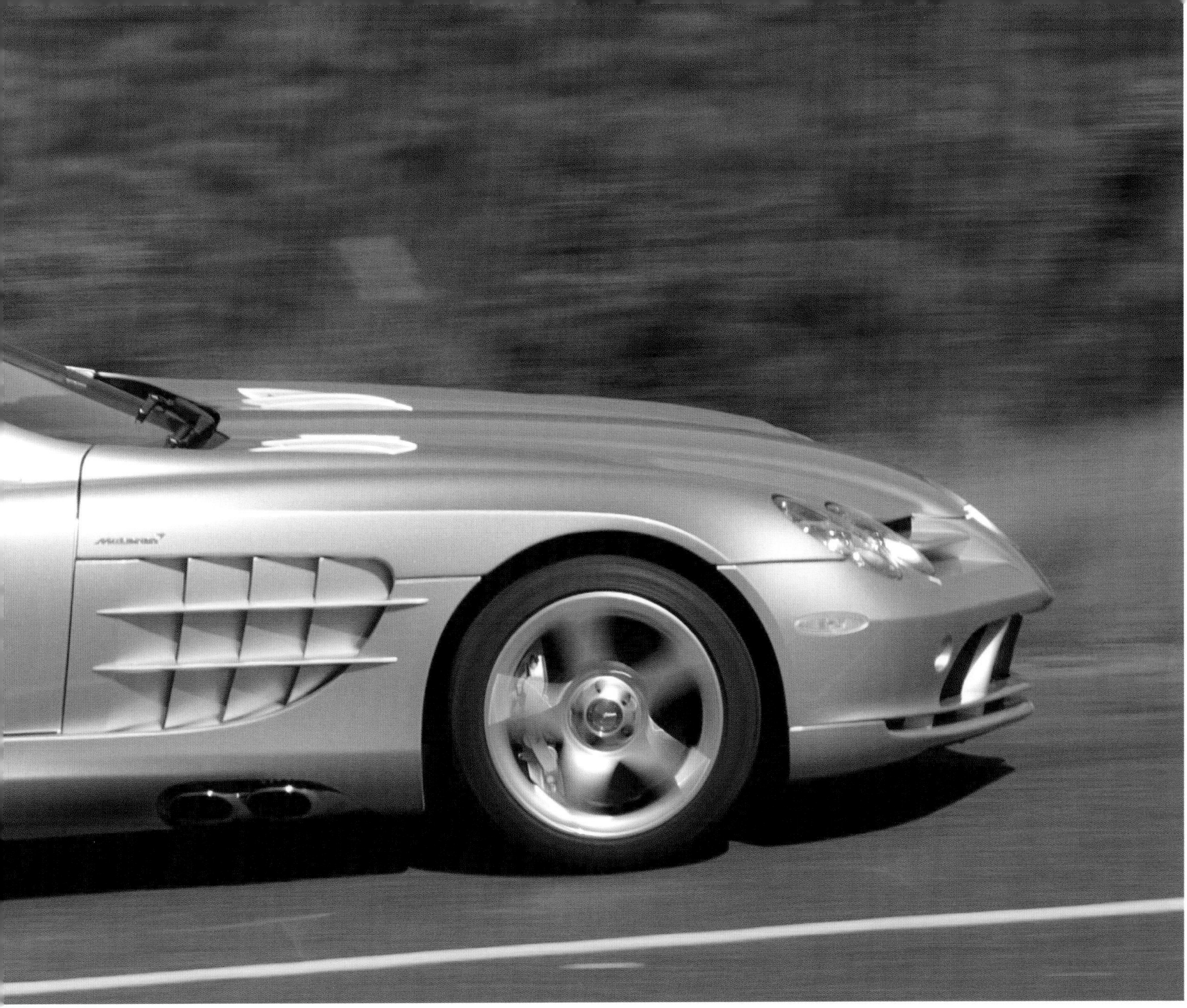

Ferrari Enzo, Mercedes figures the SLR has longer legs. The automaker will build 500 annually for the next seven years, so young entrepreneurs reading this right now still have time to grow their businesses quickly enough to afford one before the last SLR slides off the assembly line.

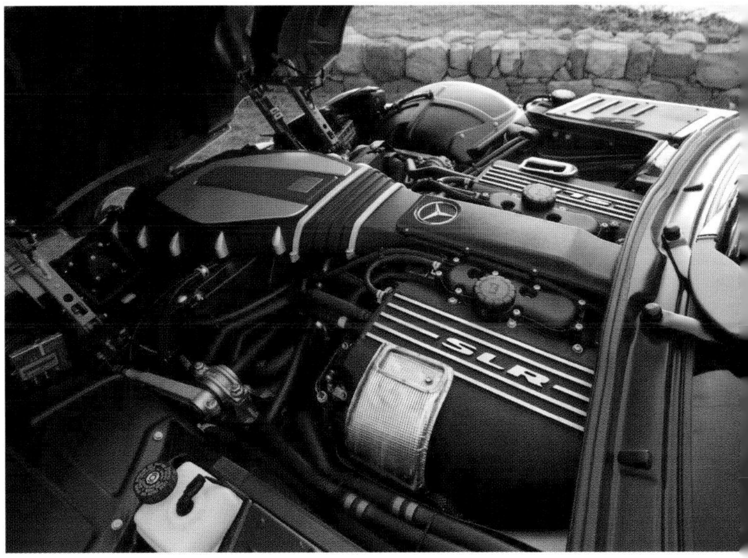

Will the SLR evolve during those model years? While the first two years of production had solid orders before SLR No. 1 was made, how much the Mercedes changes over the years might depend on its long-term reception in the marketplace.

While the first SLRs will only be offered with a silver or black exterior, the company will eventually widen that palette. There will also be an extensive customizing program à la Maybach that will allow SLR buyers such options as custom leather for the interior. And we hear the supercharged V-8 is good for several hundred more horsepower, though it's uncertain what the point would be, given the SLR's current performance, which is already breathtaking.

Remember, ignition on, thumb up the little flap...push down on the button...

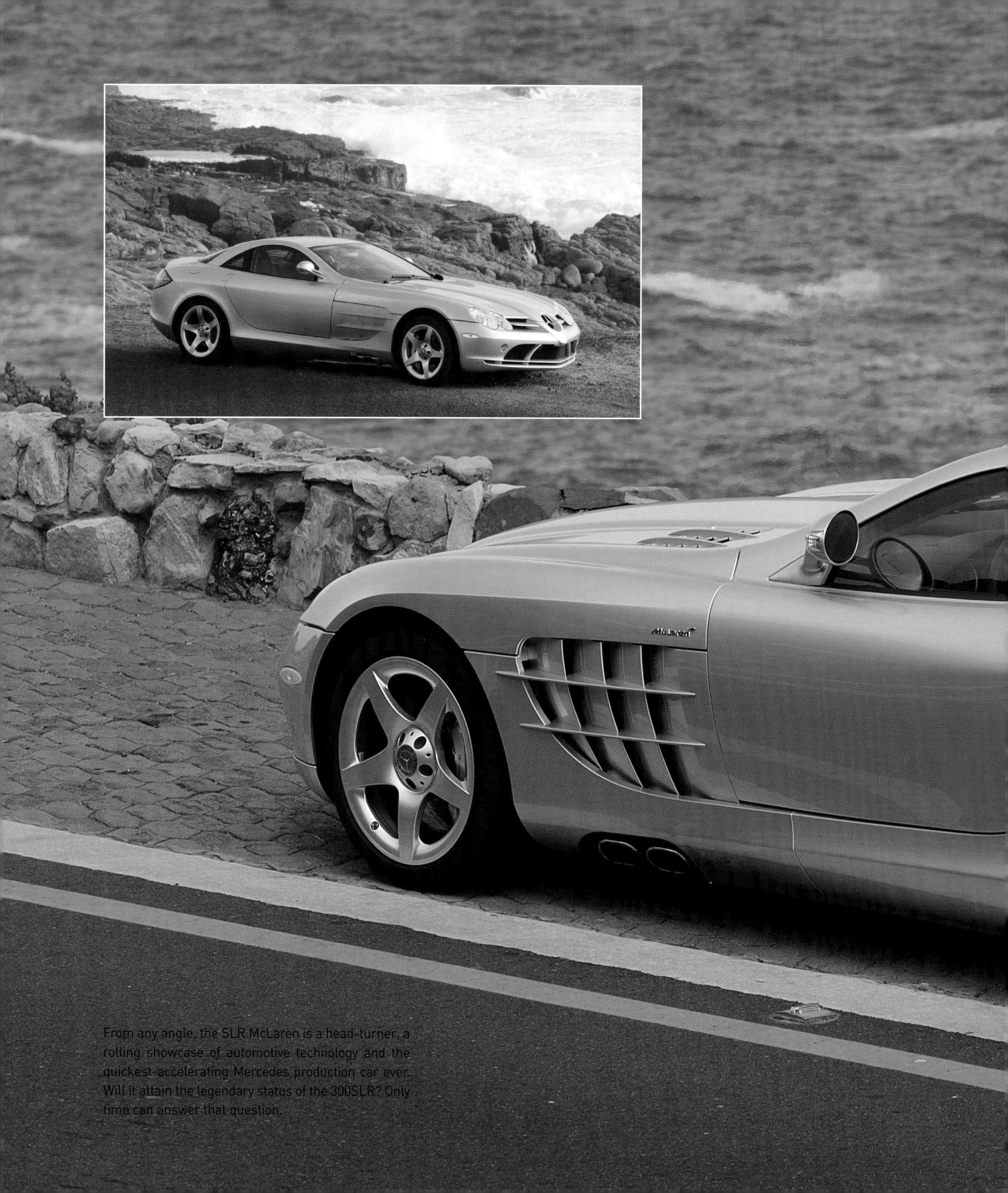

From any angle, the SLR McLaren is a head-turner, a rolling showcase of automotive technology and the quickest-accelerating Mercedes production car ever. Will it attain the legendary status of the 300SLR? Only time can answer that question.

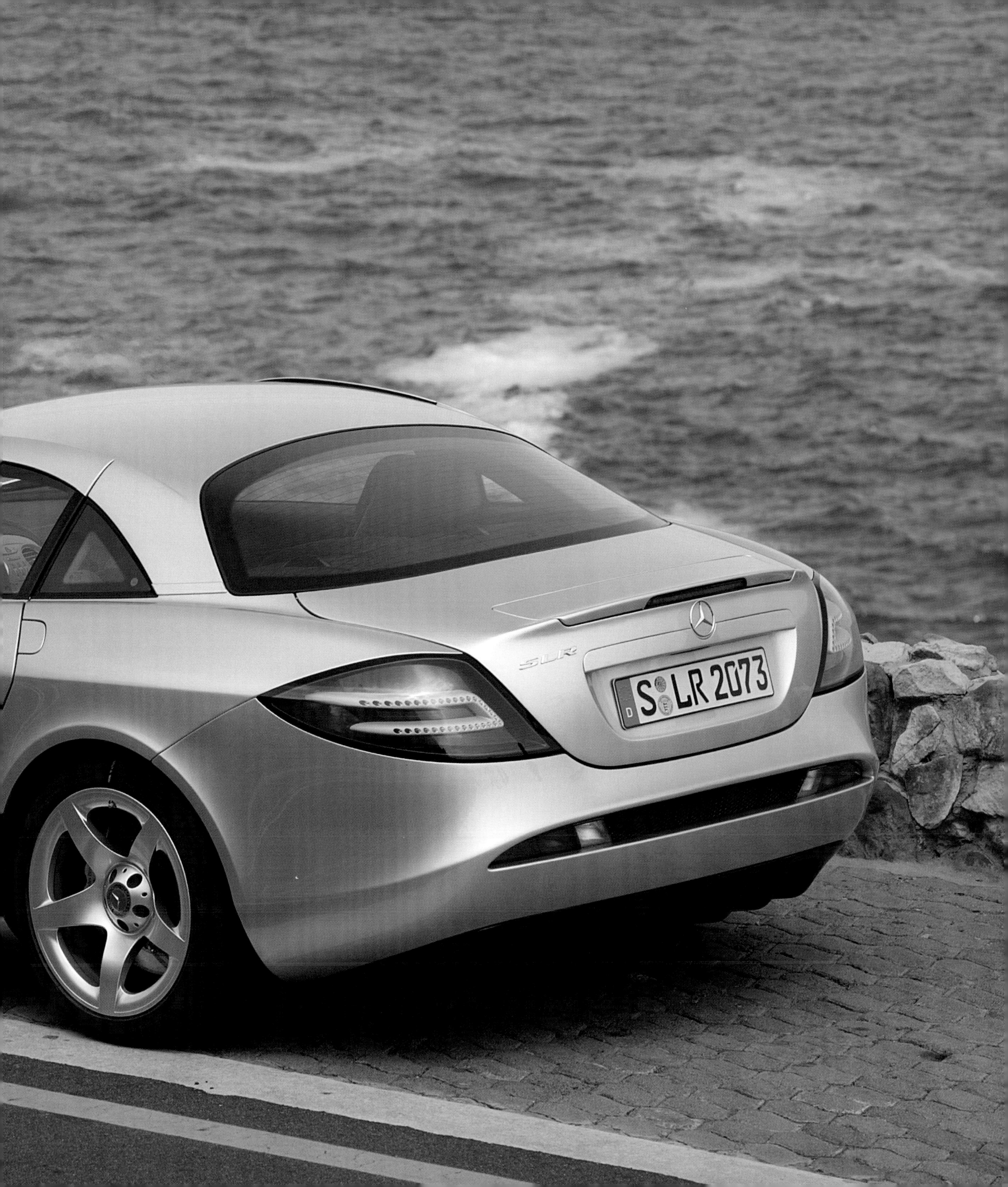
SLR
S LR 2073

PORSCHE 911 GT3

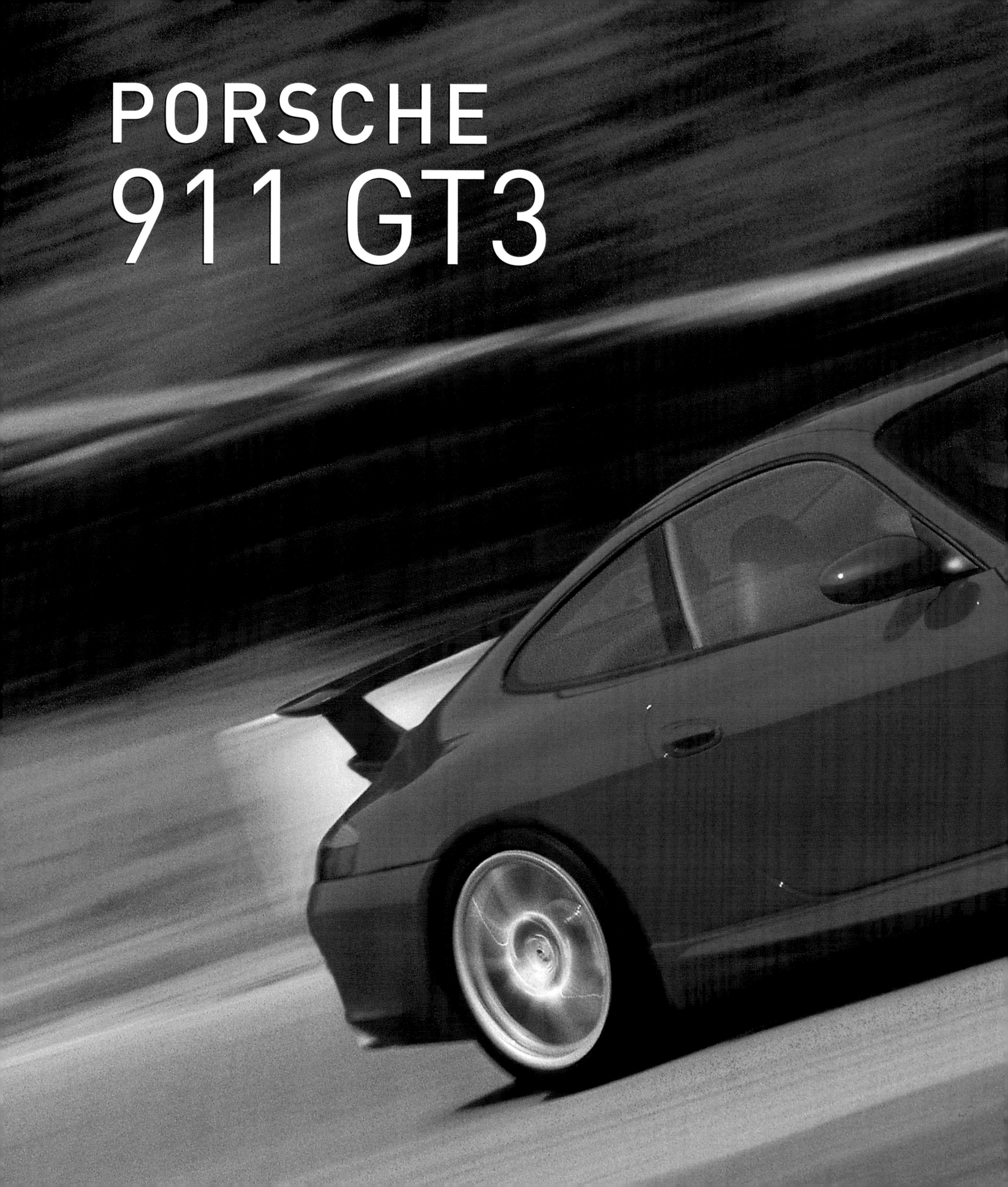

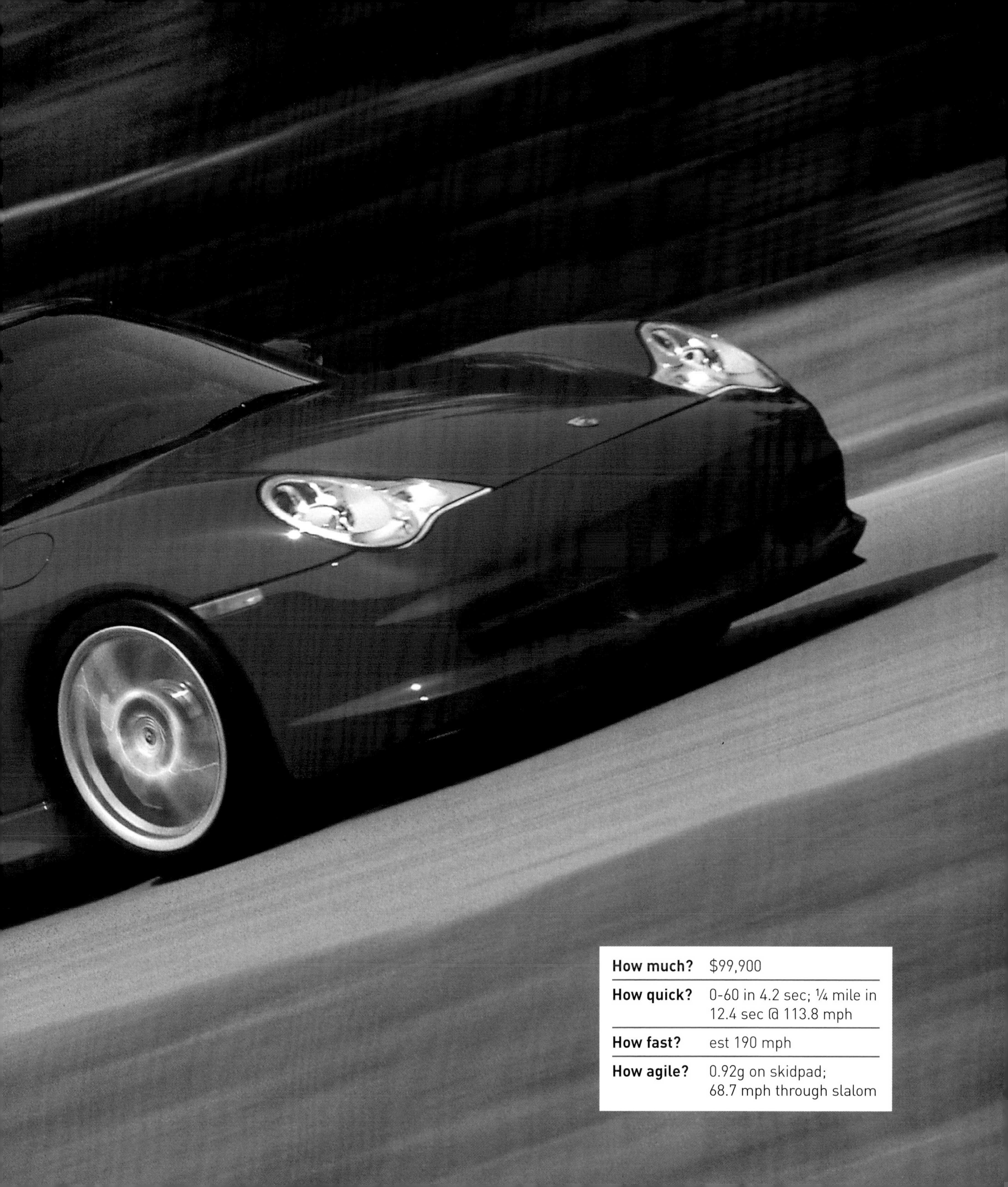

How much?	$99,900
How quick?	0-60 in 4.2 sec; ¼ mile in 12.4 sec @ 113.8 mph
How fast?	est 190 mph
How agile?	0.92g on skidpad; 68.7 mph through slalom

RETURN OF THE 911 DRIVER'S PORSCHE

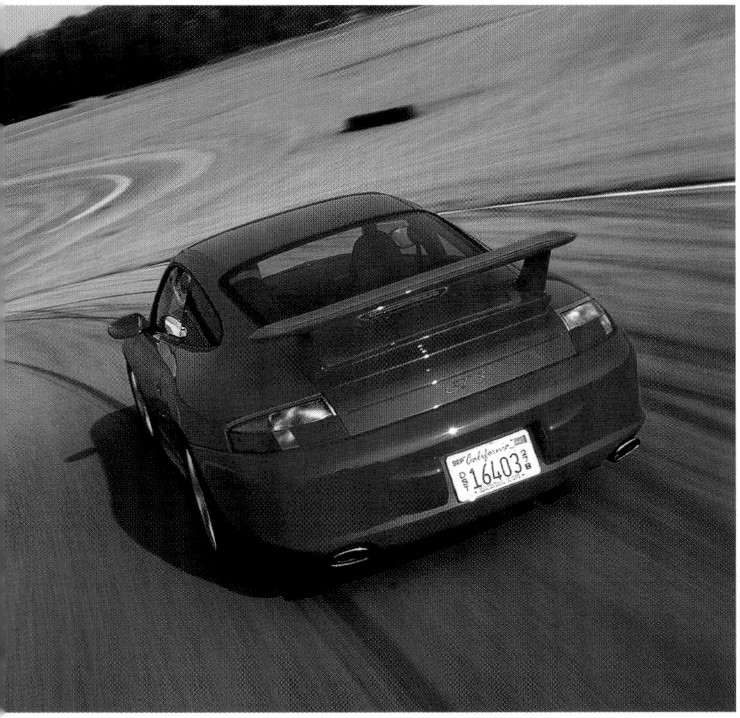

ABOVE: Photographing a GT3 on a racetrack (in this case, Virginia International Raceway) is second nature, as this is the 911 that time-trialers and track-day enthusiasts will gravitate toward.

BELOW: "GT3" is Porsche-speak for the quickest normally aspirated 911 model ever.

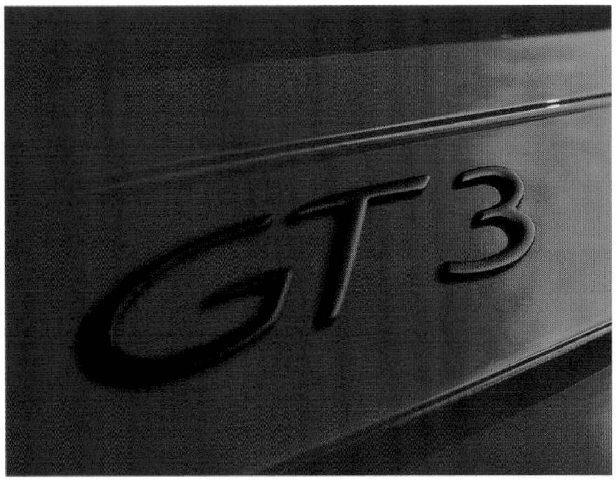
GT3

THE PORSCHE 911 HAS BEEN DESCRIBED as "a bad idea, executed brilliantly" because of its tail-biased weight distribution that stems from its rear-mounted flat-6 engine. Since its introduction in 1964, much has been done to tame its tail-happy tendencies—a lengthened wheelbase, wider rear wheels and tires, a switch from semi-trailing-arm rear suspension to a multilink design—to the point a 911 has become almost too docile for some purists. For this small but vocal group, Porsche has responded with the 380-bhp GT3, a track-ready, fully adjustable variant that's the quickest normally aspirated 911 in the lineup. More important, it's a car that demands significant driver skill to extract the utmost from its capable chassis. If you're a purist, you wouldn't have it any other way.

"A rear-engine, rear-drive sports car? No way, no how, it'll never work." Or so the thinking went as early critics questioned the wisdom of the Porsche 911's unorthodox layout. How could a car with its engine hanging over the rear axle do anything but go straight?

Now some four decades later, the 911 continues to defy conventional thinking by getting better with each new generation. In current 996 guise, Porsche's oldest model line enjoys its broadest appeal to date, offering a unique blend of sports-car performance and GT manners. Forty years of evolution have not only turned the 911 into a faster car than its predecessors, but also a much more composed and civilized one.

Civility is certainly not a bad thing, but for hard-core 911 drivers, sometimes it can be too much of a good thing. Compared with previous iterations, some feel this latest, more driver-friendly version has taken some of the old-school challenge out of driving a 911 quickly.

For this cadre of serious 911 devotees, Porsche has created the 911 GT3. Originally developed as the basis for Porsche's GT3 Cup and GT3 RS race cars, the street GT3 is pure sports car. It's faster and more responsive than a standard Carrera, more involving than the Turbo and quicker around a corner than the GT2. Like the famous '73 Carrera RS 2.7, the light, lean GT3 exists solely as a driver's car.

A simple turn of the key immediately tells you there's something different going on in back. Blip the throttle and the car shudders slightly, the exhaust instantly barks in response. The engine sounds menacing, almost air-cooled in nature. A quick look at the numbers shows the GT3's 3.6-liter flat-6 pumps out 380 bhp at 7400 rpm and 285 lb.-ft. of torque at 5000. Better still, it revs to a remarkable 8200 rpm.

To achieve such high rpm, Porsche engineers have gone to great pains to reduce the engine's internal reciprocating mass. If it moves and can be lightened, then it has been. The pistons, piston pins, valves and titanium connecting rods have all been pared down to save weight. This enables the engine to

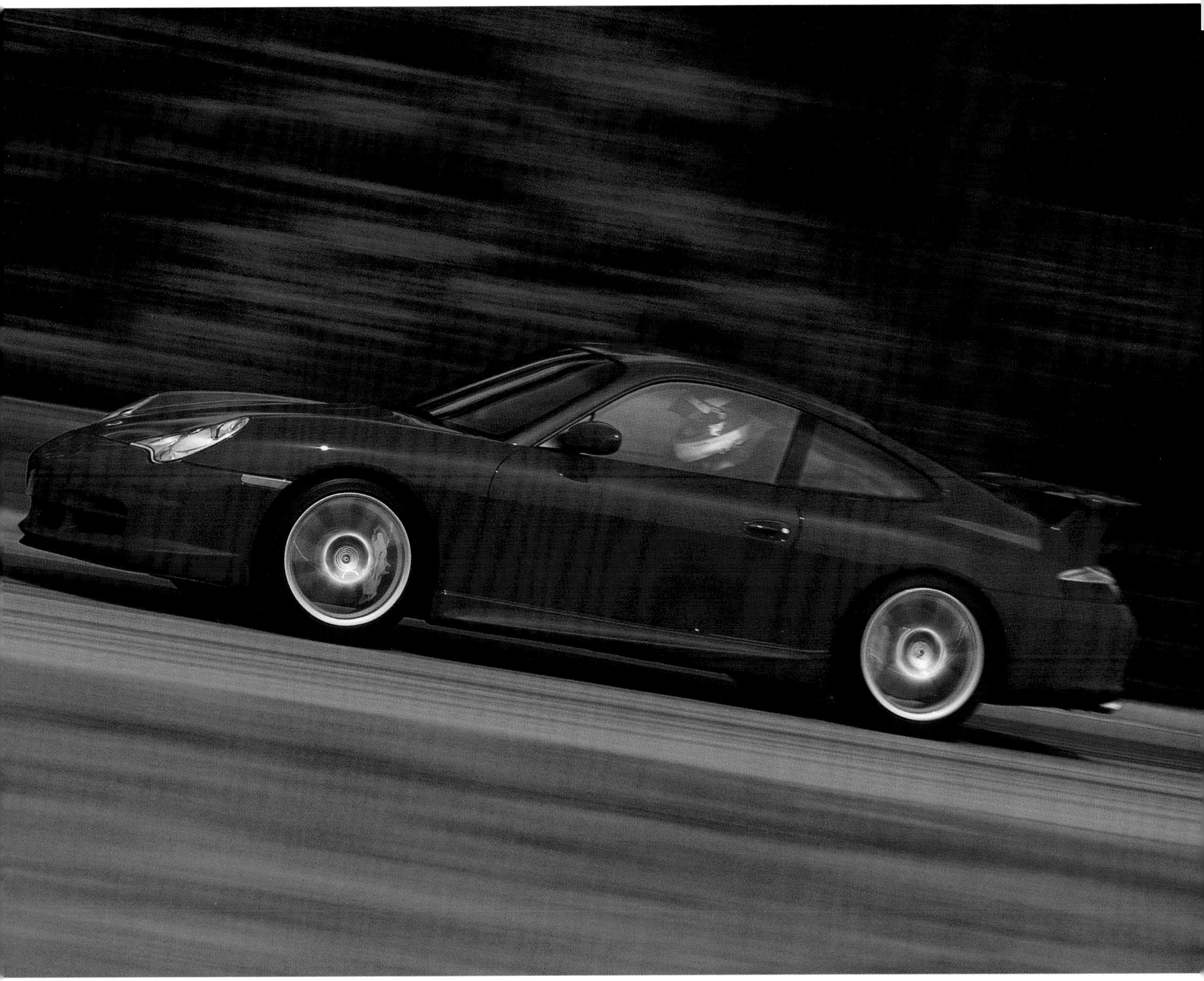

rev more freely, along with significantly improved throttle response. Even the crankshaft's vibration damper has been removed, itself netting a 5-lb. reduction in rotating mass.

Other enhancements over the standard Carrera include a new two-stage resonance intake system, revised engine management, different cams, a new VarioCam system with a wider range of timing adjustment and a less restrictive exhaust. The standard dry-sump lubrication system has also been upgraded to handle the increased lateral loads associated with track driving; a total of five pumps are used to provide the necessary oiling.

ABOVE: True 911 "aficionados" will recognize the GT3 by its 10-spoke 18-in. wheels, lower ride height and distinctive rear spoiler. Of course, the metallic bark of its flat-6 engine is a giveaway too.

OPPOSITE: The power sports seats shown here are fitted for North American cars, but the Europeans get more serious (albeit less comfortable) thin-shell buckets. Instrument graphics and silver appliqués for shifter and handbrake are other GT3 touches.

BELOW: Not a stripped-down race car by any means, the GT3 does without the rear jump seats but maintains most amenities like power windows, air conditioning and a decent sound system. As with any modern 911, there's just the right balance of sportiness and functionality.

Out in the open, the GT3's 380-bhp bark translates into serious speed. One trip through the gears quickly highlights the engine's rev-happy attitude and excellent flexibility. Strong midrange pull starts at around 4000 rpm, then builds to a crescendo from 6000 right up to redline. Revs climb with an unbridled sense of urgency accompanied by the edgiest exhaust note this side of the Carrera GT.

Grab a gear at 8000 rpm and the close-ratio 6-speed transmission delivers a quick, crisp and refreshingly mechanical shift. Similar to the GT2's gearbox, the GT3's unit features steel synchronizers in 3rd through 5th gears, plus its own oil/water heat exchanger. After the gear oil is cooled, it's sprayed on the individual gears as required, effectively controlling gearbox temperatures. Compared with the standard 911, shifting requires a little extra effort, but feels more positive and direct. Gear ratios have also been spaced to suit the engine's higher-revving capability, which helps the GT3 streak from 0–60 mph in a blistering 4.2 seconds and reach a top speed of 190 mph. It's interesting to note that the GT3's power-to-weight ratio is actually better than the 911 Turbo's, yet the Turbo is slightly quicker to 60 mph through launch traction afforded by its all-wheel-drive system.

To ensure none of the engine's enthusiasm gets lost in translation to the chassis, the GT3's suspension setup is tuned for speed over comfort. Firmer

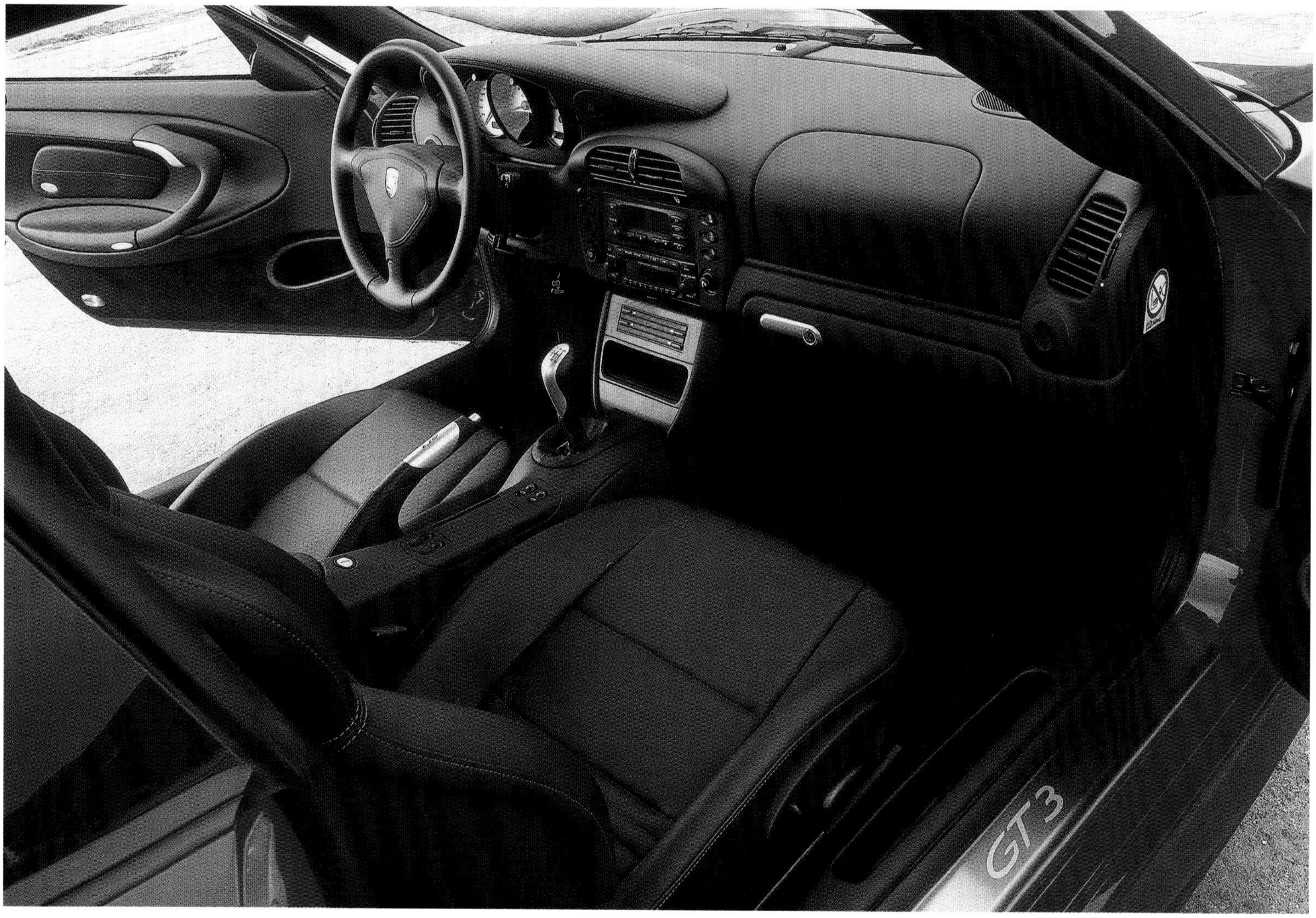
GT3

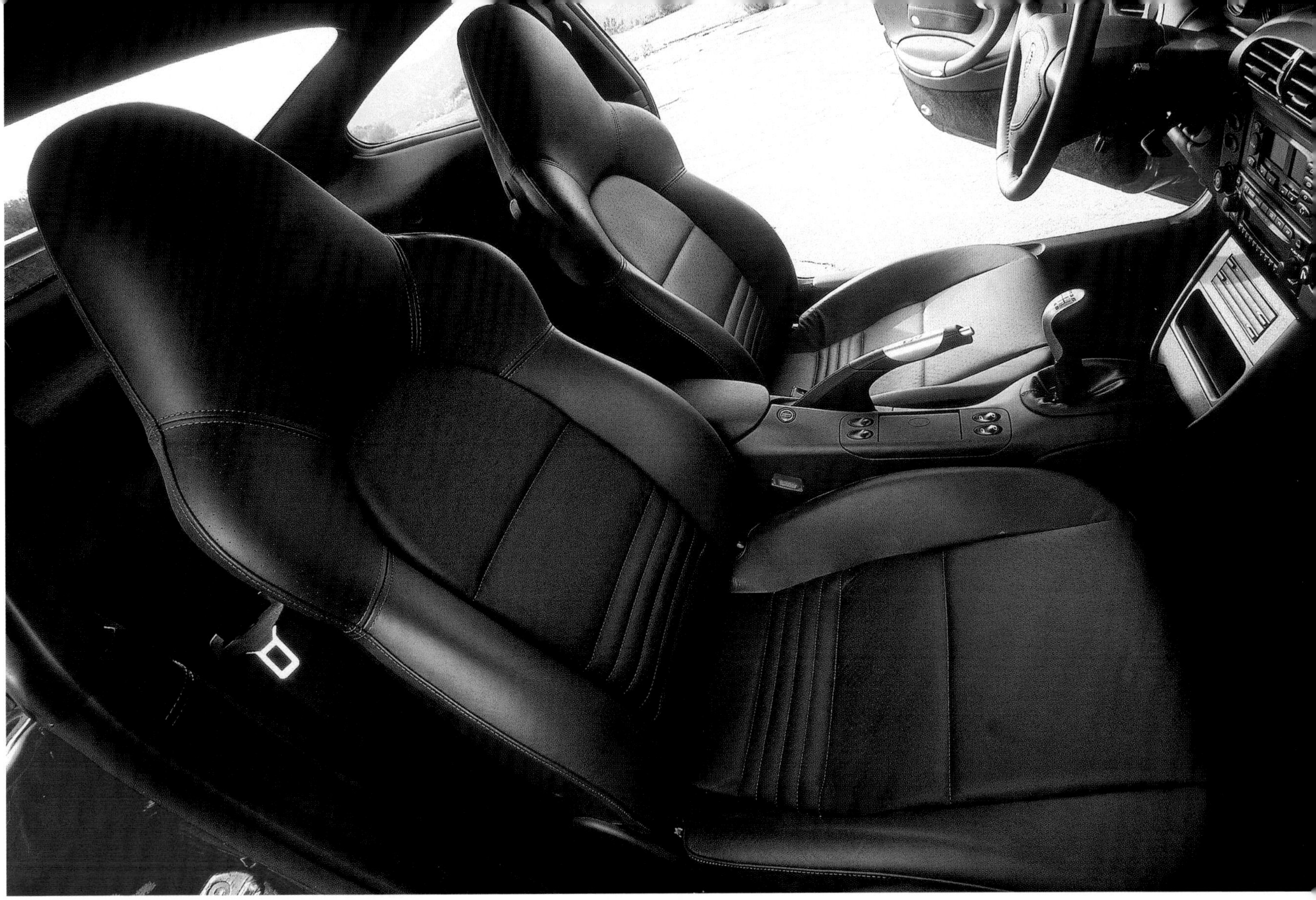

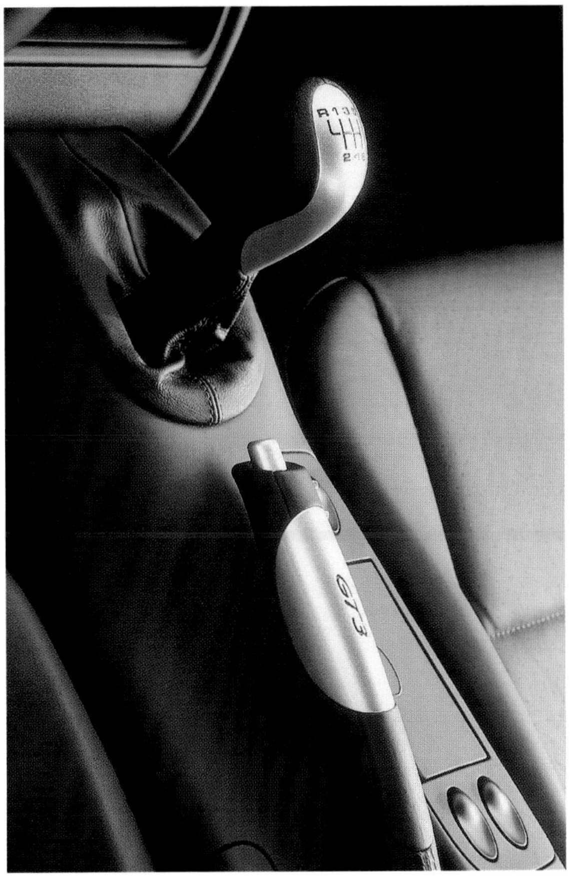
GT3

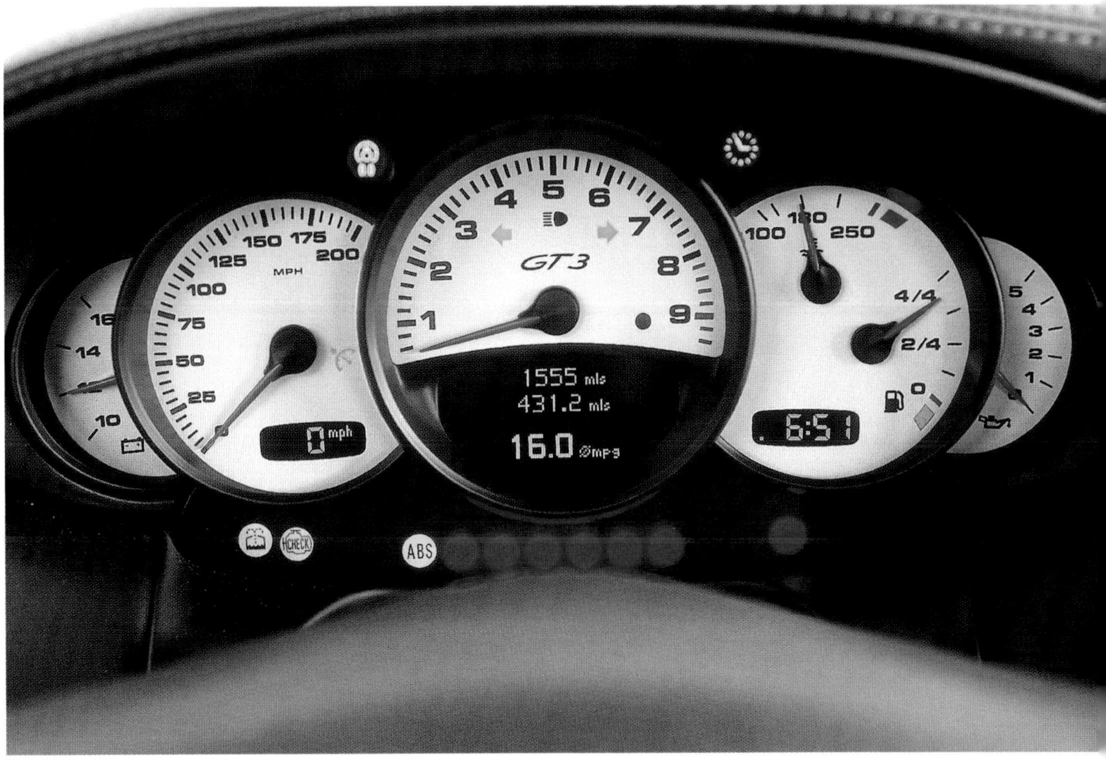
GT3
MPH
1555 mls
431.2 mls
16.0
ABS

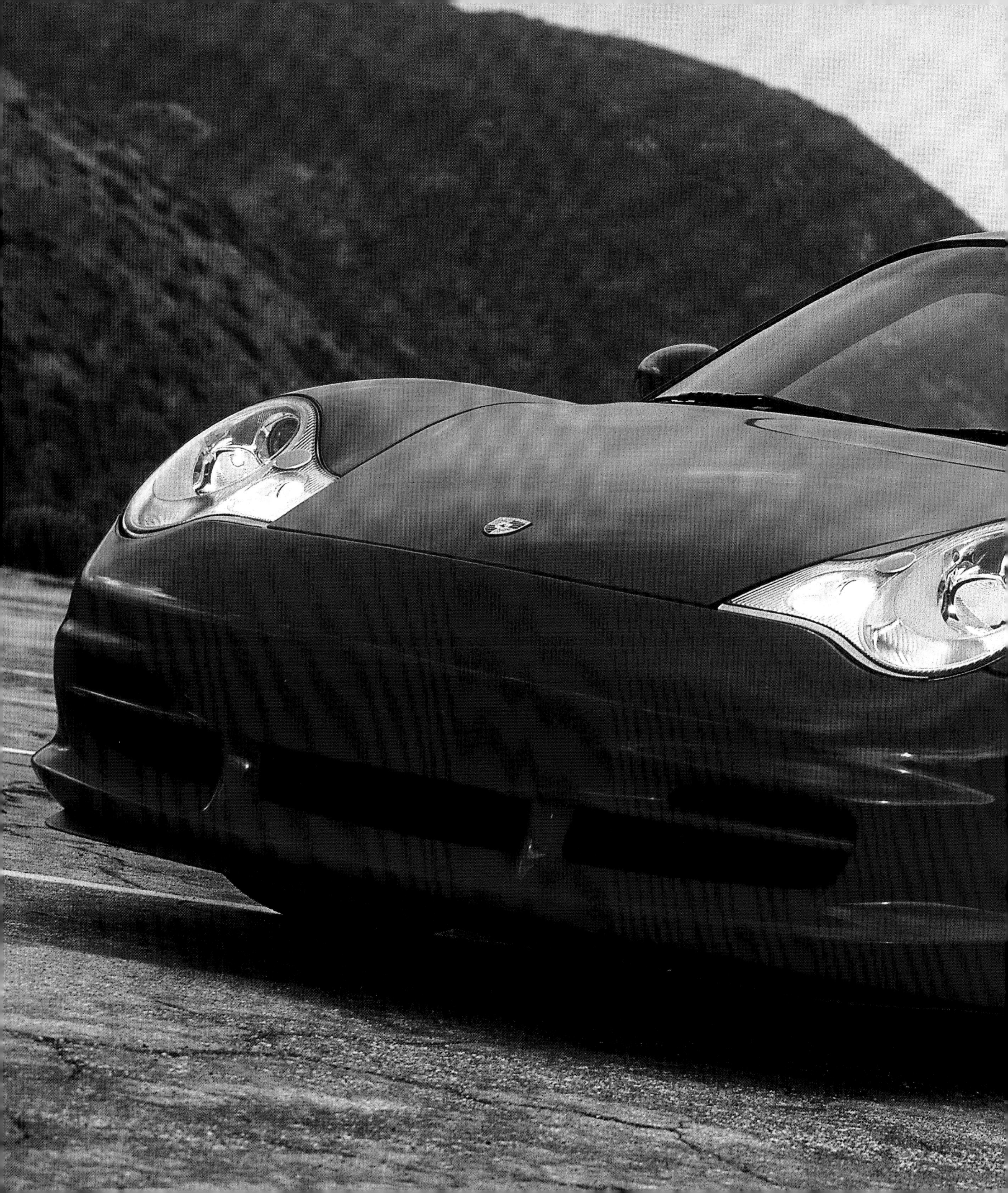

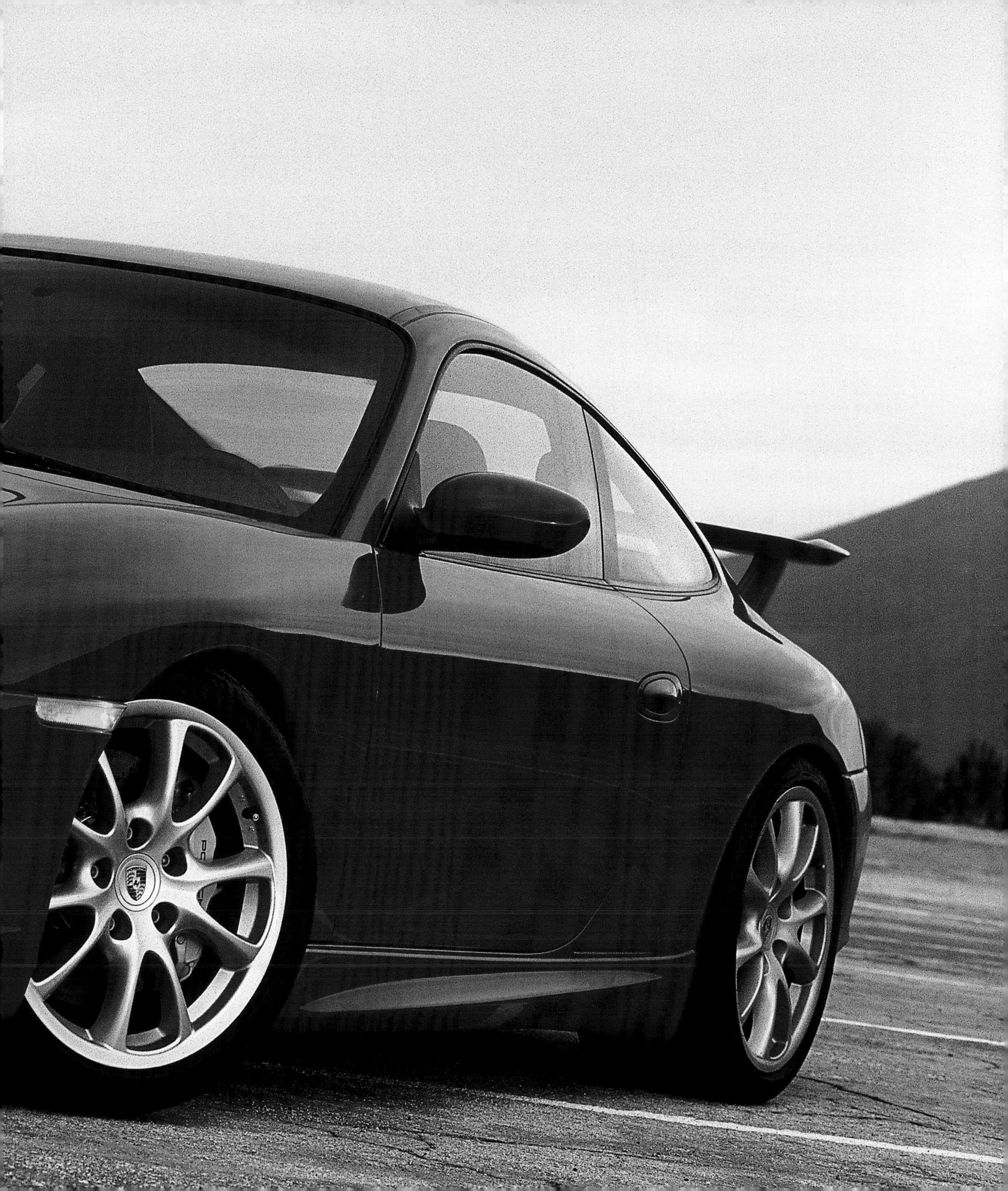

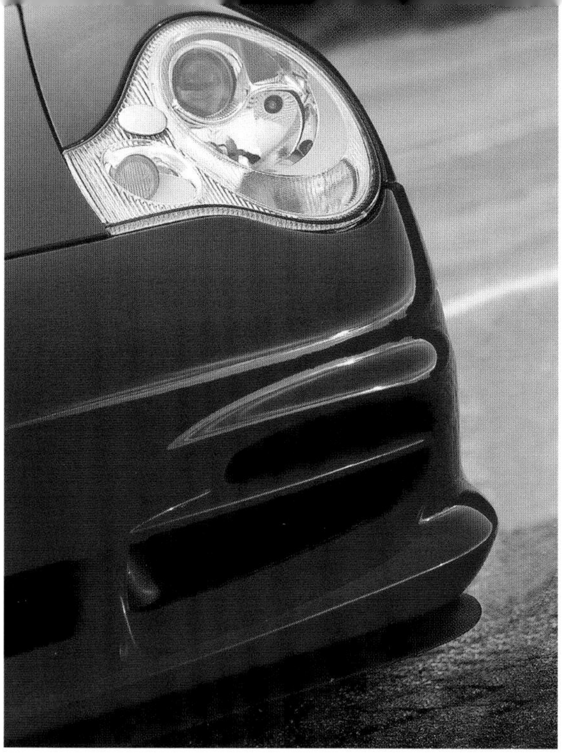

shocks, springs and anti-roll bars maintain an intimate connection with the road, yet manage to retain enough compliance to keep from being unbearably harsh. This setup also lowers the car by 1.2 in., dropping the center of gravity accordingly. Rubber-isolated strut-top bearings are replaced with steel uniball counterparts to reduce deflection under extreme cornering loads. For the track-driving aficionado, camber and ride height can be changed to suit street or track use, while 5-position front and 4-position rear anti-roll bars add an extra level of personalization to suit different tracks, conditions or driving styles. Also, the suspension is designed to accept commonly used racing springs for greater ease of setup.

Braking is handled by massive 6-piston calipers up front (with 13.8-in. rotors) and 4-piston stoppers (13.0-in. rotors) in back. Performance is never in question with zero fade and trademark 911 stability, stop after stop. ABS steps in as needed and serves as the only electronic driving aid on the GT3. There's no traction control or stability control here, not even as an option. For the well-heeled and weight conscious, the GT3 can be ordered with Porsche Ceramic Composite Brakes, which add an extra $8150 to the price tag, but offer a weight savings of nearly 40 lb. As an added benefit, we found that they generated only small amounts of brake dust.

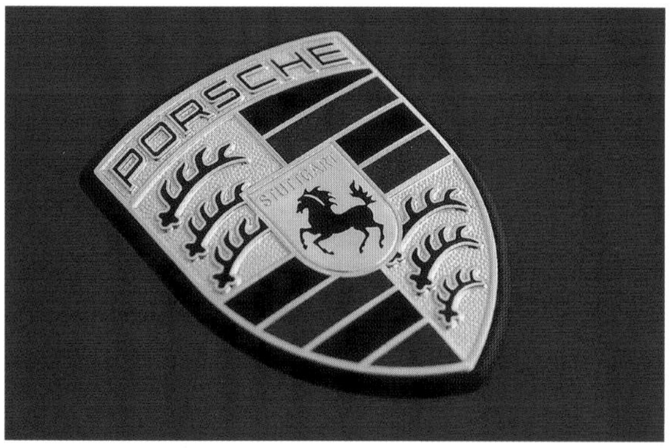
PORSCHE

Hit the road (or track) and the GT3 comes to life in a wonderfully harmonious sonata of speed. Chassis and drivetrain work together as a whole, frenetically rushing you from one corner to the next. It still possesses the 996 platform's stable nature, but thanks to its stiffer, more responsive chassis tuning, everything feels more direct. Any changes in throttle inputs have an immediate effect on chassis dynamics. Roll out of the gas slightly in mid-corner and the front tucks in while the tail lightens up. Roll back on and rear grip returns. Like its racing brethren, the GT3 can be braked hard and deep into turns, repositioned with a little throttle modulation, then happily drifted out at exit.

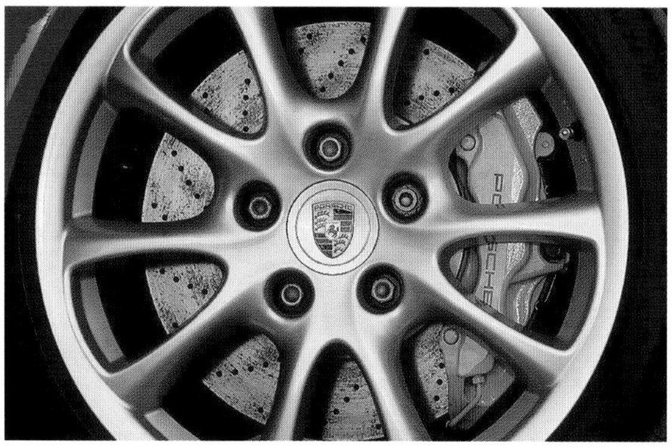

For more casual motoring, the GT3 makes no secret of its sporting intentions. The track-tuned suspension and ultra-wide tires (235/40ZR-18 front, 295/30ZR-18 rear) tend to follow pavement seams and undulations on anything but the smoothest surfaces, giving the car a somewhat active nature on city streets and back roads. This behavior is noticeable at first, but quickly forgotten as it becomes yet another part of the GT3's special personality.

At any speed, the close connection between engine and chassis requires smooth steering, throttle and brake inputs. Ham-fisted driving normally forgiven in a Carrera isn't as easily tolerated in the GT3. This is not a machine that suffers fools gladly. It demands respect from all who sit behind the wheel, rewarding the skilled pilot with a driving experience unequaled by any modern 911.

Inside, the cockpit is standard-issue 911, save deletion of the sunroof and

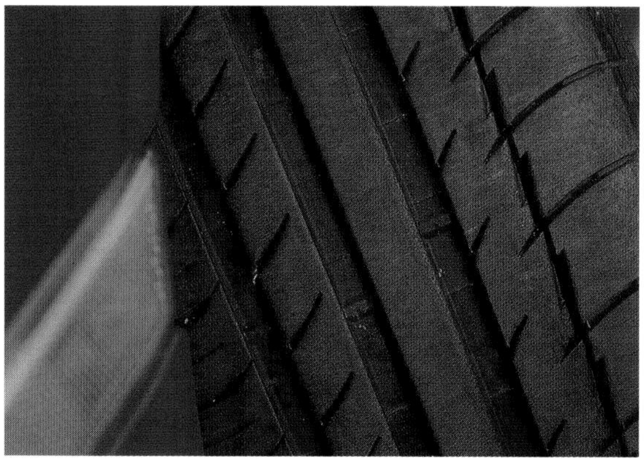

While the sum is greater than the parts, the GT3 nevertheless has nice parts. **FROM TOP:** front fascia styling is derived from GT3 Cup race cars; Porsche—there is no substitute; massive aluminum calipers clamp the optional ceramic-composite rotors; the car-to-road interface of the generous Michelin Pilot Sport tires.

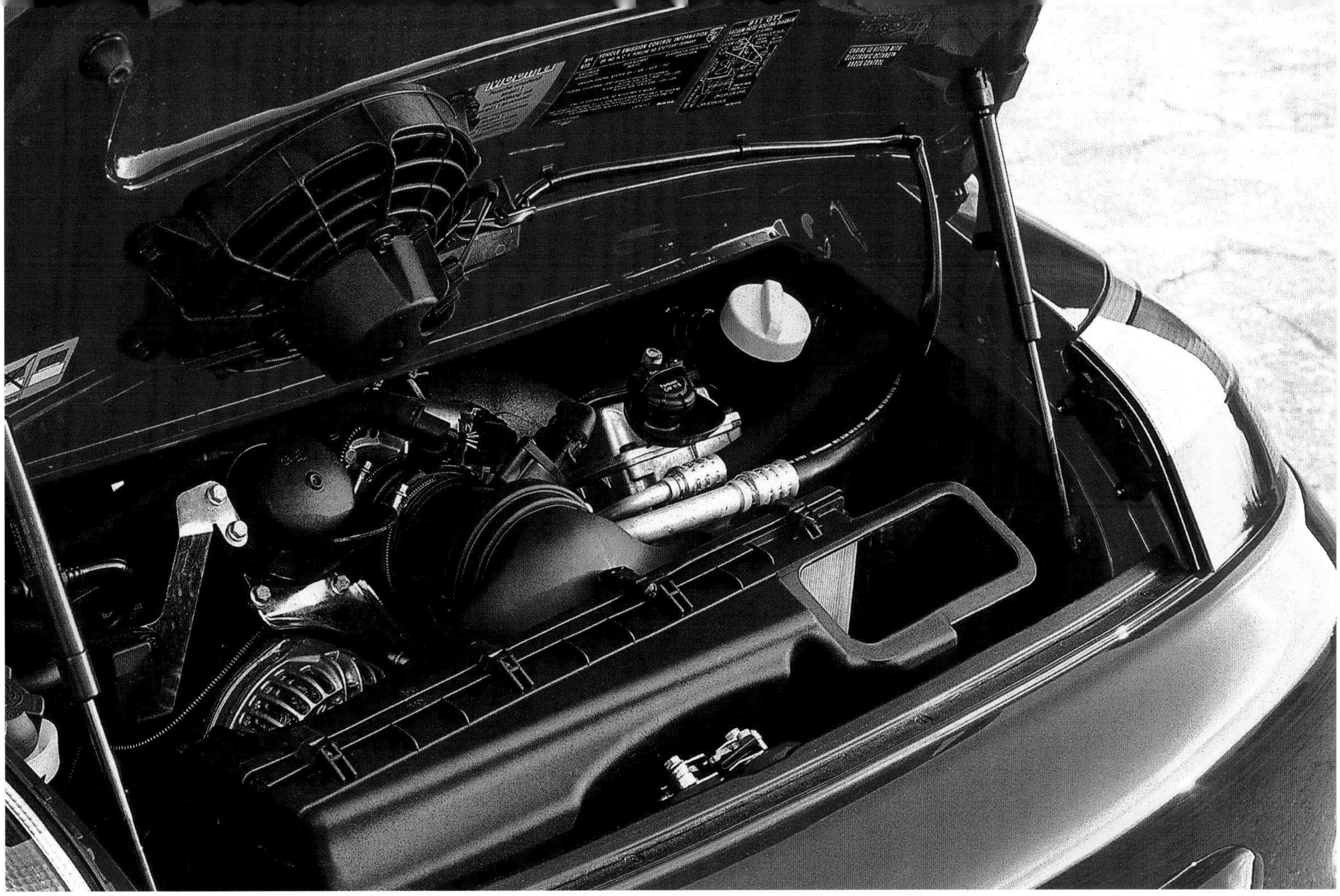

back seat to reduce weight, and a black Alcantara headliner. The radio/CD, power windows, central locking and air conditioning all remain for the sake of comfort and convenience. They're joined by Porsche's excellent power sport seats, which add a welcome show of support during serious cornering. For the slightly more hard-core European market, thin-shell leather-covered sports seats, weighing 20 lb. less than the standard 911 Carrera seats, are fitted, and stereo and air conditioning systems can be deleted at no cost.

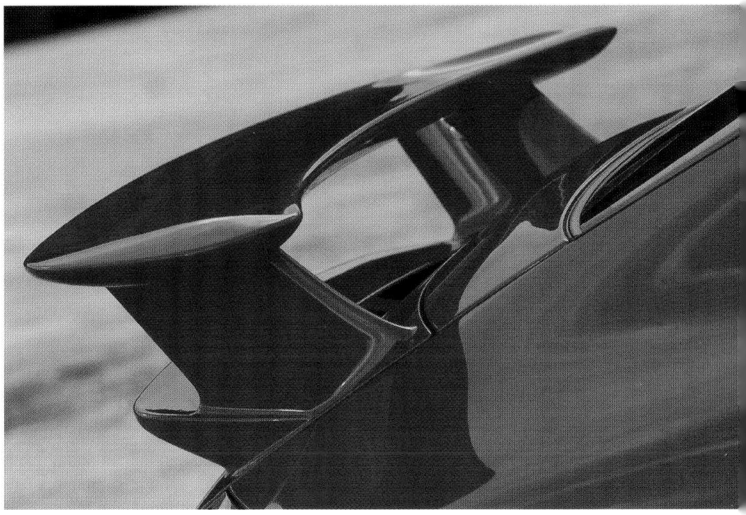

TOP: What you can see of the 3.6-liter flat-6. What you can't see are its more radical camshafts, lightened internals and less restrictive exhaust, all of which enable an 8200-rpm redline and an output of 380 bhp. Rear wing stands proud of the bodywork, and is adjustable for incidence.

Externally, the GT3 profits from lessons learned in the heat of Porsche Supercup competition. A GT3 Cup-derived nose, aerodynamically optimized side sills and a fixed rear wing quickly identify the GT3 as more than just a tarted-up Carrera. Underneath, three large composite panels streamline airflow from the front axle to the engine, and help the GT3 achieve a slippery 0.30 coefficient of drag. Functionally, the new bodywork reduces high-speed lift at both ends of the car while also providing additional airflow to the front brakes and radiator. The wheel design is also new, a look the GT3 shares with the '04 GT2. If we could delete any part of the bodywork, it would be the small, black plastic lip spoiler affixed to the nose, as it tends to scrape on anything but the shallowest of driveway entrances. It's designed to be easily removable, though.

2004 allocation of GT3s is 750 cars for North America. Priced at $99,900, Porsche's latest (and greatest?) 911 isn't cheap, but given its stirring performance, will most surely sell out.

In this latest iteration, the 996 platform finally gets to show its full potential. Quicker, stiffer and graced with an intoxicating new powerplant, the 911 GT3 clearly illustrates that Porsche still knows how to build a true driver's machine.

PORSCHE
CARRERA GT

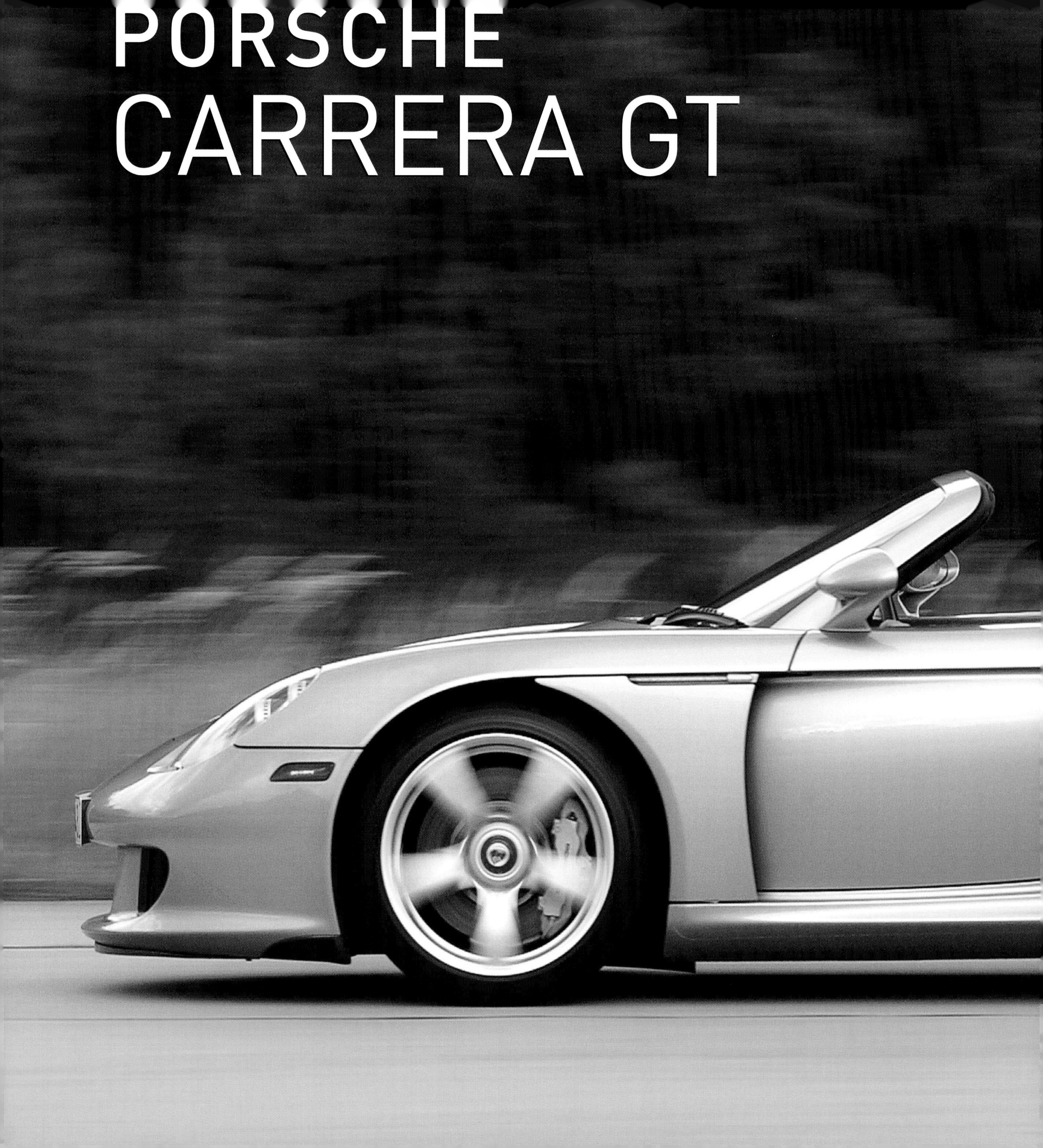

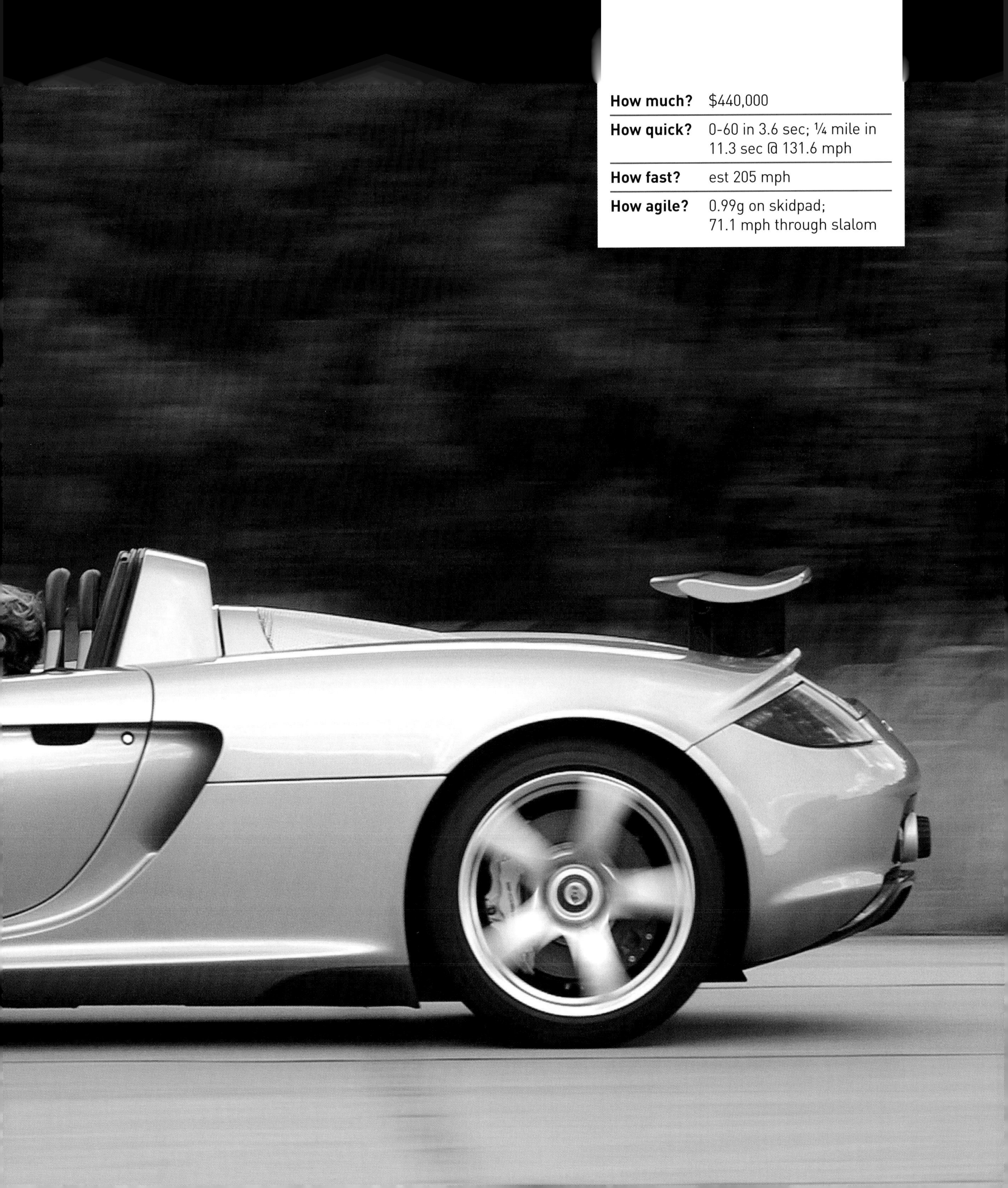

How much?	$440,000
How quick?	0-60 in 3.6 sec; ¼ mile in 11.3 sec @ 131.6 mph
How fast?	est 205 mph
How agile?	0.99g on skidpad; 71.1 mph through slalom

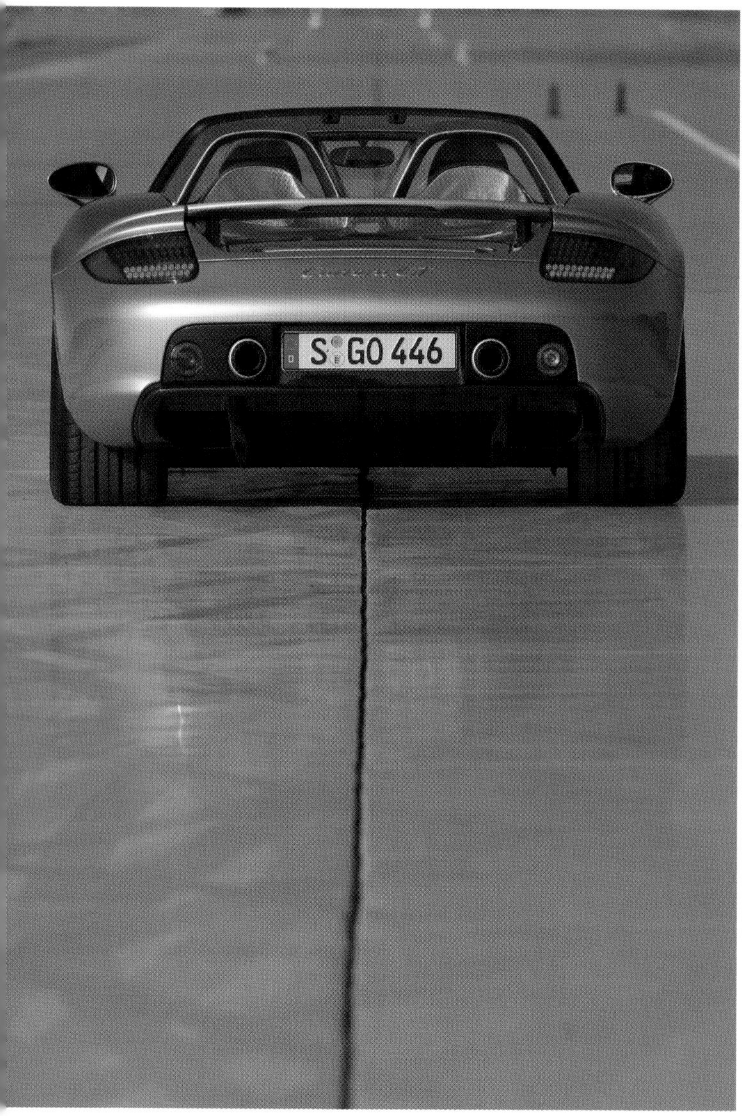
S GO 446

ABOVE: Though fully licensed for the street, the Carrera GT's race-car origins simmer just beneath the surface. Look no further than the downforce-generating diffuser beneath the twin tailpipes.

BELOW: If you need more proof, consider that the word Carrera means "race" in Spanish. Here, it's spoken with a German accent.

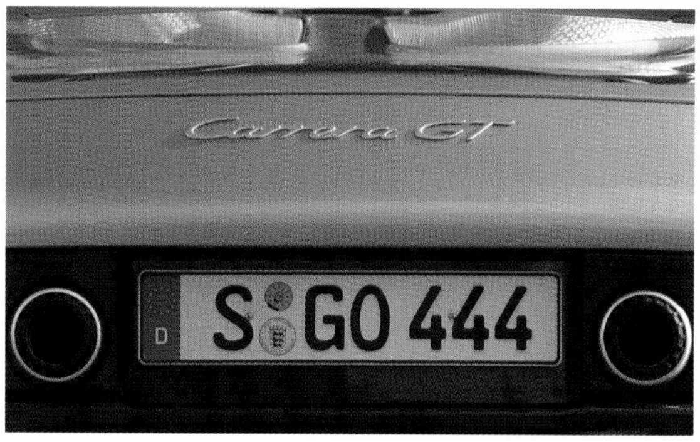
Carrera GT
S GO 444

LE MANS RACER FOR THE STREET

IN RACING AS IN LIFE, when one door closes, another oftentimes will open. And so it is with Porsche's stillborn Le Mans racing prototype, which never turned a wheel in competition but now provides the basis for an astoundingly capable supercar, the Carrera GT. Not since the Porsche 959 that bowed at the Frankfurt auto show of 1983 has the Zuffenhausen-based firm produced a car so singularly focused on raw speed, and so technologically advanced. After all, a race-tuned 605-bhp V-10, a carbon-fiber-reinforced-plastic chassis and ceramic composites for both the brake discs and clutch friction plate are a far cry from the first Porsche, the 356 "Gmünd coupe" of 1948, assembled from modified Volkswagen Beetle components in an abandoned Austrian sawmill.

When Porsche announces that it is to build a super sports car, everybody listens. Especially when it's a car that represents the sum of all the engineering know-how from the famed Zuffenhausen carmaker, steeped in racing heritage and with a highly regarded reputation for producing outstanding road-going sports cars. It's no wonder that since the 2000 unveiling of the Carrera GT supercar concept at the Paris auto show, the enthusiast world has been anxiously awaiting the car's official introduction. Well, it has finally arrived.

The fundamental objectives set forth by Porsche engineers for the Carrera GT are the same as with any race car: It must have a lightweight and extremely stiff chassis, with the entire package having a low center of gravity. Initially, studies were done with the chassis made of steel and aluminum, but ultimately carbon-fiber-reinforced plastic (CFP) was selected to meet the weight and stiffness targets suitable for high-performance driving dynamics. The Carrera GT is the first road-going production car to have not only its entire monocoque chassis and exterior panels constructed from CFP, but also its rear subframe that serves as both the engine cradle and as the mounting platform for the suspension. Special attention has been paid to the subframe because of its operating environment near the power unit. As with the rest of the chassis and body, where optimized carbon-fiber weave orientations have been specifically chosen to maximize load-bearing ability and ease of shaping, the complex single-unit CFP subframe also has aluminum honeycomb elements sandwiched in for better heat resistance. According to Porsche, despite the GT being an open roadster, it boasts bending and torsional stiffness greater than that of a modern coupe, and with the tub weighing just slightly over 220 lb.

With a lightweight and stiff race-carlike chassis comes a suspension design and tuning that are track tested and proven from Porsche's winner of the 1998 24 Hours of Le Mans, the 911 GT1. Unlike the MacPherson struts employed on 911 road cars, the Carrera GT uses all-around upper and lower A-arms to precisely control and optimize wheel articulations through various load conditions. Pushrods feed the forces from the wheels into the inboard-mounted springs and dampers via stainless-steel pivot levers. The levers are also where

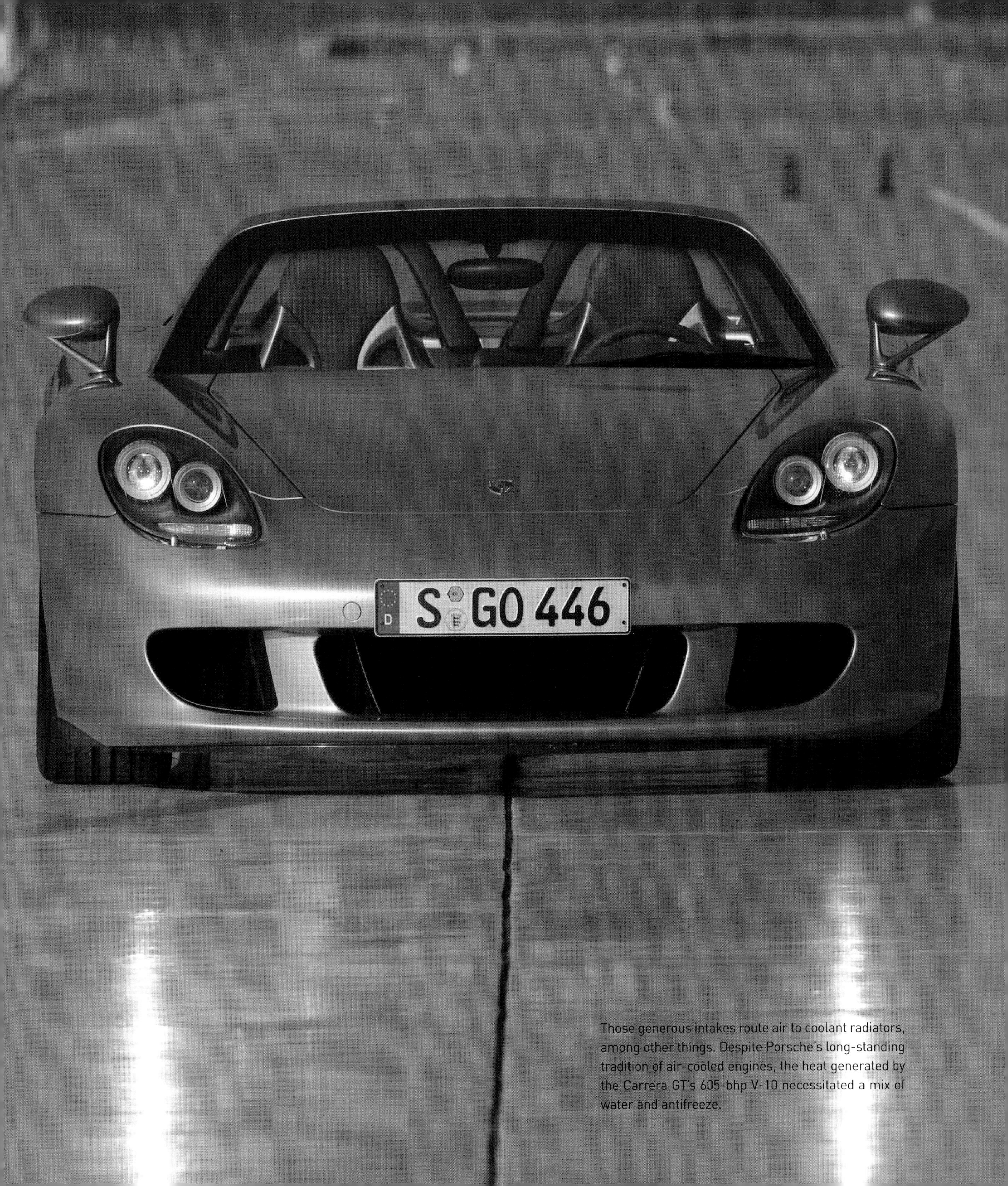
S GO 446

Those generous intakes route air to coolant radiators, among other things. Despite Porsche's long-standing tradition of air-cooled engines, the heat generated by the Carrera GT's 605-bhp V-10 necessitated a mix of water and antifreeze.

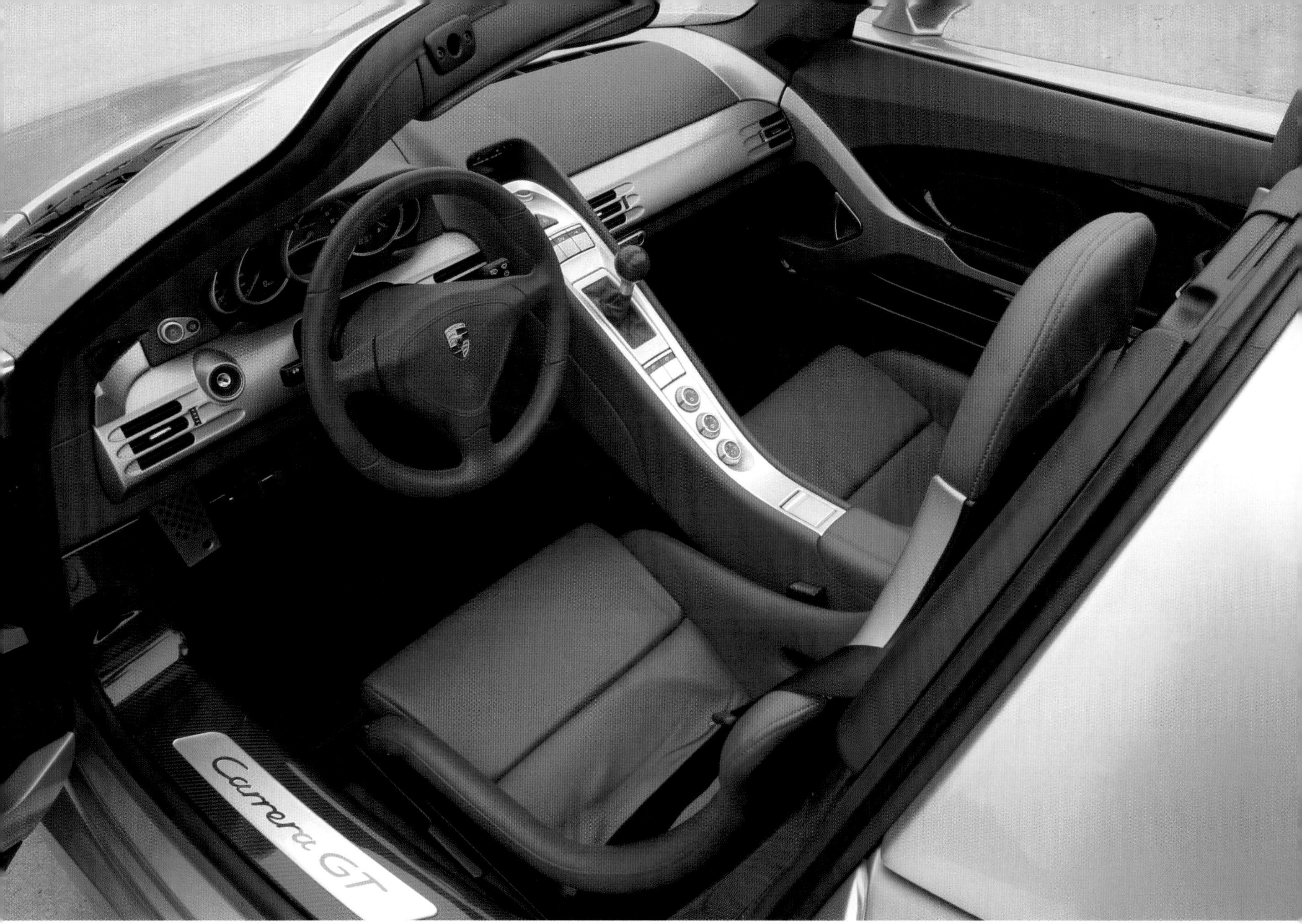
Carrera GT

ABOVE: The Carrera GT's interior won't seem completely foreign to those familiar with the 911's. High-arching center console and wide, carbon-fiber sills are departures, though.

the left and right suspensions are tied together with an anti-roll bar. By separating the spring and damper movements from the wheel-control arms (a common practice in motorsports), precise suspension motions and tuning are possible for both low and high speeds.

The Carrera GT rides on forged magnesium wheels with specially designed front 265/35ZR-19 and rear 335/30ZR-20 Michelin Pilot Sport 2 tires. These asymmetrical tires feature stiffer inside tread blocks for better wear and wet traction, while the outside softer compound allows for superior dry-weather handling. For stopping power, 6-piston aluminum monobloc brake calipers bite into the 15.0-in. ceramic composite discs at all four wheels, the same Porsche Ceramic Composite Brakes (PCCB) used on 911s.

For crash safety, the Carrera GT's carbon-fiber passenger cell is designed to absorb extreme impact energy, and the top layer of the interior is covered with Kevlar to prevent CFP from splintering and intruding into the cockpit. The doors are reinforced with steel tubes, as are the A-pillars with high-strength steel and the B-pillars with more composite components to protect the occupants in case of a rollover. High-strength stainless steel extends forward and rearward, mated to the aluminum bumper structures not only for added protection but also for ease of repair after a frontal or rear-end collision.

By increasing the bore of the 5.5-liter engine originally developed for Porsche's Le Mans racing program, the new 5.7-liter V-10 boasts abundant power from its position amidships in the Carrera GT. Weighing in at just 472 lb., the high-strength light-alloy block and heads are designed as a load-bearing unit, with water and oil channels fully integrated into the casting whenever possible. Controlled by Motronic ME 7.1.1, Porsche's VarioCam continuously adjusts the intake camshafts to optimize combustion and ensure maximum power output from low to high engine rpm. Instead of using liners, the cylinder bores are coated with Nikasil (a combination of nickel and silicon). The pistons are connected to the crankshaft via titanium connecting rods. And dry-sump lubrication is used not only to guarantee performance under extreme driving conditions, but it also allows the power unit to sit just 3.9 in. above the car's underfloor and further lowers the vehicle's center of gravity.

Rated at 605 bhp at 8000 rpm and 435 lb.-ft. of torque at 5750 rpm, the V-10's enormous power is sent to the transversely mounted 6-speed gearbox without going through a normal two-mass flywheel or a conventional clutch. Instead, torque is first transmitted via a patent-pending hollow main input shaft with an inner thin solid rod acting as a torsional spring to dampen any fluctuations in power output. Without the heavier flywheel setup, the engine is eager to free-rev quickly like a race car.

From the torsional output shaft, the Porsche Ceramic Composite Clutch (PCCC) acts to smoothly couple the crankshaft and the gears. To keep the V-10

ABOVE: While overlapping gauge cluster follows 911 practice, those bottom-hinged alloy pedals, **BELOW LEFT**, are stand-alone works of art. High-mounted shift lever in the magnesium center console selects ratios of the 6-speed transverse gearbox.

FOLLOWING PAGES: Engineering and aesthetic excellence come together everywhere you look. The yellow paint of those 6-piston brake calipers signifies ceramic-composite rotors; third high-mounted brake light neatly integrates with the twin roll hoops; and taillights incorporate an array of quick-reacting LEDs.

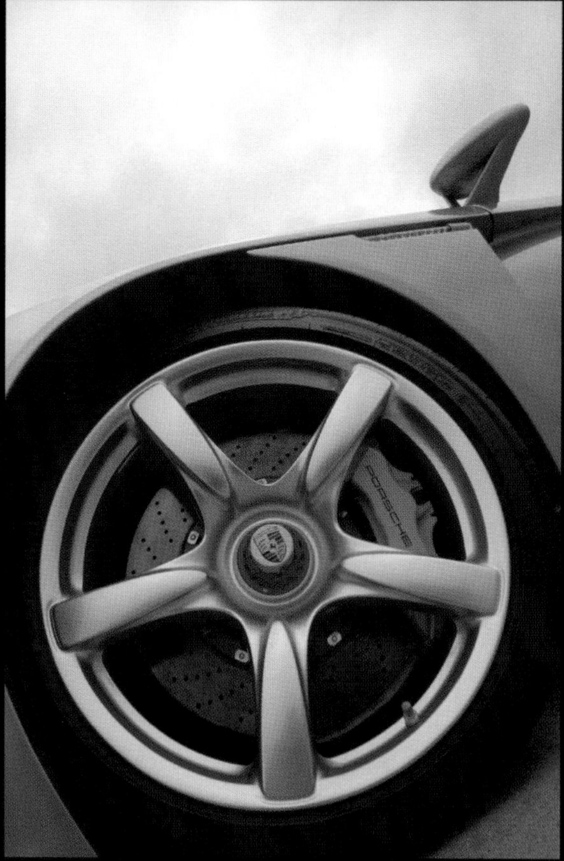

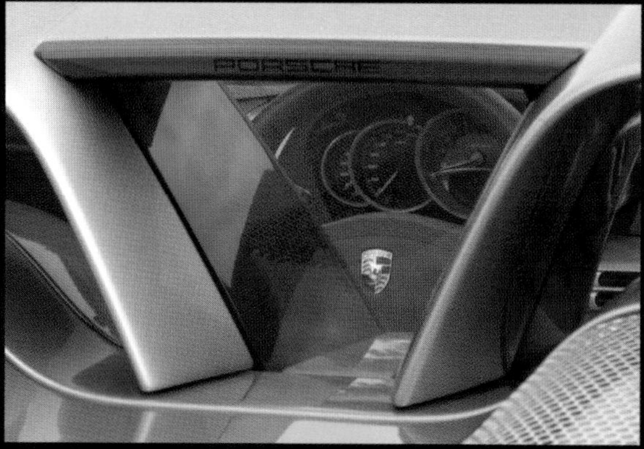
PORSCHE

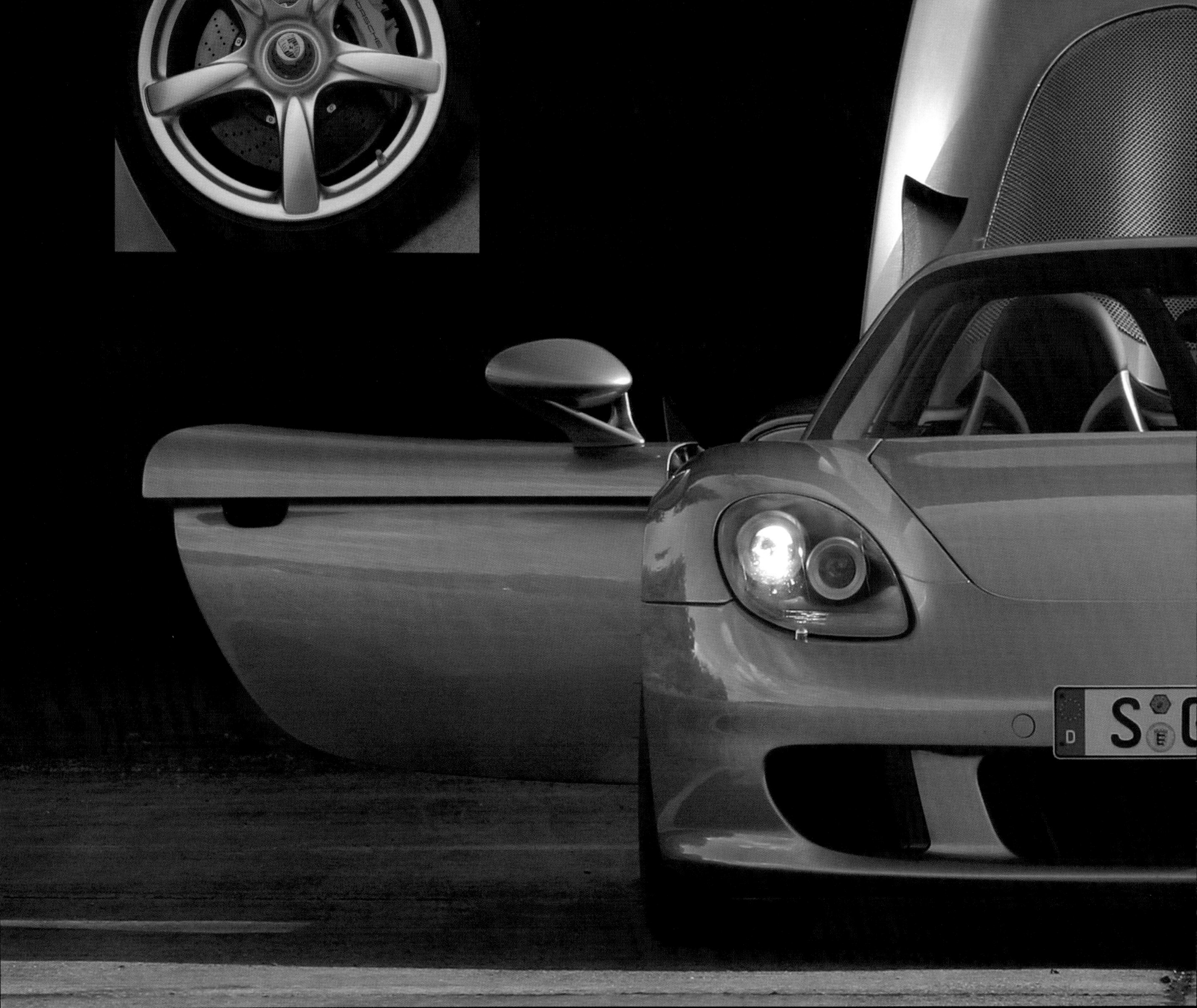

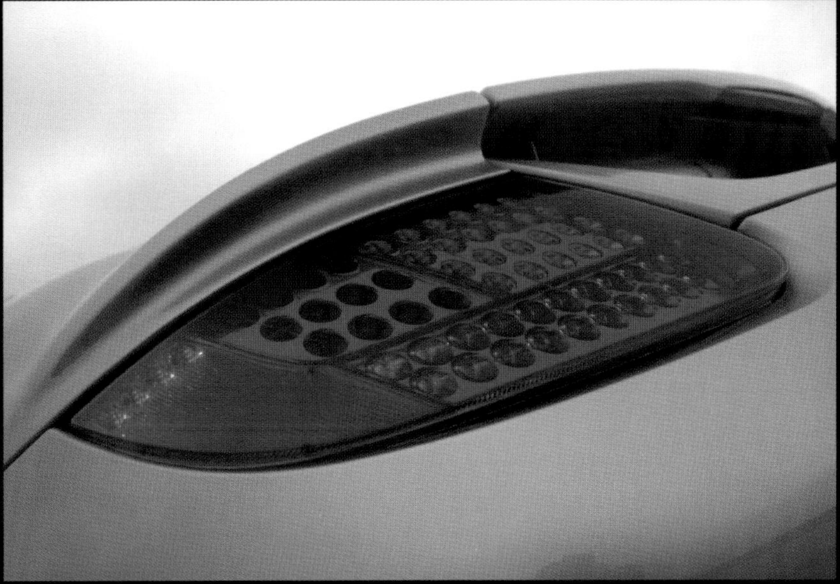
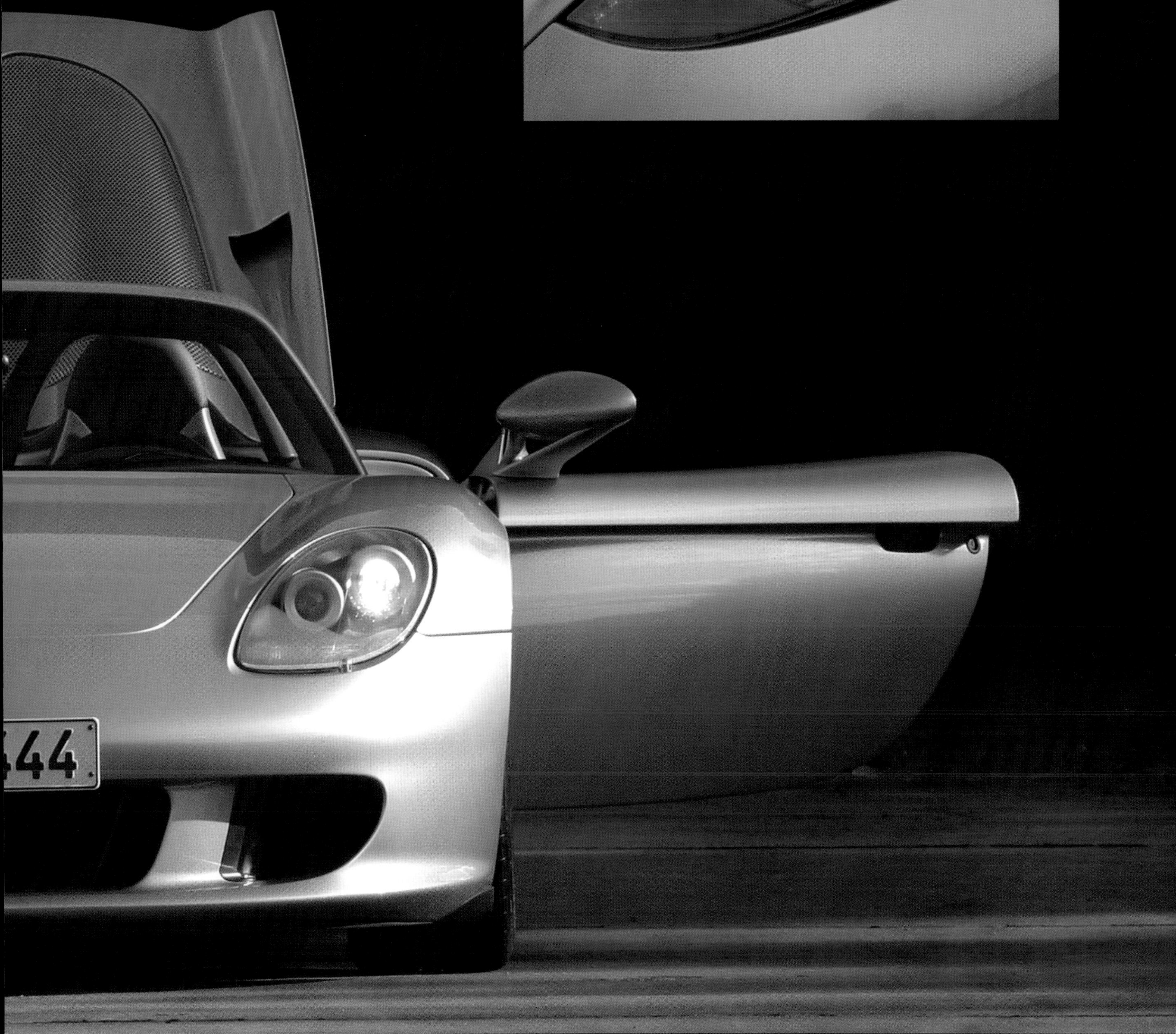

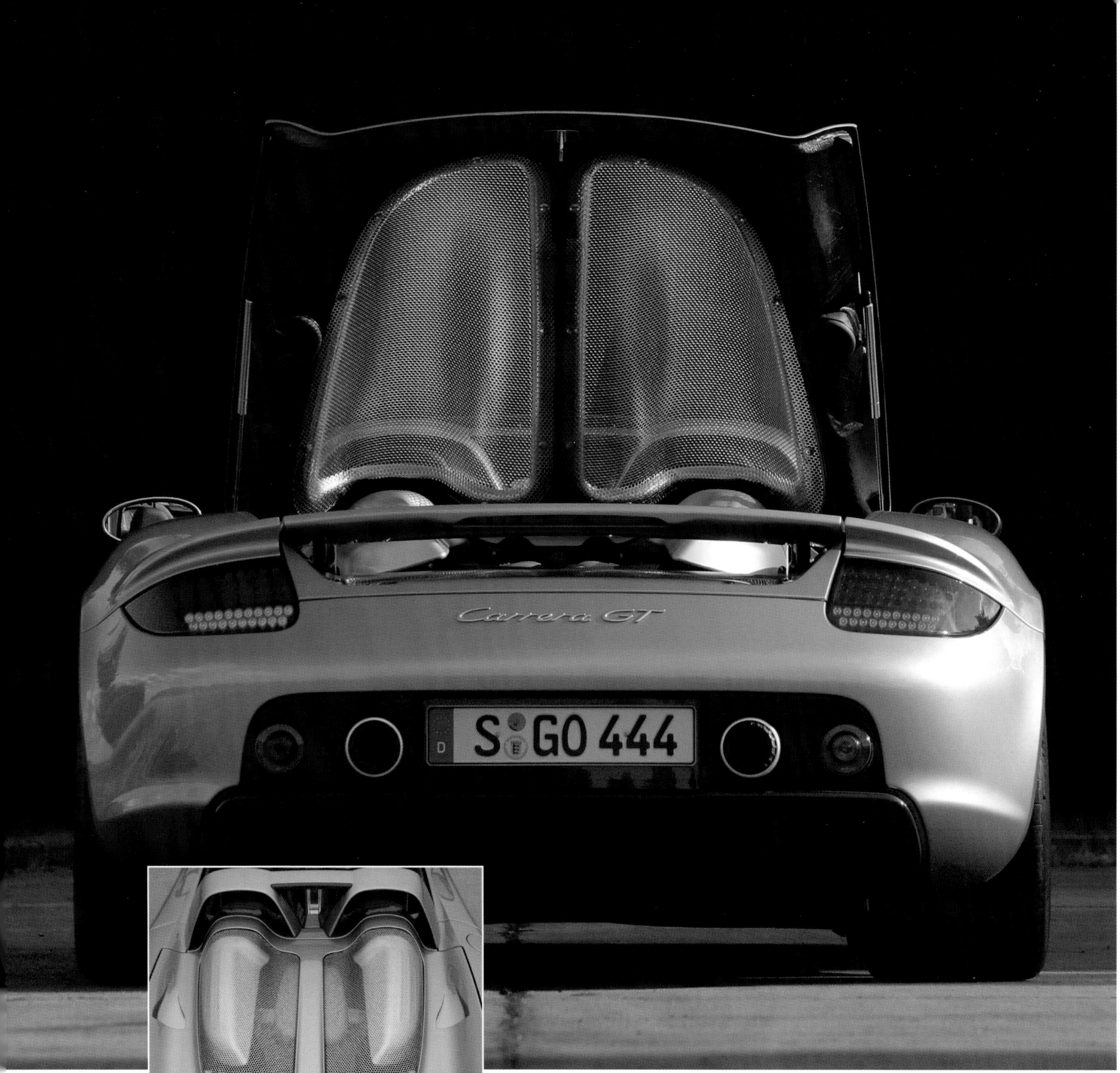
Carrera GT
S GO 444

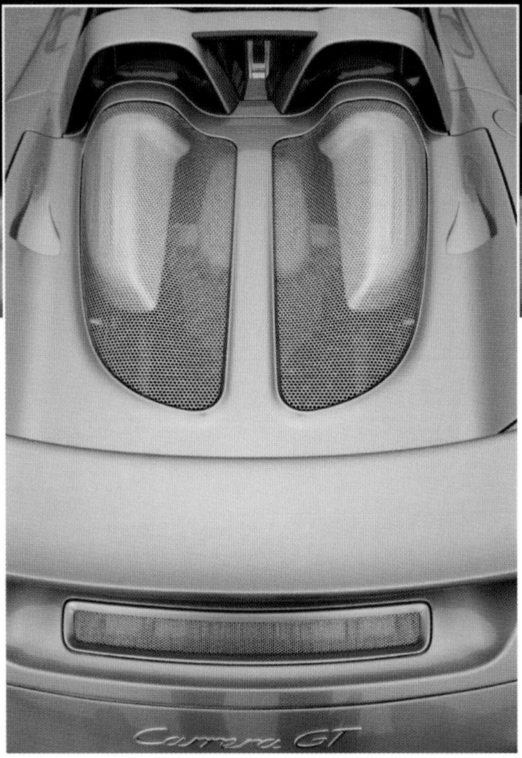
Carrera GT

as low as possible in the car, a small-diameter clutch is needed. Multiplate carbon-fiber racing clutches would seem to be the answer, but they're plagued with a short service life. So engineers borrowed their experience from the Porsche Carbon Ceramic Brakes and applied the same concept. The Carrera GT's PCCC consists of two ceramic plates with four titanium backing plates. It weighs only 7.7 lb. compared with the 911 Turbo's normal 15.4-lb. unit. The ceramic clutch also sports an impressive exterior diameter spanning only 6.65 in., in comparison with a typical one measuring about 15.0 in. For optimal off-the-corner acceleration, a limited-slip differential resides at the rear axle to properly distribute torque to the drive wheels.

On the outside, the Carrera GT's styling shows a strong family resemblance up front. The rest of the wide, low-slung roadster body sports an elegant but athletic look. On the inside, the instrument panel is similar to its 911 sibling's, but the flowing curve of the molded magnesium center console is unique.

Slip inside the supportive carbon-fiber/Kevlar leather seat, turn the ignition switch positioned characteristically to the left of the steering wheel, and the V-10 comes to life with precision and quickness. Right away the immediacy of the engine wanting to rev to its maximum 8400 rpm is apparent. In fact, the powerplant revs so easily that it is not unlike a high-revving motorcycle. While the unusually high position of the gearshift on the center console may appear awkward at first, once you are seated and extend your right arm forward you'll notice how easy it is to use the short-throw shifter. With the bottom-hinged clutch pedal requiring a sensitive touch, rolling away smoothly in 1st gear requires patience and practice to avoid stalling the engine.

On the road, the Carrera GT's ride is taut, with its suspension adequately soaking up most of the imperfections on the asphalt. On twisty roads, the super Carrera maintains excellent composure. There is little body roll as the Porsche winds through the apex with confidence. The steering effort is moderate and the feel is linear, providing good feedback from the pavement. There is tremendous lateral grip available from the Carrera GT, so as the speed builds through the corner, there is never any sense of the car wanting to swap ends. Not unless you romp on the throttle on corner exit and unleash the full V-10 power. While there is no yaw control to save you, traction control is present to limit wheelspin if you are too anxious with the gas pedal. In our testing later, the GT sprinted from a standstill to 60 mph in 3.6 seconds.

On the track, the Carrera GT is ultra fast and beautifully balanced, especially in the hands of Walter Röhrl, Porsche's veteran test driver and former World Rally Champion. On a former Soviet airbase outside of Berlin in the Brandenburg forest, the GT reached 200 mph easily on a 1.2-mile runway, with plenty of space left to slow down. The super Porsche blasted across the concrete slabs with rock-solid stability and nary a hint of high-speed lift or swaying. There is so much power from the V-10 that even starting out in 1st gear, then immediately upshifting to 6th, the GT can still accelerate to over 150 mph covering the same distance. Given more room, the factory claim of a 205-mph top speed seems well within reach.

To demonstrate the GT's outstanding road-holding ability, Walter took journalists for thrill rides on a road course set up around a few of the giant aircraft hangars. In professional hands, the super Carrera dances through each apex at every corner with utmost smoothness. Every steering input produces an immediate response, fluid and confident, with or without traction control turned on.

Interested in taking a Carrera GT home? It will set you back $440,000 with the total production run capped at 1500 units. Porsche says that between one-third and one-half of all GTs will come stateside. The good news is that if you want to drive this ultimate Porsche road-going sports car, they are still available at the dealers. Better hurry!

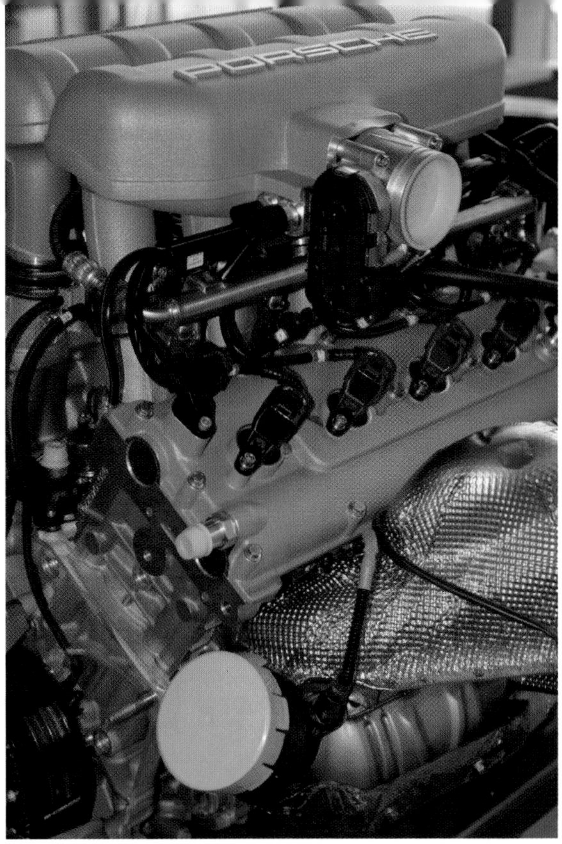
PORSCHE

ABOVE: Originally developed for endurance racing, the Carrera GT's 5.7-liter aluminum V-10 has Nikasil-lined bores, dry-sump oiling, titanium connecting rods and makes 605 bhp.

BELOW: Here, the carbon-fiber engine subframe is visible, which also serves as a mounting point for the rear suspension.

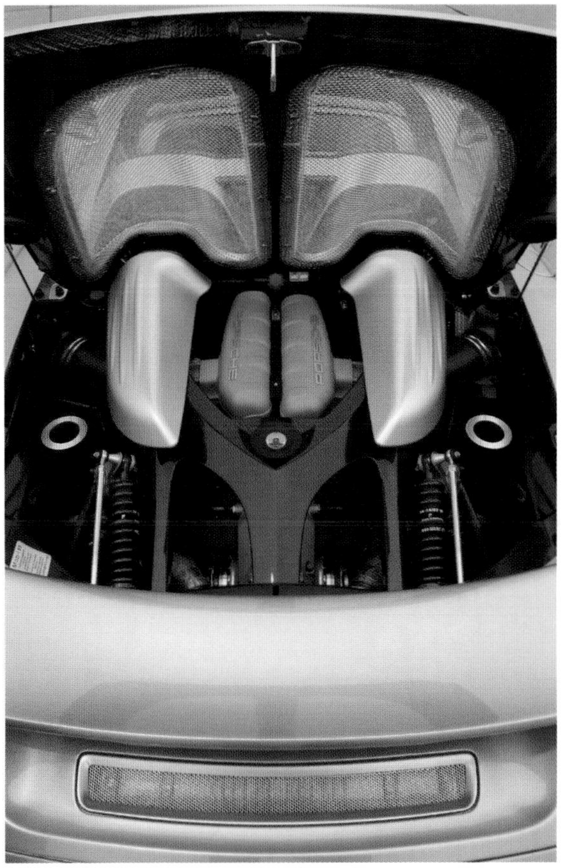

THE INSIDE STORY FROM ROAD TO TRACK

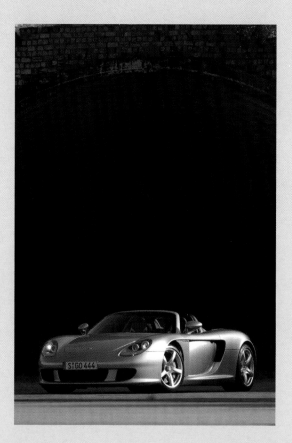

The Carrera GT was developed from an open-cockpit racing prototype designed to Le Mans LM 900 regulations requiring a minimum weight of 900 kg. Unfortunately it was never raced, following Porsche's decision to suspend its factory-backed racing activities. The first experimental prototype had proven to be very competitive, and rather than cancel the entire project, the racing bodywork was replaced with a superb roadworthy roadster body, which became the star of the 2000 Paris motor show.

Its future was uncertain as Porsche CEO Dr. Wendelin Wiedeking insisted that the car would be produced only if it could be made at a profit. He was confident it could be done, proved by the fact that development work has never ceased to make the car both road legal and acceptable to buyers willing to pay nearly a half-million dollars for it.

Le Mans racing prototypes must, by regulations, have a minimum weight of 900 kg (1984 lb.) without fuel. It was obvious that as a road car meeting worldwide safety and emissions regulations and minimum customer requirements—including full leather trim, airbags, sound and navigation systems, etc.—the Carrera GT would be heavier. Even though the untrimmed body is all carbon fiber, it is considerably stronger and heavier than a racing body and has two seats instead of one. Add the large windscreen, the large doors with power windows and you have probably added at least 330 lb.

In the racing car, the engine was rigidly bolted to the monocoque. For noise and vibration reasons, this is unacceptable in a road car. In the GT, the engine is rubber-mounted in a carbon-fiber subframe bolted to the monocoque, which also carries the rear suspension. Herbert Ampferer, Porsche's competition manager, says the subframe added 100 lb. and that the V-10 engine itself is 66 lb. heavier than the racing unit. In addition, a heavy catalytic exhaust system matching the engine's power is unavoidable and no modern car can do without ABS and a brake booster (both forbidden at Le Mans). In the end it all adds up to more than 925 lb. and a car that, despite having recourse to the most sophisticated lightweight materials, weighs 3043 lb. without fuel, or 50 percent more than the racing version.

As to the adoption of a 68-degree angle between the two banks of five cylinders, Ampferer said that it was not chosen because in the racing version the engine's width was critical for space reasons. In the early 1990s, he said, Porsche started the development of a 3.0-liter racing V-10 that was never produced. On that occasion a huge number of computer-aided calculations and real-time experiments were made to find out which cylinder bank angle and which of 16 possible firing orders would provide the best compromise between maximum efficiency of the intake and exhaust systems and the lowest possible vibration level, and the result was 68 degrees, as adopted for the new engine. As the crankpins remain at 72 degrees to each other, the firing intervals are irregular, alternating between 68 and 76 degrees, but this is undetectable, both by ear and feel.

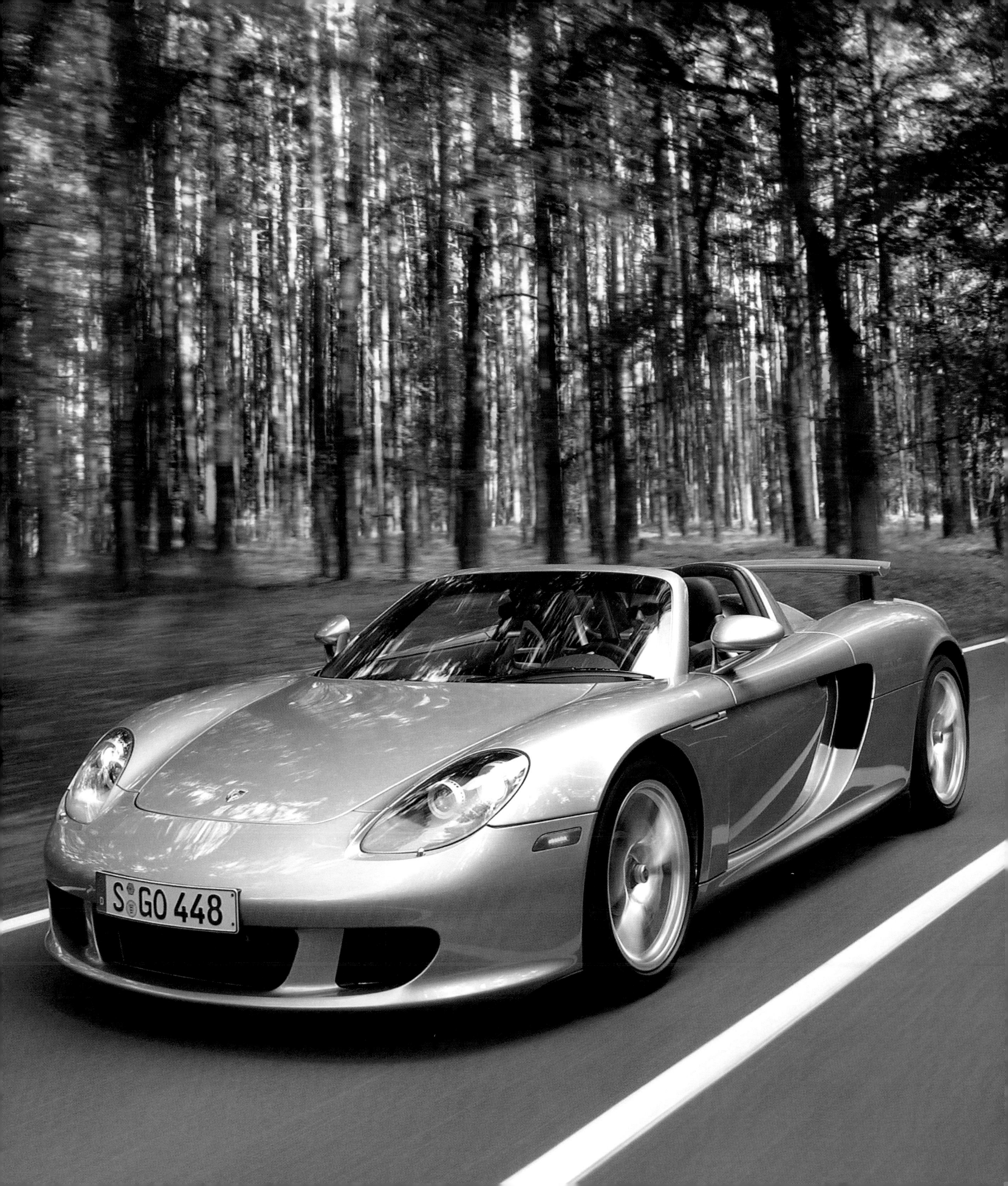
S GO 448

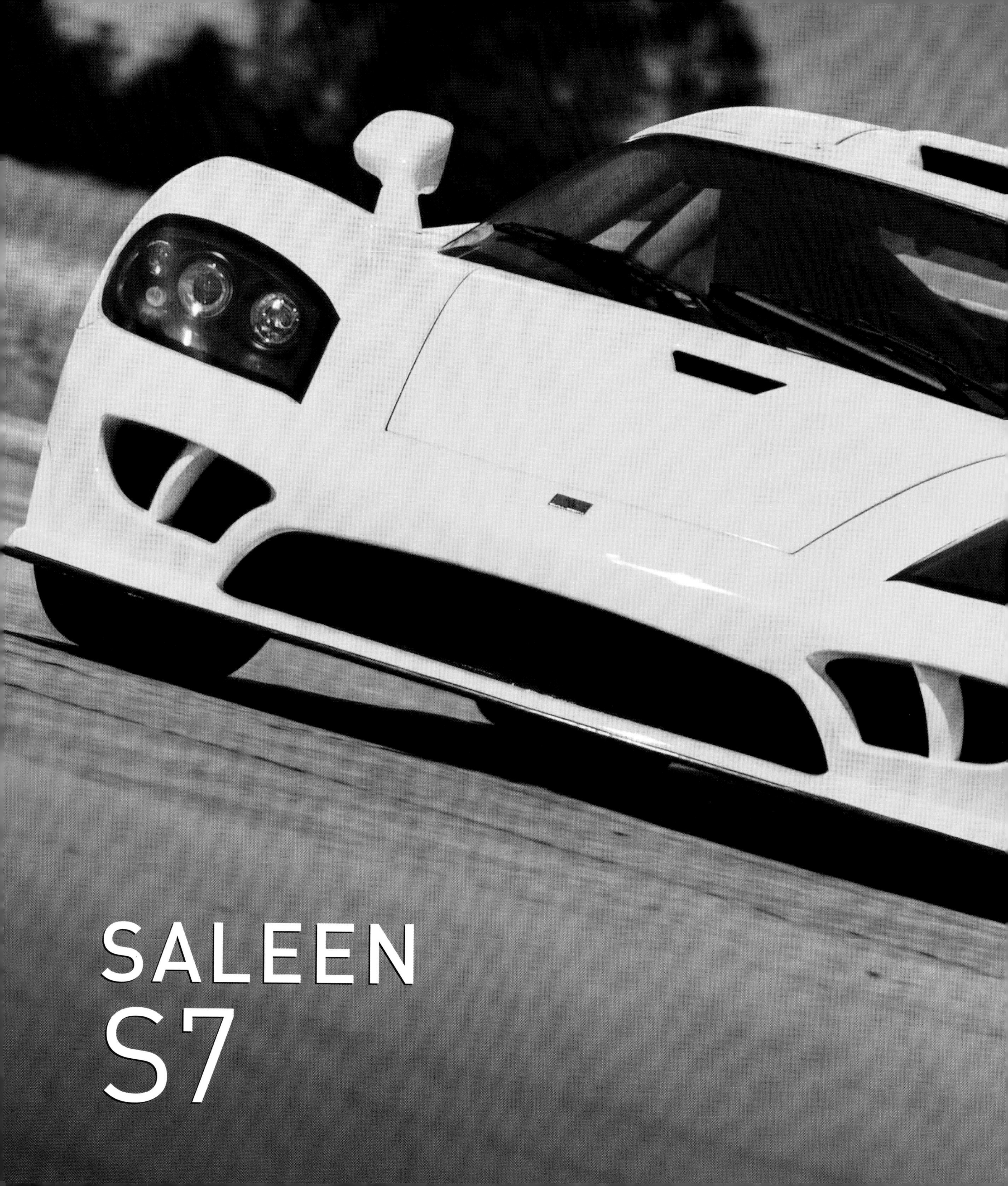

SALEEN S7

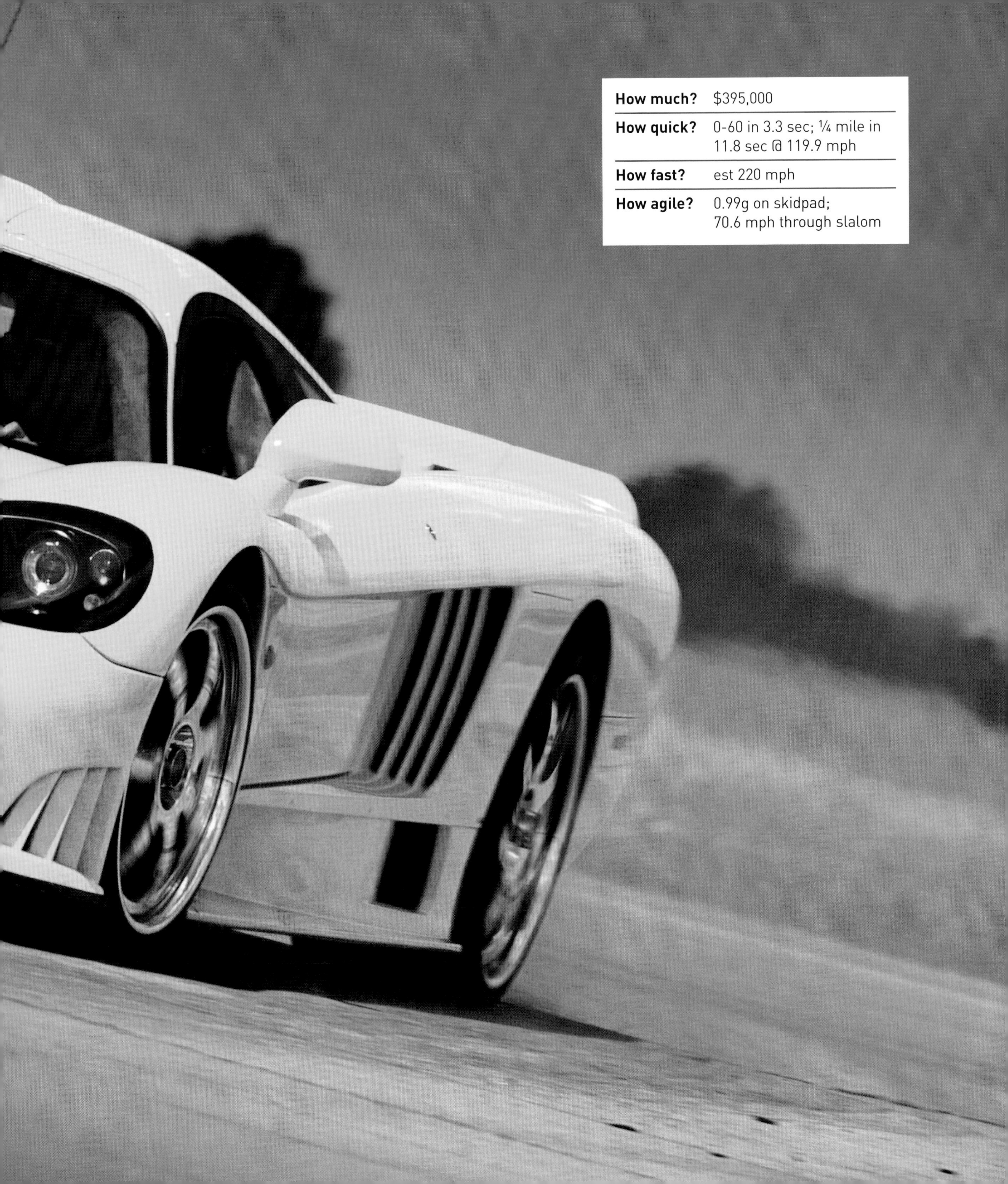

How much?	$395,000
How quick?	0-60 in 3.3 sec; ¼ mile in 11.8 sec @ 119.9 mph
How fast?	est 220 mph
How agile?	0.99g on skidpad; 70.6 mph through slalom

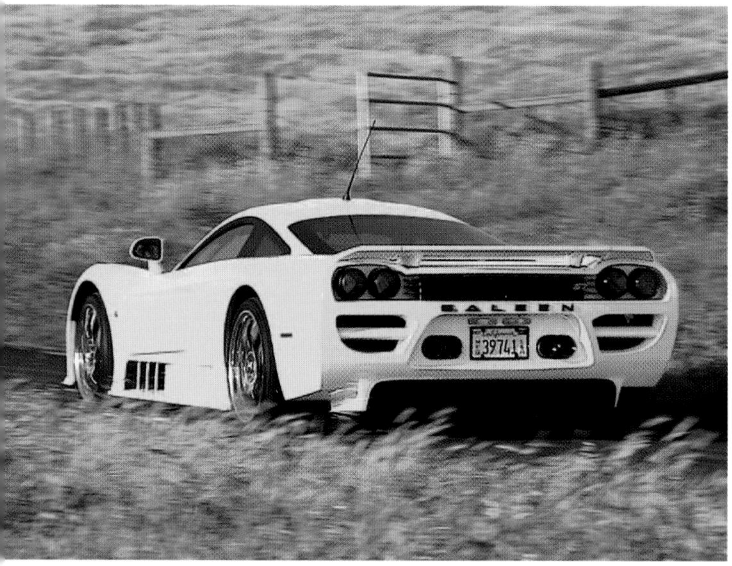

ABOVE: The S7's amply perforated tail helps the 7.0 liter V-8 engine keep its cool. No doubt, there's plenty of heat generated when speed exceeds 200 mph.

BELOW: The S7 badge is subtle, but the rest of this American-built exotic more than compensates.

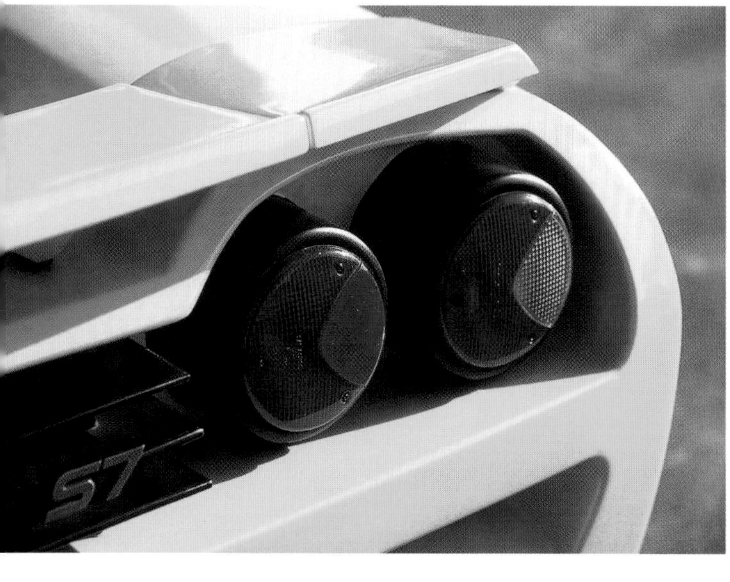
S7

PATRIOT MISSILE

AN INSPIRATION TO EVERY SCHOOLKID who's ever doodled a swoopy sports car during class, the Saleen S7 is the realization of one man's dream. Although his name is nearly synonymous with performance-modified Ford Mustangs he's built, Steve Saleen found it impossible to resist the urge of designing and crafting his own supercar. And he's succeeded where others have failed, manufacturing a uniquely American exotic, powered by a thundering 7.0-liter 550-bhp pushrod V-8 and generating race-car levels of aerodynamic downforce—no surprise, really, as the S7 road car is a gentrified version of the racing machine that has proven itself in endurance competition. And the S7 looks the part, whether it's driven down Main Street or the Mulsanne Straight.

"It's really there for sentimental reasons," says Steve Saleen, referring to the only part that his $395,000, 200-mph-plus S7 supercar shares with the Ford Mustang—a lower window channel buried deep within the featherweight carbon-fiber door. It's a nice gesture, seeing as Saleen's exclusive high-performance versions of Ford's pony car have made him a household name among Ford loyalists, and a demigod at Ford club gatherings. In 2003 alone, he sold nearly 900 Saleen Mustangs through selected Ford dealerships, in various states of chassis tune, power and appearance.

As we circle a stoutly triangulated space frame of 4130 chrome-moly tubing gusseted with panels of honeycomb aluminum at the Saleen factory, it's obvious that this is no Mustang. Later, with Steve riding shotgun in our fully assembled S7, we tap the full 550 bhp and the car explodes like a round out of a chamber to a very un-Mustang-like speed of 165 mph. On this necessarily deserted section of road, the suspension compresses mightily and the steering tightens, as the car is generating its full 2870-lb. curb weight in downforce here...and it's champing at the bit for more throttle. I have no reason to doubt the 200-mph claim. The sound is thoroughly intoxicating too, with 7.0 liters of dry-sump aluminum V-8 transitioning from coarse rumble to maniacal shriek with every flight to the 6500-rpm redline. This thing flat moves, and feels locked in a slot at triple digits.

Later, we attack a favorite tree-lined canyon road, throttling in the huge 3rd-gear thrust from turn to turn. It's remarkable how the front aero enhances turn-in, and how a car that seemed so unmanageably wide at first can be guided so obediently in its lane. We're flying along at ridiculous speeds, and the mammoth Pirelli P Zeros have hardly squawked in protest.

Geez, in the span of several hours I think I've used my entire fun allotment (and good karma with police) for the year! Steve is grinning too—and deservedly so. He's succeeded where many others have failed, in building a no-holds-barred American supercar that's crash-tested, OBD-II certified and emissions-legal in all 50 states. It's also a true race car for the street, de-

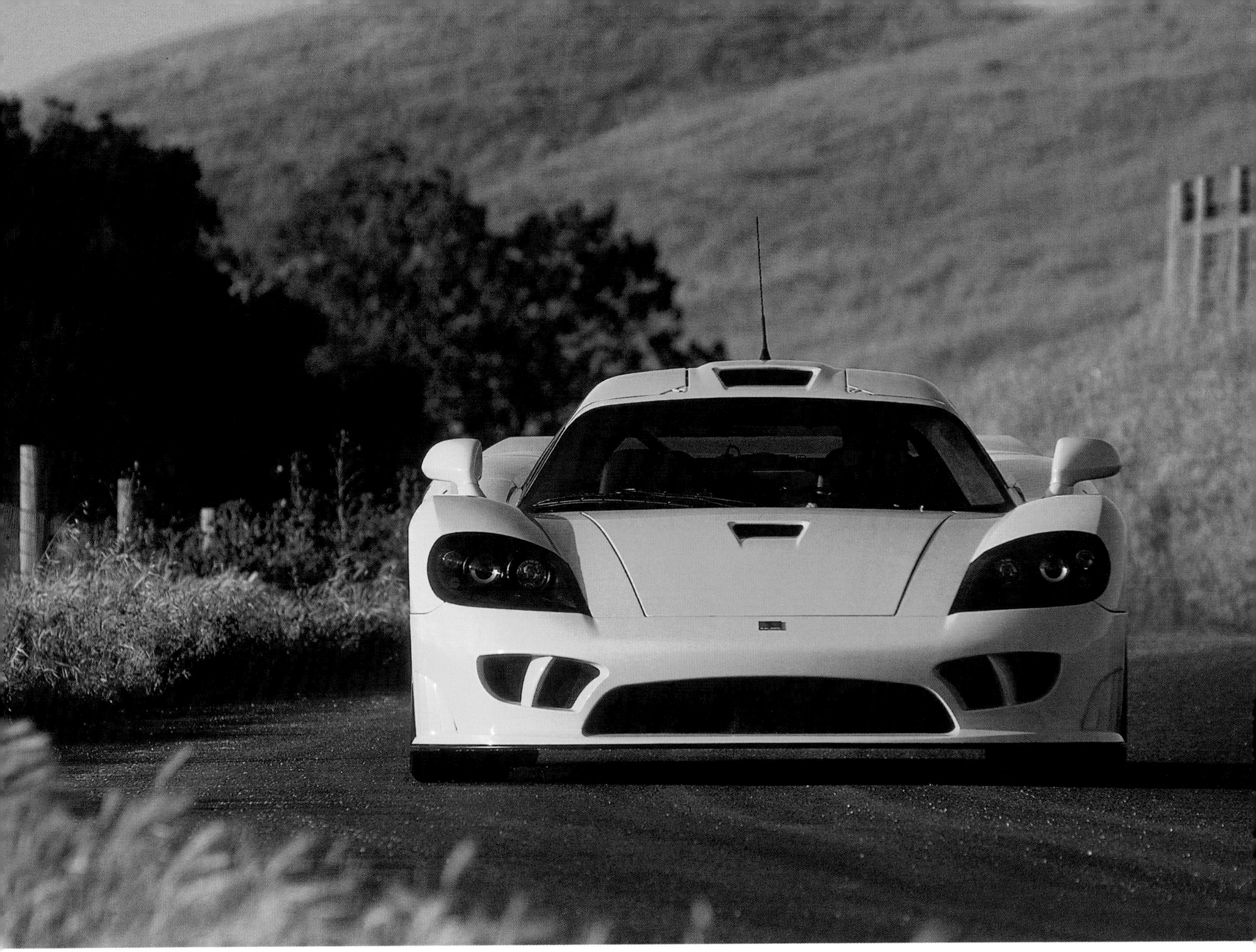

signed without compromise around its considerable downforce package, that makes the Lamborghini Murciélago feel positively posh by comparison. That's purely intentional, as the whole Saleen crew is proud of how close the chassis is to the S7 race car's, the track-proven alter-ego that won 19 out of 32 races in 2001, including a victory over the factory GTS Corvettes in the 12 Hours of Sebring.

As the factory tour continues, it starts to become obvious why the S7 costs as much as it does. Billy Tally, Saleen's enthusiastic vice president of engineering, holds up a front suspension upright that's been CNC-machined from a solid aluminum billet, its elegant latticework of openings designed to admit cooling air to the brakes. It's one of hundreds of like-machined parts that are hand-assembled, welded and jigged up on the premises. Only the immaculately done carbon-fiber bodywork is done off-site, though it's painted in Saleen's booth. Saleen admits that the English Midlands is the epicenter for this work: "The weave pattern is better-looking, it's lighter, and it's stronger."

ABOVE: The S7's extreme width is apparent here. Yet as downforce increases with speed, the Saleen starts to feel narrower and more agile.

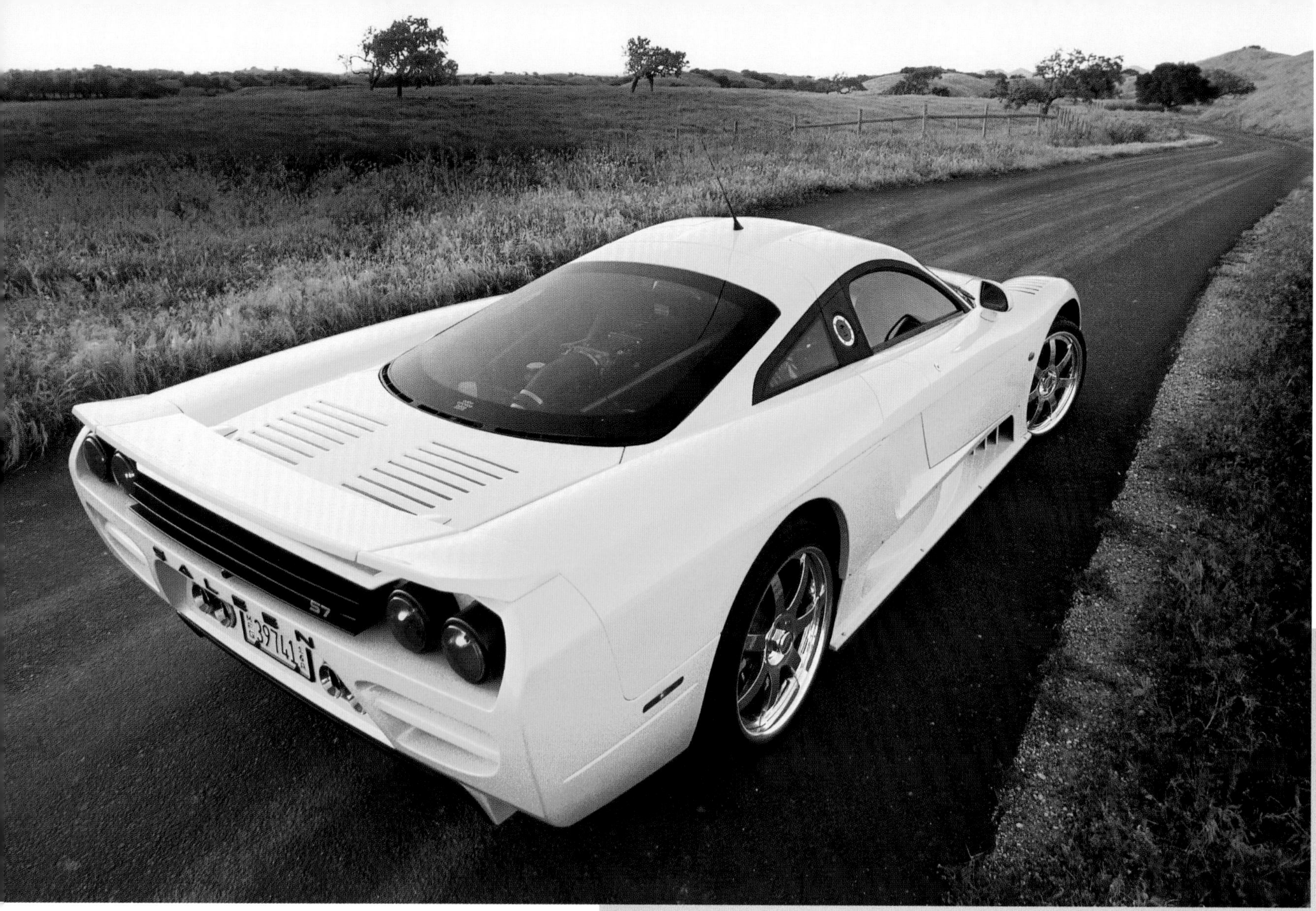
S7

ABOVE AND RIGHT: The S7's carbon-fiber bodywork seems to stretch rearward for miles, with the cockpit pushed up toward the front wheels for an immediate view of the road. Built around producing lots and lots of downforce, the S7's body is festooned with vents, slats and ducts that channel, admit or evacuate air.

OPPOSITE, TOP: The mid-mounted V-8 breathes through this duct, positioned at the leading edge of the roof.

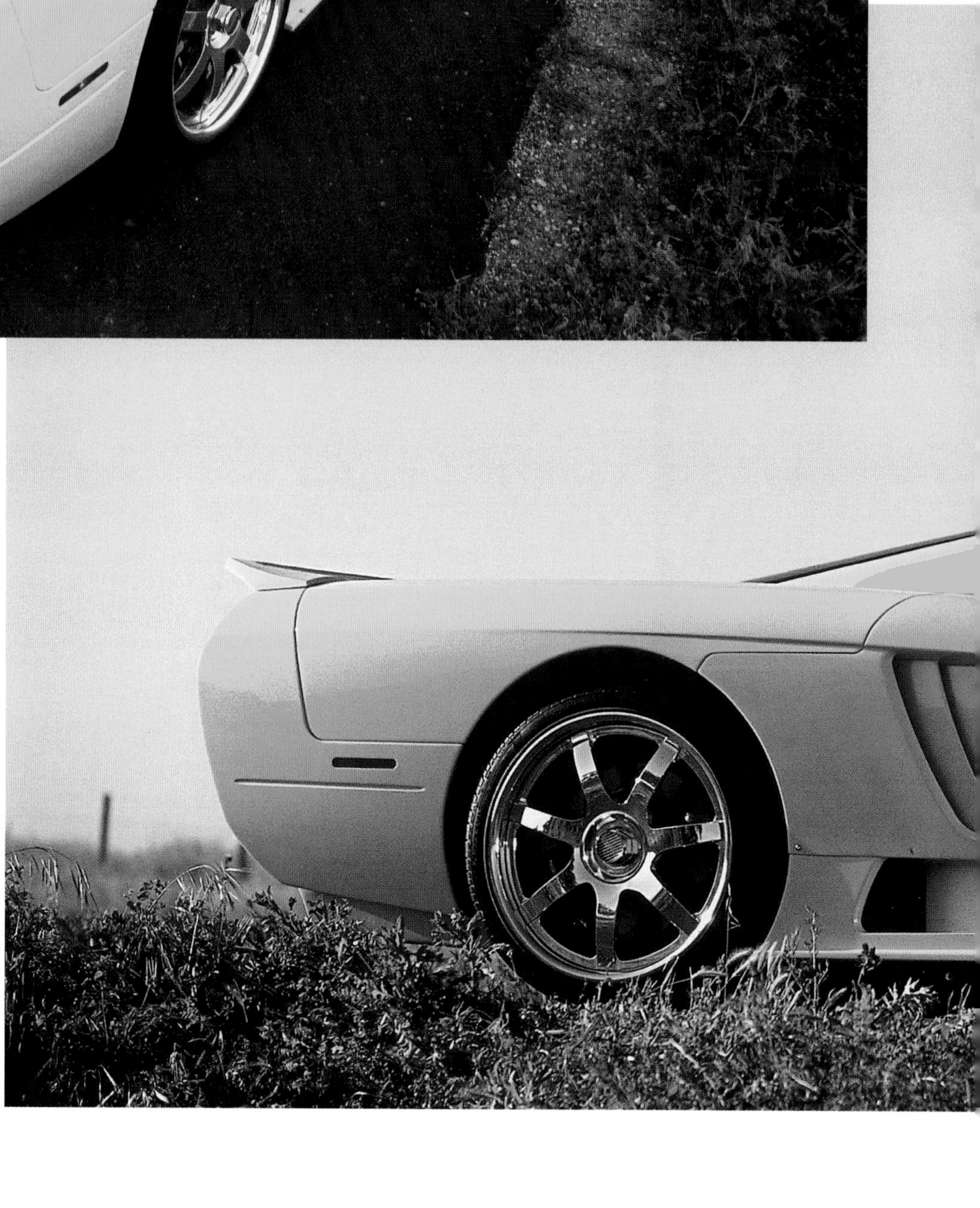

We move to engine final assembly, where Steve clears up the misconception that the 7.0-liter V-8 is Ford-based. The aluminum block is a Saleen-exclusive lightweight casting that has small-block external dimensions with big-block capacity. "I did borrow Ford bore centers so I didn't have to re-invent head gaskets and some other bracketry," explains Steve. Tally points with obvious pride to an S7 cylinder head and pokes a finger in the gaping ports, the exhaust valve seats done in beryllium. "It has the best heat conductivity of just about any metal on the planet," he says, adding that with ultra-precise computer machining of both ports and combustion chambers, most heads are within 0.5 percent of one another on the flow bench.

Out of the shop and back in the S7 (chassis No. 17), we have a chance to sample the amenities, as there are power windows and door locks, fabulous-smelling Connolly leather, very effective heat and air-conditioning systems, and a silver-trimmed, white-face gauge cluster inspired by Steve's own Breitling wristwatch. There are small luggage compartments front and rear, which beautifully show off the carbon-fiber weave and are shaped to accom-

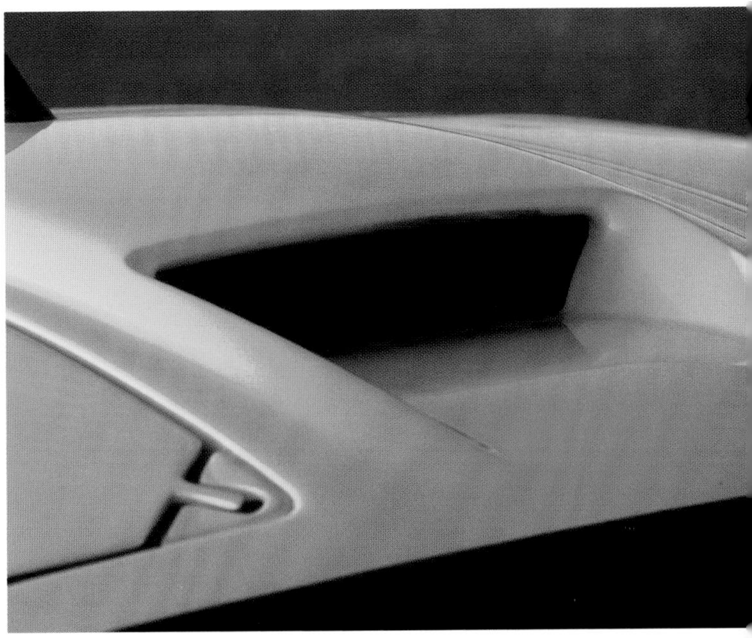

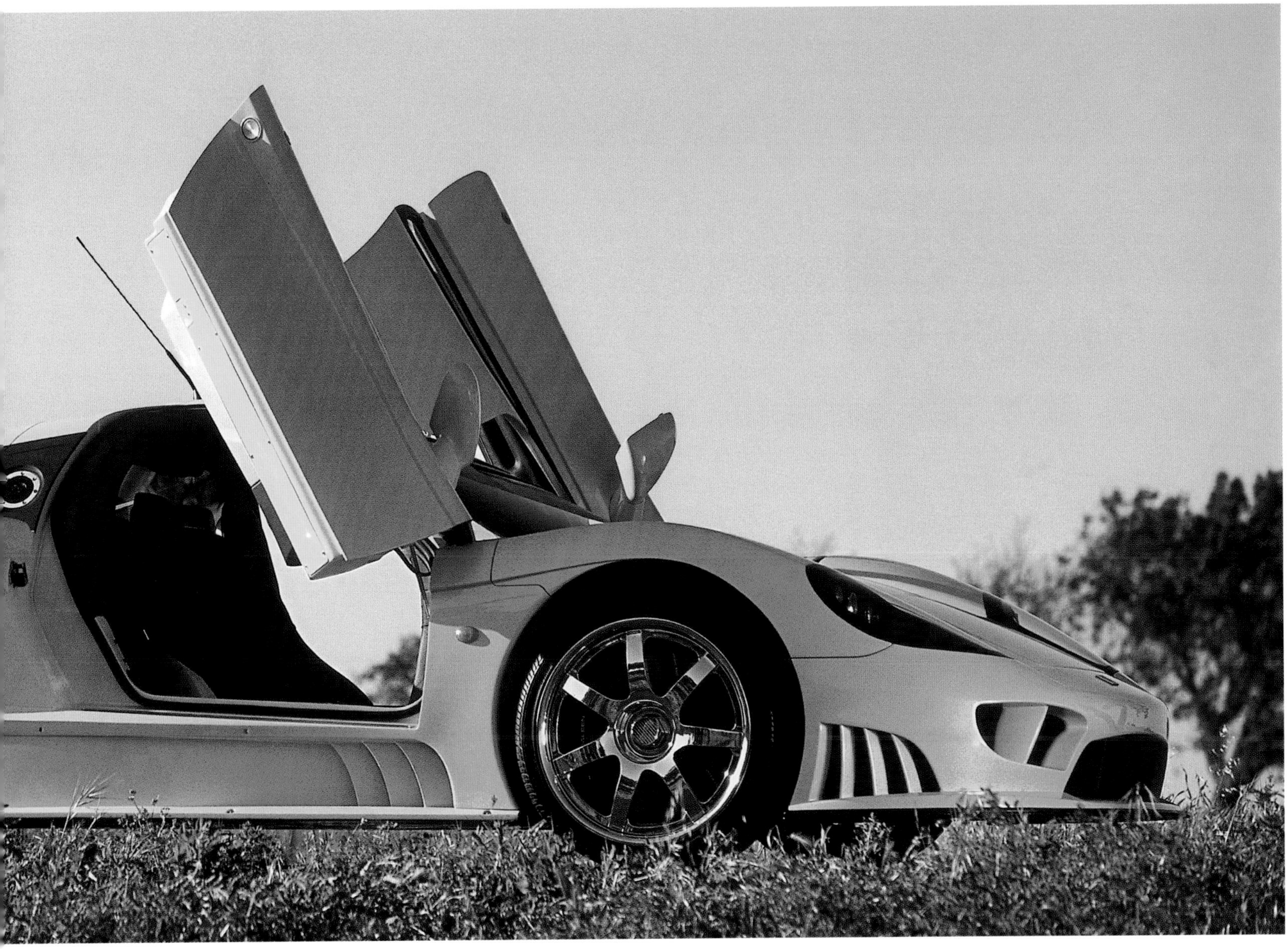

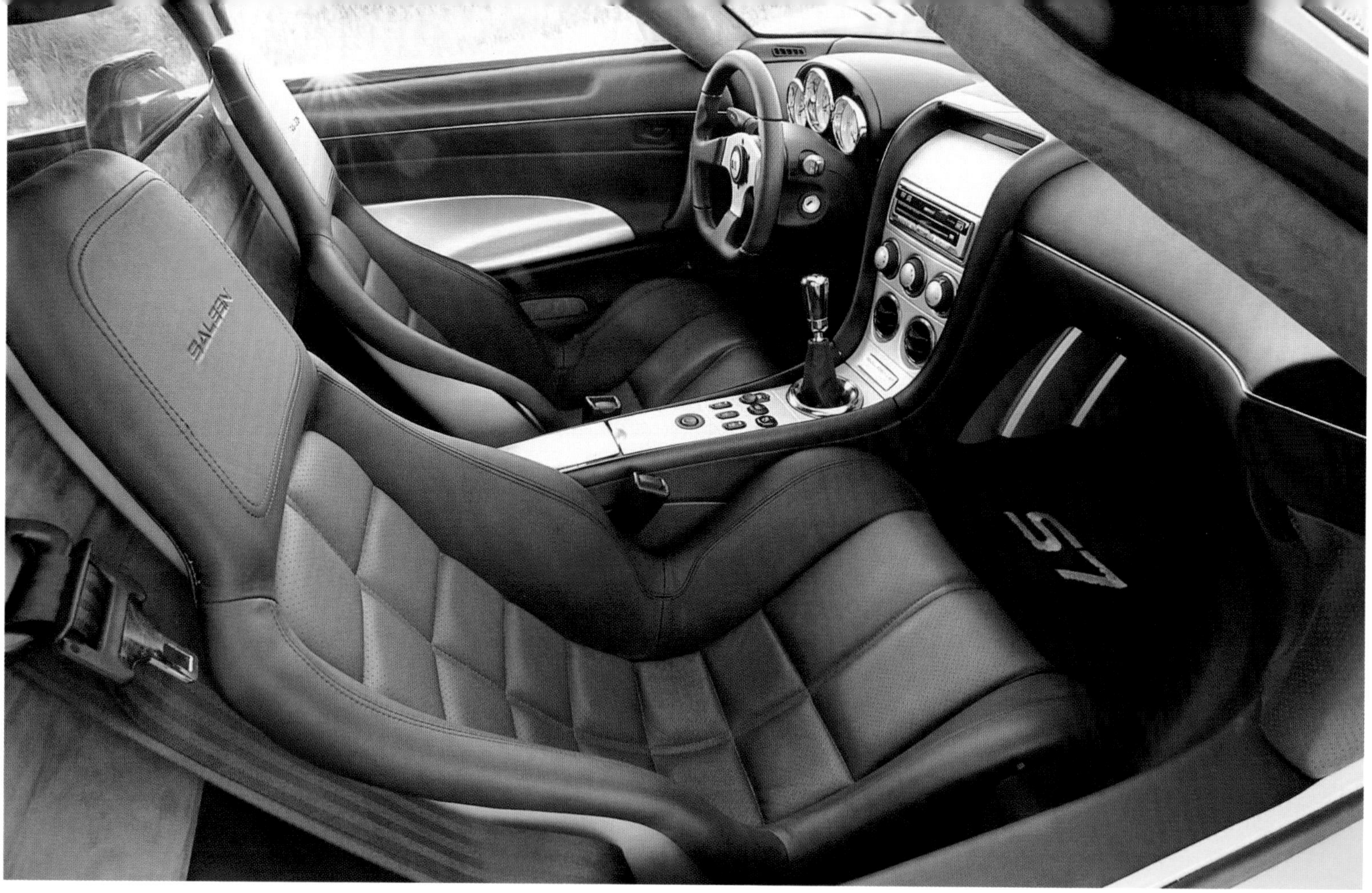
SALEEN
S7

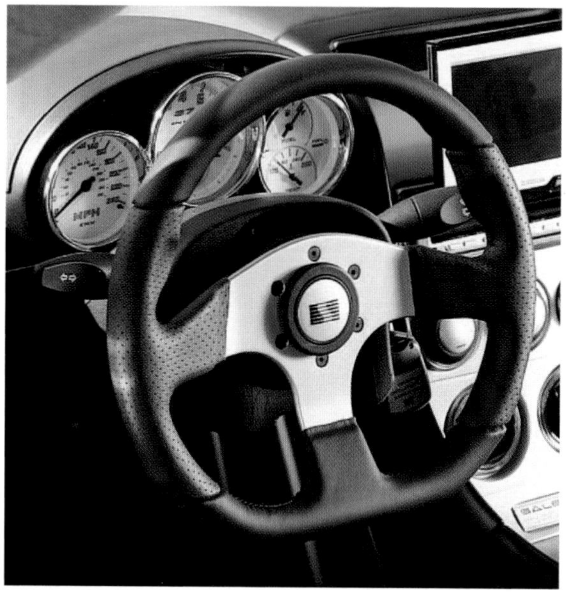

modate the three-piece set of fitted luggage that is included with the car.

The luggage isn't the only thing that's fitted...the driver is too. The leather-wrapped, fixed-shell seats are non-adjustable fore-aft; rather, the AP-sourced pedal cluster can be manually bolted in one of eight positions. Leather-covered seat pads can be added or taken away according to driver girth and preference, and the small-diameter wheel is adjustable for tilt. As part of the purchase price, Saleen flies the buyer and spouse first-class from anywhere in the U.S., puts them up at the local Ritz-Carlton for two days, takes them on a tour of the Saleen shops in Irvine, California, and fits them to the car. Last, Steve takes them on what he calls an "acclimatization drive."

This is necessary. For a number of reasons.

First, there's a certain technique requiring some flexibility to enter the car. The doors tilt forward on a diagonal hinge line, like a Porsche 962's, and if you attempt to put just one leg in the footwell and hoist yourself into the off-set-toward-center driver's seat, you'll do the splits like Mary Lou Retton. No,

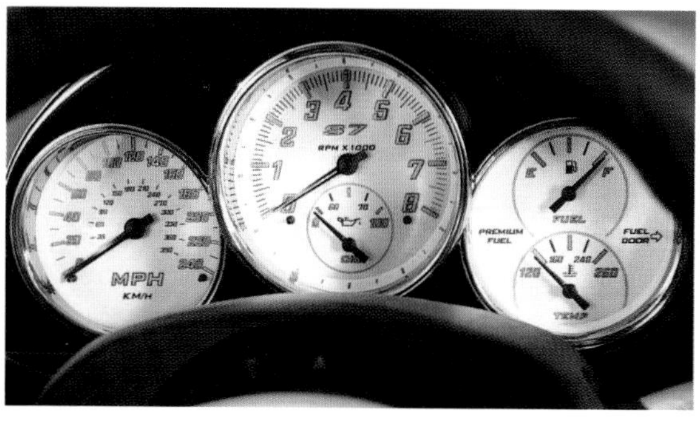
S7
MPH
KM/H
FUEL
TEMP

CLOCKWISE FROM RIGHT: The S7's aircraft-style fuel filler; classy instruments inspired by a Breitling wristwatch; a suitably chunky 3-spoke steering wheel (that's Saleen himself in the rearview camera display); and lightweight seats that, along with the pedal cluster position, are custom-fitted to each driver.

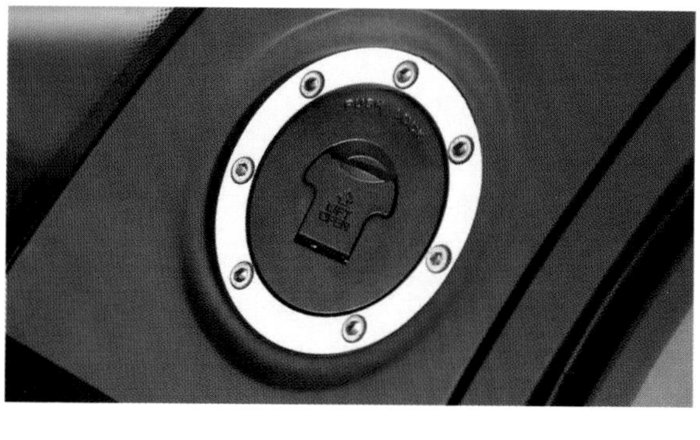

PORSCHE CARRERA GT

SPECIFICATIONS

Base price, 2004	$440,000
Curb weight	est 3530 lb
Wheelbase	107.5 in.
Track, f/r	63.5 in./62.5 in.
Length	181.6 in.
Width	75.6 in.
Height	45.9 in.
Fuel capacity	24.3 gal.

ENGINE & DRIVETRAIN

Engine	dohc 4-valve/cyl V-10
Displacement	5733 cc
Bore x stroke	98.0 x 76.0 mm
Compression ratio	12.0:1
Horsepower (SAE)	605 bhp @ 8000 rpm
Torque	435 lb-ft @ 5750 rpm
Fuel injection	elect. sequential port
Transmission	6-speed manual

CHASSIS & BODY

Layout	mid engine/rear drive
Brake system, f/r	15.0-in. vented & drilled discs/15.0-in. vented & drilled discs; ABS
Wheels	forged alloy; 19 x 9 1/4J f, 20 x 12 1/4J r
Tires	Michelin Pilot Sport 2; 265/35ZR-19 f, 335/30ZR-20 r
Steering type	rack & pinion, power assist
Suspension, f/r	upper & lower A-arms, pushrod coil springs and tube shocks, anti-roll bar/upper & lower A-arms, pushrod coil springs and tube shocks, anti-roll bar

PERFORMANCE

0-60 mph	3.6 sec
1/4 mile	11.3 sec @ 131.6 mph
Top Speed	est 205 mph
Braking, from 60 mph	124 ft
Skidpad	0.99g
Slalom	71.1 mph

PORSCHE 911 GT3

SPECIFICATIONS

Base price, 2004	$99,900
Curb weight	3160 lb
Wheelbase	92.7 in.
Track, f/r	58.5 in./58.9 in.
Length	174.6 in.
Width	69.7 in.
Height	50.0 in.
Fuel capacity	16.7 gal.

ENGINE & DRIVETRAIN

Engine	dohc 4-valve/cyl flat-6
Displacement	3600 cc
Bore x stroke	100.0 x 76.4 mm
Compression ratio	11.7:1
Horsepower (SAE)	380 bhp @ 7400 rpm
Torque	285 lb-ft @ 5000 rpm
Fuel injection	elect. sequential port
Transmission	6-speed manual

CHASSIS & BODY

Layout	rear engine/rear drive
Brake system, f/r	13.8-in. vented discs/13.0-in. vented discs; ABS
Wheels	cast alloy; 18 x 8 1/4 f, 18 x 11 r
Tires	Michelin Pilot Sport; 235/40ZR-18 f, 295/30ZR-18 r
Steering type	rack & pinion, vari power assist
Suspension, f/r	MacPherson struts, lower A-arms, coil springs, tube shocks, anti-roll bar/multilink, coil springs, tube shocks, anti-roll bar

PERFORMANCE

0-60 mph	4.2 sec
1/4 mile	12.4 sec @ 113.8 mph
Top Speed	est 190 mph
Braking, from 60 mph	119 ft
Skidpad	0.92g
Slalom	68.7 mph

SALEEN S7

SPECIFICATIONS

Base price, 2003	$395,000
Curb weight	2870 lb
Wheelbase	106.3 in.
Track, f/r	68.8 in./67.3 in.
Length	188.0 in.
Width	78.3 in.
Height	41.0 in.
Fuel capacity	19.0 gal.

ENGINE & DRIVETRAIN

Engine	ohv 2-valve/cyl V-8
Displacement	7008 cc
Bore x stroke	104.8 x 101.6 mm
Compression ratio	10.0:1
Horsepower (SAE)	550 bhp @ 5900 rpm
Torque	525 lb-ft @ 4000 rpm
Fuel injection	elect. sequential port
Transmission	6-speed manual

CHASSIS & BODY

Layout	mid engine/rear drive
Brake system, f/r	15.0-in. vented & slotted discs/14.0-in. vented & slotted discs
Wheels	forged 2-piece alloy; 19 x 9 1/4 f, 20 x 12 r
Tires	Pirelli P Zero Rosso; 275/30ZR-19 f, 345/25ZR-20 r
Steering type	rack & pinion, power assist
Suspension, f/r	upper & lower A-arms, coil-over springs w/ adj tube shocks, anti-roll bar/upper & lower A-arms, coil-over springs w/ adj tube shocks, anti-roll bar

PERFORMANCE

0-60 mph	3.3 sec
1/4 mile	11.8 sec @ 119.9 mph
Top Speed	est 220 mph
Braking, from 60 mph	125 ft
Skidpad	0.99g
Slalom	70.6 mph

ACKNOWLEDGEMENTS

This book would not be possible without the tireless efforts of "Road & Track" Librarian Jane Barrett, Art Director Richard M. Baron, and Assistant Art Director Tanya Owens Nuchols; the keen copyediting eyes of Managing Editor Ellida Maki and Editor-in-Chief Thos L. Bryant; the design talent of Patricia Fabricant; and the clear-minded coordination of Filipacchi Publishing's Publisher, Dorothée Walliser.

CREDITS

Aston Martin Vanquish: story by Patrick Hong; photos by Guy Spangenberg

Bentley Continental GT: story by Thos L. Bryant; photos by Stéphane Foulon

Dodge Viper SRT-10: story & sidebar by Matt DeLorenzo; photos by John Lamm & Jeff Allen

Ferrari Enzo: story by Patrick Hong; photos by John Lamm

Ford GT: story by Patrick Hong; photos by Allan Rosenberg

Lamborghini Gallardo: story by Patrick Hong; photos by Marc Urbano

Lamborghini Murciélago: story by Patrick Hong; photos by Guy Spangenberg

Maserati Coupe Cambiocorsa: story by Andrew Bornhop; photos by Ron Perry

Mercedes-Benz SLR McLaren: story & photos by John Lamm

Porsche Carrera GT: story by Patrick Hong, sidebar by Paul Frère; photos by Stéphane Foulon & Guy Spangenberg

Porsche 911 GT3: story by Kim Wolfkill; photos by Marc Urbano

Saleen S7: story by Douglas Kott; photos by Brian Blades and John Lamm

Captions and introductory text for each car by Douglas Kott

Road & Track® is a registered trademark of Hachette Filipacchi Media U.S., Inc.